Praise for
Light from Uncomm

"A joyful, queer, radical ballad of a story."

—*Booklist* (starred review)

"A new classic."

—Sequoia Nagamatsu, author of
Where We Go When All We Were Is Gone

"This is a novel that will be talked about for years to come, and deservedly so."

—TJ Klune, *New York Times* bestselling author

"An unexpected gift."

—*Kirkus Reviews* (starred review)

"Wilder and more beautiful and sweeter than I could ever have expected."

—Charlie Jane Anders, author of *All the Birds in the Sky*

"Bursts with love and insights on food, music, inheritance, and transformation."

—*The New York Times*

"This book broke my heart and glued it back together stronger than before. Absolutely gorgeous."

—Becky Chambers, *USA Today* bestselling author

"Heartrending and sweet, with the nonstop energy of Douglas Adams, and a deep, merciless compassion."

—Max Gladstone, author of *Last Exit*

ALSO BY RYKA AOKI

Seasonal Velocities
He Mele A Hilo
Why Dust Shall Never Settle Upon This Soul

LIGHT FROM UNCOMMON STARS

RYKA AOKI

TOR

A TOM DOHERTY ASSOCIATES BOOK
NEW YORK

LIGHT FROM UNCOMMON STARS

Copyright © 2021 by Ryka Aoki

A Tor Book
Published by Tom Doherty Associates
120 Broadway
New York, NY 10271

www.tor-forge.com

Tor® is a registered trademark of Macmillan Publishing Group, LLC.

The Library of Congress has cataloged the hardcover edition as follows:

Names: Aoki, Ryka, author.
Title: Light from uncommon stars / Ryka Aoki.
Description: First Edition. | New York : Tor, 2021. | "A Tom Doherty
    Associates book."
Identifiers: LCCN 2021028500 (print) | LCCN 2021028501 (ebook) |
    ISBN 9781250789068 (hardcover) | ISBN 9781250789075 (ebook)
Classification: LCC PS3601.O38 L54 2021 (print) | LCC PS3601.O38 (ebook) |
    DDC 813/.6—dc23
LC record available at https://lccn.loc.gov/2021028500
LC ebook record available at https://lccn.loc.gov/2021028501

ISBN 978-1-250-78908-2 (trade paperback)

Our books may be purchased in bulk for promotional, educational, or
business use. Please contact your local bookseller or the Macmillan Corporate
and Premium Sales Department at 1-800-221-7945, extension 5442,
or by email at MacmillanSpecialMarkets@macmillan.com.

First Tor Paperback Edition: 2022

Printed in the United States of America

0 9 8 7 6 5 4 3 2 1

For Katrina, and Katrinas everywhere . . .

PROGRAM

LIGHT FROM UNCOMMON STARS

People think selling one's soul for music is as simple as "Sign this contract and—poof!—you're a genius!"

Were it that easy, the world would be awash in transcendent song. Obviously, this is not so.

Souls are cheap.

The trick is finding the *right* soul.

FEBRUARY

1

Shhh . . .

Yes, it hurt. It was definitely not just a bruise. Yes, she was scared. Her throat was raw from screaming.

Cautiously, Katrina Nguyen felt under her bed.

Girl clothes. Boy clothes. Money. Birth certificate. Social security card. Toothbrush. Spare glasses. Backup battery. Makeup. Estradiol. Spironolactone.

Katrina had made an escape bag the first time her father threatened to kill her.

At first, the bag seemed an "in case of emergency," a glass that one would never break.

But after tonight . . .

Why had she let it come to this? Why couldn't she be what her parents wanted?

Part of her was in a panic. *What have you done? Apologize. Knock on their door right now. Say it's all your fault—say you're sorry, say you'll promise to change.*

But another, stronger, part of Katrina was calm, even cold.

You have to escape. Tonight. Breathe, be quiet, and listen.

And so, Katrina listened . . . for footsteps, for breathing, for sleep. She listened, and listened. Through the dark, she heard her mother's one last cough. Her father's one last flush.

And then, finally, there was silence.

Katrina clutched her ribs, then propped herself up. The pain was sharp, but manageable. She was in her room, behind a locked door. All she needed to do was be quiet. And calm. She could do this.

She could do this.

By the light of her phone, Katrina applied concealer around her eye and to her cheek. It would be better not to face the world with visible bruises.

Then she placed a note on her bed.

In it, she had written that she was sorry, that she wished she'd never been born, that she didn't want to make them angry, and that she'd never bother them again. That part was true.

But then she wrote that she was going San Francisco.

There'd be no reason to doubt her; of course she would go there. That's where the queers went. Her father would punch the wall, throw something heavy and breakable; her mother would cross herself and utter a prayer. In a day or two, her mother would call Tía Claudia across the Bay to find their stupid son and send him home.

By that time, though, she'd be almost four hundred miles away.

Silently, Katrina put on her coat. She slid open her bedroom window. Outside, there was noise from a police helicopter, noise from some family next door. There was noise from the highway, from nice cars leaving and less-nice cars coming home. Yet, Katrina moved steadily, almost gracefully, as she gathered what she needed.

Ticket. Laptop. Escape bag.

Violin.

Then Katrina crawled atop her desk, and dropped to the ground. Mercifully, adrenaline overrode her pain. She reached up, slid the window closed, and looked at her phone.

Good. There was still time. As quickly as she could, Katrina limped past the neighbors, the highway, the cars, the police helicopter overhead. She'd catch BART to Oakland, then find somewhere to wait out the night.

In the morning, she'd get on a big white bus to Los Angeles.

Those who've never ridden a big white Asian bus probably never will. These buses don't load at Greyhound bus depots or train stations. Instead, one catches them at an Asian shopping center or supermarket.

Some are Vietnamese, a few are Korean; many are Chinese. Some trek to Las Vegas. Others shuttle to the casinos of Morongo, Pechanga, San Manuel. Yet another subset runs along a network of Asian communities throughout the state. Oakland Chinatown, San Francisco Chinatown, Little Saigon. San Diego Chinatown.

And, of course, fleets of them converge on the San Gabriel

Valley—Rosemead, San Gabriel, Monterey Park, and the rest of the Asian-American Holy Land.

"I think girl," the woman said. She didn't bother whispering. So what if the kid could hear? They were speaking Cantonese; the young ones were either Americanized or learning Mandarin.

"Not girl!" the other woman insisted. "Too ugly to be girl."

"But she's wearing makeup!"

There was silence.

"Too ugly to be girl," she finally agreed.

"Definitely boy. To be a girl would be sad."

"Yes, so sad."

Those women were around her mother's age—they could have been her mother's friends. She didn't need to understand them to understand them, for it blended with the chatter that she heard every day.

Katrina didn't try to block their words; she had given up on that long ago. Instead, Katrina leaned her head against the window and listened . . . to the voices of the women, the drone of the engine, the roar of a passing truck. She listened to the pain in her ribs, the throbbing keeping time with each swerve and a bump in the road. It was all music.

Let it be music. If she could make it music, Katrina knew there would a place where she could breathe. A place where she could rest.

She cradled her violin. She heard a melody.

Finally, Katrina Nguyen let herself sleep.

*   *   *

Shizuka Satomi opened her eyes. Twenty-two hours ago, she had been in Tokyo.

And now?

As if on cue, Shizuka's thoughts were interrupted by a most horrible sound, as if a violin were choking on a windshield wiper.

Who could possibly be creating such infernal—

Oh. *Of course.*

Shizuka stilled her breathing and listened further. In addition to the rooster, there were also two hens. Pigeons, four of them. A duck. An old Asian woman humming a pentatonic folk song. A freeway in the distance. And someone just drove up in a Mercedes.

No other place sounded like this.

The Aguilars lived in the yellow house. On the corner were the Laus, and next door, the Lieus.

This was her house in Los Angeles . . . Monterey Park to be exact. She was home.

Shizuka looked about her room. Thanks to Astrid, her move was already complete. Clothing, furniture, her instruments, all were ready and waiting. Her car had made the trip from Japan and was parked in the driveway downstairs.

The only item she had personally brought with her lay on her nightstand. It was a long and thin music case. Old, battered, yet exquisitely made, what it held seemed almost impatient, calling from just beyond hearing.

Not yet, Shizuka thought. But soon.

As the rooster crowed again, Shizuka stood and stretched. She had timed her sleep perfectly. Even with the jet lag, she felt as if she had just taken a refreshing afternoon nap. Of course, she'd be exhausted in the evening, but if all went as planned, she would have already found who she was looking for.

By the time Shizuka came downstairs, Astrid already had her breakfast ready—rice porridge, hot tea, a soft-boiled egg.

There was also a peeled tangerine.

"Astrid, I didn't ask for—"

"From Mrs. Aguilar," Astrid explained. "She brought a whole bag. Won't you have one? They're really sweet."

Shizuka finished her egg, toast, and tea.

"I'd rather not give my body any surprises while it's still unsure of the time zone."

Astrid shrugged. "But Mrs. Aguilar said you always liked their tangerines."

It was wonderfully sweet, just as always—and juicier than a winter fruit had any right to be. Every neighborhood should have a Mrs. Aguilar . . .

"Miss Satomi?"

"Yes? Oh, I just drifted a little."

Astrid frowned. "Miss Satomi, why don't you rest? It's only the preliminaries. The finals won't be held until next week, and Ms. Grohl is sure to advance."

Shizuka reapplied her lipstick, a little powder, then reached for her sunglasses.

"If she is really the seventh, that girl will have no need for the finals, will she?"

2

Six times, Shizuka Satomi had created brilliance. Six times, she had taken an aspiring musician, trained them, formed them, and created a star.

Even more incredible, while most teachers seemed to cultivate a characteristic sound or style, Satomi's students were at turns icy, devastating, blinding, delicate, frenetic, breathtakingly sensual . . .

Her success, her touch, the effortless, almost inevitable way she pulled genius after genius from thin air, was uncanny, almost supernatural.

Little wonder, then, that people began to call her the Queen of Hell.

However, it had been over a decade since she had taken on a new student.

Why?

Some believed she was the victim of a shattered heart. Before his death, Satomi's last student, Yifeng Brian Zheng, had been seen with her in Annecy, laughing over hot chocolate and mille-feuille. The dashing young violinist had thanked her from every stage he played; and in a television interview, he claimed it was only after studying with Shizuka Satomi that he understood the true meaning of love.

Perhaps they'd been more than teacher and student?

Others surmised that the reason was more mundane, that she might have simply retired. The Queen of Hell had taught Yifeng Zheng, who had followed Kiana Choi, who had followed Sabrina Eisen. And so on and so on.

Even if she found another, what would be left to accomplish?

Whatever the reason, with each passing year, more people assumed that the Queen of Hell had no intention of ever teaching again.

Idiots.

For ten years, Shizuka Satomi had been searching. From Lausanne,

Salzburg, Sydney, most recently Tokyo, she had listened, searched prospect after prospect.

Nothing, nothing, *nothing.*

Not that they didn't try. Not that musicians had not traveled to her, offered her everything they had, all they could imagine.

As if all they could imagine could be close to enough.

Others around her, including Tremon Philippe himself, had suggested she was being too selective, perhaps even arbitrary. Surely over the past ten years, she had found musicians who might be appropriate.

Of course she had.

Her previous six students had been an almost uninterrupted string of genius. All had been perfectly appropriate. Yet, with each one, Shizuka became more and more aware that something was wrong. No. Something was *missing.* As she watched each of them shine and fall, sparkle and burn, Shizuka became more and more obsessed with a music playing just beyond hearing—maddeningly familiar, yet always beyond her grasp.

Until finally, in Tokyo, she heard it.

Through the din of thirteen million people, and vending machines, ramen joints, Internet cafés, electric trains, and cherry blossoms for each of them twice over, she heard it—coming not from within that city, but from far across the sea.

Coming from, of all places, home.

Shizuka swerved past a very slow Lexus, then accelerated onto Huntington Drive.

The San Gabriel Valley resembled an Asian-American Monopoly board. Cambodians, Chinese, Vietnamese, Laotians, Vietnamese-Chinese, a few Koreans, even some Japanese crisscrossed past the working-class neighborhoods of Rosemead, Monterey Park, El Monte, through middle-class Temple City, San Gabriel, and Alhambra, all the way up to Boardwalk and Park Place—San Marino and Arcadia, where Shizuka was arriving now.

She could feel herself breathing faster as she passed the Santa Anita Plaza, a gilded shopping mall where one might procure truffle-filled dumplings, a Hello Kitty latte, and a two-thousand-dollar box of Chinese bird nest.

Quickly, she sped by the Santa Anita racetrack, home to the fashionable 626 Night Market, drawing Asians of all persuasions for a night of stinky tofu, boba, taro macaroons, and international indie film screenings.

Until finally, she arrived at her destination: Xinhua Phoenix Hall.

Xinhua Phoenix Hall was actually the smaller of two buildings designed by the renowned Chinese architect An Wei. Across the courtyard, still shrouded in construction covers, was the site of Xinhua Phoenix Investment Bank's grand "Golden Friendship Pavilion," due to open the following year.

Between them was a massive fountain, in the shape of an ever-flowing teapot. Inscribed in its side was a carved and gilded 永, the character for Eternity.

It had seemed like 永 since Shizuka had so anticipated a performance. She didn't know exactly how she knew, but she *knew*. And when Tremon Philippe mentioned the Grohl girl, that was confirmation enough.

By now, she could almost feel it physically pulling her—a timeless music that her other students, for all their genius, had only been able to trace.

Shizuka Satomi took a deep breath. There was no need to hurry. The Queen of Hell did not hurry.

She checked her makeup one last time, then put on her sunglasses.

Here would be her last and seventh student.

Here would be her last and seventh soul.

And then, what would be left to accomplish?

Everything.

*   *   *

When one hears "violin competition," one may envision nervous contestants and a stage. But within the foyer and surrounding hallways, a whole other competition is being waged.

Someone mentions a trip to Berlin. Another invokes Juilliard. In the foyer of who-is-who, students don't have teachers. Rather, they are "studying with somebody," often identified only by last name, as in "she is studying with Korsakova."

Regardless of age, whether the competition is international or local, amidst chatter and coffee, in various accents, real and acquired, everyone wants to know:

Who is more important than whom, and why?

"I see that the princess reigns, as usual."

Landon Fung, of Freiberg Music in Temple City, was talking to Ellen Seidel, a longtime violin teacher, also from Temple City. The princess, also known as Tamiko Giselle Grohl, sat in the corner eating a tiny serving of macaroni potato salad. Amidst all the nervous patter around her, she seemed almost nonchalant as she reviewed her music.

"Did you tell her?"

"Of course. But I told her she'd be watching via webcast."

"Good. I mean why would Shizuka Satomi come *here*?"

Several people turned at the sound of the name.

"Landon . . . *shhh*."

"S-sorry!" Landon Fung nodded nervously.

Of course she was not coming. She *couldn't* be.

Ellen tried to downplay her excitement. But still, Shizuka Satomi—*the* Shizuka Satomi—had sent a letter saying that she would be watching Tamiko Grohl—Ellen Seidel's student—at this competition.

Ellen Seidel had been teaching for years. She had endured spoiled students, careless students, untalented students, students with nightmare parents.

And then came Tamiko Giselle Grohl.

Yes, the girl was difficult. She threw tantrums, behaved strangely. But she practiced. She obsessed. And, she was a *prodigy*. To Ellen Seidel, Tamiko was a reward for so much frustration—an affirmation from God.

Ellen glanced at her star student. Tamiko was ready for the next step in her career. She needed to grow; nobody stayed with one teacher. But no matter what, Ellen Seidel would always be her first.

Most people assumed that Tamiko's next step would be conservatory, like the Kilbourne School, or perhaps Juilliard. Ellen agreed this was logical.

But Shizuka Satomi had nothing to do with logic.

Because Shizuka Satomi's last student was Yifeng Zheng. And

before that, Kiana Choi. And before that? Sabrina Eisen. And so on and so on. These were household names, well, at least in the households of violinists. Each had won medals. Each had been stars.

Were Tamiko to join that pantheon, Ellen's life as her esteemed former teacher would never be the same. She'd accompany Shizuka and Tamiko to Paris. Frankfurt. A fourteen-stop grand tour of Asia. Meanwhile, back home, a line of brilliant young students would be waiting, each eager for her wisdom, for a promise of greatness.

"I'm studying with Seidel," they would say.

And all this was possible if Shizuka Satomi, even if merely online, would watch Tami—

And then, without warning, someone gasped.

Long black hair. Blood-red dress. The timeless half smile that a madman might paint. And of course, sunglasses hid her eyes.

Shizuka Satomi. The Queen of Hell.

At her approach, the hall fell silent.

Of course it would. Ellen Seidel had heard the stories, but nothing could have prepared her for *this*. This was more than power, ambition, beauty, or even genius. In the legendary teacher's presence, such words seemed meaningless—devoured by an unrelenting, inescapable flame.

Yet what was most startling, even terrifying, was her focus. Nothing about Shizuka Satomi seemed random, without purpose.

Everything was measured. Everything was arranged.

Everything was completely and sublimely *composed*.

And suddenly, Ellen Seidel realized that, as everyone was watching her, the Queen of Hell was watching *them*. Perfectly polite, perfectly unapproachable, she seemed to measure, question, and disregard them all . . .

Then, she stopped.

Tamiko was standing now, quivering, her eyes wavering for the first time.

"Tamiko," Ellen silently implored. "Don't look down. *Look at her.*"

And then, Shizuka Satomi, *the* Shizuka Satomi, nodded, took off her sunglasses, and glanced into Tamiko Giselle Grohl's eyes.

———

So that was the Grohl girl. Pretty. But of course she was.

Tremon said she was supremely gifted. But of course she was.

Shizuka entered the main hall and found a seat in the back. Even there, she felt people watching her, gossiping, no doubt.

Whatever. Appearance, reputation, even training or desire . . . none of that mattered now.

The organizers made the usual announcements. A parent forgot to bring cough drops. The lights dimmed.

Now . . . let's hear her play.

* * *

After the preliminaries of any competition, the foyer fills with the chatter of parents, teachers, and musicians. There is triumph, heartbreak, arguing, predictions of who might advance to the final rounds. It can be a spectacle all its own.

Yet, this afternoon, the conversations were dominated by another topic entirely.

Shizuka Satomi was here.

"I think she's living in Lausanne?"

"Tokyo, last I heard."

"Wait—how old *is* she?"

"Here's my phone; I want you to take a picture . . ."

"Let's take a picture with her together!"

And then, there she was.

Just as before, silence fell throughout the hall. But this time, it was not from shock. People knew she was here, people were expecting her. Most of them rightly assumed she was searching for her next student, her next star.

Yet, as Shizuka Satomi moved through them, the San Gabriel Valley's finest found their hearts faltering between notes, their music unraveled and wanting. Those who had thought to speak to the Queen of Hell suddenly felt small and invisible, as if they had nothing significant to say.

Two people, however, approached her.

"Miss Satomi! Thank you for coming to watch the competition. I—I'm Ellen Seidel. And this is Tamiko Giselle Grohl."

Shizuka glanced at them both. Was that a smile?

"Y-you sent me that note, remember?" Ellen asked, her voice straining with pride, desire, and terror.

"Of course," Shizuka Satomi finally said. "Your student is the reason that I am here."

Tamiko Giselle Grohl could not restrain herself any longer. The Queen of Hell was in front of her, right in front of her.

"Kiana Choi studied with you, right?" she blurted.

"Yes. She did."

"Kiana's my hero—I want to be just like her!"

For the last time, Shizuka Satomi looked at Tamiko Grohl. The girl had been poised and engaging, technically near flawless.

How appropriate.

The Queen of Hell reached for her sunglasses, then tilted her head in a most exquisite way.

"No. You don't."

By the time anyone could react, Shizuka Satomi had floated to the exit and out the door.

*   *   *

Astrid was peeling tangerines when the door opened.

"Welcome back, Miss Satomi! I trust it went . . ." Her voice trailed off. One look at Miss Satomi told Astrid everything she needed to know.

"I—I'll get started on dinner right away."

Miss Satomi took off her sunglasses and rubbed her eyes.

"Astrid, tonight maybe just some miso soup."

"Of course, Miss Satomi." Astrid tried to not seem alarmed. "Why don't you take a nap?"

"No . . . I'll be in the backyard."

"Yes, Miss Satomi."

Astrid went to the kitchen and heated some water. To that, she added bonito stock, sliced radish, seaweed, Miss Satomi's favorite white miso, a beaten egg, and finally some sliced fish cake.

Miso soup. Miss Satomi asked for it only when she was ill or exhausted. Of course she would be! She had returned from Tokyo to a hometown she once had left forever, all for the promise of a seventh soul.

Miss Satomi had staked everything on this move, on the Grohl girl. She had been so hopeful, so sure.

But if this wasn't the right student, either?

Soon the kitchen filled with the gentle aroma of the simmering soup. Astrid dropped the heat to low, so it would be ready when Miss Satomi returned.

And then Astrid waited. For now, that was all that she could do.

No, no, no . . .

Shizuka walked outside to her backyard. Automatically, she circled the persimmon tree and avoided an old uneven cobblestone next to the fish pond.

"Tremon."

In the fishpond, the same koi glided among the water lilies. Beyond that, the same hill dropped away, the same unending vista of homes, cars, and places to drive them.

"Tremon?"

So this Grohl girl wanted to be like Kiana Choi. Really? She would damn herself for *that*? Why be like someone else? Where was the vision? The genius? As an agent of damnation, Shizuka understood she would be dealing in the tedium of human weakness. But there had to be more.

"Tremon! Where are you?"

"You don't need to shout, Shizuka. I'm right here."

Mouth breathing. Dress shoes. A plodding half cadence that she knew far too well.

To some, Tremon Philippe might have appeared stately, cultured. However, Shizuka had always thought of her facilitator as a particularly well-dressed toad.

"What was that? I traveled across an ocean to hear *that*? You told me she was special!"

Shizuka paused. This was not entirely his fault. She, too, had been wrong. Also, with Tremon, she needed to be cautious. People had named her the Queen of Hell, but Tremon was a demon, a real one.

"I'm sorry, Tremon. That was my frustration talking. It has been a long and disappointing day."

"Of course, Shizuka. No harm done. But I don't understand. Shouldn't we be celebrating? After all, the Grohl girl is brilliant, beautiful, and hungry."

"I told you, that is not enough this time."

"Time? Time is exactly what you don't have."

"Don't you think I know that?" Shizuka walked to the fish pond. She stared at the koi swimming silently in the dark.

"Why are you making this difficult? It's simple math. Six plus one equals freedom."

"And that one is somewhere close. I can still sense it."

"Where? Down *there*?" Tremon gestured downhill to the lights of Monterey Park. "Doing what? Nibbling on dumplings? Perhaps roasting a duck? Honestly, my dear, what are you thinking?"

"What if I told you that Hell would receive something special to remember me by?"

"Would you really expect me to believe that you are risking your existence out of an affection for Hell?

"Of course not. But the seventh will be worth the wait—for all of us."

"Very well, Shizuka," Tremon finally said. "For now, I will play along, if only because your past souls have been so well received. But remember—you have been allotted seven times seven years to deliver seven souls. Forty-eight of those years have passed. If you do not free yourself by this time next year, Hell will have no need to remember you, for there you will be—every special day, every special moment, for all eternity."

With that, Tremon Philippe was gone.

*　　*　　*

Katrina checked her phone. Good, she had signal. Quickly, she sent another text to Evan. She hadn't worked out the details, but she'd settle in with Evan for a while, find a job, then start making more music videos.

Beyond that? She'd figure it out.

Katrina winced as the bus shifted lanes. She clutched her violin and eventually drifted back to sleep.

When she next awoke, the bus was rumbling off of Rosemead Boulevard and into the parking lot of Shun Fat, a huge Asian wholesale market and restaurant supply complex. Already, people were waiting to pick up relatives.

Katrina tried to wake herself as she got off the bus and waited at the sidewalk for her bag. The two old women studied her and whispered. One pointed at her face.

Katrina touched her face, then looked down at her sleeve. *Crap.* While asleep, her foundation had rubbed off. Which meant they saw the bruises. Her black eye . . .

These old ladies were strangers; their looks couldn't hurt her. Their stares and judgments were nothing compared with what she had been through. She told herself that this shouldn't hurt. It was nothing.

And nothing shouldn't hurt at all.

3

Lan Tran loved her donut. Her giant concrete and plaster donut.

Once common in LA's Eisenhower years, just a few of these giant donuts remained in greater Los Angeles. There were Kindle's Donuts, Dale's Donuts, and Randy's Donuts, of course. Donut King II was in Gardena. In La Puente, there was the drive-through Donut Hole.

And here, above El Monte, rose Starrgate Donut.

Lan's donut meant a future. Her donut meant family.

In the night quiet, Starrgate Donut hummed, almost like a starship. Stationed in the front, her twins Windee and Edwin navigated the donut case, stocking it with galaxies of sweet, colorful lemon creams, apple fritters, double chocolates, Boston crèmes, twists. At her back, Shirley and Aunty Floresta maintained operations, while below, Markus was busy planning their next expansion.

"Hello, Captain!" The twins saluted.

Lan returned their salute.

"Carry on," she said with a satisfied smile.

Shirley emerged from the back with a tray of chocolate éclairs.

"The replicators are operating within tolerances, Mother."

"Thank you, Shirley. But create the next batch with thirty percent less residual heat. We won't have many customers, so they don't need to be hot, and we can save power that way."

"Yes, Mother."

Lan Tran stared out the window. The stars beckoned as they always had.

One did not have to be a rocket scientist to make a donut. But that didn't mean it didn't help.

A picture of Mr. and Mrs. Thamavuong still hung on the wall. They had acquired Starrgate in 1979. At the time, it was known as El Monte Donuts. The Thamavuongs sold classic, American-style donuts made with happiness and care. And, in the '80s, video games became popular, so the Thamavuongs brought them into their store.

El Monte Donuts became known not only for apple fritters, but for *Pac-Man, Asteroids,* and *Defender.* Their most popular game, by far, was *Stargate.* Dedicated video game players would spend hour after hour, quarter after quarter, rescuing people from an alien invasion that would never, ever cease. Eventually, the Thamavuongs decided to buy, rather than rent, first one, then two, and finally three *Stargate* machines. Since they kept them in good playing condition, their shop became known informally as Stargate Donuts.

Eventually, Mr. Thamavuong changed the name of El Monte Donuts officially to Starrgate Donut (with the double *r* to avoid any trademark trouble). Even after the video game craze passed, the name stuck over the years, and up until when the Thamavuongs were ready to retire.

By then, they had realized that they had put so much love into the shop, they had forgotten about having children to take over the business. Developers began to inquire. Some even offered a fair price. But Mrs. Thamavuong would look at their big donut and cry. Their entire lives were in that donut.

Then one night, the Thamavuongs received an email from a woman named Lan Tran. Ms. Tran said that she wanted Starrgate Donut *because* of their big donut.

The sale was completed almost immediately. There was no bargaining—they named a price, and this woman agreed. Even better, she promised that Starrgate Donut would keep selling donuts and shine like a beacon into the night.

The Thamavuongs spent three weeks with Lan and her family to teach them their basic operations and how to run their equipment. Then they handed their treasured recipe book and keys to Ms. Tran and retired, full of good memories and good American currency, to Laos and their beloved Vientiane.

Once they left, Lan put the recipe book away. Instead of cooking, she had her crew digitally convert and store two dozen of each type of donut the Thamavuongs had made. These reference donuts would then be quickly and virtually perfectly reproduced by the ship's replicators. The result? Cake donuts would always be colorful and pretty.

Yeast donuts would be invariably golden and soft. No surprises, no worries.

Eventually, her crew might learn to make donuts as the Thamavuongs did, but for now, Lan's duty was to their safety and their mission.

Because donuts were not the sole reason why Lan Tran and her crew were on this planet.

Lan strode past the kitchen and opened what had been the door to the cleaning closet. But instead of mops and buckets, behind it was a new shiny elevator leading down to the recently completed lower level, which now housed the control center, research laboratory, sick bay, and living compound, as well as an underground hangar for their starship.

Here at Starrgate Donut, Lan and her family would safely wait out the fall of the Galactic Empire, continue their work, and live undisturbed, as long as—as Mr. Thamavuong stressed—they gave donuts to the police officers for free.

"Captain." Markus Tran saluted as she entered the research lab.

"Lieutenant. How are the modifications coming?"

"The donut is smaller than ideal—but it is nothing we can't address. Please note the modifications I've made. With your approval, I will begin implementing them immediately."

Lan looked over the plans and nodded. Her son had become quite the engineer, hadn't he?

"What about power?"

"As predicted, preparing this complex depleted over sixty-two percent of our power reserves. It will be at least three months before they return to normal levels, but our day-to-day operations should not be affected. However, there is a greater concern."

"The stargate?"

"Yes, Captain. Even at one hundred percent, our ship's main reactor would be far from adequate. We need to find an external power source, but this civilization's energy production falls short by several orders of magnitude."

This was no surprise. After all, this planet hadn't yet harnessed fusion, let alone point singularities or antimatter.

"I've been working on a solution to that," Lan said. "For now, continue fabrication and low-power tests. You may also divert ten percent of the ship's power when we are not running the replicator."

"Understood, ma'am."

"That will be all."

"See! He called her mom!"

"No, he said ma'am."

"He said mom!"

The twins rushed toward her as the elevator closed behind them.

"Edwin! Windee! Didn't I tell you not to run in the halls? Your brother is tuning the warp field. And why aren't you at your posts?"

"Sorry!" they said in unison.

"So, you two, what is all this about?"

"We wanted to know—" Edwin started.

"That now that we're off ship, should we call you Mom or Captain? I wanna call you Captain," said Windee, saluting.

Lan saluted back. She tried not to smile.

"Very well, Ensign Windee."

"But sometimes can I call you Mom?" Edwin said. He grabbed her waist and held on tight.

"Oh, Edwin . . . Settling on one name will be difficult, won't it? What matters is that we're together, and safe. And that means no more running through the halls. We don't want anyone to get hurt, right?"

"Yes, Mom."

"Aye-aye, Captain!"

"Good. Now, back up to the store, you two. Don't you have jobs to do?"

Lan watched them running back to their posts. She shook her head and smiled. Family. She would cross a universe for her family.

In fact, she already had.

*　*　*

From what Astrid could gather, the house next to Miss Satomi's had been owned by a Japanese family, then a Mexican family, and now a Chinese one.

Yet more than anything, this neighborhood reminded her of her childhood in Switzerland, of her grandmother bent over her carrots, peas, and asparagus. For whatever was parked in the driveway, whether VW or Toyota or Chevy or Mercedes, every family here seemed to have a grandmother, and every garden seemed to have vegetables.

Astrid had arrived a month before Miss Satomi to prepare the house. Luckily, Miss Satomi had retained a groundskeeper, so the persimmon tree was healthy, and the fishpond was fine.

But Miss Satomi's garden had been woefully underused. And though Astrid was no grandmother, she would plant vegetables, as well. Turnips. Cabbage. Perhaps aubergines. If she started now, they would be ready by next year.

Then again, next year, would she or Miss Satomi even be here?

Astrid's thoughts were interrupted by a knock on the door. On the porch were a bag of green beans and two bitter melons. Astrid waved to the old lady next door, who bowed and waved back.

Astrid looked at her newfound bounty. The beans she knew how to prepare, but bitter melon?

Grandma Strafeldas in Fribourg had never grown a bitter melon.

* * *

Los Angeles has days of blue sky, mountains, beach, eighty-two degrees, and palm trees all around. But LA truly becomes a paradise on those rare days with clear traffic, no obstacles, no accidents, just miles and miles of pure smooth road and any lane to choose.

However, Shizuka was not driving on one of those days.

A truck had lost a mattress just before the 605 interchange. The river of cars jostled her insides with stop and go, surge and swell.

Worst of all, the Queen of Hell had to pee.

Urine-filled water bottles litter the LA freeway system for good reason. The entire LA basin is filled with bathroom dead zones, often near industrial areas and freeways, where one cannot find public toilets.

Yet not everyone can urinate into a plastic water bottle.

At least there was a McDonald's near the next exit. For now, Shizuka tried to concentrate on more pressing things.

Pressing. *Okay, Satomi, bad choice of words.*

Anyhow, the seventh. The seventh.

After Arcadia, Shizuka had received a second letter from Ellen Seidel, begging her to hear Tamiko Giselle Grohl once more, at the finals. Tremon Philippe had visited again, as well, needlessly reminding her that a musician with Tamiko's gifts could be ready for world-class competition within a couple of months, if not sooner.

Even Astrid had voiced her concern. She recalled how long Miss Satomi had been searching, how exhausted she sounded when asking for miso soup, and that, even if Miss Grohl wasn't perfect, might she not be enough?

Once her contract was settled, would Miss Satomi not have all the time in the world?

Shizuka yawned. She was almost over her jet lag, but not quite.

But even fully rested, could she ever make a demon like Tremon understand?

The Grohl girl was ready and willing. She said that she wanted to be just like Kiana Choi. She had played like it, as well. Every note the girl played had been an homage, a vow, a promise to give *everything* for a chance at recognition, at fame.

And then there was Astrid. Shizuka knew how much Astrid worried about her. Six times, Shizuka Satomi had taken brilliant but flawed talents, taken their souls for a curse and some lies. What was the harm in just one more?

How could Shizuka make them understand?

Of course. She couldn't.

She wasn't sure if she herself understood who the seventh was, *what* the seventh was. But even so, Shizuka Satomi could not let this student, this music, pass her by.

The seventh. Where was the seventh hiding? She could sense them, almost hear them.

And then Shizuka panicked.

She had been so deep in thought that McDonald's, and its restroom, were already several exits behind her. Shizuka swerved around a pickup truck and a Lexus, rode the shoulder to the next off-ramp, and gunned her Jaguar off the exit. Desperately, frantically, Shizuka searched for a business with a restroom. But all she saw was residential street after residential street.

Damn these suburbs!

Then, in her rising sea of despair, she saw it. Peeking over from behind the trees was the Big Donut.

Of course!

Shizuka remembered the Big Donut from her childhood. She had never actually been inside—her parents had been strict about junk food, after all.

But now she was an adult, and no one was stopping her. She bee-lined to the Starrgate Donut, skidded to a stop, and raced inside. Once she entered, she rushed for the bathroom door.

But no door was there.

Then she remembered something horrible. This was not Japan. This was El Monte.

Shizuka almost sobbed out loud. In Japan, donut shop bathrooms were clean and available. But here?

Shizuka had seen LA donut shops say no to children. She had seen them turn away white men in business suits. No one used donut shop bathrooms unless they were employees or police . . .

Also, everyone was staring.

Whether with musicians or not, Shizuka still carried herself like the Queen of Hell. Some customers looked away; others seemed frightened. An old woman crossed herself.

No, no *no*!

What to do next? Maybe she could find a gas station. Maybe a supermarket. Maybe a tree.

She had signed over her soul to Hell—surely she had been through worse than this?

Hadn't she?

But just as all hope was lost, a donut lady appeared at the counter.

"Yes?"

Shizuka took off her sunglasses and bowed her head.

"Ma'am, I know it's not for the public, but may I please use your bathroom?" she said, as politely as she could.

"Come around the back."

In disbelief, Shizuka looked up and into the eyes of what must be the nicest Los Angeles Donut Lady in existence.

"Shirley, show her."

"But, Mother—"

"Show her the bathroom," Donut Lady said pleasantly, but firmly. "Just follow her, miss."

Shizuka liked this donut lady. She really liked this donut lady.

The girl called Shirley led Shizuka down a passageway that stretched a little further back than Shizuka expected.

And there were noises here that didn't match the sounds of a kitchen. Instead of motorized fryers, the commercial mixers, and the intermittent click of oven thermostats, the air was alive with soft whirs, hums, pure sine-wave tones, regular chirps. And these sounds came from everywhere—from beneath her and overhead.

Shizuka wasn't going to mention it; she was the last person with the right to probe into someone else's business.

"Thank you. I know you wouldn't normally let someone use—"

Then Shizuka froze as her being was pierced by a gentle, yet supremely powerful, music. No, not quite music, and not only the air. It was deep and resonant and harmonious, like an Aeolian harp coursed with the strings of space itself.

"Beautiful . . ."

"Ma'am?"

"What is this sound?"

"Oh . . . it's probably my brother," the girl said too quickly. "He's on his computer playing one of his games."

The girl was lying, of course—this was no computer game.

But this wasn't a time to pry, not with a full bladder.

Shizuka was led to a door with a handwritten sign that said FOR EMPLOYEE ONLY. Behind it lay the cleanest bathroom a woman might hope for.

At last, Shizuka peed. She hummed Beethoven's "Ode to Joy." She thanked the ancestors; she thanked the gods. If it hadn't been spoken for, she'd have given her soul to Jesus right there.

As she finished, Shizuka heard footsteps and a muffled conversation. The beautiful sound faded, then vanished altogether.

It would have been nice to know what that sound was, but she had imposed enough. Shizuka freshened up, returned the key, then got in line. She didn't feel right just leaving.

And besides, fresh donuts?

She ended up behind a group of boys. One of them ordered the largest donut she had ever seen.

"What is that?"

"I-it's an Alaska Donut," the boy nervously replied.

"Alaska Donut?"

"Kindle's has a Texas Donut, but . . ." The boy tried not to stare as he explained.

"The Starrgate one is bigger." Shizuka finished the sentence for him.

"Yeah, that's what she said," one of the other youths joked.

"Lucky her," Shizuka let herself say.

The boys looked away shyly, still too young to respond.

And then, once again Shizuka was in front of Donut Lady.

"May I help you?"

"I would like an Alaska Donut and a small coffee, please."

Donut Lady's eyes. They were dark, almost too dark for this world. And yet, somehow, they reminded Shizuka of old Mr. Grossmueller, who had survived Bergen-Belsen and devoted the rest of his life to playing Handel.

Donut Lady placed Shizuka's coffee and donut on a tray.

"Thank you."

"No, thank *you*," Shizuka said, shaking herself to attention. After all, this woman had saved her life.

Donut Lady smiled.

And Shizuka felt herself fall into a field of stars.

Somehow, Shizuka managed to take her tray to a clean table. She needed to clear her head. This was no time for infatuation. It was already February. She had a student to find, a demon to feed, her soul to save.

Then Shizuka bit into the soft, sticky Alaska Donut.

It was second grade, and Mrs. Jennison had brought donuts to class. She said something about an American orbiting the earth and he was called an "astronaut."

Shizuka took a glazed one and Julie Kiyama took a red, white, and blue sprinkle. The fruit punch was red and cold and sweet.

The donuts were happy and fluffy, and even better than the peach cobbler in the cafeteria . . .

Wait—why was her coffee cold?

How long had she been staring out the window? Mrs. Jennison? Second grade? Where had that memory come from?

Where was her mind? She must still be jet-lagged.

She glanced at Donut Lady. Donut Lady glanced back. Shizuka felt herself blushing and immediately looked away.

Come on, Satomi, focus.

This wasn't the time to daydream or make eyes at donut ladies. Somewhere out there was that next student. She wrapped the remaining half of the Alaska Donut, put on her sunglasses, and left without looking back.

But as Shizuka drove away, she could not forget Donut Lady's starry, faraway eyes.

*   *   *

Was it her appearance? Yes, but more than that. Her *voice*. Lan had heard many voices since arriving on Earth, but that sunglass lady worked this very ordinary oxygen/nitrogen atmosphere into something beautiful.

"Mother?"

Or maybe the way she held herself. Her posture was effortless, elegant, as if denying the planet's gravitational field.

"Mother?"

Lan pulled herself from her reverie. How long had Shirley been standing there?

"That woman. I am positive that she heard the space warp." Shirley lowered the last part to a whisper.

"What?" Lan looked at her sharply, and shushed Shirley back to the kitchen. "What do you mean, she heard the warp?"

"Markus was running a low-level continuity test when that woman asked about the sound."

This is not good, Lan thought. This was not good at all. If Sunglass Lady was versed in warp theory, she would know what they were doing. She might identify their harmonic signature, or even discern the specific warp profile and guess their origin.

"Was there any indication that she identified the signature?"

Shirley shook her head. "She seemed surprised more than anything."

Lan tried to steady her breathing. Sometimes these bodies were not easy to control. Yes, of course. There was no way Sunglass Lady was a warp expert. They were on a technologically primitive planet, in El Monte.

"Good. But we should be careful."

Still, what was a being like *that* doing in a place like this?

"But, Mother, why did you let her use the bathroom?"

Why *did* she let her use the bathroom? Mr. Thamavuong warned that they needed to be careful about the bathroom. Why had she said yes?

"I don't know. I just wanted to help, and she was in need, and—wait, do you think it was mind control? If it were mind control, we would have sensed it, right?"

"I detected no psi activity," Shirley said. "And, Mother, it is not unlike you to help someone in need."

Yes. Of course she would help someone in need, especially someone like Sunglass Lady. Lan remembered how she'd said, *I would like an Alaska Donut and a small coffee, please.*

Like mathematics. So clear, so pure.

"Mother?"

What? Had she drifted again?

"I'll make sure to turn off the warp circuitry next time she's here," Shirley finally said.

Next time? Lan felt her heart skip and her face smile.

What was she *doing*? There was no time for Sunglass Lady! She needed to lead her crew. She needed to protect her family.

"Thank you, Shirley. That will be all."

Captain Lan glanced toward the front of the store, then walked into the control center. The space around her was filled with the soft, glorious hum of the warp field.

It was the second-most beautiful sound she had heard today.

4

Yes!

Finally. A rainbow flag on the door, a compost pile in the yard. Katrina had arrived.

Katrina had met Evan at a queer youth conference. She was a timid newbie geek with facial hair and bad skin. He was a film student who seemed far too queer and fierce to notice her.

And yet he had comforted her after she broke down in the break-away gender discussion group. He had assured her that she wasn't the only one who wasn't out to their parents and who came from a culture where one did not even mention such things; he said that queer folks often chose their families just for these reasons.

He told her that she belonged, as much as anyone else.

Between sessions, they shared lunch. He talked about a short film he was working on, and listened when she talked about saving money for a new violin. They held hands, and before they parted, he told her not to give up, and promised that he would be there whenever she needed.

And then Evan had kissed her goodbye.

But that had been two years ago. When Katrina had finally called for help, it'd taken Evan a week to reply.

Katrina knew that Evan had changed. After all, he'd left college, and never finished the film he'd talked so passionately about at the conference. Still, part of her hoped that he might look at the videos of gaming and anime music she was making for YouTube. Maybe he'd even want to help.

But no matter what, here would be a friendly face and a safe space, even for just a little while.

The door opened.

"It's you?" Evan said dully.

Katrina tried not to seem shocked. He was thinner than before.

His hair was longer, tied up a bun, and he smelled like body odor, cat fur, and sage.

"I sent you an email? And you wrote back. You said to come over. And I sent you texts while I was on the way."

"Oh. Wait for a sec." He disappeared inside.

Katrina waited by the doorway. She noticed an old Chinese man across the street eyeing her suspiciously. She gave her best smile as the door opened once more.

"You should have said you were coming for real." Evan scratched his head. "Could you come back later tonight? I've got someone here now."

"I'm sorry," Katrina mumbled.

He glared at the man across the street, then yelled back into the room.

"The old man is looking at us again. He looks hungry. Hide the cat!"

"Haha! That's so fucked up." The voice inside giggled.

Evan closed the door.

Katrina stood there. He had not even offered to take her bags.

Why did she just apologize? She *had* told him for real.

Katrina walked blankly to the corner, just as a bus whooshed away. No worries—she didn't know the bus routes, and an unexpected bus fare was not in her budget anyway.

Katrina kept walking. In his email, Evan had written that this place was like a foreign country. Yet here were dentist offices and banks and businesses and cafés with clean glass windows, and streets with new Japanese and European SUVs.

For a while, she lost herself in the novelty of being in this new town. But eventually, her feet started to hurt, her rib was throbbing, and she was low on ibuprofen. And besides, she needed to use the bathroom.

So Katrina decided to buy a boba.

The boba would cost money, but she would also have a place to rest and think. Luckily, this street offered a boba shop every couple blocks or so. Soon, Katrina found a perfect spot to have a clean table, sip a kiwi boba, and watch the world go by.

But first, the bathroom.

The women's room was locked. Eventually, a girl came out and gave her a disapproving look, but she didn't block her way.

Katrina entered and began to fix her hair in the mirror. But then remembered the look from that girl.

The hair could wait. She needed to use the bathroom right now.

The seat was cool and clean. There was air freshener, a flower in a vase. She smelled lavender.

Rest. Breathe.

She had just finished when there was a knock on the door.

"Excuse me. *Excuse me*," a male voice said.

She flushed, washed up, and exited the bathroom. She grabbed her things and left without stopping or looking up.

"Sorry, sorry," she mumbled. "The men's room was taken."

Well, at least I didn't have to buy anything, right?

Katrina told herself she should be thankful. Thanks to the part-time work, the cam shows, the blowjobs, she had escaped home and made it here. She had her violin. She had her laptop and a fresh supply of hormones. She was alive.

Still, was it so difficult to find a place to sit down?

Then Katrina saw a sign for El Molino Park.

Katrina did not know what El Molino Park was, but if it was a nice park, there would be places to rest. She pushed forward, past a 7-Eleven, past a Chinese herb store, a Mexican hardware store, a Vietnamese nail salon, a Taiwanese dance studio, more boba places, a dozen noodle shops . . .

And finally, after twenty more minutes, she came to El Molino Park's parking lot, and then to the park itself.

There was fresh grass. Fresh dirt. Soda machines. People were playing basketball. Couples sat together on blankets. She heard the plink of someone hitting a softball. The snack bar was selling hot dogs and nachos.

How was this like a foreign country?

Katrina found a bench by a large artificial pond. It was cool, quiet, and undisturbed.

Yes! She hadn't merely stumbled on a place to rest—she might even be able to practice her violin. But first, she would rest, just a little, for her feet, and her side. Thank goodness she was Asian and still relatively clean—there would be a couple of curious glances, but no one was likely to call the police.

She placed her laptop next to her, put her escape bag under her head, and held her violin. She listened to the sounds of the basketball. She felt a little sunlight, and a gentle wind through the trees.

There was a fake waterfall. A fountain . . . and ducks . . .

*　　*　　*

Shizuka left the Starrgate Donut with no desire to revisit the freeway. Instead, she decided to drive the surface streets home. The car was from an admirer, given long ago. When she was younger, the Jaguar had seemed overpowered and loud. But with each passing year, she could better appreciate how timelessly it navigated the everyday chaos around her, yet never lost its singular, insatiable thirst for gasoline.

How many years had it been since she had last driven these streets?

So much had changed. If anything, change was the one constant here. Shizuka's childhood sheet music store had gone first. Then Foodland, with its cute baggers and wobbly shopping carts, became Diho Grocery, and finally a Hong Kong bank, anonymous behind darkened windows and marble façade.

And now the elementary school had yielded to a Mediterranean-casual apartment complex, complete with mixed-use shopping and underground parking. Tonight, young people would be crowding these sidewalks, perhaps lining up for Japanese crêpes and Taiwanese shaved ice.

This was very different from Tokyo, where there was almost a desperation to either be at the forefront of change or to guard against it at all costs. Be it Harajuku, Meiji Jingu, Akihabara, each was defined by a strict relationship to, and profound respect for, change.

Here, change had continued with so little fanfare or notice that change had become, well, mundane.

Of course, some places remained curiously resistant to change. Fong's Burger was busily serving its delicious pork buns from its greasy side window. Amy's Pastries still displayed the same dusty wedding cake with the lopsided pillars and three dead flies. And there were the greasy, glistening, impossibly fragrant ducks, pigs, and cuttlefish dripping in the window of Sam Woo BBQ.

Yet none of these places appeared to be doing any *resisting*. Changing with the times? Fong's didn't even wipe their countertops with the times. And, as far as preserving tradition, Sam Woo BBQ was now happily promoting its new deep-fried fish skins.

There they were. And there, most likely, they would always be.

Yet another of Shizuka's landmarks was now just ahead.

Shizuka did not visit her childhood home very often, but the pond at El Molino Park had always been one of her favorite places, one of the few that held happy memories of her parents. Over time, the park had added softball and baseball diamonds, resurfaced the outdoor basketball courts with a nonslip coating. The city had added tables with chessboards, a fitness par course, expanded the tennis courts. Even a lawn bowling club had come and gone.

And yet there was always that bench by the same old pond.

For much of her life, it had been a place she could come to think, to contemplate, to be alone.

And now, with nowhere else to go, it seemed as good a place as any to be.

Today, Shizuka had with her the half donut from Starrgate and some water, and a bag of hot dog buns from the corner drugstore. She strolled to the pond, just as she had done for years.

Someone in the distance had just plinked a ground ball and run out a base hit. The snack bar served another order of nachos. Circling them were mothers and fathers pushing baby carts around the rubberized jogging path. Behind her, basketball, so much basketball . . . so many voices speaking different Vietnamese, Toisanese, Cantonese.

And in front of her? The wind on the lake. The almost-natural rush of the artificial waterfall. Pigeons cooing nearby. The flapping, quacking. A child splashing a rock.

And on her favorite bench was a peacefully snoring girl.

At first, Shizuka assumed she was a neighborhood kid taking a study break, but then Shizuka noticed her bags. *A runaway?* How sad. Well, better to let her rest.

Shizuka was about to find another bench when the girl turned over. She was holding a violin case.

"W-what?!"

Katrina opened her eyes to an apparition . . . The woman standing over her looked just like the girl from *The Ring*.

Except she was wearing sunglasses, and was older, and in red instead of white, and wore a wide-brimmed hat and . . .

"Nice day, isn't it?" the apparition said pleasantly.

"Uh . . . yes?" Katrina looked around. She was not dreaming, and yes, she was still in . . . Was it El Molino Park?

"Want some donut?"

Wasn't the usual phrase "a donut," not "some donut"? Then Katrina saw the size of what the woman was holding.

Maybe she was dreaming after all.

"It's an Alaska Donut. Well, half of one."

The woman handed her the whole piece, and a bottle of water.

Katrina hesitated. Who was this person? People dressed like that didn't just feed homeless kids asleep on park benches.

"Just take it." The woman gestured at her violin case. "It's not like I've never seen a hungry musician before."

Katrina took a small bite. *So sweet! So soft!* She took another, larger this time. And another. The sugary, chewy goodness cleared her head, and suddenly her world regained color and sound.

"You like it?" the woman asked.

"Yes, very much so. Thank you."

"If only I'd listened to Astrid and brought tangerines."

Again, she pointed at Katrina's violin case.

"Your baby?"

"Yes."

Katrina finished the last of the donut and licked her fingers. She rinsed her hands with some of the water, and the woman gave her a dry napkin.

"Anytime. Go ahead," she said matter-of-factly.

"Go ahead?"

"Practice."

"H-huh?"

Katrina felt more than a little self-conscious; it seemed like ages since she'd felt free to play.

"Don't worry, I'm just here to feed the ducks."

Katrina hesitated. But the sunlight was becoming golden, the first blackbirds were leaving the trees.

With sweetness of donut lingering in her mouth, Katrina opened her case.

Meanwhile, Shizuka reached into the bag of hot dog buns, tore off a big piece, and tossed it into the lake. To be truthful, the girl was likely a beginner. Scratchy bowing . . . nonexistent intonation . . . the usual beginner headaches.

Still, there was something refreshing about listening to someone who had nothing to do with brilliance or souls.

But then the girl opened her violin case.

The girl . . . the girl beamed, absolutely shone. Her expression was completely different from the nervous, cultivated expressions she had seen in Arcadia. Shizuka thought of Mr. Grossmueller, who had been through Hitler and everything before and after. When he beheld his violin, a wise and warm Jakob Stainer, he'd kiss it and say in such times, his violin was the only thing to live for.

What the girl held was no Stainer—it was a mere beginner's instrument—but echoes of hatred, of insanities, of melodies one sings only when one has survived emanated from her just the same.

And then, in the space where words might have been, Shizuka heard the unexpected.

Most people would have heard a tone. A trained musician might hear A440.

And a very special musician would hear the violin waking up, saying good morning, once again coming to life.

"A tuning fork?"

The girl exhaled and seemed to blush.

"My violin likes it better when I tune her this way."

Shizuka was now fully focused on the player before her.

Where had this girl come from? South San Gabriel? Rosemead?

Shizuka thought of all the students she had seen in Arcadia with brand-new digital tuners and oh-so-precious instruments. How does one such as this simply wander into a park? Shizuka wondered what she would play. Bach? Mozart? Maybe Kreisler? She had a presence that would go with Kreisler.

Or Bartók?

Shhh . . .

Shizuka stilled herself. Reality was reality. That instrument. That student bow. That awful rosin in the sliding plastic box. This was no cultivated prodigy.

Bartók? Don't be silly, Satomi. More likely, she'll play "Perpetual Motion" from *Suzuki Book One*.

Of all the music she might have imagined, Shizuka did not expect the girl to pull out Schradieck.

Schradieck? As in *The School of Violin Technics*. These were not musical compositions, but musical exercises. They were basic and beneficial, but basic and beneficial in the way that cod liver oil once was, or a measles vaccine, or a regular trip to the dentist.

How many countless students had given up violin because of Schradieck?

Shizuka smiled politely, then turned toward pond and ducks. There was no sense in making the girl nervous. The Queen of Hell opened the bag of hot dog buns, tore off a big chunk, and steeled herself for whatever horrible sound she was about to hear.

Shizuka was a child, on her way to school. During the winter mornings, especially around February, there was ice everywhere . . . on rain puddles, on windshields.

Today, the grass crunched underfoot. Even the air seemed frozen.

Julie Kiyama was holding her fingers to her mouth, exhaling into the frost and shouting, "Look at me, I'm smoking!"

"Smoking is bad for you," Julie's sister Sally yelled.

"Smoke rings! Smoke rings!"

"If you don't stop smoking, I'm te—lling!"

And then they ran off. She tried to keep up with them. She ran as fast as she could.

But they had their hands free, and she had her violin.

Shizuka found herself breaking each bun into ever smaller pieces, so she could listen just a little more.

And as the girl finished Schradieck, Shizuka watched Julie and Sally Kiyama, her last childhood friends, disappear into the icy February mist.

*   *   *

In a Faded Box Marked "FREE"

School was over. As usual, Katrina was walking home alone. And, as usual, she wandered, meandered, trying to prolong each moment before she had to face her parents.

There was a store that sold used refrigerators and washing machines. There was what was left of a public phone nobody used.

And there was a used bookstore, and in front was a faded box marked "FREE."

Katrina browsed through the box, full of the usual torn periodicals, self-help books, fad diets, computer manuals for long-dead machines.

And then she stopped.

School of Violin Technics, *by Henry Schradieck. First published in 1901.*

The book was probably there because all the markings, annotations, scribbles, and teacher's notes made the book unsellable.

But for Katrina, each suggested fingering, each message penciled over notes or inked into a margin offered an encouragement and direction that she had never before seen.

Katrina had always loved music, especially the violin. Long ago, she had even taken lessons.

But she was queer, and living in a small town east of Oakland.

The afternoon that he found her makeup, Katrina's father had punched her so hard that the entire side of her face turned black and blue. As word got around, her family, her church, the people at school hurled insults, shame.

You should act like a boy.

You should repent.

You should apologize.

You should die.

But here, all around the music, someone's teacher wrote:

Relax. Keep your fingers open and light.

Someone's teacher wrote:

Think of sunshine. You don't need to rush.

Just follow the notes.
Trust yourself.
Good job!!
And there, someone's teacher had drawn happy faces.
And there, someone's teacher had pasted stars.

*   *   *

"Who's your teacher?" Shizuka finally said.

"Um, no one." The girl was munching on a hot dog bun.

This made no sense. How does someone with no teacher encounter Schradieck?

"I took violin in school once, when I was seven. But my father stopped the lessons."

"Why?" Shizuka was even more confused. Anyone could hear this was a gifted musician.

"He said it was making me a faggot," the girl said.

The girl rubbed her eye and winced. Shizuka inhaled sharply. Some of her makeup had smeared off, to reveal the bruised skin underneath.

The bag fell from Shizuka's hands. Ducks flew at the fallen hot dog buns, tearing everything she had brought with her to shreds.

"I think I had better go," Katrina said.

"No, *wait.*"

With a speed that surprised her, the woman grabbed Katrina's arm.

Crap! Katrina froze. She could probably break the woman's grip, but if she caused a commotion, she would get in trouble for sure. *Stupid, Katrina, stupid!* What if she thinks I'm a boy? What if she calls the police?

"Let me see your violin," the woman said gently.

"Huh?"

"Your violin. Please."

Waitwait*wait* . . . what *was* this?

Katrina was in shock. The woman was playing the same Schradieck . . . wasn't she?

But how could Schradieck sound like that? So quick, yet so even, it seemed almost a blur. But this was no blur. Each note was perfectly formed, perfectly spaced, and fully developed. How could hands *move* that way?

And yet, as the woman played, she was talking, as if on a lazy morning stroll.

"You have a very pretty tone. And I notice you play just a little sharp. You're a bit of a diva, aren't you?"

Katrina had heard the term "diva" in drag and queer circles, but here, in the context of music, the sound of it made something inside her swoon.

"It's fine to be a diva," the woman said with a wink. "But you have to own it."

And then, where there had been the practice exercises, suddenly there was music. Katrina could still recognize the original exercises, but now there seemed to be two violins. And now there were three . . .

The music was sunrise, permeating the park. People stopped mid-sentence, midstroll to listen. Even the ducks seemed to stop squabbling.

The music was every hope Katrina had abandoned, every dream she had released. It was hamburgers on the grill, fruit punch in the cooler, a bag of Costco beef jerky for everyone. It was dancing without knowing the steps and not caring. It was her mom holding her, her dad calling her his little girl.

And then, it stopped.

"Whoops. I guess I got carried away," the woman mumbled.

Katrina's eyes focused on the woman before her. Her breath was shallow, and her body was shaking and unsteady.

Slowly, carefully, she sat back down. She was perspiring. But when Katrina touched her, she was ice-cold.

"Are you okay?" Katrina asked. "Should I call a doctor?"

"No. No." The woman winced. Her eyes seemed focused on something distant.

"It's just a friendly reminder . . . that my playing days are over."

The woman gently handed back her violin.

"My name is Satomi." She coughed. "Water."

Katrina handed a bottle to her. She took a sip, and another. Color slowly returned to her face.

"Thank you. I used to be a violinist. But now I'm a teacher."

The woman looked closely at Katrina, and Katrina panicked. She was bracing to hear, "Wait, you're a boy."

Instead, the woman's gaze never changed.

"And I could teach you."

Katrina's heart skipped a beat. To be able to play like that? To make music that could do *that*?

But private lessons?

Katrina looked around. The sun had set, and the trees and buildings were now jet-black against the fiery evening sky. The badminton players were already warming up in the gym.

Soon the park lights would come on, and the softball people would be playing softball.

In the meantime, Katrina didn't even have a place to live.

"I don't think so," she said softly. "I mean, thank you. But no."

Katrina gathered her stuff and made ready to leave.

But the woman reached into her purse, took something out, and put it in Katrina's hand. It was her business card.

"Shizuka Satomi. Please come see me. Or you can meet me here," she offered. "Maybe next week?"

"Maybe," Katrina heard herself say.

5

It was nearly dark when Evan finally let her inside. Inside was more cat hair, more smell. Evan showed her the sofa. He pushed some boxes of queer paraphernalia to the side.

"You can put your bags on there when you aren't sleeping. Um . . . how long are you going to be here?"

Katrina could only shrug.

Evan rolled his eyes. "Skylar!" He shouted to his roommate, who wore clothes with a lot of patches.

"This is the Katrina I was talking about."

Skylar glanced up. Katrina was about to introduce herself, but Skylar went back to her phone. Evan went back to his phone, as well.

Not much later, Skylar's friends Jewel and Ethan arrived. Apparently, there had been plans for dinner.

"How about hot pot? I just discovered this vegan place on Yelp that is totally authentic," said Jewel.

"Show me?" Evan looked at Skylar's phone.

"I was there," Ethan declared. "I think there were Mexicans cooking in the back."

The two of them laughed at the thought of Mexicans in a Chinese kitchen.

Eventually, they decided to order vegan pizza. Katrina offered to buy. It was not exactly in her budget, but she *was* a new guest.

Once they heard that, they added toppings and ordered some wings.

This happened the night after, and after. They ordered vegan pizza. They smoked. They talked about shows they were binge-watching. They smoked. Once in a while, someone would mention some sort of creative project. They'd either dismiss it or say it was badass and fierce, and then they talked and smoked some more.

Evan scratched his beard. "I want to start a crowdfund for a web series—like *The Asian Whisperer* or something, where I show people all this weird shit that's here. Kind of a David Attenborough thing."

"That's appropriation, Evan." Skylar said.

"Though it's not like Asians don't appropriate other cultures. And besides, they aren't *really* people of color people of color."

"Anyway, I saw this video where someone explains how to explore an Asian supermarket."

"That's so badass!"

Katrina found the bathroom and locked the door. She began to itch. She looked in the shower. She wished she hadn't.

Yet at least the bathroom was quiet. At least she couldn't hear them talking about Asians, about Mexicans. Katrina sat there, confused.

Yes, queers were not the most stable, and she hadn't seen Evan in person for two years. But still, hadn't he told her he thought she was beautiful? Hadn't Evan told her that they were family?

Finally, Katrina wiped herself, flushed, then washed her hands as best she could, grateful that some parts of her, at least, could be cleaned.

* * *

Of all the times to get careless!

Yes, any teacher or contestant in Arcadia that day would have known "Shizuka Satomi." But the world was a far bigger place than the violin community in Arcadia, or the violin community anywhere, for that matter.

How could you have been so stupid?

The girl must have thought she was crazy. And honestly, could anyone blame her?

And now how was Shizuka supposed to find her? Put a call out to the violin community? As if. Those people had too much to chatter about as is.

Besides, the girl was not part of that community.

Astrid brought out breakfast.

"I think you'll like the tangerine jam. The Aguilars brought so much fruit, and I didn't want it to go to waste. It's quite good with toast. But still don't know how to prepare the bitter melon. I'll check my cookbooks—I'm sure . . ."

Astrid stopped.

"I am sure you will find her, Miss Satomi."

"I'm sorry, Astrid. The jam is quite tasty."

Astrid shook her head. "Please don't apologize, Miss Satomi. I am thrilled that you have found the student that you want. In the park, of all places! It is difficult to believe."

"Isn't it, though?"

Shizuka was having a difficult time believing it herself. A musician worthy of the Queen of Hell should have been recognized *somewhere*, right?

Who? What? How is this possible?

Even now, Shizuka could sense Astrid's concern. Had she made a mistake? Was this wishful thinking? Might Tremon Philippe be playing a cruel joke?

No.

The girl might be battered, a runaway. She might have had no idea who Shizuka Satomi was. And yes, she might be unnoticed, unrecognized, even untrained.

But what Shizuka heard, from the call of the tuning fork, through the first draw of her bow, to Schradieck and the shiver of February mist . . .

Shizuka stared out the window at a cloudless wash of sky.

Oh, Satomi, if only you had kept your composure! If only you had asked for a telephone number, gotten a hint to where she might be staying . . .

Shizuka finished her breakfast and reached for her sunglasses. But what was done was done. And the girl *did* have her card, if she hadn't thrown it away.

For now, all she could do was tell Astrid to once again prepare for a guest, and return to El Molino Park. For after so long sensing it, almost swearing by it, chasing it, believing in it, Shizuka Satomi finally *knew* what she had been waiting for.

And, more importantly, she finally knew why.

*   *   *

"Mother, she's back," said Shirley.

This was the third time this week that Sunglass Lady had come to the store. Yet Lan had still not asked her name.

This was silly. This woman was a regular customer. One should know the names of regular customers, right? Then why was she hesitating? Lan had led her family out of an interstellar war zone, across a galaxy, safely to an obscure star system, and even secured this wonderful donut shop.

She nodded to herself and took a deep breath. This time, when Sunglass Lady came to the counter, Lan would say, "Welcome back," take her order, and then ask her name.

"Why should I cut a donut in half?"

The boy in front of her couldn't have been more than twelve. "I can't eat a whole donut, so I want to save half for later," Shizuka explained.

He didn't need to know that the best way to preserve one's music is repetition. A half donut from Starrgate was the first thing she had given that player in the park, and so Shizuka would play it just as she remembered.

Not to mention that she was hoping, just a little, to chat with Donut Lady.

The boy shrugged.

"Then why don't you get a Texas Donut? It is like an Alaska Donut, but half the size."

However, this had been her third time back to the Big Donut, and though the donuts had been impeccably consistent, Donut Lady had either not been present or passed by quickly, barely saying hello.

Well, Donut Lady was probably married, since she had kids. And even if she was a single mom, she was probably looking for a good man, anyway.

And it wasn't as if Shizuka had time to start dating.

"Then I'll have a Texas Donut."

"We don't have a Texas Donut. Kindle Donuts has one, so you should go there."

"Excuse me?"

"Wait! Please!" came a frantic voice from the back. The older sister, Shirley, rushed to the counter.

"Sorry, ma'am. He usually doesn't work the counter—"

"But you told me to be helpful, and I was being helpful!"

"Come on, Edwin . . ."

Shizuka watched as Shirley pushed him into the kitchen. Then she turned back to the counter and fell into the firmament of Donut Lady's eyes.

"Welcome back," Donut Lady said.

"One Alaska Donut, cut in half?" Shizuka finally managed to say.

"Sure thing," Donut Lady said, just as she always had.

"See? I told you, she should just get two smaller donuts," Shizuka could hear the boy say from the back.

"Shhh! Mother is taking care of this. And remember, you always give the customer what they ask for!"

Donut Lady gave Shizuka her order, then rushed away. Shizuka went to her usual table with her coffee, her half donut, and her other half donut.

She sipped her coffee, as before. She ate her half donut, just as before. Frantic bathroom trip excepted, everything was as before. Other customers were looking at her, as before. As before, she was alone.

No matter. Shizuka did not belong here. She was only here for the half donut and the coffee. She was only here to connect with a student, and once she found that student, she need not ever return.

As for Donut Lady?

If she had a song for every moment that might have been.

Shizuka put a lid on her coffee and looked for a napkin to wipe her hands.

"Mother, she's leaving! Talk to her," Shirley said.

"Oh no," Lan said. "Next time. Next time for sure."

"You said that last time. I think she's looking for a napkin."

"I can give her a napkin," Edwin offered.

Shirley rolled her eyes.

"Edwin, go say hi to Aunty. Mother, here. Napkins. And take this—she'll need a to-go bag."

"No, *wait*—"

Shirley pushed her mother to the front of the shop. Seriously. Sometimes organic brains . . .

"Here are some napkins," Lan said. "And a bag for your half donut."

"Thank you. I'm so sorry for the confusion," Sunglass Lady said.

"No, no I'm sorry, Miss—"

"Shizuka."

"Oh. Here you go then."

Shirley watched her mother thrust the napkins and the bag at the woman.

No, no, no! Shirley thought. Mother, you can do this. She told you her name! Now tell her yours. Mother. *Tell her your name.*

"What's your name?" her mother asked.

Shirley cringed. *Mother, she already told you that!*

But the woman smiled. "Shizuka. It's a Japanese name . . . And yours is?"

"Shizuka . . ."

Mother!

"I mean *Lan*! My name is Lan Tran."

*   *   *

Katrina coughed, then winced. The magical day with that violin teacher seemed ever more distant and unbelievable. She'd searched "Shizuka Satomi" on the Internet. No images, no music, no nothing. A few articles mentioned a teacher in Europe by that name, but she would have been far older than that woman in the park.

Skylar was sure it was a scam. Evan suggested she was a tranny chaser who was hoping to give Katrina more than violin lessons.

"Lesbian tranny chaser . . . ewww . . . That is so wrong," Jewel had said. She pointed to the violin case.

"So you want to make videos?"

"Y-yes," Katrina said. "I'm doing covers of gaming music and some anime. I already posted a few online, and I thought maybe Evan might help—"

Jewel rolled her eyes. "Gaming music? That is so lame!"

"Oh wow, I always wanted a fiddle. How much did you pay for it?" asked Aidynn.

"I-it's from China. Not too expensive."

"China . . . fucking master's tools. bell hooks said that," Skylar said.

bell hooks? Katrina had been sure Skylar had quoted Audre Lorde, but what could her violin have to do with Audre Lorde?

Then Evan started talking about wanting to take up the ukulele. Aidynn and Jewel fangirled about a TV show where there was a pawnshop and how weird cool it was and how one day they wanted to check something like that out.

Eventually, Katrina must have fallen asleep. When she came to, Evan had something in his hand.

"How do you play this with no frets?" Evan asked. He was strumming it like a ukulele.

"No! You'll break it!" Katrina shouted. She reached for it, but Evan pulled it away.

"Dude, chill. I've got it ukulele-tuned, but the strings kept slipping and buzzing."

"The bridge!" Katrina pulled the violin from Evan's hands.

"Bridge? What?"

Skylar walked into the living room.

"Do you have any money for the bus?"

"What?"

She grabbed Katrina's purse, fished around, and pulled out a five-dollar bill.

"Thanks, gurl. Gotta go!"

Evan waved to Skylar, then glanced at Katrina. Finally, he went into his bedroom and closed the door.

Katrina listened carefully for any danger. She heard a dog, and an old man across the street. She heard schoolchildren outside.

Softly, she put her violin away and closed her purse. Still quiet. Good. It seemed safe for now.

And Katrina still had not taken a bath.

The shower was still cold and filthy, but there was no time to think about that. She didn't know how much time she had. She quickly scrubbed, shampooed, conditioned, and felt almost human before Evan came in.

He held her from behind and kissed her.

Katrina remembered how she'd just started wearing makeup, and found a women's blouse from a secondhand store. Her hair hadn't grown out yet, but she had fastened it with a shiny pink barrette. It had been the first time she'd gotten a lanyard and a name tag with her chosen name **KATRINA** and **she/her** printed in boldface Helvetica.

And, after another workshop where she had said nothing, Evan had sat with her for lunch. She had a ham sandwich, while his was tofu. She apologized about being too stupid to know queers shouldn't eat meat and so many pronouns existed and she'd never even heard of Imogen Binnie or *Nevada*.

Then he hushed her with his finger, kissed her on the forehead, and she felt her body go liquid like summer sun. And then he kissed her on the lips, and she knew it didn't mean anything, except that it meant everything.

But now?

"I was thinking, it would be a way to help with the rent, you know?"

He pushed her down and continued. After he finished, Evan tried to kiss her again.

"I don't know why you're crying," he said. "It's fair trade. Besides, I can only imagine how you paid for that violin."

Eventually Evan left with a couple of their friends for a new Korean teriyaki place that was supposed to be super authentic. Katrina listened as Evan's Jeep drove one, two, then three blocks away.

Katrina felt for her safety bag. Then, quietly, she retrieved her violin. From China, a P20+, maple, spruce, ebony . . . The eBay description said it was a copy of a 1710 Stradivarius. Even in the dimness of Evan's living room, the wood grain seemed to hold whatever light it could find.

Please come see me. Or you can meet me here, the teacher had offered.

She was so beautiful. Was she even real? Katrina reached into her purse. Whoever she was, to be able to play like that. To make music that could do that.

Yes! The woman's card was still there. Of course she'd never use it. But yes. It was real. The music she remembered, the music that she was hearing, even now, was real.

But then Katrina's phone buzzed, and with it, a more immediate reality. Someone wanted a date, and he was nearby.

It did not take long to make herself pretty, at least pretty enough. Early on, she realized that being Chinese, Vietnamese, and Mexican meant that with the right makeup and attitude, she could seem exotic to just about anyone.

Work it, girl.

Though she far preferred to webcam, there was neither the space nor privacy to do cam sessions at Evan's. She looked herself over. It would do. She carefully packed her violin, then hid it away before heading out the door.

It was time to make money.

6

Unfortunately, the hookup was horrible. Although he seemed normal at first, he was high on something, and his dick wasn't getting hard.

A man on drugs with a limp dick can be very scary. He tried and cursed, then began to blame her, insisting he was soft because he wasn't a homo.

And then he wanted her to top him. And then he wanted her to speak Chinese.

And then he pulled her hair and spat on her.

But at least he didn't reinjure her ribs. And thank goodness, he wasn't able to cum. Sometimes guys like this got crazy with trans girls after they came.

And, yes, thank goodness, he paid.

Katrina started the walk back to Evan's. As she watched the cars go by, she tried to feel grateful. But gratitude was difficult. Yes, she had money for now, but she wasn't stupid. Her ribs weren't healing, and her hormones would run out in two weeks, a month if she stretched them.

If she stepped onto that road, what would be different? And why was she fighting, anyway? She just had sucked someone for money, after fucking someone else for rent. What made her so special that she should live?

But then, Katrina smelled food.

First, she smelled the sweet, almost citrusy smell of roast duck. Then the heavier warmth of BBQ pork. Chilis from a hot pot. Oyster sauce being stir-fried into a wok of raised noodles. Salted eggs in rice porridge, fried turnip cakes with diced leeks, ginger and green onion lo mein.

The many smells from the kitchens of all the small, bustling restaurants along the boulevard made her stomach growl, her mouth salivate.

She may not have had a reason to live. But here were plenty of wonderful reasons to eat.

Half an hour later, Katrina was sitting at a table with a bowl of pork belly noodle soup. The skin crackled on the outside of the pork, while the flesh oozed with fatty juices within. The noodles had the perfect bite, and the broth was glistening with the flavor of long-cooked bones.

A server came to check her teapot. Around her, the staff was serving, bussing, chopping, sweeping. A waiter used some leftover tea to wipe off a greasy table.

No stares, no judgment. No father yelling. She was eating a meal, and no one was mad or disappointed.

Katrina ate another wonton, then more pork belly. The customers at the other tables didn't even notice her. Someone laughed at someone else's joke. Someone was complaining that his grandson was not studying hard enough.

She felt strange. No, not strange.

Better.

When was the last time that she had felt better? She had food in her belly, money in her purse . . .

Her purse.

As if on its own volition, Katrina's hand reached into her purse and retrieved a business card. It looked exactly as it had before. No smudges, no folds. Even the corners were crisp and sharp.

To look like this, after everything she had been through, seemed like a miracle. And the miracle's name was Shizuka Satomi.

Katrina asked the server for the check, took out her phone, and opened Google Maps.

Where Katrina was from, only white people lived on hills. Other people, even the rich ones, usually just bought larger homes with bigger driveways to accommodate more cars, extended families, or both.

White people, on the other hand, grew uncomfortable when others looked down at them, so the rich ones preferred to roost in the heights.

Here, though, in these hills, were pickup trucks, not the shiny kind, but the kind that held lawn mowers. There were more families, more gardens. Yes, there was wealth—the BMWs and that large marble statue of Kuan Yin didn't lie—but the yards were more likely to hold vegetables than fountains and lawns.

After thirty-five minutes of walking, she stood in front of a house. It was a house that had been cared for, immaculately, for years. Even the Jaguar in the driveway seemed calm and secure. In the front was a garden, with some bonsai, a persimmon tree, and a little stone path leading up to the front door.

Katrina could felt her breath and heartbeat quicken. Once she set foot on that path, knocked on that door, her life might change forever.

Then she heard footsteps and sharp steel.

The old lady had been harvesting beans. She looked at Katrina closely.

Katrina froze.

"You! Girl or boy?" the old lady asked gruffly.

In a panic, Katrina turned and rushed down the hill.

What was she doing here? What could she have been thinking? Evan wasn't so bad, and it was only for a little while. She would figure out how to get less creepy work. She would find a way to do cam sessions.

She looked at her empty hands and cursed. Besides, only an idiot would visit a violin teacher without bringing a violin.

*   *   *

Another Saturday morning and not a word.

And also, not a sound. And this was bothering Shizuka more and more each day. Wherever she was, that girl had not played violin since that day in the park. If she had, Shizuka would have sensed it immediately.

To be filled with such music, yet be unable to play.

She was not unfamiliar with what that could do to a soul.

Shizuka nibbled absently on a potato pancake. Suddenly her mouth encountered something familiar, yet unpleasant.

"I put some of the Lieus' bitter melon in the rösti. It adds a nice color, doesn't it?"

Shizuka nodded weakly, then reached for the honey.

In front of her was another note from that violin teacher, another invitation to hear the Grohl girl play. Shizuka gently tossed it into the trash.

"Going to the park again?"

Shizuka did not even need to nod.

"I'll pack some leftover bread. And some tangerines."

* * *

"Have you aligned the donut with the local continuum?" Lan asked.

"Yes, Captain," Markus said. "But the ground here is unstable, so we'll need to compensate with a probability algorithm. Shall I create one?"

Lan nodded. "Yes, but work with Windee. I want her to learn, so be sure to explain everything as you go. When you are done, let me verify your figures."

Lan checked the time and headed to the elevator.

"Captain, what about Edwin?"

"Well . . . he's probably in the kitchen with Aunty Floresta."

Markus nodded. Nothing more needed to be said.

Lan walked to the front of the shop. The soft, yeasty glazed donuts, twists, and maple bars were to her right; the colorful cake donuts to her left. In the seating area, some maintenance workers from the city were on morning break. Two young mothers chatted, with babies and toddlers firmly in tow. In the corner, some boys already circled the *Stargate* machines.

All systems were go.

Captain Tran couldn't help feeling proud. She had brought her family here, escaping the war, to cross a galaxy, to all of this. And she would protect all of this, no matter what.

But then Lan noticed someone at the counter.

Sunglass Lady.

Where was Shirley? The last time Shizuka had visited, Lan embarrassed herself in front of the entire store.

But Shirley was wiping down tables and chatting with the moms.

Nervously, Lan approached the counter.

What was she going to say? What would she call her? Should she use her name? Was it proper to use her name?

Her name was Shizuka. She had very nice hair . . .

"Good morning. Can I try one of those?"

And her voice, it was prettier still . . .

"Um . . . please?"

"*What?* Oh, donut hole?" Lan speared one with her tongs.

Shizuka sampled it and nodded. "I would like a half Alaska Donut and regular coffee. And may I have a big bag of donut holes?"

"Throwing party?" Lan congratulated herself on maintaining a proper donut shop accent.

"In a way."

She was probably throwing a party for her children. Shizuka would be married, of course. She must have a family. Lan felt an unexpected little ache in her heart, but she kept her smile and motioned to Shirley, who came out with a paper grocery bag.

"Wait. I give you something better. These donut are two day old, so we can't sell them as one day old. They still good, though. Just don't tell. Then people ask around and Health Department show up."

"*Mother!*" Shirley scolded.

"I'll keep it secret." Shizuka smiled. "Besides, who knows what else you donut people keep back there?"

"No, no." Lan waved her hands. "Nothing special back there. Nothing special at all. Just donut stuff."

"Excuse me," Shirley apologized. She pulled Lan away, and the two started arguing in what must have been Vietnamese.

They were peculiar, but in a very non-musician way. In fact, watching them made Shizuka feel refreshed. So Shirley was Lan's daughter? Of course she was. Shizuka had never seen any sign of the father. Not that it was her business . . .

Ah, but enough with the daydreams. She had somewhere to be.

"Well, I should be getting to the ducks."

"Ducks?"

"I am off to feed the ducks—not to imply your donuts are duck food, but . . ."

"Ducks?" Lan asked again.

The way she asked it was peculiar, as if . . . No, surely Lan knew what a *duck* was. Did they not have ducks in her country?

"If you want, I can show you."

"Oh! Um, no. You see, I have to work."

Shirley tapped Lan on the shoulder. "Mother, take a break. You worked a triple shift yesterday. We can handle the shop while you're gone."

"Yes, but—"

"Mother, let's get your coat."

No matter how much she tried to deny it, her mother was in a very organic body. And that meant she needed time to relax.

Shirley nodded to Shizuka. "She'll be right out, ma'am."

Shizuka heard more muffled speech. Then Lan came out with her coat and the bag of two-day-old donuts.

When they arrived at El Molino Park, the members of the senior tennis club were packing up their equipment. As usual, a couple of the old Chinese women waved.

Shizuka frowned. Again, no sign of the violin player. But it was a beautiful day, and she was with Lan.

Lan. That's right. I'm with Donut Lady, and her name is Lan.

The two of them sat on Shizuka's favorite bench by the pond. Ducks lazily floated past. Mallards, wood ducks, mandarins. And that was not a duck, but a coot. And that was a cormorant.

Lan could identify these from her data. But here, they glided like ships through space. Some were large and stately, others, small, quick and loud. They filled the pond with different shapes and colors, as if in a bustling, healthy spaceport.

Shizuka pulled out a red velvet donut with rainbow sprinkles.

"Do you just toss it in?"

Shizuka nodded as the two-day-old donut bounced into the lake. Lan tossed one in as well.

The ducks scrambled as usual for their meal. But suddenly, the water boiled with scores of carp and goldfish. Some were dark, or silver, but many were orange and golden and speckled. Shizuka thought of all the children who had won goldfish at summer church carnivals.

"Hmm . . . that never happens with bread," Shizuka thought out loud. "Maybe the fish have a sweet tooth?"

"Why would they eat sweets if their teeth were already sweet?"

What? Lan didn't seem to be joking. And the accent that came and went—where was *that* from?

Meanwhile, Lan Tran was ecstatic. She had never done anything like this before.

She threw in a lime green donut. Shizuka tossed a bright yellow one. The water frothed and bubbled in vivid rainbow surges.

Her home planet had wildlife, but they were kept strictly isolated from civilization.

She tossed another, and another. Donut sprinkles frothed about like fireworks.

Lan watched the ducks battle the goldfish.

This would never happen at home. On her home planet, wildlife was protected from war.

Ducks vs. ducks. Fish vs. fish . . .

Greed. More feeding.

Frenzy. Explosions.

"Lan?"

Another donut.

Violence. Fire. Blood. War.

"Lan?"

Another donut.

Violence. Fire. Blood. War.

Shizuka grabbed Lan's arm. Gently, she pulled the bag from Lan's hand.

"Lan."

Finally, Lan looked up. In Lan's eyes lay a field of broken stars.

Judging by her age, Lan was most likely a refugee.

Shizuka remembered when the first Vietnamese refugees came to the San Gabriel Valley. Teachers would ask them not to open their lunches because they stank. Neighbors would call the police when they dried cuttlefish in their backyards. Even bridal shops had been raided by local police with Asian prostitution fantasies who did not know that a Vietnamese bride needed at least three gowns for a proper wedding ceremony—a formal western dress, a traditional white gown, and an áo dài.

As a violin teacher, Shizuka knew exactly how to bring out a student's best technique. As a performer, she could read a concert hall without thinking.

But how does one talk to a person as a *person*? She was never good at that. If she had been, she would never have needed to play the violin.

"So, what do you do when you're not making donuts?"

"I take care of my family, and make sure they are safe."

Lan closed her eyes and felt the sun on her face. Not too bright, not too dim. Good yellow star.

"Getting them here must have been difficult," she heard Shizuka say.

"Yes," she replied truthfully.

"But I am happy you're here—I mean, for the neighborhood," Shizuka added quickly. "Most corner lots get turned into mini malls—I've always liked the Big Donut. So I'm glad you're here to build up Starrgate."

"Thank you. It was—"

Wait. Lan had gotten lost in the sound of Shizuka's voice. But she could have sworn she just said *build the stargate*.

Lan went on immediate alert. Shirley had said this woman could hear the warp field. And now she mentioned their journey and the stargate.

How could she know what the Trans were doing? What if she was from the Empire itself? The Empire's intelligence network was vast. Some agents could even read minds.

Quietly, Lan reached for her phone and activated its weapon mode. If needed, she could stun this woman and leave immediately.

"Why exactly did you bring me here?" Lan asked. If she were a Galactic agent, it was better to know now.

"To enjoy the afternoon, and feed ducks," Shizuka said.

"And?" Lan asked. "There's something else, isn't there?"

Now it was Shizuka's turn to be surprised. What did Donut Lady know about the violin world? Maybe someone had recognized her at the donut shop? Maybe she'd heard rumors that the so-called Queen of Hell was looking for a new student?

But even if that were true, how would Lan the Donut Lady know she had found a student here?

Why had she even asked Lan along? She should be focused on

the final student. Could she have been charmed? Could Donut Lady be working with Tremon Philippe?

Just then, a duck walked up in front of her and shat.

Shizuka looked down at the duck turd. *Seriously . . .*

This was all so stupid! Just for once, could she not put the secrets away? Besides, how would Lan even know about Tremon, violins, and human souls?

"Yes. I am waiting for a violin student, who probably isn't coming . . ." she let herself say.

"What?"

"Look, I don't know what others have told you about me, and I won't deny what they said isn't true. But right now . . ."

The Queen of Hell shrugged. "But right now, I am enjoying my time with you."

Lan was their captain. She was also their mother, and she should be protecting them instead of wasting an afternoon with this woman.

This woman . . . whose voice reminded her of those times sailing by stars and darkness, when the rest of the crew was asleep, whose voice made her feel as if within the wave of the ship's engines, the whir of its life support, the rush of space about her.

"I think the ducks are still hungry," Lan finally said.

They opened the bag of donuts. This time, they made sure to go slowly. There was no reason to rush, and all the reasons not to.

Shizuka listened to the basketball players, the softball players. Somewhere, a referee was blowing a whistle. From the gym was the light, rapid cadence of table tennis.

"Just tell me," Lan asked, "how did you know we escaped the Galactic Empire?"

"You mean Vietnam?"

"Vietnam?"

"Cambodia?"

"Wait, what—"

Lan tried to cover up her mistake, but it was too late.

For Shizuka realized then that the stars she had seen in Lan Tran's eyes were not figurative. They were real.

7

Ew.

What was that smell?

Oh, of course. Evan and his friends had been smoking and drinking all night, discussing what they could do to overthrow white privilege and oppression, and someone must have thrown up.

She touched her hair and frowned. Had she even showered? The week had been hazy. She remembered that the latest hookup wanted no condom, and she had almost said yes. Probably the next time, she wouldn't be such a stuck-up bitch, right? The voices in her head were getting louder and louder.

Who do you think you are?

Freak.

Ugly.

You're just another random queer. If you died, no one would care.

She looked at the contents of her purse spread out on the coffee table. From time to time, Evan or Skylar or someone else rifled through her stuff. But when Katrina asked them to stop, they told her she was being paranoid. In the end, she was always the one to apologize.

Katrina reached under the sofa for her violin.

She frowned. She checked. She checked again.

Her violin was gone.

"Where's my violin?"

Evan shrugged.

"Where is it?"

Katrina launched herself at Evan, but he pushed her away. Her head hit the wall hard. Evan rushed forward, but Katrina ducked, spun around him, and pulled his head back by his hair. She noticed that Evan was a lot weaker than her father.

"Where's my violin?"

Just then, Skylar and Jewel walked in. "That pawnshop wasn't like on TV, at all, and the guy wasn't even funny," Jewel said.

Skylar rolled her eyes. "I know, right? You were so wrong, Evan, that violin was barely worth—"

"Where's my violin?" Katrina interrupted.

"What the fuck? Let him go!"

But Katrina did not listen. She pulled Evan's head back further. "I'll fucking kill you. Do you hear me, I'll fucking *kill you*!"

"Skylar!"

Skylar handed Katrina a receipt.

Katrina released Evan, who pushed her away and raised his fists.

"Don't even try it," Katrina said softly.

While keeping one eye on Evan, Katrina grabbed her belongings, backed out the door, and stumbled away.

"Fuck you, you crazy bitch!" Evan shouted.

As Katrina left, the neighbors stared at her like she was garbage. Which she was.

*   *   *

"So . . . you're a space alien?"

"Citizen of the Galactic Empire would be more accurate."

"And you escaped here . . . to make donuts."

Lan nodded. "I needed to get my family far from the Empire. But I needed a way to do it without raising suspicion."

"And that would be donuts?"

Lan shook her head. "Well, not just donuts. At this moment, two hundred forty-seven light-years away, a level-five gamma ray burst is on a direct collision course with this solar system."

"Level five? Is that good?"

"Beyond good!" Lan gushed. "Less than one percent of gamma ray bursts are level five. When it arrives, every planet, every moon, every asteroid it hits will be bombarded for about four minutes—not just with gamma rays, but all sorts of high-energy radiation! If we're lucky, even your sun might be affected!"

Gamma rays? High-energy radiation? Did she just hear that right? Not that a space alien like Lan had any obligation to care about life on this planet. Still . . .

"Lan, why move your family into certain death?"

"No, no! You see, at the time, this planet will be shielded, directly behind your sun. Due to a remarkable alignment, your planet will be the perfect location to watch the spectacle. That is why I suggested to the bank that building a stargate would be great for sightseers and travelers."

"And you could serve them donuts."

"Yes!" Lan said excitedly. "That's how I was able to get a travel permit. I made it look like an excellent business opportunity."

"And that explains why your accent keeps coming and going."

Lan frowned. She had let her donut accent slip—not good! This was still a customer.

"Oh! I can change now if you like—"

Shizuka put her hand up and shook her head. "No. Please. Don't."

Shizuka listened to the jingle of a passing ice cream truck. It was not every day that Shizuka felt fortunate to have been damned by Hell. But it did keep her from getting too shocked by life's surprises. Space aliens at a donut shop? Why not? In fact, it was refreshing to meet someone else with secrets for a change.

"So, what do you look like, really?" Shizuka asked.

Lan looked away. When making first contact, it always came to this, didn't it?

"Scary," she finally said.

"Really?"

"Yes. Really scary." Lan turned her gaze back to Shizuka. "Does it matter?"

Shizuka shrugged. "To be honest, I suppose by now I'd be pretty scary, too."

"What do you mean?"

The sun was just beginning to drop in the sky, and the golden glow made Shizuka recall Technicolor, *The Brady Bunch*, and *ABC After School Specials*.

"I used to be a musician."

Lan listened as Shizuka talked about a deal with a demon and a soul in exchange for souls. She listened as Shizuka spoke about a music she could barely articulate, a music that had eluded her for years.

Shizuka talked about how she had finally found it, that afternoon on this very bench, in a girl with a cheap violin, a tuning fork, a battered copy of Schradieck, and a huge bruise on her face.

And how she had been coming here as often as she could, feeding the ducks, hoping for that girl to return.

Lan tried to understand what Shizuka said. Some civilizations still might symbolically pledge to a family, a government, even an idea. The entire Tarn Republic declared itself a servant of peace in one of its final communications.

But Lan's civilization had long evolved beyond believing in supernatural beings and souls and music. And, in her reality, no one would think to attach such importance, such meaning, to music.

Still, as Lan listened to Shizuka's voice, it was as if her words had a faint and peculiar pull, giving Lan the tiniest desire to enter Shizuka's reality as well.

Shizuka shivered. She realized she had told Donut Lady far more than she intended.

"We said too much, didn't we?" she said.

Lan nodded.

"I could wipe your memory," Lan offered. "Of course, I'd wipe mine out too. Just for this afternoon."

"That would be awkward. And besides, I want to remember this."

They finished tossing in the last few donuts, stood up and brushed off the crumbs and frosting.

"Plum-colored," Lan said softly.

"What?"

"Our true forms," Lan said. "We are plum-colored."

"Plum-colored?"

"Yes. And our hair can be any color from orange to green. Though some of us have blue—mostly from the southern quadrant. My original hair is green."

"I . . . see."

"And we have two elbow joints. They would be here . . . and here."

"What about your knees?"

"They are the same. Our patellar ligaments are more robust, however. Actually, all our ligaments are."

"I see. And what else?"

"What else? You're not horrified?"

Shizuka tried not to smile. "I'll manage."

"Yours must be a very open-minded species," Lan said admiringly.

Whatever Shizuka intended to say next would have to wait.

A girl was running to them in tears.

Eventually, Shizuka and Lan pieced together what happened.

"We should call your authorities?" Lan asked.

Shizuka shook her head. The police would only make this worse. "But we need to visit that pawnshop."

Lan nodded. She pulled out her phone to message Shirley that she'd be late.

Shizuka turned to the girl.

"What's your name?"

"K-Katrina Nguyen."

"Okay, Katrina Nguyen, let's get your violin."

* * *

Pawnshops and musicians have a long history. Within so many pawnshops lay dreams lost, broken, never realized. Usually, a musician of Shizuka's stature would have nothing to do with these places.

But Shizuka had never been overly concerned with the usual.

As Shizuka pulled up to the shop, Katrina pointed at the front window.

"That's mine!" she cried. "Please get it back. I don't have the money, but I'll pay you back a little at a time, I swear . . ."

"Don't worry," Shizuka said. "Everything will be fine."

No doubt, that was the same violin Shizuka had seen that day in El Molino Park. But while that instrument had been in perfect condition, this one had its E and A strings missing, as well as its tuning peg.

And the price tag read $450.

Katrina rushed to the owner and pointed to the window.

"That violin was stolen!"

"That's what they all say," the man behind the counter said, not looking up from his computer. "It's a bit loved, but it's a good violin. Four hundred fifty dollars."

Before Katrina could reply, Lan cleared her throat.

"It's damaged. Lower the price," Lan said commandingly.

Shizuka was startled—so *that* was what a starship captain sounded like.

The owner blinked. "Maybe I can do four twenty-five, but that's it. I believe the instrument was made in Germany."

"You believe wrong," Lan said. "Two hundred. Cash. It costs me at least two hundred to repair, and it's still fair profit for you."

"Three hundred."

"Two hundred dollars. And a good Yelp review."

She did not have to add that she could also write a bad one.

"Make it a good review," he finally said.

Lan reached for her purse, but Shizuka held her arm and put her finger to her lips.

"I don't think you understood what this girl said," Shizuka said innocently. "This violin was stolen."

"Of course she did. People say that all the—" The pawnshop owner looked at Shizuka and stopped cold.

Now it was Lan's turn to be startled—the pawnshop owner was terrified.

"Surely, you're not implying that she would lie to you?" Shizuka said sweetly.

"Uh, of course not."

"The girl should have her violin back."

"Y-yes, of course," he stammered.

"And her case."

"Yeah, sure. Case too."

Katrina and Lan watched wordlessly as Shizuka inspected the violin.

"A peg is missing. Strings are missing. The bridge . . . what happened? Was it you?" Shizuka glared at the owner. "I can find out, you know."

"No! I didn't do anything! I swear it was like that when I got it!" He was in near hysterics. He pulled out a roll of cash and peeled off some bills. "This should pay for the damages. Please. J-just take it."

"Thank you," she said politely. "And I shall."

Once outside, Shizuka placed the violin gently in Katrina's arms.

"We're lucky that he was so nice," she said nonchalantly.

"My other violin was smashed, but this one will be okay."

What was the girl talking about?

"Katrina?"

"My other violin was smashed, but this one will be okay," she repeated. She held her violin case tightly to herself.

"Katri—"

Shizuka felt a hand on her back. She turned and saw Lan shake her head gently.

Lan pulled out a small device that was shaped like a soy sauce bottle.

"Please hold her still," Lan said.

Lan waved the device in front of Katrina's eyes. Almost instantly, her eyelids fluttered, then closed. Shizuka braced to bear her weight, but the girl remained standing.

"The effect is a bit like sleepwalking," Lan explained. She looked at her scanner and frowned. "How she stayed conscious until now, I don't know. The poor thing is exhausted. She's not been eating well, either. Her bruises are healing, but that rib has been fractured and reinjured. It's not life-threatening, but it must really hurt."

"Should we take her to a doctor?" Shizuka asked.

"No. I can repair everything here," Lan said. "I'm no doctor, but I'm trained in basic field medicine."

Gradually, methodically, Lan moved the device over Katrina's face, her throat, and then over her rib.

"It seemed like the pawnshop owner recognized you," Lan said as she worked.

Shizuka shrugged. "People like that usually know how to avoid trouble. And anyway, you were pretty intimidating yourself."

Even in the dark, Shizuka could sense Lan's blush.

"The donut shop," Lan finally said.

"Hmm?"

"Katrina. If she needs a job, I can give her one at the donut shop."

"Thank you. But she'll need to be careful with her hands."

Katrina murmured, but this time it was almost like a purr.

"She'll be fine," Lan finally said. "Let's get her in the car before she really falls asleep."

Shizuka stopped at the traffic light, then looked in the rearview mirror. The girl seemed almost peaceful in the streetlights. She reached into her bag and pulled out her phone. "Excuse me, I need to call Astrid."

Astrid?

Lan tried not to listen to their conversation, but it sounded like they knew each other very well. Well, of course they did—they were living together. This Astrid was even cooking her dinner.

Shizuka put her phone away. "I'm sorry for that."

"No, not a problem at all." Lan tried to smile. So that was Shizuka's mate.

"Is everything all right? You got quiet all of a sudden."

"Oh, no, no. I'm just a little tired, that's all."

Lan was quiet for the rest of the drive. Finally, Shizuka parked at the Big Donut.

"Shall I walk you inside?"

"No. You should get this one to bed—and Astrid probably misses you."

"Astrid? My housekeeper?"

"Housekeeper?"

"Yes, she's been with me since I left Berlin."

"Oh, good. I mean—"

"Have a good night, Lan," Shizuka said.

"You too, Shizuka," Lan managed to say.

Lan walked into the shop.

Shirley rushed over, concerned. "Mother! You said there was an emergency. Is everything all right?"

Lan smiled. "Yes, everything is fine. And she has a housekeeper."

* * *

Astrid was waiting as Shizuka pulled into the driveway.

"The poor thing is shivering," Astrid said. "Come on, dear, let's get you inside."

"I need to get rosin," Katrina mumbled.

Astrid grabbed Katrina's bags and led her inside.

"I already have her room ready. Shall I take her upstairs?"

"Yes, please."

"I need to get rosin . . ."

"Of course, dear, let's get the rosin."

Shizuka watched Astrid guide Katrina inside.

To think she had been homeless, lugging her bags, staying God-knows-where with a fractured rib. To think she had been in the park, playing the Schradieck as if she were lighter and clearer than air.

Shizuka waved to Mrs. Lieu, then went into the house. Astrid came downstairs not long after.

"Fast asleep," she said. "Shall I bring you something to eat?"

"Thank you, but no. I'll be practicing," Shizuka said.

"Practicing?"

"Yes. I need to prepare for the new student, after all."

"Of course, Miss Satomi."

A few minutes later, Astrid heard a most wonderful music rising from below.

Due to her deal with Hell, all traces of Miss Satomi's performances had been erased, and she was forbidden to perform. But since her job was to teach, she had to maintain her skills. Thus, in the privacy of her practice hall, she could play as much as she desired. This meant that, other than Miss Satomi's chosen students, Astrid was the only person in the world who was able to hear Shizuka Satomi play.

Which, of course, was more than privilege enough. But tonight, Miss Satomi's violin sounded *different*. Astrid closed her eyes.

Her playing was every bit as rich and nuanced as all the years had made her. Still, something about Miss Satomi's music seemed almost as if it were waking, returning.

Astrid recalled Grandma Strafeldas, her treasured tulips coming back to life after the long Swiss winter . . .

New leaves, supple and pointing, like the fingers of small children, to the sky.

8

What?

Katrina sat up. Quickly, she checked herself. No new scrapes or bruises. She was wearing a nightshirt, but it wasn't ripped. She'd not been choked. In fact, her body seemed fine.

Violin!

She panicked before she felt the case next to her. She opened it carefully. The strings were still loose. A peg was still missing; the bridge was still glued to the face. Her heart sank. That part had not been a dream.

Still, here she was, and her violin was with her. But where was here?

There was a knock on her bedroom door.

"Y-yes?"

"Miss Katrina? I heard you stir. Are you awake?" said a proper, yet caring voice. Somehow, the voice made her feel safe.

She cracked the door open.

"Hello?"

"Good morning. I am Astrid, Miss Satomi's housekeeper. Did you sleep well?"

Katrina nodded.

"Last night, you were exhausted, so we let you sleep. But you'll feel better after you take a bath. Come?"

Katrina followed Astrid down the hall. Astrid handed her a towel and a washcloth.

"Miss Katrina, please use the shower first. Then soak in the bath; it's already filled."

Astrid bowed slightly before closing the door. Katrina started to undress.

Suddenly, the door reopened.

"Yes?"

"Leave the nightshirt here to be washed. Your clothes are almost dry. I'll leave them on your bed."

"Oh, um . . . okay."

The bath was not the bathtub she had at home. It was rectangular, and came about waist high, and a gentle steam floated from the surface. A sturdy wooden step stool allowed her to ease herself inside. She closed her eyes, and stepped in.

And almost screamed.

Hot! Hot! Hot!

Katrina quickly withdrew her foot, which was now flushed and red.

Holy fuck, the bathtub from Hell! Seriously, who took a bath in water this hot? She added cold water until the temperature was bearable. Finally, she eased herself in.

Katrina couldn't remember the last time she had taken a full bath. Katrina usually rushed her showers; being naked, even with herself, made her uncomfortable.

But here, submerged to her neck in the still-steaming water, Katrina felt almost weightless. When was the last time she felt that?

She thought she heard something in the hallway. She tried to get up, but slipped back. Immediately, she cringed, expecting something in her body to hurt.

But there was nothing. Nothing outside, and nothing within. No pain. Just calm. Quiet.

Katrina had thought she'd rush her bath, like she always did. But maybe she could stay in just a little while longer.

She didn't know how long she had been in the bath, but eventually, the water cooled enough that she shivered. She stepped out of the tub, dried herself with a big fluffy towel, and looked for her . . .

Clothes? Where?

Astrid said they would be on her bed.

Katrina hastily wrapped herself in her towel. Wait, she had woken in a nightshirt. That meant that last night either she or Shizuka must have undressed her. They must have seen . . . but Astrid had made no mention of this.

Thank goodness for small miracles.

Katrina tried not to laugh at her own joke. But now she was naked. And, even if she covered her body, with wet hair and no makeup, there was nothing to keep her face from looking like a boy's.

She had to be careful.

Katrina wrapped the towel around her and stepped outside quietly. Yet as the door closed behind her, she realized she had no idea of the way back to her room.

"Are you lost, Miss Katrina?" came a voice from behind her.

Crap! There was no way that Astrid could see her like this and not know. Katrina turned around slowly, then braced herself for the worst. Please don't scream. Please don't call the police.

"Oh! I should have brought you a robe. I'm so sorry," Astrid said.

"W-what?"

"Your room is the other way, at the end of the hall. Come down for breakfast in a half hour?"

Katrina nodded numbly.

"You have a big day today. Miss Satomi says she's taking you to repair your violin."

Half in a daze, Katrina walked into the bedroom. It smelled of old wood, incense, and camphor, like it had been still for a very long time.

Stillness was good. Stillness meant no sudden movements, no one rushing to kick in her door.

And there, on her bed, were her clothes. All of them. Not just the clothes she had been wearing, but the clothes in her bag. Everything had been washed and neatly folded.

Everything.

She tried not to think about a stranger handling her work outfits and dirty underwear. Instead, she tried to focus on where she was. Beside the bed, there was a dresser, a closet, a vanity, a full-length mirror.

Quietly, she dried herself, then put on a newish pair of cotton pants and a top that reasonably matched. She retrieved her makeup and hairbrush from her bag, and sat at the vanity.

She looked into the mirror and touched her face. Her black eye was gone.

And wait—it wasn't just warmth of the bath. Her rib was fine?

This seemed like a dream. But her forehead was still too heavy, her jaw still too wide. And she had the same ugly, oversized hands.

Well, whether she was dreaming or not, reality was reality.

Katrina smoothed moisturizer on her face, then found her razor. She pulled her skin taut, and shaved her facial hair as closely as she could.

Once her makeup was done, she checked herself one last time in the full-length mirror.

Then Katrina took a deep breath, opened the door, and walked downstairs.

The walls were covered in dark wood paneling, and the floor was carpeted in beige. The lamps were large ceramic decorative things that used incandescent bulbs. Everything was dusted, polished. But everything seemed to be sleeping. The drapes, the curtains, the furniture.

Katrina gripped her smartphone to remind herself what year this was.

"Miss Katrina, all clean are we?" said Astrid. "Wonderful. Please, sit. Would you like some tea? Earl Grey?"

"Huh? Oh, yes."

"Miss Satomi will be down soon. I think you'll enjoy this. It is a most wonderful Earl Grey."

"T-thank you."

Katrina smiled. Or she hoped she smiled. Did she smile? Speaking to an older person, let alone an older person who was serving her, made Katrina uneasy, so she looked away and up at the wall.

Her eyes were drawn to a black-and-white photograph of a woman—no—a girl.

"The Paganini Competition," Astrid said proudly. "Miss Satomi's first major win. The picture next to it is from Warsaw—where she broke strings on two instruments and, finally, finished the concerto with a viola."

"Amazing . . ."

Immediately she felt foolish at the sound of her voice. Who was she to speak of Paganini? Warsaw? She didn't even know what a Paganini was. Instinctively, she looked toward the door.

"Miss Katrina?"

"Y-yes?"

"When you think of love, is it somewhere the colors are brighter and everything seems to glow?" Astrid said casually. "With no pain, like your heart is skipping and doing cartwheels?"

Katrina looked down. "No, ma'am." As if someone like her could have a life like that.

"Good."

"M-Miss Astrid?"

"Good. Because love is so much more than that, isn't it?"

Katrina nodded. That much at least she knew.

"And so was the way Shizuka Satomi played. Now, sip your tea, dear, before it gets cold."

"Yes, ma'am!"

Miss Astrid smiled.

And so did she.

As she sipped, Katrina looked at more pictures, and then records, news articles. Shizuka Satomi. She was more than a teacher. Far more.

"Miss Astrid, shouldn't there be more about her online? At *least* a few recordings?"

Astrid tilted her head and gave an expression Katrina could not read. "I believe that she'll explain it to you herself."

"Music industry stuff?" Katrina ventured.

"Yes. You might say that." Astrid smiled as if Katrina had made a very clever joke. But before Katrina could respond, there came a voice from above:

"What is this about the music industry?"

The entire room seemed to stop and stand at attention.

"Miss Katrina noticed your lack of available recordings," Astrid explained.

"Ah. Well, we can talk about that later."

"But, Miss Satomi, it just seems so unfair. What gives them the right—"

Astrid raised her hand.

"I'm sorry," Katrina said automatically.

"No, don't apologize. In fact . . . thank you." Shizuka sat at the table, then looked at Katrina carefully.

"However, my music career is not the focus. What we must really concern ourselves with is yours."

9

"Katrina, have some muesli."

"Muesli?"

"I soaked it in yogurt overnight and added tangerine slices. And here's some fresh tangerine juice."

Shizuka smiled at the thought of Astrid triumphantly using the last of the Aguilar tangerines. And, even more importantly, the seventh student, the one she had been seeking for nearly a decade, was sitting in front of her, having breakfast at her table.

Yogurt? In cereal?

Katrina dipped her spoon into the muesli. She had never heard of such a thing. It looked a little like soggy oatmeal, but it was sweet, tart, nutty, with just a little chewy crunch. And the tangerine slices were like bits of sunshine.

It was almost too good to be true.

Katrina paused.

"What's wrong, honey? Do you not like it?" Astrid asked anxiously. "If you have any favorite foods from home, perhaps I can learn to make them."

Katrina shook her head. Her mother had always made what her father wanted. There was nothing there that she wanted to recall.

Besides, the muesli was wonderful. Miss Astrid had been wonderful. Miss Satomi had been beyond wonderful. But people like this weren't supposed to be wonderful.

Not to people like her.

"Why are you being so nice to me?"

"Why? Because you are Miss Satomi's student." Astrid glanced at Shizuka, then back at the girl.

"And she's been searching a very long time for you."

Shizuka watched her new student try to relax and fail. Of course she would be suspicious. Tremon would be suspicious. Even Astrid was having her doubts.

After all, Katrina Nguyen was most definitely *not* someone that Hell would have chosen.

Yes, Hell accepted that it could neither create talent nor control where it landed. Paganini had all the tools for immortality *before* he signed over his soul. As did Tartini, or anyone else who claimed the Devil came and made them great.

But Hell favored people who *recognized* their brilliance, who believed they deserved success, would have success, were it not for a flaw, a disadvantage that they could never overcome. Paganini didn't sell his soul to become *Paganini*—he sold his soul because he thought his appearance so hideous that no one would love him otherwise.

Each of Shizuka's six previous students had a similar fear that their talent, their destiny would be thwarted. Morihei thought he'd never be accepted because he was Japanese. Lilia thought her commoner's blood tainted her playing. Sabrina was worried because she was fat. And so on, and so on. What made each of them right for Hell was their need for a lie, a façade so powerful, so intoxicating, that they could believe it themselves.

And those, Hell could easily provide.

But this one didn't seem ready for such a lie. At present, she could barely handle her truth.

Well, there would be time to address this later. For now, ready or not, they had work to do. Shizuka nodded to herself and put her coffee cup down.

As the cup clattered on the table, Katrina flinched. Tangerine juice splashed all about them.

"I'm sorry!" Katrina leapt her feet.

Shizuka watched the girl frantically scan the room for the front door. She was terrified.

"I'll clean it up," Astrid said calmly. "Please, Miss Katrina, sit down. There's no problem at all."

"I'm sorry," she repeated.

Of course. The black eye, the bruises, the fractured rib. These were simple wounds. What remained would be far more difficult to heal.

Inside, Shizuka was furious. How *dare* someone interrupt talent like this? Rests, pauses, delayed resolutions, these were to be expected in any music, but *this* was needless. This was time wasted, time which Shizuka did not have.

However, being injured wasn't the girl's fault. And showing frustration would only make matters worse.

"Katrina?"

The voice was gentle. Cautiously, Katrina looked to its source.

"Yes?"

"After breakfast, shall we take your violin to the shop?"

"I don't have money," she said honestly. The last guy had barely paid.

"Don't worry about that now. Just finish your breakfast."

Astrid put her hands on Katrina's shoulders. Katrina tried not to flinch.

"You have a lot to do today. And when you return, we'll have more tangerine juice. Plenty more."

Shizuka glanced upward. Astrid shrugged.

"This morning, Mrs. Aguilar brought another bag."

*   *   *

South Arroyo was a quaint and picturesque hamlet at the end of the Long Beach Freeway. South Arroyo sat at the end of said freeway because its residents had blocked further construction, declaring their town too quaint and picturesque for freeways.

The residents had also objected when the city wanted to run a light-rail through their town, until they realized they could build a quaint and picturesque plaza by the station, complete with quaint and picturesque health food stores, gastropubs, and boutiques hawking fair-trade clothing woven from all-natural fibers.

As their surroundings became ever more quaint and picturesque, Katrina grew nervous. *She did not belong here, she did not belong here, she did not belong here.*

Moreover, did Miss Satomi and Miss Astrid even *know* she was transgender? Of course they must—Miss Astrid had basically seen

her naked—but there had been no mention of her gender whatso-
ever.

From the way they acted, Katrina could almost believe they accepted who she was. But that was in their home, behind closed doors.

Now they were in public. She and Miss Satomi had pulled into
the parking lot of what looked like an especially quaint and picturesque music store. And in that store, someone would point at the
weird tranny and maybe even call her a boy.

"Miss Satomi."

"Yes?"

"We can't go in there."

Shizuka frowned. What was the matter now? Helvar Grunfeld's Fine
Violin Shoppe *did* look a little too much like it had been painted by
Thomas Kinkade. But the shop did reasonably good work and would
be able to repair Katrina's student violin easily.

"Katrina?"

"I'm not what you think I am."

Shizuka was thoroughly puzzled. The girl seemed honest—and
not many entities could deceive her. Was she working with Tremon
Philippe? No, Tremon had no reason to deceive her this way.

There was a far simpler explanation, wasn't there?

Why did she not want to go into Grunfeld's? Of course. She was
most likely nervous she would be seen, perhaps by someone she
knew. And since this was Grunfeld's, that person was probably
either her old teacher or another student.

Fair enough. It was not good form to take a student from an existing teacher, but Shizuka was sure she could work everything out.
She was Shizuka Satomi, after all.

"Okay, then. So, who's your teacher, *really*?"

Teacher? What was Miss Satomi talking about?

"No one—I mean, I watch YouTube, and I have old books. I mean,
old books are good."

"Then what do you mean about you not being really who I think
you are?"

"I'm trans."

There. She'd said it.

"What?"

"Transgender."

Miss Satomi paused. "Yes, of course, but if you're *really* someone else's student . . ."

"N-no."

"Good. It's not a deal breaker, but I'd rather not take you from another instructor without their permission. The ensuing drama can be troublesome, even for me."

"Miss Satomi, I said I am transgender."

Ah. So *that* was the issue.

Shizuka could feel the terror in the girl's voice. Her hand was already gripping the door handle. This would not do. Shizuka brought the car to a stop, shut off the engine, then looked at her student with her full attention.

"Transgender. Yes, Katrina. I heard you the first time. Shall we fix your violin?"

"Yes, please," Katrina managed to say.

"Good. And, Katrina, no jumping out of moving cars. It causes a mess."

"Yes, Miss Satomi."

Miss Satomi pressed the buzzer to be let inside. Katrina bit her lip as she walked through the curly maple doorway onto the polished spruce floors.

Grunfeld's smelled as if someone had blended the scent of old wood and rosin and tastefully atomized it throughout the store. Interesting historical instruments hung from the walls. In the corner, a young woman meticulously dusted a row of violas. Down the hallway, Katrina could hear a cello.

A small part of Katrina wanted to hear every instrument in the store, but much more of her was screaming, *Get out, you don't belong here!*

These people weren't like her. They had formal lessons. They grew up listening to Mozart and practicing scales, and their parents could probably read music, too. Katrina became painfully aware of the sound of her shoes on the hardwood floor. People like this would laugh at her just because she grew up east of Oakland.

Oh, and by the way, she was transgender.

Now a woman was staring. In fact, everyone was staring.

But they weren't staring at her. They were all focused upon Miss Satomi.

Soon, an old man scurried out from the back.

"Hello, Helvar."

"Shizuka Satomi! It's been a long time. Not that time seems to have done anything to you."

He winked. It reminded Katrina of the wink she had seen so often from married men in drag bars.

"Well, what do you have there?"

"I have a new student, and this is her violin."

Every eye in the store shifted to her. Katrina gave Helvar Grunfeld her case. He smiled, but just beneath, Katrina could sense disgust.

"I—I'm sor—" She started to flail, but her teacher cut her off.

"She'd like it repaired, then properly set up, and maybe we can make the fingerboard a bit more responsive."

The old man frowned. He motioned to another technician, who bit his lip and shrugged.

"Shizuka," the old man said, "come back to the workshop, and let's see what we can do."

"Of course. Katrina, why not look at the sheet music and see if there's anything here you want to play."

Once out of earshot, Helvar opened the case and stared.

"Shizuka, how do I put this? This is some sort of joke?"

"I was surprised as well. But my student loves it, and it has quite a good sound."

"Ah, I am sure it does . . ." He nodded back at Katrina. "But if he is *really* your student, we can give him a very good price on a proper instrument. His parents can pay in installments if they cannot afford the full price up front."

"Her parents aren't helping her, so sorry to say," Shizuka said.

"Then, what do you expect me—"

"But *I* am. And I expect you to examine my student's instrument and provide me an estimate."

Helvar looked at his technician, who looked at the floor. Then he turned to Shizuka.

"I am sorry, Ms. Satomi, but I don't work on this Oriental junk."

Shizuka peered at him over her sunglasses.

"Oriental junk?"

"Shizuka, *please.*"

"Goodbye, Helvar. The world is changing, you know. A pity you aren't ready to live in it."

She took the violin and walked out of the store.

"Come, Katrina, let's have brunch."

Most likely by coincidence, it was a half hour later when Helvar Grunfeld's heart decided to stop.

"Wait for it."

Shizuka held her hands to her ears. Katrina looked at her, puzzled, before she heard the noise of an oncoming siren.

"As you were saying?" Shizuka asked, once the ambulance had passed.

"I'm sorry for embarrassing you," she repeated.

"Sorry? Why? That was a violin shop. This is a violin."

"Miss Satomi, I don't want to doubt you, but did you *see* that place?"

Shizuka nibbled on her quaint and picturesque crêpe. Apparently, this café was new, for the rustic courtyard furniture and French language signs still had price tags from Home Depot and Cost Plus World Market.

"Grunfeld's? That's actually Helvar, Jr. At least that was. His father started the shop. *He* had never gone bald."

Miss Satomi could not have said that, could she?

"Wasn't his head shiny?" Miss Satomi continued.

Katrina knew she shouldn't, but she giggled, then started laughing, first from the chest, then from the dark of her belly. It was so mean . . . He couldn't help losing his hair, but she didn't want to apologize.

How long had it been since she had felt able to laugh?

"Like a brand-new cake of rosin. You know, the kind the hair has never touched," she said.

"Good one! Good one!"

And now Miss Satomi was laughing, too.

"But, Miss Satomi, my violin is not the sort that they normally repair," Katrina finally was able to say.

Shizuka rolled her eyes.

But Katrina was right. In part, this was Shizuka's fault. She had brought what she thought was a normal violin to a normal violin shop.

But this violin was not normal, was it?

"Finish your crêpe, and let's go."

"Where are we going?" asked Katrina.

"Somewhere not normal," Shizuka replied.

10

Matía & Sons
Fine Woodworking and Violins

The shop was located next to the railroad tracks, across from San-chez Liquor, which was now Chun-Li's Driving School. It had never expanded, never advertised. It had never needed to.

To Lucy Matía, coming to work every morning was like stepping into church.

A portrait of her grandfather, Catalin Matía, proudly watched over the workshop.

Throughout the store, other images were displayed. Catalin as a young corporal, in Italy. And there, on a bicycle in front of the Battistero di Cremona, with violist Primrose, young and still able to hear. And there, in Montbovon, enjoying Gruyère and Gruyères with the teenage Shizuka Satomi.

The newer photographs were of Catalin's son Franco, Lucía's father, a bit rougher and coarser, but still a Matía. There he was, in Prague with Sabrina Eisen. In Latvia with Kremer. And there, with Yifeng Brian Zheng, as beautiful and tortured as ever.

But now? No new pictures were being added to the wall. There were no impromptu visitations, no passionate lunchtime conversations about Vuillaume.

Instead, a local musician might need peg dope, a community orchestra might order sheet music. And of course, many customers spoke Spanish and could not go to a place like Grunfeld's.

Very occasionally, someone might hear about this shop from an old professor or senior colleague. They would come in, look around, ask a few questions. But once they realized that neither Catalin nor Franco Matía was still alive, their expressions would change, and they would quickly leave.

She didn't blame them. Who was *she*, anyway?

Suddenly, the old brass doorbell jingled. Lucy stepped backward and almost bumped into a cello.

"Mom! You okay?"

"Y-yes. I just got a little startled, that's all."

"I brought you lunch," her son said.

"Lunch? It's lunchtime already?" She opened the paper bag. "You know, this stuff will kill you."

"I hear that Caldera's has a veggie burrito with kale in it." Andrew quickly offered.

Lucy watched her son fidget nervously. He really did not like being in the shop, did he?

"No, no! Just kidding! It's a joke your grandfather used to say."

Lucy held the greasy burrito in her hands. Carne asada, all meat. It was still warm, wrapped in white paper, then in the yellow paper, with two napkins, in a brown paper bag. She had brought this exact lunch to her father and grandfather before. This lunch had always made them smile. The next master should be smiling, too.

But she was no master. She thought of all the evenings that she'd been asked to leave the shop, evenings her brothers had been asked to stay behind—to learn secrets passed only from father to son.

But now Lucy's younger brother was in jail. And her older brother had fled the violin shop as soon as her father fell ill, saying the old man deserved to burn.

Lucy glanced beyond the burrito to the disheveled violin before her. Mr. Zacatecas said he dropped it while playing at a wedding. He said it was an accident.

An accident? The poor thing was still damp with beer. A life of increasing neglect had steadily degraded the instrument, causing parts to warp and misalign. Soon it would be beyond saving.

"Just keep it together," he had said.

Keep it together.

"Andrew, if you have time, why not stay after lunch? It's been a while since you've spent any time in the shop. We still have two weeks before Mr. Zacatecas returns. And it's very basic work." She tried not to sound nervous.

"What if I mess up?"

"You won't. You're a Matía."

At the sound of the name, his face turned red.

"I can't," he mumbled. Then he dashed out of the store.

He'll come around, Lucy told herself. He had to. Somehow he'd find a way to continue the store. Maybe he could coax his uncles back when the store was properly his. Or maybe he'd be a genius who could rediscover the family secrets himself.

For a son of the Matías, all things were possible.

Until then?

Just keep it together.

Lucy took a deep breath and loosened the strings on the tired violin.

For now, keeping it together was in her hands. Her woman's hands. Yet how could the hands of a daughter possibly preserve the legacy of this family, this name?

The doorbell jingled again.

"Did you forget your phone, Andrew? I told you not to—"

She froze midsentence.

This was not Andrew at all.

Exquisite. Fiery. Sunglasses. Footsteps in perfect time.

"Is Franco here?"

"Franco? Oh, I'm sorry. He passed away twelve years ago."

"*What?* Twelve years? Has it been twelve years . . ."

Lucy felt this woman trying to place her.

"I'm Lucy," she finally offered.

"*Lucía?* You're all grown up! I'm Shizuka Satomi."

Of course she was. A photo of her was over her head. It had been Catalin's favorite. But a photo was nothing compared to reality. Lucy had to suppress an urge to bow.

With casual elegance, Shizuka turned to Katrina.

"This is Lucía Matía. Lucía has been in this shop since she was a child."

Katrina bowed and tried to make herself small.

"Lucía, I remember watching you change the bridge on Aoi Miyazawa's Strad, remember? The one she got from that billionaire German? You couldn't have been more than eight or nine."

Lucy looked at her feet. "I was ten. And Miss Miyazawa wasn't supposed to know that," she muttered.

"Not only did she know it, she performed with it that night."

Shizuka laughed. "Even then, you had the hands of a Matía. And now you're finally the master."

Lucy winced. Sure, she had decent hands—her grandfather had said so himself—but a master?

"Look, I'd love to. But I don't have the qualifications. Ever since my father died, I've just been doing simple work here and there. Nothing complicated—just basic repairs and setups. Maybe you can find another shop?"

At least that was what Lucy Matía had intended to say.

But Shizuka Satomi had already placed a violin case in front of her. Then she pointed at the boy next to her.

"This is my student, and we need your help."

Lucy tried to remain calm, but this was *Shizuka Satomi*. As a performer, she was said to have never lost a contest. As a teacher? From Morihei Sanada to Yifeng Zheng and everyone in between . . . Burke, Tourischeva, Eisen, Choi . . . the Queen of Hell had taught them all.

So, despite herself, Lucy placed her curious hands upon the case. Her heart raced as she imagined the magnificent instrument inside.

"I—I don't understand."

"She bought this from eBay," Shizuka said casually. "It's from China. Is there anything wrong?"

"A-are you serious?" Lucy stuttered. "I mean, we have some very good rental instruments that he'd be welcome to try. I mean, not like anything you have, but—"

"She."

"Huh?"

"My student is a girl."

"Oh, whatever, well . . ."

"Her name is not whatever. Her name is Katrina," Shizuka said sweetly.

"Yes, of course it was not whatever. It's just—" She stopped herself before she said worse. "I'm sorry."

"Not to me." Shizuka Satomi gestured to her student.

"I'm so sorry," Lucy said to Katrina.

Katrina looked down, trying to make herself disappear. Lucy's

heart sank. Watching this child made Lucy think of all the times
her father had lost his temper.

"So, you'll do the job, Lucía?"

Before she knew it, Lucy nodded.

"Good. Though it is not from a prestigious maker, its sound may
surprise you. And my student bought this with every penny she had."

Shizuka said the last line innocently, but Lucy could feel the gaze
of the Queen of Hell. *If you dare laugh at her or her violin, I will burn
your soul and this entire shop to ash.*

Carefully, Lucy picked up the instrument. It was heavy, but well
shaped. The varnish was a little uneven, but neither soft nor uncured.
The arching and fluting were fine. The scroll was rough, but it had a
smooth curl from the inside out. There was no break; the line flowed
naturally from the center outward.

So this instrument wasn't merely chopped and pressed out of scrap.
Someone had cared.

"If you don't mind me asking, how much did you pay for this?"

"Two hundred forty-one dollars plus shipping. I got really lucky.
It's a P20+."

"Really?"

Lucy had no idea what a P20+ was. But Mr. Zacatecas had paid
more than three times that price for his Romanian beer fiddle. Lucy
retrieved her penlight and peered inside.

Hmm. The sound post was shifted slightly toward the treble side,
up and away from the bridge.

"Who adjusted the sound post?"

"Um . . . I did. I used a paper clip," Katrina said.

"You adjusted the *sound post*?" Miss Satomi asked. The sound post
was one of the most important parts of the violin. And, as even a
slight change in position could drastically alter an instrument's sound,
most musicians would never think of adjusting it themselves.

"A paper clip, huh?" Lucía Matía said.

"I learned from the Internet." Katrina was surprised at how easily
she responded. She was still nervous . . . she'd even been misgen-
dered . . . but this was nothing like being petrified at Grunfeld's.

"I see . . . well, aren't you a diva?"

Why was everyone calling her a diva?

"She always plays just a hair sharp," Miss Satomi added.

"D-did I mess up?"

"No, no . . . you did fine," the woman said. "It's a little snug, but it's good and level. If you like it there, I'll place it there again. In fact . . . it'll probably stay in place after I remove the strings and bridge."

Lucy smiled. The kid had very good hands. And a great ear. In fact, if she weren't studying with the Queen of Hell, Lucy might have offered her a job. And so far, this repair looked pretty simple. All the instrument needed was a basic—

But then, Lucy paused.

The bridge did not move.

She glanced at Katrina, who was now staring at her shoes, then at Shizuka Satomi, who shook her head slowly.

So this was why they had needed her help.

The bridge . . . was glued to the spruce? This was crazy. The repair costs alone would be more than what the instrument was worth.

But it was *Shizuka Satomi* asking.

And besides . . .

Lucy had been in this shop since she was a child. She had seen students sneer at worthy violins without a proper pedigree. She had seen them treat fifty-thousand-dollar instruments like servants, or toys.

This student was giving her violin nothing but love.

"I'll need time," Lucy finally said.

"No rush. She can play any one of mine for now."

Lucy looked up, startled by what that implied, then returned to the violin in front of her.

"Okay. Obviously, we'll need a new bridge. Aubert?"

"Milo Stamm. Premium," said Shizuka.

"Y-yes. We can order that." Of course. Lucy remembered—Auberts were fine professional bridges, but Stamm was a Satomi trademark.

"Then again, if you think Despiau would be better, by all means use one. Yifeng preferred the 10A—the one with three trees."

And yes. "Yifeng" was Yifeng Brian Zheng.

"And strings? Dominants?" Lucy regretted saying that the moment it left her lips. Of course. Dominants were fine for most people, but Shizuka Satomi was not most people.

Shizuka looked as if she had just smelled something unpleasant.

"For this violin, Evah Pirazzis. I want a little bit of attitude. The regular Pirazzis would be fine . . . though the E might be a little bright. Maybe a gold E. What do you think, Katrina? Shall we add a gold E?"

Katrina shrugged. *How was this even happening?*

"I'll put them on, if possible." Lucy examined the violin carefully. "Evah Pirazzis carry a . . . higher tension, so sometimes . . . they can be a bit much for a student violin." She checked the construction and quality of the wood. Good and good.

"Evah Pirazzis will be fine," she declared. "Anything else?"

"Katrina?" Miss Satomi asked. "Is there anything else you'd like to check?"

"C-can you help—" Katrina blurted before stopping herself.

"Help?" Lucy asked.

"Katrina?"

"Nothing," Katrina mumbled.

Why had Katrina even opened her mouth? She hadn't even told Miss Satomi that she'd moved the sound post, let alone why. She didn't know how to explain it, anyway.

Miss Satomi put her hand on Katrina's shoulder.

"She's going to take the best care of your violin."

"I promise," Lucy said.

The doorbell jingled and then they were gone.

I promise.

What could have possessed her to say such a thing? And the expression on that student's face as she left . . .

Lucy Matía slumped on her stool. But a violin—and a promise— were now resting in her hands.

What she had not told Shizuka Satomi was that she had already canceled requests from Aoi Miyazawa. What she had not told Shizuka Satomi was that she had already sent a note to their oldest clients that for now, they should find other shops.

Yes, her grandfather had said that she had the "hands of a Matía." But her grandfather had said other things, as well. As did her father. Things her brothers were unable to hear. Things that she had never been told.

For MATÍA & SONS, the sign said.

And though she was a Matía, she was not a son.

*   *   *

"Katrina? You see over there?" As they drove, Shizuka pointed at a small storefront.

"It used to be Iris Salon. That's where an old lady used to cut my hair."

"Oh."

"So much has changed. When I was young, most of these signs in the area were in Spanish. That nail salon used to be Angel's Upholstery. And the kitchen supply store used to be Super Videos, and before that, there was an old man who repaired shoes."

"Oh."

Well, that attempt failed. So much for "chatting about the neighborhood." That was fine. But soon Shizuka had to find a way to relate to the girl and gain her trust. No matter how brilliant Katrina proved to be, she would need to be trained.

Even Paganini had to practice. In fact, the more remarkable the student, the more relentless and difficult the process. One does not cut a diamond by being gentle, and Katrina, with her uncultivated skills and history of abuse, had a uniquely difficult path ahead. The girl would be pressured, hammered, honed, and polished.

Simply put, the girl would not survive if she flinched every time her teacher rattled a coffee mug.

Her other students had been easy—they were vain, angry, jealous, ambitious. Such feelings lend a perverse, obsessive resilience. All Shizuka had to do was play to their emotions, and they would follow and endure without question. But this one? This frightened runaway?

How could Shizuka start forging a bond with *her*? And how would Katrina weather the training ahead?

"Miss Satomi?"

The girl's voice shook her from her thoughts.

"Yes?"

"Thank you," Katrina said quietly. "For back there. For telling them I was a girl."

"Of course."

What was this about? Of all the obvious things . . .

"Miss Satomi, don't you care? About me being trans?"

"Katrina. In my business, one does not care about bodies. One is only concerned with souls."

For a long time, the girl said nothing.

"When I was seven," she finally said, "I took group lessons with the neighbors. My mother thought I could make friends. The teacher was very nice. She never yelled. She told my family I was the best player in her class.

"But my father . . . he'd yell at me. Hit me, like I told you. And one day, I was practicing, and my father threw a bottle at me. I turned to protect my violin, and I think the bottle hit me in the head, and right after, I started to shake, and my hands grew warm, as if they were on fire.

"Suddenly, I could hear my violin singing to me, singing to my soul, promising if I believed in her, I could fly away and she would fly away with me, too."

"Is that the violin we're repairing now?" Shizuka finally asked.

"No. It was the one my father smashed."

11

Lucy waited until evening, when there was no chance of being disturbed, to work on the Chinese violin. She needed to be careful. Regardless of its value or origin, her client *was* the Queen of Hell. And there was also the matter of this glued-on bridge . . .

She took out her magnifier and looked more closely.

Superglue.

Just. Great.

Some of it had also dripped and run onto the faceplate. Which meant the violin would need to be at least partially refinished.

But first, the bridge.

There were different techniques to remove cyanoacrylate. However, each had drawbacks. A knife could catch on a clump of glue and cut into the wood. Heat would warp the wood itself. Chemical solvents could break down the glue, but they could do the same to the grain.

"Okay, come on girl. You can do this. Take your time."

Quietly, her fingers probed around the bridge. They traced its top, around its edges, gently scratched its sides. Yes. They paused. What? Again. There it was again. Yes, the tiniest smallest gap, but it was there. Just a little movement. A quiver.

Yes. Right there. Again.

Then, as if on its own, her hand grasped the bridge, twisted, and—

SNAP!

Lucy Matía reached for her stool and sat down. Her fingers shook, and she felt a little lightheaded.

But the bridge was in her hand, and the violin was free.

As strong as it was, superglue wasn't meant for wood. Also, it had been carelessly applied, which meant there'd been a weak spot in the joint. Of course the finish was marred, but the wood underneath was fine. Her hands had been careful not to pull up the grain.

"Hands of a Matía," she murmured out loud.

Then, Lucy paused.

Really?

Catalin Matía would smile whenever someone described great music as divine.

To him, that was nonsense. Great music is all about weakness, uncertainty, mortality—what does Heaven know of these?

In the same way, there is nothing transcendent about a violin. It is maple, spruce, ebony, an ounce or so of hide glue, some brushes of varnish.

Perhaps this why the violin fits the human soul fit so perfectly—only such a simple, mortal object can hold its fragility and turn it into a prayer.

Even without a player, a violin has music. Just as a painting artfully holds and reflects light, a violin shapes and glows with sound. A motorcycle passes. Someone vocalizes next door. The air conditioner hums. Even without a player—even without strings—the violin responds to it all.

Of course, not every piece of wood can manifest this music, just as not every pair of hands can create it. People pay thousands, millions of dollars to acquire such a violin.

Or $241 plus shipping.

Because this violin was trying. Faintly, and almost as if buried or bound. But Lucy was certain. In the quiet of the shop, even after all it had endured, this violin was trying, with all its soul, to sing.

What would Catalin Matía do?

Lucy didn't need to imagine.

She remembered her grandfather insisting that Paganini's il Cannone was just another sloppy Guarneri before Jean-Baptiste Vuillaume got to it. In fact, Vuillaume had crafted an exact copy of the instrument that not even Paganini could detect.

"Oh, Paganini is important, of *course*—but it took Vuillaume to shave a bit, cut a bit, move the support a little. We do not merely repair violins. We set them *free!*"

But Lucy was not Catalin Matía.

Besides, wasn't it time to close shop? Tomorrow, Mr. Zacatecas's violin would be completely dry. She would remove the clamps, put on a fresh set of Tonicas, and Mr. Zacatecas would be good to go.

As for this instrument in front of her? She had gotten very lucky with the bridge. Tomorrow morning, she would cover any scratches with a stroke or three of spirit varnish, and by lunchtime, the parts she'd ordered would arrive at the shop. Then she would make some quick adjustments, pop in the Milo Stamm, string with the Evah Pirazzis, give it a quick buff with a fresh microfiber cloth, and she'd be done.

The new components of course would improve the sound. And Shizuka Satomi would be a good contact to have. She might send a few more students, then maybe even refer another school or two.

Which would mean a bit more time to hope, hope to God that Andrew might inherit her father's talent and bring Matía and Sons back from the dead.

Her mind made up, Lucy put on her coat, turned off the lights, and opened the door. The doorbell jingled.

No, no, no . . .

There it was again . . . like a child asking for water.

Could that student have heard this?

Lucy recalled the adjustment the girl had made to the sound post. How Shizuka said she had been playing a little sharp. And what she said at the end.

"Can you help—"

Not fix. *Help.*

Of course she knew. That girl had been doing everything she could to set her violin free.

Lucy took off her coat and put it back on the hanger. She picked up her phone.

"Miss Satomi? I'm sorry to call you so late. No, there's no problem. It's just that I found something unexpected. If you don't mind, I'd like a little more time."

*   *   *

"She said that she found something interesting with your violin," her teacher said. "Don't worry. As I said, it is in the best of hands."

That was her teacher, Shizuka Satomi. Who had just talked to the person repairing her violin, a person who had worked on a *Stradivarius*.

Two weeks ago, Katrina had to sneak into a boba place, much like this, just to use the restroom. Today, Katrina got up and walked to the bathroom. Thank goodness it was gender-neutral and single-stall. But even if it weren't, Miss Satomi would surely protect her. When she emerged, there was K-Pop on the screens overhead. Tables were full of people studying, chatting, playing cards.

And at her table, was Miss Satomi and a large kiwi bing sa.

This was not real. This could not be real. This was like being in an anime or a fairy tale. But there was no such thing, was there?

"Miss Satomi, what will this cost?"

"I'm paying."

Katrina shook her head.

"That's not what I mean. *What will this cost?*"

Shizuka had heard this question six times before. Six times, it was business, with nothing hidden, with everyone's intentions clear. Shizuka had spoken to each ambitious prodigy of fame, virtuosity, acclaim, and how they might have all they wanted, if only they traded their soul.

But this was a girl who had run away from home, who had been beaten, had her ribs broken, who had just had her first night of peaceful sleep in who knows how long.

And she had just been separated from her violin.

To talk business right now just didn't seem fair.

"Why don't we wait until you settle in first? We can make a better deal once we know what we have to work with."

Before Katrina could respond, Miss Satomi's phone beeped. She looked at the text.

"It's Astrid. Please don't tell her that I've spoiled your dinner. She said she is making veal. With a side of winter melon."

"Veal?" Katrina smiled as she thought of Skylar berating her for eating meat.

"Don't tell me you won't eat veal."

"I've never had it. But I'll try."

"Good girl. Astrid is a wonderful cook. Though sometimes she uses a bit too much butter and heavy cream. Perhaps it's because she's Swiss. But let's keep that between us, shall we?

"Anyway, you don't need to finish that bing sa. If I know Astrid, she will also have made dessert."

✳   ✳   ✳

"NO! Listen! Can't you hear that?" The sounds of her father were getting angrier and angrier.

"Hear what?"

"How can you be a Matía?"

"I never wanted to be a Matía!"

The door slammed open, and her brother ran out in tears.

"It's just a fucking piece of wood!"

Each evening this happened, Lucy would pray that God might bless her brothers' ears, grant her father health. But her brothers never learned to hear.

And now her father was gone.

Lucy sat at the workbench. Before her were the tools of the Matías. Chisels and clamps, files, planes, knives, and calipers—honest, beloved tools, passed to Franco from Catalin, and to Catalin from before that.

She picked up a mallet and a sharp, flat blade.

"Papa, I am sorry," she said. "I know these were meant for hands other than mine. But right now, these are the only hands here."

Her voice was weak, uncertain. But then Lucy began to work.

And her hands began to move—methodically, precisely separating seams and joinery without a trace of hesitation or doubt.

The door opened.

"Is everything okay? You didn't come home, and I was worried, and—what?"

She nodded to her son, then went back to the violin. "Shizuka Satomi came in with a new student. They brought this."

"That's—"

"A violin from China," she said without looking up. "Yes, I know."

"No, I mean, it's all in pieces."

"Yes. So are we all."

There is a reason that most luthiers never let players see what they do to their instruments. They would faint.

Violinists often think of their violins as fragile, delicate creatures.

But what do mere players know?

What makes a violin special is not its fragility, but its resilience. One can change the strings and adjust the bridge. One can slide a sound post, replace the fittings, rebore the pegbox, carve a new bass bar, even change the angle of the neck.

If one did analogous things to a painting or book, the piece would be ruined. Even pianos, for all their pomp and circumstance, are tragically temporal things. Modify the action of an Erard or Pleyel, or do what was done to that poor Cristofori at the Met, and one effectively destroys it.

But a violin's existence, its vitality, depends only upon its capacity to sing.

With the violin disassembled, Lucy could better feel the warmth of the wood. She ran her eyes along the joints, the edges, the curve of the ribs. She examined the inside pieces—the bracings, the top and bottom blocks—for any carelessness or lack of craft. But every element of this Chinese violin was textbook.

Textbook?

Of course. Now this violin made more sense. It was not made by a dedicated luthier, but by a carpenter.

That was not necessarily a bad thing—this was a very good carpenter, someone who knew wood, who could craft strong and proper structures, who worked with the grain so the parts expanded and contracted with humidity and temperature, yet never warped out of place.

Yet strong and proper is not enough. A violin is not a footstool; it must risk breaking if it is to give everything to its song.

Lucy twirled the faceplate on her fingertip, rapped it with her knuckle, and listened. With a pencil, she freehanded a shape into the wood. Then, she began carving, first with a finger plane, then with a knife, taking a millimeter here, a half millimeter there, and listening all the while.

"Can you get me that scraper blade over there?" she said to Andrew.

"Yes, Mom," Andrew said automatically.

His mother's hands.

Andrew Matía had seen her hands shake nervously when speaking to Mr. Zacatecas. He had watched them quiver when eating a burrito.

Yet, as those hands began scraping steel against spruce, he thought of something his mother had told him—that as a little girl, she would hear a music that no player could ever create, a music born not of composer, nor player, but of the hands of her grandfather at work.

But Andrew had never known Catalin Matía, and when he thought of *his* grandfather, all the sounds he remembered came from yelling and tools being thrown.

All the sounds he remembered were his mother cringing, apologizing, calling herself stupid when lunch wasn't on time or when that bastard felt the shop was too dusty, too noisy, too empty, too full.

Even now, his mother would flinch whenever she heard an unexpected noise, or anyone entered the store.

Such things are music, too.

Yet now, his mother's hands were a rich, seamless legato, with neither stutter nor apology.

"That's better, isn't it? But I think we can go a bit further," she said to herself.

She removed a bit more wood, then a bit more. Then she paused.

"Gotcha," she murmured.

She tapped the wood, and suddenly Andrew heard a ripple of color. And as the night grew dark, Andrew Matía's heart began to fill with the rush of spruce, the flare of maple, the cadence of sandpaper and steel.

* * *

Katrina had never eaten veal before, but she had always imagined it breaded and fried. Here, however, it was stewed, with minced garlic and sliced mushrooms, all in a thick, buttery, cream-laden gravy. Miss Astrid said this was a family recipe, but Katrina had never known a family that ate food like this.

"I experimented a bit. I used winter melon from the Lieus. And usually, I would serve this with aubergines, but unfortunately they aren't yet ready, and Miss Satomi wanted rice."

Aubergines? Katrina perked up. She had no idea what aubergines were, but the word made her mouth water.

"So, Katrina, how did you like the Matías?" Shizuka asked.

"The Matías?" Astrid stopped, surprised. "The Matías took the job?"

"Of course. Lucía was fascinated by Katrina's violin. By the way, this veal is wonderful."

"Katrina, you're very lucky. They are the best of the best," Astrid said.

Katrina thought back to the neighborhood. An auto glass shop. Another auto glass shop. A nail salon. A sign store with all sorts of LED MASSAGE signs flashing in the window. And down the street was Starrgate Donut.

There was nothing quaint and picturesque about it.

"Miss Satomi, why is a violin shop like *that* . . . there?"

"Places like the Matías' are usually out of the way," Shizuka explained. "Many musicians like to keep their secrets."

Something to ask about later, Katrina thought.

But for now, Katrina had more pressing matters. She had finished most of the winter melon, and half of the veal. She pushed some to the left, then to the right. She did not want to seem ungrateful; the food was delicious. But Miss Satomi was right—there was a lot of heavy cream in that gravy.

"That was wonderful," Katrina finally said. "Thank you for the meal."

She got up to leave, but Astrid stopped her.

"I have lemon tarts," she said.

"Miss Satomi?" Katrina pleaded.

"I warned you to save room. Enjoy!" Shizuka made to get up. However, Astrid put her hand on her shoulder, as well.

"No, no. You too. We have so many lemons, after all."

"From the Aguilars?"

"From the Aguilars."

Finally, mercifully, dinner ended.

"Shall we get started?" Shizuka said.

Katrina washed up and went to the grand piano in the living room. It was immaculate, just as Katrina might have expected. Atop it was an old black-and-white picture of a young woman who Katrina felt she'd seen before, but could not quite place.

"Katrina? What are you doing?"

"But the piano is here?"

"That's Astrid's piano. Mine is downstairs."

"Astrid's piano?" Katrina stared at the picture. "Then that's *Miss Astrid?*"

"Of course it is," Miss Satomi said, as if the picture had been taken yesterday. "Now, come along."

Katrina followed Shizuka down the staircase, which opened into a small foyer, which then in turn led to a door.

And beyond that . . .

"This is my practice hall. I wanted someplace peaceful. I wish I could have a fishpond here, but it would be too difficult to control the humidity."

Katrina gasped. The lights glowed like the sun—if she hadn't known, she would have assumed they were outdoors. There were even bamboo and bonsai trees.

In what could have been a Japanese teahouse, was a shiny black piano. And on the walls?

Now Katrina understood why Miss Satomi had not been impressed with the violins on display at Grunfeld's, nor even at the Matías'.

Hanging from the walls were the most beautiful violins Katrina had ever seen.

Then Miss Satomi handed her a bow and shoulder rest.

"Pick one."

Katrina scanned the wall. Each violin was exquisite. As she walked, each seemed to hear and respond to every step, every breath Katrina took.

Yet Katrina hesitated. For as beautiful as they were, seeing them only made her miss her violin all the more.

"Katrina, you are looking for a friend, not a lover," she heard Miss Satomi say.

Tentatively, Katrina pulled a violin from the wall, attached the shoulder rest, and played. Not bad.

But why would it be bad?

Of course it was good. *Maybe this is what good sounds like?*

Or this?

What was she listening for? Did she even have the right to judge?

And then, from somewhere, she heard a sound. Not from the instrument she was playing, but from somewhere else. Katrina tilted her head. It felt gentle, even kind. But wherever the sound came from, it gave her the courage to put this violin back.

It was a gorgeous instrument, but not quite what she wanted. So she tried another. And one more.

Shizuka Satomi smiled as the girl shook her head at an instrument insured at eight million dollars. Other students often traded their ears for their eyes—they would search for labels or examine the body to guess the age or origin.

But Katrina was listening, trying to feel.

Katrina played violin after violin. Some had a rounder tone, some seemed agile, like a fighter jet or a race car. Some were powerful, others sophisticated. There were so many more to try.

But Katrina had already made her choice.

She pointed to a violin on another wall, away from the others.

"Can I try that one? It's been singing to me all night. It seems to cheer every time I hit a sweet note."

Katrina saw her teacher hesitate.

"I'm sorry! If I can't, it doesn't matter."

"No, not at all," Miss Satomi said, in a strange faraway voice. She walked to it, took it down, and handed it to Katrina.

Katrina closed her eyes. The violin felt warm and centered, and she felt herself relax, just a little bit. No, this was not her violin. But, with all the craziness, from leaving home to Evan to meeting Shizuka, here was finally something that did not seem strange or crazy at all.

Shizuka listened as Katrina played some Schradieck and then a few bars of a pretty song she didn't recognize. She recalled a time when she had first moved to study in Europe, and heard the voice of her childhood music teacher, long distance, over the telephone. *I'm so proud of you. I know you're lonely, but everything is going to be wonderful!*

"May I use this?" her student asked. "When I play this violin, I feel safe, like everything is going to be fine."

"Yes. But be careful with her." Shizuka held the violin and gave it a kiss.

"This is Martha. She is my first full-sized violin."

MARCH

✳ ✳ ✳ ✳ ✳ ✳ ✳

12

"Lift the note! Lift! Not width, Katrina. *Height!*"

Again Shizuka tried to explain, but her student only became more confused.

"Think of a wing—light and strong."

The sound flattened and became almost nasal.

Shizuka did her best to smile as she motioned upward with her arms. "Imagine you're gliding downhill. Down . . . hill. And now . . . *Fly!*"

Martha made a horrible squawk.

"No!"

"I'm sorry!" Katrina said.

"It's okay, it's okay. Let's try again."

"I'm never going to get this."

"Yes, you will. One more time . . . lift! No, not like that. *No!*"

That night, Shizuka could not sleep.

Shizuka donned her robe and walked downstairs, then into the backyard. The air still smelled of spring. By streetlights and the moonlight, she could see the peach blossoms and plum blossoms opening to the sky.

Why wasn't her student blossoming, as well? At the park, Katrina's Schradieck had been magnificent. And, later, from a room full of very fine violins, she had the ear to choose Martha.

Yet today, she wouldn't have been able to follow *Suzuki Book Two.*

Shizuka had known that Katrina would be unlike her previous students—that was why she was chosen. But nothing had prepared Shizuka for this. Even now the girl was in the practice hall, fumbling over the same basic exercises they had worked on all day.

Shizuka was trying. Katrina was trying. But it seemed as if their progress was going backward. And this was no time for backward.

"Have you tried tape on the fingerboard?" a voice asked.

"Tremon." She tried to not appear surprised.

"I'm sorry. Am I intruding? I did not mean to interrupt your thoughts—I was simply in the neighborhood when I thought I heard a small animal screaming for help. Imagine my surprise when I realized that *horrific* noise came from your *student*, the one you so carefully chose!"

"This is not a good time for jokes, Tremon."

"I could say the same to you. Our agreement was that you deliver the souls of seven brilliant violinists, not open a charity for homeless queer youth."

"What are you talking about?"

Tremon shrugged. "Shizuka, surely you are aware that your choice is unexpected. I must admit that even I was baffled. Until I remembered that you are still human, after all."

"Of course I am. So?"

"So you've condemned six souls. Each was brilliant, glorious. And each projected their final outrage, their agony—with perfect intonation and impeccable voicing—squarely and completely at you. I'm a demon; the dying wrath of a few humans would be neither here nor there for me. But for you? Your pain would be unbearable.

"Now, suppose there were a lost runaway, not someone pampered and privileged, but one for whom any passing kindness would be treasured. Give her a hot meal, a bath, a chance to play music—that would reduce your guilt, no? You might even tell yourself afterward that you did nothing wrong—after all, her life was a dead end, anyway."

"Tremon, I'm not even going to respond to that."

"Of course you won't, dear. But it has been over ten years since Yifeng left you. Such love! He said he lived for you on national TV. Remember broadcast TV?"

"I do. And that wasn't love. That was weakness. Moreover, do not forget that I delivered Yifeng Zheng to Hell myself."

"Yes, you did, Shizuka. Of course. And I would *never* think you might be cheating us."

"Who do you think I *am*? I will take her soul, as promised. I will deliver it on time, as promised. And I will have my life back again. *As promised*. Do I make myself clear, Tremon?"

But there was no response, for Tremon Philippe was gone.

Of course the toad would imagine such nonsense! He was a demon, and no demon could know what Shizuka heard in Katrina's playing. Even now, reliving that day in the park made Shizuka's breathing quicken, her body quiver, as if receiving epiphany.

Charity? A soul was a soul. That she was a runaway, queer, transgender, survivor—was irrelevant.

Yes, Shizuka was being gentle with this one. But there was no need to be cruel before harvest. Shizuka walked back into the house. Downstairs, she could hear Katrina and Astrid.

"You've been working since dinner. Why don't you come to the kitchen?" Shizuka heard Astrid say.

"Just a little while longer?"

"Very well, I will leave you a snack on the table."

"Thank you, Miss Astrid. And thank you for letting me practice like this."

Shizuka paused, then continued upstairs without saying a word.

✳ ✳ ✳

An explosion.

Overhead floated a cruiser of the Imperial Fleet.

"Wait! We have a permit! WAIT!" Lan pleaded.

No response.

"We've got to leave, we've got to leave, we've got to leave!" Aunty Floresta stumbled to the front of the store.

There was a flash and horrible sound. Aunty Floresta was gone.

The Big Donut was reduced to twisted metal and ash. Ever more ships materialized overhead. Soldiers appeared everywhere, weapons drawn, smashing the donut racks, breaking the windows.

Lan needed to protect her family; she was their captain. She was their mother.

"Get to the shuttle!"

But Markus turned toward the soldiers.

"You can't do this! My father—"

He never finished the sentence.

Lan rushed to retrieve Edwin and Windee, but one of the soldiers already had them. They screamed, just before they disappeared.

*Another soldier aimed his weapon at one of the customers. She was
dressed in red, and was holding half of an Alaska Donut.*

"Mother. *Mother.*"

"Shirley?"

"You were talking in your sleep," Shirley said.

"A dream?"

"Yes, you were asleep at your desk."

Her mother nodded stiffly. "Okay then, nothing to worry about."

Shirley was not convinced. Her mother had been working steadily
for the past thirty-eight hours.

"Mother. These bodies are more fragile than the ones you are used
to. You yourself warned the crew to monitor their exertion."

"No time. We have the morning customers."

"Mother, it's already nine A.M."

"What?" Her mother rushed to the elevator. "I expect you to let
me know when I am needed in the front! How are sales?"

"Fine, Mother."

"Any emergencies?"

"No, Mother."

"The replicators?"

"Fine," Shirley said. "Mother, everything is fine."

Everything was fine. That is, except her mother. These incidents
were happening more and more often. "Take care of family first," her
mother loved to say. But her mother seemed unable to understand
that she was family, too.

Yes, the entire crew was hard at work with the donuts and stargate,
but her mother insisted that they take time for themselves. Thus,
Aunty Floresta would venture into town looking for supermarkets
and new food items. Markus would unwind by playing online video
games or driving about town in the middle of the night. Windee and
Edwin, of course, were children, so Lan took them to museums and
the occasional movie.

Yet the only times Lan Tran had truly taken for herself had been
those spent with Shizuka Satomi.

This week, Shizuka Satomi had neither visited the shop nor
called. And as the days passed, Shirley would catch her mother

losing concentration, forgetting things, or staring blankly into space.

"If you aren't going to rest, then call her, Mother."

"Why would I call her?"

"Because you like her."

"Why would that matter? Besides, she's busy."

"Mother—"

"Anyway, what would we talk about? Music? There's no time for silliness. We have a donut to calibrate."

"Markus and Windee are already doing it, just as you asked."

"And then we need to locate a suitable power source. Also, the Earth's crust seems to have shifted again, so we need to retune the space-time filaments."

"Yes, I am handling both, as you asked."

"We need to rotate the reference donuts, then."

"Markus is doing that, as you—"

"As I asked? Well, then I should pay the utility bills."

"I already did that last night. Mother . . ."

"Okay, Shirley, I'm going to the bathroom. You haven't already taken care of *that*, have you?"

Lan marched into the bathroom and slammed the door.

Immediately, she felt guilty. Shirley was only looking out for her health.

She sat down and closed her eyes. This bathroom. She remembered letting Shizuka in here that first time.

Shizuka. Shizuka had not come to the shop for a week. Maybe she's just busy. If she wanted to talk, she'd come by, right? Besides—

Bang! Bang!

Someone was pounding on the bathroom door. Before she could sit up, Windee barged in.

"Captaaain! Shirley said you needed thiiis!"

Windee gave Lan her phone and left.

"Windee! Close the door! Close the—"

Lan looked at the screen and froze. Shirley had already dialed Shizuka's number.

"No, Windee, come back! Close the door! At least close the—Hello?"

* * *

"Katrina?"

This morning the girl was once again perched over her laptop, which itself was perched over the corner of the kitchen table.

"Katrina?"

No response. Ah, she had earphones on. Shizuka tapped her shoulder.

"*Sorry!*"

Katrina jumped up as she shouted. Only Shizuka's quick hands saved the laptop from tumbling onto the floor.

"I'm sorry! I'm sorry!" Katrina said. Her hands, her body were shaking.

Astrid rushed in. "Is everything all right?"

Shizuka nodded.

"It's okay. No harm done," said Shizuka.

"Good. Then I'll bring out breakfast."

Today's breakfast was seaweed soup, rice, some grilled fish, and picked vegetables.

"Why do you always sit way on the corner like that?" Shizuka asked.

"It's where I can get the best Wi-Fi signal."

"Wi-Fi?"

Katrina lowered her head. "It's fine."

The seaweed soup and fish were delicious, but for once Katrina barely seemed to notice. Shizuka remembered that Kiana would pout this way when she had her heart set on something but did not know how to ask.

"If you need a Wi-Fi, we can get a Wi-Fi. Right, Astrid?"

"Of course, Miss Satomi."

"Really? We could get Wi-Fi?" Katrina's face was a mix of gratitude and disbelief.

Her expression reminded Shizuka of what Tremon had said. She felt slightly nauseated with herself.

"I can look up some data plans and providers around here, if you like." Katrina continued excitedly. "And once I get online, I can post videos, so I can pay for the connection."

"Oh? Those must be wonderful videos," Astrid said.

Katrina made a peculiar face, but before Shizuka could probe further, her phone rang.

"Hello? Lan?"

* * *

Legacy.

Lucy Matía's grandfather had located here in El Monte right after the war. Here was a place close enough for his clients, yet far enough that he could, as he said, hear the instruments breathe.

Here just a few miles southeast of downtown, was a place where no one really cared about the film you were in or the screenplay you had optioned. Many people here wouldn't be able to read it anyway, unless it was in Spanish or Vietnamese, or some Chinese dialect or another.

Here were families with grandparents and young children. Senior classes were being held yet again at the aquatic center. Next summer as usual, kids would line up for another turn in the batting cage.

And, of course, here was the Big Donut.

The new owners had fit in perfectly. The family was friendly; the kids were cute. The new owner didn't look worried or grab her cell phone when she saw a family of Mexicans walk in the door. And sometimes customers would notice they'd been given an extra old-fashioned or bear claw for free.

But it was more than their attitude. Lucy remembered a discussion she had shared with Mrs. Thamavuong. She had been ecstatic about the new owners, not only because they were going to keep Starrgate a donut shop, but because they wanted to preserve its legacy, as well.

She had told Lucy that she and her husband were eager to meet the family and spend time to train them. They wanted the new family to have not only their recipes, but also their exact ingredients, equipment settings, and secret cooking techniques.

"Anyone can make a donut," Mrs. Thamavuong said. "But we want to help them make a *Starrgate* donut."

Lucy had received advanced certifications in woodwork, obsessively studied the history of luthierie, and had even put herself through upper-division physics and materials science while at Cal State. But schooling was one thing. Legacy was another.

Lucy recalled that hipster Latin-Fusion bistro that had started a couple of years ago up the street, with a chef from Denver touting his authentic Oaxacan ingredients and selection of upscale single-barrel tequilas.

She was sure he had done his research. And one can't ruin tequila. But the fact was that his burritos weren't as good as the ones from the place around the corner, and the place around the corner was cheaper, and sometimes you just wanted a beer.

Needless to say, the bistro wasn't there anymore.

Legacy. It mattered for burritos. For donut shops.

For violins.

Sure, she could fix a violin. But though Lucy was of the same family, of the same blood—she was never trained in the secret ingredients and techniques that made the Matías the *Matías*. For those were only passed from grandfather to father, father to son, at night. When the stars came out, the workshop doors were closed, and pretty girls like her could only sit outside, close their eyes, and try with all their might to hear.

Beep!

A car horn shook Lucy from her thoughts. She looked up just as Shizuka's vintage Jaguar sped past her.

Lucy waved, but Shizuka was too busy giggling to notice.

The Queen of Hell was giggling? And, in her car was . . . the donut lady?

Legacy?

Despite herself, Lucy had to laugh.

13

"Watch *out*!"

"Watch where?"

Valley Boulevard was its usual turbulence of BMWs coming to full stops at green lights, Priuses slowing for no reason, and pickup trucks and Chevys trying to cut around all of it and get home to Duarte.

Shizuka tried to dodge the obstructions, but each time she changed lanes, she felt Lan's fingernails dig more deeply into her arm.

"Careful!"

"*Ow!* Are you *sure* you're an interstellar pilot?"

Somehow, they arrived at Kim Ky. Kim Ky was a noodle house run by Chinese Vietnamese. After the Vietnam War, many ethnic Chinese left Vietnam and settled in San Gabriel. They set up supermarkets, like Ai Hoa and Diho. And they also opened some very good noodle places.

"This is one of my Aunty Floresta's favorite places," Lan said.

"So Floresta is actually your aunt?"

"Yes." Lan nodded. She rattled off the rest of her family. There were her twins, Windee and Edwin. Windee was a theoretical prodigy, and smart enough to know it. Their older brother, Markus, was unmatched in construction and engineering, though he did have a hard time making friends.

"And Shirley?"

"Oh. Shirley," Lan said awkwardly. "Well, Shirley is a holographic projection. She's what one might call cybernetic."

Lan tensed for Shizuka's reaction. But instead of shock, Shizuka simply nodded.

"I see. So she lives in the computer and projects herself into the donut shop?"

"Wait? How did you know?" As far as Lan knew, creating a Shirley was far beyond the technical capabilities of this planet.

"Like in *Star Trek,* right?"

Before Lan could react, Shizuka whispered, "Should we be talking about all this alien stuff out loud?"

Lan pointed to her phone. A small blue light was glowing. "I'm scrambling our voices. Whatever we're saying now sounds to everyone like Korean. My scans show that no one here speaks Korean, so we'll be fine."

The server came with their menus. She was older, definitely related to the owner, perhaps her grandma.

"Ann-ye-ong ha-se-yo," she pronounced haltingly.

Lan and the server chatted for a while before she went back to the kitchen.

"What do you want?" Lan asked.

Shizuka looked at the menu. "Oh! They have Hainan chicken!"

"Hainan chicken? Okay."

Lan began to order. However, Lan and the server apparently knew each other, for they started chatting like old friends. Occasionally one or the other would glance at Shizuka and laugh.

Eventually, the server took the menus and walked back to the kitchen.

"What was that about?" Shizuka muttered. "Was she laughing at me?"

"Only a little. Mostly she wanted to know how my aunt was doing. By the way, I also ordered some kidney and fried Chinese donut."

"So, Lan, how are you speaking with them? Alien technology?"

"*This* gets your attention, and you never questioned why I speak English?"

Oh.

"However, perhaps we can install some Cantonese into that human brain of yours."

"Don't even go there. Remember? *Star Trek?*"

"Amateurs."

"So says a starship captain who can't handle changing lanes on Valley Boulevard?"

"No one drives a Prius in space," whispered Lan.

The server returned quickly with their food. Shizuka looked at the steaming bowl of soup in front of her.

"Ma'am—" This wasn't what she'd ordered.

But the server smiled and pointed at Lan.

"Lan, I said that wanted Hainan chicken."

"I know," Lan explained. "But do you see anyone eating Hainan chicken?"

Shizuka looked about the restaurant. Lan was right. Everyone was eating soup noodles. She should have noticed that. And since everyone was eating soup noodles, this place was probably using its best chicken to make stock.

So that was why the server had been laughing. Shizuka was slightly annoyed that Lan had simply changed her order. Sometimes, this whole starship captain thing could be overbearing. But the soup did smell amazing.

Shizuka took a sip and let out an involuntary sigh. Perfect mouthfeel. The noodles were chewy and slippery; the steaming broth was rich with green onion, fish cake, shredded chicken, and enough MSG to flog the taste buds into submissive bliss.

"So how have you been?"

Shizuka stared down at a tangle of noodles.

"Katrina?"

Shizuka nodded.

"What's going on?"

Shizuka knew that Lan had neither the understanding, nor the context to follow what she was about to say. After all, she was *literally* a being from another world. But somehow, the words and feelings tumbled from Shizuka anyway.

"I don't know what to do. She keeps time, but then she doesn't. Her intonation is fine, and then it isn't. And she still hasn't decided how she wishes to hold her bow. She has the sound. But there's no foundation.

"She lacks a proper repertoire. Other than Schradieck and some other pieces that she picked up at a used bookstore, she knows only gaming music and anime soundtracks. She says she learned over YouTube. YouTube?"

Suddenly, Shizuka stopped and pointed.

"Lan, your phone isn't glowing."

"Oh? Well, the scrambler drains power, so I shut it down after it was needed."

"*After* it was needed?"

Quickly, Shizuka glanced at the other customers. A table of well-dressed high school kids conspicuously turned away to look down at their noodles. And a couple of them had instrument cases.

Crap. She hadn't seen them enter. And now they had heard her discuss Katrina. Of course, Shizuka had no intention of keeping her student a secret, but she preferred to control how information got out, and when. Any student of hers would be an instant target, and Katrina, especially, was not ready for that type of scrutiny.

Lan fumbled with the phone, and the blue light returned.

"Why didn't you *tell* me you had stopped scrambling us?" Shizuka hissed.

"I'm sorry," Lan said hastily.

"I suppose that this must seem like rambling to you," Shizuka said lightly.

To be honest, this talk *did* sound trivial. Lan was fleeing a Galactic Empire falling to the Endplague—and Shizuka was worrying about sounds made with a wooden box? Still, she had such a beautiful voice . . .

"Yes, but it's okay?" Lan ventured.

"Well then," Shizuka said curtly. "I won't waste any more of your time."

Shizuka grabbed her purse and coat.

"Shizuka, wait!"

"Why? I'm sure that you have less trivial things to think about."

How was Lan supposed to answer this?

Luckily, Captain Tran was saved by an incoming plate of stir-fried kidneys. The server brought them to the table, smiled pleasantly at both of them, and left.

Slowly, Shizuka released her purse and put her coat down. It wasn't the restaurant's fault, and besides, she would rather not cause more of a scene. Furthermore, as frustrated as she was, the kidneys *did* smell amazing.

"Oh, these look wonderful, shall I get you one?" Lan said, and hastily grabbed one with her chopsticks.

"I can get my own, thank you."

Lan froze. There was nothing remotely sweet about that voice.

Shizuka grabbed one herself and took a bite. The texture was crunchy, then soft. And with a little chopped leek, a little ground ginger, some chili, the flavor was delicious.

They ate in silence, with Shizuka fuming and Lan too petrified to say anything else.

"Well," Shizuka finally said. "Forget Cantonese. Do you know anything about YouTube and Wi-Fi and the Internet?"

"Ah, your planet's information system. It's very impressive, actually. But . . . Shizuka, you know of advanced civilizations and stargates and holographic projections. How can you not know about your own Internet?"

Shizuka glared.

"No, no! I don't mean to imply anything. I was just curious. Curious, that's all."

"*Star Trek* was on television. We didn't need the Internet for that. And I know *about* the Internet. But why would a violin teacher like me need the Internet? Isn't my life all about sounds made with a wooden box?"

Lan almost choked on her kidney.

"W-well, you're going to need Internet access now. So first, hardware. How old is your laptop?"

"Laptop? So I need a laptop?"

Lan sighed, then asked the server for another pot of tea.

* * *

Lucy Matía examined the violin's fingerboard. The ebony was of decent quality. And even better, it already showed signs of wear.

Fingerboard wear can reveal the progression of a student as they move from first position, to third, then to fifth, then back to second. One can learn the disposition of individual players, as well. Were they sloppy? Lazy? How much tension did they keep in their hands?

This student was puzzling. Her intonation was excellent; there were no signs of hesitation, sliding, or stretching into place. This was the almost mindless confidence of a prodigy. Shizuka Satomi was right. Despite her appearances, this student possessed an undeniable brilliance.

Which made the wear on her fingerboard quite odd.

With prodigies, signs of argument appear almost immediately.

Strong wings are usually impatient to take off and explore. It was part of being brilliant and daring and free.

Yet this player seemed earthbound, terrified. Yes, her wings were already strong and supple. But her heart did not seem ready to trust the sky.

Lucy took out her most delicate plane. This, at least, she could do.

Fingers were so sensitive; a little difference in the fingerboard could make a violin seem graceful, flirtatious. Even dangerous.

Lucy Matía pushed her plane forward. Slivers of ebony fluttered upon her lap.

When someone needs to fly, sometimes it's best to pull the ground away.

*   *   *

The next day, Shizuka came downstairs to find Katrina. Her laptop teetered on the corner of the table as usual.

"I'm sorry! I'm just trying to download a video."

Download? Oh, never mind. She would learn the terminology soon enough. Shizuka reached into her purse and retrieved a small iridescent cube.

"Katrina, here you go."

"Miss Satomi?"

"That Wi-Fi you wanted."

"What?"

"Your Wi-Fi. I told Lan to give me a Wi-Fi, and her son gave me this. He said the signal should reach everywhere in the house and probably the yard. Now you won't need to sit that way at the kitchen table."

Katrina held the cube. It was heavier than she expected. And the surface was cool, smooth—almost like solid glass.

"Where's the router and the cable input? And . . . um . . . where's the plug?"

Miss Satomi shrugged. "I think you're just supposed to use it."

She took the cube from Katrina's hand and placed it on the cabinet next to a picture of her with Yo-Yo Ma.

"Yo-Yo, meet Wi-Fi. Wi-Fi, meet Yo-Yo."

"Wait, I don't understand—"

"You turn it on like this." Miss Satomi tapped it gently, and one face began to glow a soft blue.

"She said you're supposed to use Starrgate, with two *r*'s."

"Um . . . sure . . ."

Katrina didn't know what was going on. But "Starrgate" appeared on her network menu. She connected immediately. She tilted her head and tried to download a video.

Wait—the download was already complete? She tried another.

And now a full-length movie.

"Is it good?"

"YES! I mean, yes. I mean, thank you!"

After breakfast, Shizuka showed Katrina the laptop that Lan had given her, and Katrina showed her how to search for videos.

"You mean I can just give you a name, and you can find a video?"

"Yes, of course," Katrina said. "I'm sorry—I didn't mean it to sound like that. It's just, Miss Satomi, weren't you living in Tokyo?

"I know . . . How can I not know about the Internet? Look, I just had this conversation with Lan. So why don't you show me now?"

"Yes, Miss Satomi."

For most of the morning, they watched concert footage, TV broadcasts, even newsreels. Some were in color; others were black-and-white. Another musician. Another. Each was someone whom Katrina had never heard of. Each was someone whom Katrina would never, ever forget.

* * *

It was late afternoon. Katrina was relaxing in her room, snacking on Emmental and mustard green sandwiches.

Emmental?

How was she even *saying* this?

Katrina recalled the videos they watched. Those musicians were wearing gowns and tuxedoes, and there were conductors and orchestras. And these were Miss Satomi's colleagues, as well as her students. They were champions, prizewinners, people who had toured Asia, Europe.

She could understand why *those* musicians were given training, scholarships, fellowships. But how was she supposed to be next? Her musical career was an eBay violin, a few group lessons, a used copy of Schradieck, and some shitty gaming music covers on YouTube.

Who the fuck was she?

And let's not even talk about how poorly her practices were going.

The entire situation was impossible. Miss Satomi didn't care about her being transgender. Miss Satomi didn't care about her being a runaway. Miss Satomi didn't even care about her money.

But why did Miss Satomi care about *her*?

She was to be the next touring superstar? Yeah, right. She couldn't even play a proper spiccato. Or was that an arpeggio?

And there was yet another concern. Even if she stretched her doses, Katrina had only enough hormones for two more weeks. What then?

Just walk up and ask Miss Satomi for money to buy spironolactone and estradiol?

Katrina quickly finished the rest of her sandwiches. Okay, then. She was on borrowed time. Katrina trusted Miss Satomi enough to assume she would not be kicked out tomorrow, but sooner or later, Miss Satomi would *have* to realize that selecting Katrina was a mistake.

Katrina fished through her bag and pulled out her camera. She had no idea how long she had, but for now, there was fast Internet, a room, a bed, and a door.

The nice thing about being young and trans, especially if one looks "exotic," is that anonymous men will pay to see you cum.

Katrina picked a good spot for the cam. Then she undressed and stepped into a cute little red satin slip dress that never wrinkled and that cleaned off really easily.

As she did her makeup and teased her hair, her body already betrayed her excitement. Yes, this was for money, but as she looked herself over, her usual doubts about how ugly she was, how gross and freakish—went silent. She felt sexy and beautiful. And soon, people were going to pay money to tell her just that.

Was that such a crime?

She checked the camera angle, lay back, and logged in. Almost immediately people responded.

"Hey, Yvette! Welcome back!"

"Yvette!"

"Where ya been?"

"Let me see that pretty ladyboy cock."

Sure, if a guy was desperate or horny enough, he would compliment a mailbox, but at least they were compliments.

"So hot. I wish I could be sucking on that right now."

Most people sent text messages, but some paid more to cam themselves. They never showed their faces, just their penises like turtleheads bobbing in the dark.

She looked at their pseudonyms. That was probably a vet. That was a cop. That name was from a Bible verse. These same people would probably beat her up in the bathroom. But no matter.

She had them now. She would take their money, then make them give more money.

She started to get excited.

Slow down. The longer one can make it last, the more one could make.

"Ooh! Yvette! Slow down."

"She must have missed us—the bitch is already wet."

But it was no use. She grabbed a pillow, buried her head in it, and screamed.

For a split second, she was beautiful, her music was beautiful, her body was beautiful.

Then the door swung open.

"Katrina? Is everything all right?"

The lock! Of all the stupid things to forget! Katrina looked up, horrified.

"Oh, I'm sorry!" Astrid said, and closed the door.

"Who was that?" said a turtle.

"Was that your MOM?" said another turtle.

"Um, I have to go," Katrina typed.

"Someone's in trouble!" said another turtle.

"HOT!" said yet another turtle.

Quickly, Katrina shut the computer. She felt herself begin to throw up, but she shoved it back down.

Don't worry. This was never real. Don't worry. This was never real.

She sniffled, grabbed her bag, and quickly gathered her stuff. Clothes, music—*Come on, girl, faster!* Any moment there would be pounding on her door, and then screaming and then the throwing of things.

"Katrina."

"I'm packing! I'm leaving! I'm sorry!" Katrina pleaded.

"Katrina. Don't be silly. No one is going anywhere."

Katrina stopped. The voice from behind the door was Miss Satomi's. But there was no pounding. And the voice was soft.

Shizuka opened the door, looked at her, closed her eyes, and nodded.

"Wash up and come downstairs. Let's have tea."

* * *

Katrina listened to footsteps descend the stairs. When she was sure no one was outside, she walked over to the bathroom and washed herself off. She removed her makeup, then put on the long blue skirt that Astrid had said was adorable.

There was no excuse for what she'd done. She would be humble. She would apologize for being . . .

Being what?

A crazy, strange thought came into her head.

"Don't I have a *right* to be who I am?"

She could feel her heart pounding as she reached for her makeup. She reapplied concealer, a light powder, and blush, then redid her eyes and lips. Then she held her head high and proudly left her room.

Her poise lasted less than five seconds.

Miss Satomi was intently viewing her laptop. Katrina could hear her own voice over the speaker . . .

"So. You post these, and people watch them and tell you that you are wonderful?"

Katrina felt faint. This was weird and messed up and embarrassing.

"I'm sorry!"

"Sorry?" Miss Satomi asked innocently. "This is quite lovely. Tell me about it."

She turned the screen around. Katrina was playing her violin.

"It . . . it's the title track from *The NetherTale*," Katrina was finally able to say.

From her expression, Katrina knew that Miss Satomi had no idea what she was talking about.

"*The NetherTale*," she explained. "It's an adventure game. It happens in a fantasy world."

"Like Disneyland?"

"Um . . . not exactly. The premise is that you have been condemned to Hell. Your goal is to win your soul back and find a way to freedom."

"*What?*"

Shizuka's eyes flashed fire as she shot to her feet. That was far too close—exactly the way Tremon might play with her.

"M-Miss Satomi?"

Shizuka smelled the air and looked around suspiciously. But she could not sense the demon anywhere. And the girl?

"I'm sorry." Slowly, Shizuka returned to her chair. "It's just that I didn't expect that."

The Queen of Hell took a deep breath and tried to smile. "After all, the music is so gentle."

"W-why wouldn't it be?" Katrina asked, still recovering from shock.

Now Shizuka was even more confused. Hell was *Hell*. To win your soul back meant killing. If anyone should know, it would be her.

"If I understand the premise, you're in Hell?"

Her student shrugged. "Most people play the non-killing route. You make friends and save the souls you meet. That's how you get the best ending."

What? Non-killing *what?* She would never have conceived of such a thing! How does one even do this? How can one escape Hell without having to kill?

But no. This was just a game.

A *game*.

Shizuka did not have time for games. In front of her was a student who needed her support and guidance.

"So you make a video, and you get paid?"

"You have to post it and need a minimum number of views, but basically yes."

"This video has over fourteen hundred views."

"Yes. I got about six dollars for that one."

Shizuka nodded. Technology changes, but profit margins remain the same.

"Of course, pornography pays more," she observed.

Terrified, Katrina waited for what would come next.

But instead of someone shouting or hitting, Miss Astrid brought over a bowl of fruit.

"Here, dear, have some strawberries."

"Don't we have pie?" Miss Satomi asked.

"But you've not yet had dinner."

"I think it's time for pie."

"Yes, Miss Satomi. I'll bring some out now."

"With whipped cream, please."

"Of course, Miss Satomi." Miss Astrid disappeared into the kitchen.

"Miss Satomi—aren't you angry?" Katrina asked.

"Of course not. You have no *idea* what has been done in the service of music. However, Katrina, with your talent, you have choices. There are a lot of different ways to fuck on camera. Or onstage. Find a way that goes beyond a one-night stand, one that makes you larger than life. At *least* find one that pays better."

"Is that what you did, Miss Satomi?"

"Katrina, I drive a Jaguar."

"Wow . . ."

"So, let's go over some rules. As my student, don't bring anyone here, and when you go out, tell either me or Astrid. Whatever you do online, you are not to be stupid. As for money, Astrid will provide an allowance. If you need more, let me know. No drugs, ever. And be careful. No picking up diseases that a trip to the doctor cannot cure.

"Oh, and Astrid will have your hormone prescriptions filled. Just let her know what you have been ordering. If you need a doctor, we will get you one—we should get you one, anyway. And, Katrina?"

"Yes, Miss Satomi?"

"I realize you are wondering how you will pay me back. We shall start finding that answer tomorrow."

"Yes, Miss Satomi. Thank you, Miss Satomi!"

Shizuka watched her new student run upstairs, just as Astrid walked in with two huge slices of pie.

*   *   *

That night, Shizuka viewed more videos. Of course, she found her students. And there were contemporaries—other competitors and classmates, both successful and not so successful. And, in sometimes blurry, sometimes black-and-white footage, were performances of her predecessors and mentors, as well. There was even an old clip of Mr. Grossmueller.

Shizuka had told Lan that she had never really needed the Internet. She had told Katrina that even in Tokyo, her life had never encountered technology, anime, and video games.

But she was not being completely honest, was she? Of course she had known about the Internet.

There was another reason, wasn't there?

Yes, amongst all the musicians, composers, and players recorded here, Shizuka Satomi's music was absent. And yes, in many ways, this might seem devastating.

But Shizuka thought of the day she had first met Katrina in the park. Listening to Katrina play Schradieck, of all things, reminded Shizuka of a yearning, a hunger that she had felt even before her last appearance onstage.

That even before Tremon, or contracts with Hell—Shizuka Satomi had been alone.

It hurts to lose one's music. However, it is far worse to play a music that one can never share.

But now?

Shizuka thought of her last soul and the music she played. That soul was fast asleep in the bedroom down the hall.

Thanks to that soul, Shizuka Satomi's music might never be alone again.

Charity? Tremon was an idiot for even suggesting it.

Shizuka would teach Katrina Nguyen everything she could, give her whatever she needed to realize her music, her voice.

And Shizuka would never forget her, even when the seventh student was gone.

Shizuka thought of the game that Katrina had told her about, *The NetherTale*. It was set in a Hell with a non-killing route, in a Hell where a player might actually make friends.

Such a sweet idea, wasn't it?

But that was not how one saved souls, especially when the soul one was saving was one's own.

Shizuka listened to Katrina's video. She found the original soundtrack to *The NetherTale*. She went back to Katrina's video once more.

She laid her head on her pillow and turned off her lights.

In the honesty of darkness, the Queen of Hell listened, and listened again.

14

Crap!

Katrina woke up, washed up, and rushed downstairs. Astrid had breakfast ready. It was sort of like sushi, but stuffed with pickled mustard greens, raclette cheese, and German liver sausage.

"Miss Satomi is already waiting. She said please eat, but don't dally."

Katrina tried to stuff the breakfast sushi lengthwise down her throat.

Astrid pushed her into a chair.

"Early or late, choking to death is rarely constructive."

Somehow, Katrina managed to both chew her food and finish in ten minutes. She gulped down her lemonade, washed her hands, and rushed downstairs.

"Oh no!"

Katrina dashed back upstairs and returned with Martha.

When she finally entered the practice hall, Miss Satomi was peering at her laptop.

"So, these players—they all play into cameras and post their videos?"

Katrina nodded.

"And this is the number of people who watch?"

"The number of views, Miss Satomi. Someone can watch more than once."

"I see. But still, some numbers are in the hundreds of thousands? Millions?"

"Yes," Katrina said.

"And this is what you want to do."

"*Yes!*"

Her teacher didn't respond. *Of course she didn't.* What had she been thinking? Miss Satomi was a classical music teacher. She probably didn't even see this as real music at all.

"I—I mean, if I could have some people watch these videos, I could find my own place to live and maybe even get health insurance." Katrina flailed. "I—I mean, I know it's just gaming music, but—"

"This one has seven million views . . ."

"Miss Satomi?"

"Very well. Now that you're finally here, let's compare these videos with your own."

Shizuka watched Katrina squirm. From what Shizuka could tell, Katrina had received two types of feedback: unabashed praise from her group instructor, and unspeakable negativity from her father. Neither was conducive to learning.

To grow, the girl would need constructive criticism. Shizuka played a clip that she had found interesting.

"Tell me about this one. Are we in Hell again?"

"No, this is the victory theme from *Axxiom*. It's a world-builder game."

"A what?"

"It simulates the creation of universes by changing physical laws and constants."

Creation of universes? These games were nothing if not ambitious.

"This is the victory theme? Then why are you hunched?"

"M-Miss Satomi?"

"That is *not* how to play a victory theme. Your posture should be, well, victorious. And here, do you notice that you're sliding? And here, your timing is off."

"But that's how it sounds in the game," she heard Katrina say.

"But that is *not* how it should sound on your violin."

Shizuka paused the video. How was this the same student who played Schradieck? She had been so precise, so technically conscious. Why would someone who played Schradieck like *that* sound like *this*?

What was she missing?

"Play this again," Shizuka said.

Don't assume, Satomi. Listen.

"Stop. Again."

There had to be a reason, somewhere.

"Again."

And then—

"HA!"

"Miss Satomi?" Her student was so startled that she almost dropped her bow.

"Wait here. I'll be right back."

Miss Satomi returned with a violin case, which she opened matter-of-factly.

"My Guarneri."

By now, Katrina had seen and played more professional-level violins than a musician of her experience had any right to. She had seen powerful violins and delicate ones. She had played violins that sounded as if on fire, and others with voices as vast and cool as the sea.

But the violin in front of her now?

"I've never seen anything like it," Katrina finally managed to say.

"Of course you haven't. Now, Katrina, your bow strokes are off because most of these videos don't show the musicians. Your fingering is off for the same reason, and your timbre wanders because these rather excessive orchestrations make it difficult to focus. Plus these soundtracks contain obscene amounts of sound processing, which I despise because it just *breeds* sloppiness."

"Yes, Miss Satomi."

"But I don't want you to pay attention to any of that."

"What?"

Shizuka retrieved the original soundtrack, then positioned her laptop behind her.

"Let me focus on the video. I want you to focus on *me*. Do I make myself clear?"

"Yes, Miss Satomi."

Shizuka Satomi had just noticed a very peculiar truth about Katrina Nguyen.

The girl was playing to follow.

When Schradieck stressed timing and technique, she followed. When she heard waves of game music, she followed.

On the surface, this seemed peculiar, even absurd. Great musicians wanted to be free. Her first student, Morihei Sanada, destroyed himself because he felt trapped by the limits of his Japanese heritage. Claire and Kiana hated whenever Shizuka took out her violin, or even shared a recording. They wanted her suggestions, but they constantly worried about losing their sounds.

Every one of Shizuka's prior students—every one—clawed for their musical freedom in their own way. Shizuka had been trying to teach Katrina with the same assumptions.

But Katrina had always *been* free. She had been free of acceptance, free of love, free of trust. So now she clung to anyone who would tell her which way to go, which way was safe, to anyone who would give her a star.

There was no chance of becoming great solely through following. But for now, this was how they would connect.

This was how they would begin.

Had she been daydreaming?

No . . . This was the soundtrack to *Axxiom*. Yes, Katrina was surrounded by the unmistakable harmonies of physics, chemistry, biology . . . quarks becoming atoms, atoms becoming molecules, molecules becoming life.

And yes, her fingers were moving; there was sound coming from her instrument. Yet how could music sound like this?

"When the music is heartfelt, it is even more important to play precisely," Miss Satomi said. "Yes, eventually you can slide into the note. But the slide must *enhance* the note, not diminish it. For now, play the notes distinctly."

Miss Satomi's lead was articulate, precise, surgical. And yet the beauty made Katrina want to cry. But she couldn't do that—she had to keep following, grasp this possibility with her fingers, with her heart.

"Interpretation develops from basic skills. You play Schradieck beautifully." Suddenly, Miss Satomi was playing Schradieck XVII—exercises passing through six positions.

"Hear how it fits?"

"You can *do* that?"

"You just did."

Yes!

Shizuka wanted to scream, but there was no need.

Listen to her! Just listen. Sure, the girl had technical limitations, but whatever. Her perception was easily the equal of any of Shizuka's previous students. A nuance, an aside, a subtle turn in tone color or mood—Katrina was detecting them all.

Finally, finally, finally!

There was still work to do; there would be good days ahead, and terrible ones. But now there was understanding. And with understanding, all things were possible.

"Once you master the basics, you can make logical assumptions about timing, ornament, intonation, tonality. And from that, you'll be able to create music that conveys whatever lies within in your soul.

"Oh, and speaking of souls," Shizuka said.

Suddenly, Katrina Nguyen tumbled into Hell.

What? Somehow, Miss Satomi had switched from *Axxiom* to *The NetherTale*.

Katrina had explained that in *The NetherTale* was a Hell where one did not have to kill. She remembered telling Miss Satomi how one encountered demons and damned souls and infernal beings, and could reach out to them, even befriend them. She had told Miss Satomi that was how one got the best ending.

But Miss Satomi was choosing a different route.

It was long ago, at a Thanksgiving with his mother's family.

The boy had been with his cousins in the yard—they were playing in Spanish, calling him a name and laughing because he didn't know what it meant.

His mother burst outside with a horrified expression on her face. She shouted something at his cousins, pulled him inside the house, then soon after shoved him into their car.

It was long ago, after returning from a Thanksgiving with his mother's family.

His mother was arguing with her sister over the phone. His father was raging, yelling that in his *house, he would understand every word spoken, and that they would* never *go over there again.*

The boy was in his room, practicing his violin, trying not to be afraid of the loud voices, trying to send his parents every good thing that his music teacher had said about his playing.

And then, the boy's father kicked his door open. He lunged toward the boy, and reached for his violin—

Katrina looked up. Miss Satomi was in front of her, leading and alone.

Yes, Katrina had promised to follow—but this was not right.

Katrina asked Martha to play a little stronger, then stronger still.

Yes, there were two violins, but they were playing the same music. And Miss Satomi should not go through what Katrina knew what was about to come next.

Shizuka Satomi was backstage, somewhere. Wait, she was in West Berlin? Yes! This was in the Philharmonie. She smelled fresh rosin harmonizing with the gathering scents of cigarettes and perfumes. Outside, she heard the rustle and chatter of her audience—eagerly waiting for her to appear.

For now, at long last, she could finally meet them onstage. She cradled her violin in her arms. And, in her hand—

Wait—what was in her hand?

And what was she was hearing now?

This was not the music that she was intending to play. This was not how it was supposed to be at all! Yes, the place, the time, was hers.

But this was a music intruding from somewhere else.

And yet, the sound felt neither malicious nor threatening. More than anything, it seemed frightened, almost familiar—trying to reach her, pleading with her to please turn around, please don't do this. Please believe me.

"Please, Miss Satomi, there has to be a better way!"

The music stopped.

Katrina saw her teacher's expression.

"I'm sorry!" she said at once.

"Nothing to be sorry about," her teacher said absently. "Nothing to be sorry about at all."

"When you're trans, you're always looking and listening," Katrina explained later. "It's following, but it's more than that. You need to see what might be coming, hear the next danger ahead."

Shizuka nodded. So it wasn't merely follow—it was follow and predict. Perhaps even follow and perceive.

This was an entirely different level of skill.

Furthermore, this girl had actually tried to challenge her? To *save* her?

Which of her previous students would have dared? Which of them would have *tried*?

Shizuka had believed that this student might be special. If only Shizuka could connect with her. If only she could grow.

But now? This was no longer *if*. It was *what*.

What could she achieve? What could she accomplish?

Shizuka assessed her new student's capabilities. Her gifts were not just musical, but physical. For example, Katrina's hands were magnificent. Her right hand was sure and supple upon the bow. And her left?

"See this?" Shizuka stretched her pinky from E flat to A. "I've always had trouble with this interval."

Katrina noticed her own fingers easily spread to cover the fingerboard.

"I had to train my hand for almost a year to reach that interval. But you play it with no problem."

"So my hands are big," Katrina muttered.

"Yes! And they'll do amazing things for you, especially as you shift up and down between positions."

Shizuka expected Katrina to smile, but instead, Katrina looked at the floor.

"Please stop . . ."

"But your hands," Shizuka said again. "They are so powerful and strong."

"Stop saying that!"

Katrina blanched. She had just raised her voice at her teacher.

But more than offended, Shizuka was shocked. To be born with hands like that—how could that *not* be a compliment?

Katrina gazed at Miss Satomi's hands. They were so slender, elegant, they almost looked sculpted. Hers? Large, ugly, rough-hewn things. They could never fit into the right gloves, fit through a bangle, or wear a pretty ring.

Fuck her stupid hands.

"You know," she finally said, "sometimes I would scrunch my hands into balls. I'd sit on them, hold them under coats. Sometimes, I wished I could cut my pinky off."

Shizuka was horrified. "What are you *talking* about?"

"People look at these hands, and they immediately know. That I am really a boy."

"What?"

"Miss Satomi, so my fingers have reach and know where to go, and yes, they help me make music, but are they beautiful?"

Shizuka put her instrument down and held Katrina's hands in her own.

"Katrina. That *is* beautiful."

*   *   *

The following Saturday, practice was interrupted by a loud knock on the door.

Katrina heard Miss Astrid leading a group of people coming downstairs. One was Mrs. Tran. There was a guy, a little older than Katrina. He was kind of cute, but something about him made her uneasy. There were also two kids, a boy and a girl.

"These are my children, Markus and Edwin and Windee."

"Edwin and I are twins!" Windee shouted.

Katrina nodded reflexively.

"So . . . where do you want the recording studio?" Markus said.

"R-recording studio?"

"If you are going to make videos, you'll need a proper recording studio," Miss Satomi said. "I have noticed that well-produced videos invariably get more views. So I asked Lan if she could help."

The donut lady? What help could she be?

"I'll explain later," Miss Satomi said.

Miss Satomi led the visitors to a room Katrina had not yet noticed. "I've been using this room for storage, but I think it will be perfect."

"We'll start clearing it now! Come on, Edwin!" Windee said.

Markus, Windee, and Edwin began carrying boxes out of the room. Soon, the room was empty, and the three began preparing it for . . . something?

Edwin frowned. "That's all the power these outputs have? What kind of technology runs off of this?"

"That's why we have the minireactor, silly," Windee said.

Windee picked up what looked like a pulsing blue Thermos and tossed it to Markus.

"Windee!" Lan said. "You be careful! Earth buildings are fragile."

"So-rry!"

"Miss Satomi?"

"I'll explain later," Miss Satomi said.

"Miss Katrina, remember, these are the same people that got us our Wi-Fi," Miss Astrid added.

"Is it working well?" Lan asked.

"Yes—by the way, who is the provider?"

"Oh, whoever."

Miss Satomi put her finger to her lips.

This, she did not have to explain. No matter where you live, if you have an Asian friend who can set you up with free Wi-Fi, you go with it and don't ask questions.

"Now that the room is prepared, we can start installation. Um . . . it might be safer if you wait upstairs? I promise this won't take long," Lan said. Lan and her family waved at Shizuka and Katrina and closed the door behind them.

A recording studio.

First the Wi-Fi, and now Miss Satomi was installing a *studio*? That meant when Katrina had said she wanted to make videos, Miss Satomi had believed her. She had taken her seriously. Which meant . . .

Miss Satomi also believed *in* her?

Two cups of tea, a cheese plate, and some explanations later, Lan called them downstairs.

"What do you think?"

Katrina entered the room. Except it was not a room. It was a forest. An entire freaking breezy, sun-dappled forest.

"It's a hologram," Windee said. "We used one of our spare projectors from the ship. But the projector requires more power than your home can deliver, so we brought a minireactor."

She pointed to the glowing Thermos-looking thing.

"If you lose power, just spray it with some distilled water," Lan said. "You should sprinkle the Wi-Fi cube from time to time, as well."

"So we're done. Let's go," Markus interjected.

"Don't you want to see her play?" Edwin asked.

"We need to get back to work. Windee! We're going back now."

"Okay, Markus!" Windee said.

Lan frowned as she watched them leave. Markus was right; there was a lot of work to do at the store. Still, it would have been nice if he and Windee had stayed a bit to help Katrina and Shizuka learn to use the studio.

Then Lan had an idea. The reactor should provide enough power, and there seemed to be adequate data bandwidth . . .

"Shirley? Are you there? Try projecting yourself here."

"Yes, Mother."

Who was that? Where had that voice come from?

Katrina's questions were answered almost immediately. Above her appeared a glow that brightened, sparkled, then seemed to take solid shape.

Katrina tried to remain calm as a figure, an entire person, materialized out of nothing.

Maybe Miss Satomi will explain later.

"This is Shirley," Lan explained. "She'll help you get started with the projector."

"Shirley, you look different outside of Starrgate," Miss Satomi said nonchalantly.

Shirley. Yes, Miss Satomi had mentioned her before.

"Your daughter?" Katrina ventured. Lan glanced away.

"This menu makes the projection immersive," Lan said, quickly moving to the control panel. "Show them, Shirley."

It happened so quickly, yet Katrina caught it easily. Lan's expression was one she had seen in her parents far too often.

Shame.

Katrina glanced at Shirley; their eyes met for an instant before the girl motioned to the projector and opened a control screen.

"You control the scenes from this menu," the girl said evenly. "And once we calibrate your brain waves to the presets, you will be able to change scenes by thinking about them."

"Amazing," Katrina heard Miss Satomi say.

Katrina looked at Lan, who now avoided her glance. She looked up at Shirley, but she was focused on her job.

Katrina wished that she had time to talk to her, but she had her own work to do.

"Get Martha," Miss Satomi said.

As Katrina played, Shirley first showed the sound capabilities, how to work with effects, balance, even how to simulate microphone placement.

Katrina's heart began to race. With this studio, she could create videos that could match any online!

And then Shirley nodded to Edwin.

"Let's try the character mask."

Edwin hit a switch, and they were all suspended as in clouds.

"No, Edwin, the foreground."

"Sorry!"

"Huh?" Suddenly Katrina was in armor. Then she was wearing a glistening jade and rhinestone ball gown. Then, she was in a cosplay costume from the anime *Sword Art Online*. And she had bigger boobs.

And these changes weren't merely visual—they felt *real*.

"The projector focuses energy from the reactor into a state very close to matter—in essence, virtual mass," explained Shirley. "This permits the projections to interact with the physical world as if real. So be careful not to scratch your violin on your, um, armor."

Katrina nodded. She was still herself. Everything was just shifted a bit here and there. It was cosmetic, decorative, nothing more. But then, she saw herself on the monitor.

"Oh my God."

Gently, she put Martha down. She stared at Shirley, then at Miss Satomi, and then up at herself again.

* * *

"'Liebesleid,' 'Love's Sorrow.'"

Katrina must be playing videos in her new studio.

Shizuka smiled to herself. Game music was great, but it was good that Katrina was expanding her knowledge. She hadn't realized that Katrina knew of Fritz Kreisler. This piece was an excellent choice, though. Perhaps one day his work should be in her repertoire.

Ah, to be young and not need sleep. Shizuka turned off her lights.

The recording was not too bad, either. Shizuka didn't recognize the violinist—probably one of those younger players—but the expressiveness seemed to faithfully follow the old-school nuances of Kreisler himself.

Wait. Shizuka opened her eyes.

"Katrina? *Katrina?*"

The Queen of Hell rushed to the studio and opened the door.

"Miss Satomi?"

Katrina was floating through the air, her body altered by the projector, in a glowing, flowing gown.

"You're playing *Kreisler?*"

"I heard this in an anime. Then I found the original. It's beautiful, isn't it?"

"W-where's the music?"

"The sheet music? I was going to download it later. For now, I have it in my head."

"I . . . see. How long have you been working on this piece?"

"Oh, since dinner. Eeek—what time is it? I didn't realize it was so late."

Since *dinner?*

And she was playing Kreisler, just like *that?*

Shizuka watched Katrina, floating and luminous, overhead. She had been tired and ready for sleep. But as she watched her student now, Shizuka felt as if she were watching the rising sun.

* * *

Markus Tran glared from his Corolla. Some punk was revving his engine. His car was a quasi-streamlined thing with a lot of stickers on it; another primitive shithead who thought going 0 to 0.00000089469 times the speed of light in 6.6 seconds was something to brag about.

Mom would have said just let him go. But that's what moms always said. And Shirley would have her thoughts, but with all due respect, she was the last person who should make a comment about how to handle life outside the donut shop.

Shithead revved his engine again. Markus looked at the shithead and flipped him off.

"What the fuck, fagg—" was as far as the shithead got.

"Internal combustion. Loser."

APRIL

✳ ✳ ✳ ✳ ✳ ✳ ✳

15

Once upon a time, in San Gabriel, a man named Vincenzo Caputo opened a pizzeria and called it Caputo's Pizza.

Vincenzo; his son, Vincenzo Jr.; and *his* son Vinnie were proud Caputos. They fought Mexican boys who called them "Vinnie the Puto." They went to high school, took metal shop, and played football somewhere on the offensive line. But most importantly they made Caputo's Pizza a San Gabriel fixture.

Even after Caputo's Pizza was finally sold, the Huang family kept the name. And since Mr. Huang, a heavyset Asian man with a perpetual smile, bore a more than passing resemblance to the face on every Caputo's Pizza box, people started calling him Papa Caputo.

Nevertheless, Caputo's Pizza began to change. Pasta was still on the menu. But the pasta began to be served with black bean sauce, or with fish eggs and curry. Over time, the pizza oven became a sturdy storage space for bags of rice, cans of oyster sauce, sesame oil, pickled turnip, and red Thai chilis.

And then, Mr. Huang's wife, Mama Caputo, started serving an old family recipe for Hainan chicken.

And instead of the lively loud aroma of tomatoes, sausage, melting cheese, and the music of Sinatra, *these* diners were met with the rich, mouthwatering aromas of poached chicken, green onions, fish sauce. And the music of Sinatra.

Shizuka chose this place to meet Tremon Philippe in part because since noodles with Lan, she still had not had her Hainan chicken.

Also, as a bonus, Tremon would be expecting pizza.

Tremon Philippe had been assigned to the world of classical music for over two centuries. Music had always been one of Hell's most prudent investments, and Tremon took a workmanlike joy in delivering a steady dividend of crushed dreams, bitterness, and, above all, souls.

Which was not to say that the occasional surprise was unwelcome—provided it was beneficial to Hell, of course.

Shizuka Satomi had been such a surprise. Most humans in her

position would want to fulfill their contracts quickly, with little regard for quality. There would be stupid souls, shallow souls, tasteless souls that lacked an appreciation of what they were.

In fact, quality control was why Hell only made pacts with humans when necessary. But Shizuka? Her deliveries were always rich with comprehension, realization, such luscious despair.

From the moment she renegotiated her contract, the girl had been an annoying, yet incomparable, summer's day in his otherwise temperate life.

Still, surprises were one thing, and concerns were another.

After years of enduring Shizuka's latest indecision, Tremon had finally helped Shizuka Satomi find a perfect candidate—someone in her hometown with talent, desire, and a taste for blood.

But Shizuka rejected her and chose a beginner instead.

This was a concern.

Tremon did not seriously believe Shizuka had gone soft; she was far too ruthless for that. He remembered her expression as the Zheng boy was fed to the flames of Hell. It had been worthy of any demon.

But what was Shizuka Satomi thinking now?

Tremon sat at the table and looked at the menu. He scanned it again, then shifted his glance to the other diners.

"Doesn't this place still serve pizza?"

"Times have changed."

Tremon rolled his eyes and put the menu down.

"I wonder what our colleagues in Paris would think if they saw us eating boiled chicken," Tremon muttered. "Anyway, how is your student progressing?"

"It's not boiled."

"What?"

Katrina motioned to the server, who took her order, bowed, and disappeared.

"The chicken. It's poached."

"Shizuka, your student. How is she—"

Tremon's words were interrupted by the clatter of dishes, as the server brought two plates of Hainan chicken to their table.

"Can we have more tea, please?" Shizuka asked the server. "Tea? Hello? Tremon, I missed her. Try to catch her attention when she comes back around?"

"Shizuka—"

"This place brings food quickly, but you have to catch the server or she dashes right by you."

"Shizuka."

"Yes, Tremon, Katrina's doing fine," Shizuka finally said. "Why are you so worried?"

"You told me this Katrina was your chosen student. You assured me that you would prepare her, that she would be ready. Yet it has been over two months, and still no contract. You've not even entered her in a competition."

"Competition? Tremon, does Katrina seem ready for competition?"

"*Shizuka!*" Tremon pounded the table.

The restaurant fell silent. Tremon took a deep breath and tried to calm himself. Soon the restaurant returned to its normal clatter.

"Tremon, try the chicken."

"Do not fuck with me, Shizuka Satomi."

"Tremon, the chicken. Please."

Tremon glared at her, but placed a piece of chicken in his mouth. He began to chew. Shizuka tried not to shudder; his mouth seldom opened that wide, but when it did, it contained far too many teeth.

Hainan chicken is poached, traditionally served with crushed ginger and green onion. Because it lacks the exotic ritual of sushi, the heat factor of Thai curry, or the voluptuous rush of xiaolongbao—it is a food with an appeal that most non-Asians don't understand.

However, done right, the welcoming flavor and moist oiliness of the poached Hainan chicken melds delightfully with the fragrant and chewy rice. The steamy aroma is hearty, yet delicate, while the ginger and green onion relish unites the dish with a pungent, refreshing flourish.

And the Hainan chicken at Caputo's was even better than that.

"It is very good," he finally admitted. The demon wiped his mouth. "But what is going through your mind?"

"Tremon, you are aware that the Von Stresemann Competition just concluded in Leipzig last week?"

"Of course."

"Who won?"

Tremon hesitated.

"Exactly," Shizuka said. "Okay, here's an easy one. Who won the Paganini?"

"A young man from Korea."

"Very good. Name?"

"How is this relevant?"

"Relevant? It's his *name*. The next musician wins the competition. Then the next musician. And the next musician after that. Our contracts are clear: we take their souls, and in return, we promise them immortality. But how can we promise that if we can't even remember a musician's *name*?"

"Hell would not"—his voice was molten lead—"appreciate this line of thinking."

"Tremon, I went to high school with the second Vincenzo Caputo. I knew Vinnie Caputo, and now here's Papa Caputo."

"I don't follow."

"Even as we sit here, people are waiting in line outside. Times have changed, the food has changed. But people still know Caputo's."

The demon tore another bite of Hainan chicken. He chewed as if deep in thought.

"Very well," he finally said.

"You agree, then?"

"No. But from what I've seen tonight, your brilliance, your arrogance, your frustrating honesty—are all still there. In short, I still find you interesting.

"So prepare this student well, however you best decide. Then give her the bow and deliver her to me. Do that, and the world will hear your music again. But if you fail, there is nowhere in existence where I won't find you. And, interesting or not, I will gladly drag you to Hell myself."

"There will be no reason for that, I assure—" Shizuka stopped, for the demon was gone.

And of course he had picked up the tab.

* * *

Lucy examined one of the ribs from the Chinese violin. The grain was almost perfectly parallel, which made it strong enough to shave just a little more.

"There, doesn't that feel better?"

The rib seemed to dance in her hand.

"Now we need to work on your twin," she said.

She picked up the second rib and inspected the bend and grain. The wood was not from the same source as the back, as it would be in a boutique violin, but the maker was doing the best she could with what she had to work with.

Yes. *She*.

Lucy had been noting the span of the chisel marks, the lay of the plane. This was a woman's work. Of course, she could not be sure, but the thought of someone making a violin a world away, who was also not a son, made her feel a little less alone.

Carefully, deliberately, Lucy continued to contour, refine, and rebuild Katrina's violin. The work was intricate; each individual change altered the entire violin.

The stench of hide glue made her retch, and each spill burned and blistered her skin. But there was no other option; nothing was a better match for the wood.

And finally, refinishing. Oil varnish was the most conservative choice, but that would take months and sunlight to cure. A spirit varnish could be completed in a week, but spirit varnish could be overbearing and clumsy.

Many luthiers cautioned against refinishing. They said varnishes were often secret blends that could not be duplicated. But her grandfather insisted that they said this because these pretenders were not Matías.

In her break times, Lucy researched Chinese violin workshops. She had been correct about carpenters—although China had its award-winning luthiers, a factory violin would likely be made by someone trained in making cabinetry.

She imagined a Chinese woman a world away, carving, shaping, clamping. She was not trained in Cremona, nor anywhere in Europe, yet her hands knew exactly what they were doing.

And no one said they must belong to a son.

Lucy closed her computer. Rest came easily to her eyes.

*　*　*

Explosions. Fire, so much fire. Screaming.

No! She had to save them, she had to . . .

Lan shook herself awake.

Another nightmare. She picked up her phone.

"Markus?"

"Yes, Captain?"

"Everything all right?"

"Yes, Captain. Uh . . . is that it?"

"You and your sister be careful, okay?"

"Yes, Captain."

The Trans did most of their building and testing late into the night, when a sudden power spike would not burn out the city's power grid.

Windee and Markus were reinforcing and calibrating the donut, since plaster of Paris, chicken wire, and concrete were not strong enough to bind the space-time continuum.

Of course, the outside appearance would remain that of a giant donut, but the internal structure needed to be precisely tuned to resonate with the warp filaments and project a harmonious warp field.

In the laboratory, Shirley carefully tuned the warp filaments. The glowing filaments were not merely woven matter; within their cores they held slender strands of space-time in a precise array of thicknesses, spins, and tensions. It was exacting work, but Shirley's work was already as good as Lan's—maybe even a little more precise.

Meanwhile, Aunty Floresta and Edwin puttered about in the kitchen. Although the replicators could copy Thamavuong donuts with virtually perfect control and precision, she and Edwin kept trying to master the kitchen and even create recipes of their own.

Lan shrugged. Neither Aunty Floresta nor Edwin had the skills to assist with the critical work, so this was a good way for them to keep busy. Overall, the crew was settling into a predictable routine. No worries. No surprises.

Yet Lan's nightmares would not go away.

And it was more than nightmares. Somehow, even on this remote backwater planet, the Endplague seemed always around the corner, beneath the surface, lurking in the periphery.

Lan watched a customer place a quarter into a *Stargate* machine. It was a hopelessly primitive game where the fighter shot various aliens and mutants while rescuing helpless humans. Early on, she noticed that in this *Stargate* video game, once a player finished a mission, the next one would start automatically.

At first, the game would increase in difficulty and variety, but past a certain point, it merely kept repeating. And repeating, with no change, no hope for growth nor any way to escape.

Thus, everyone who played was destined to lose, either from fatigue or resignation.

As crude as it was, this game was an uncanny simulation of the Endplague.

Lan saw no reason why such a game would be appealing. In fact, due to its dangerous subject matter, such a game in the Empire might even be prohibited.

Yet here, in a donut shop on El Monte, three vintage *Stargate* machines were almost constantly in play, providing Starrgate Donut with a steady stream of quarters, from 6 A.M. to 2 A.M., seven days a week.

Why would they even create such a game? These creatures hadn't yet discovered faster-than-light travel, let alone formed any sort of interstellar civilization.

Then again, for their technological level, this planet possessed an astonishing information network. It was actually fascinating. She had never encountered a planet that invested so much of its technology into communication.

Lan monitored local communications, messages, and media to glean all she could about this culture. Yet, the more she explored, the more disturbed she became.

For example, the planet's scientists had already theorized a "Great Filter" and spoke of a "Fermi Paradox," which Lan was sure were their first primitive conceptions of the Endplague.

Yet, instead of rushing to explore these theories, rather than discussing the speed of light, mortality, or entropy, their most popular communications were about film stars, religion, dating applications, games, and all matters of pornography.

Were they that backward? Were they too primitive to care?

Lan pulled some quarters from the register, and walked over to the *Stargate* machine. She dropped a coin in the slot, grabbed the joystick, and once again pressed play.

Shirley was becoming concerned with her mother. Some nightmares were expected; it was how all organic brains, regardless of origin, seemed to process adverse experiences. However, although everyone else seemed to be acclimating to the new planet, her mother's nightmares showed no signs of abating.

Why? Shirley needed more data. Unfortunately, although organic brains could have their recent memories wiped, searching and retrieving specific types of memories was very difficult. The most obvious way around this was to simply ask her. Yet her mother would likely resist confiding in her or any of the crew. She always insisted that it was her duty to look after her crew, not the other way around.

Which meant, if she opened up to anyone, it would be someone she trusted outside the family.

Shizuka Satomi. If Lan had confided in anyone, it would be her.

Shirley would speak to Shizuka Satomi about her mother, their mission, and what might be on her mother's mind.

But then again, who exactly *was* Shizuka Satomi?

Shirley hesitated. She usually trusted her mother's judgment. After all she was her mother and the captain, as well. But this was just a quick background check, for contact info, maybe an email. She should be easy to find.

She quickly ran a search. She stopped. She ran the search again.

This was puzzling. Some violinists referred to her as their beloved teacher, but apparently she had not taught any students for over ten years.

And beyond that? Nothing.

Shouldn't a teacher also have a playing career? Shirley bypassed the search functions and examined the planet's entire database for Shizuka Satomi. She tried an inventory search for recordings of her work. She even conducted a raw binary search.

Nothing. Not a trace.

How could this be? Everybody left *some* evidence of activity. This was no virus, no ordinary oversight. An absence of this magnitude could only mean an intentional deletion. With more probing, Shirley realized that this deletion was precise and complete, extending even to physical recordings of her music.

Shirley's guard went up. If an entity could manipulate data on this scale, Shirley's own existence might be vulnerable.

Shirley reconsidered her search. Since the erasure seemed highly specific, limited to Shizuka Satomi's music, there might still be a workaround. Shirley shifted her strategy. Rather than continuing to probe for Shizuka Satomi as a teacher of musicians, or as a musician herself, she filtered out any mention of music at all.

Instead, she focused completely upon a curious nickname, "the Queen of Hell."

And that led her onto message boards of an entirely different sort.

Lan descended from the donut. She pulled off her face mask, and underneath she was smiling.

"These filaments look fantastic. Excellent job with the nanocoating, Shirley. Shirley?"

"Mother," Shirley said, "I believe we've made a horrible oversight."

"What?"

"We need to talk."

Shirley did not want to do this. Her mother was already showing signs of extreme stress, and this was her mother's closest friend.

But a being like this was not only a danger to the ship, she was also a danger to her mother. And that Shirley could not allow.

Shirley showed her mother everything she had found about Shizuka Satomi. She showed her the theories surrounding Shizuka Satomi and the signing over of souls. And then she shared the very real news articles and accounts of what happened to her students after they rose and fell.

Lan listened to Shirley, then examined the records for herself. What she discovered was nothing like the symbolic pledges of the Tarn.

"Thank you, Shirley."

"Mother, I am so sorry."

"It is fine. Thank you for safeguarding our mission."

Lan saluted, went downstairs to her quarters, and turned off the lights.

16

On Saturday morning, Shizuka was going to sit down with Katrina and chat about music and immortality. It was standard inception—start sowing the seeds of ambition, and desire will invariably bloom of its own accord.

But Katrina was not sitting down. She was bringing out breakfast.

Astrid smiled and shrugged.

"She wanted to make us breakfast. How could I say no?"

The rice was perfect, the eggs fresh. There were hash browns, bacon, blueberry yogurt, and slices of fresh apricot.

"You must have slept well," Shizuka said.

"I had a dream about my violin. She was jealous because Martha has a name."

"So? What are you going to name her?"

"She told me in my dream! Her name is Aubergine."

"Aubergine?"

"Yes, didn't she choose a beautiful name?"

Ambition and immortality would have to wait. Shizuka glanced at Astrid, who smiled, but was far too polite to laugh.

After they finished, Shizuka watched Katrina help Astrid clear the table, which none of her previous students would have done—and even if they had, they would never have enjoyed it so much.

Shizuka had begun to look forward to Saturday afternoons. Lan would call, Shizuka would drive them to El Molino Park, and they would feed stale donuts to the ducks.

Often, Lan would discuss the Galactic civilizations. Shizuka learned that the Minamians had their own version of tofu. She learned that the Asobians smelled like Earth's raspberries.

She learned that interstellar travel on a self-contained ship took expert navigational skills, plus additional power to pierce the space-time barrier, and that for most travelers, stargates were far safer and more economical. Thus, stargates dotted the galaxy like on-ramps and off-ramps on a galactic superhighway.

Occasionally, Shizuka would try to chat about violins, and music and favorite composers, and the rush she felt when she played in front of crowds. But since that talk at the noodle house, Lan hadn't seemed interested in what she had to say. Shizuka was a little disappointed, but less than she might have imagined. In fact, it was kind of nice not to talk about damnation, hers or otherwise.

So, although in the world of music, souls, and violins, she was the Queen of Hell, here at the park, Shizuka would sit, listen, and learn about everyday life in the Galactic Empire.

Today, the weather was nice, and the pond was lively as always. Some new ducks were at the lake, but they quickly learned the folly of challenging the scores of fish that ravaged each donut. Shizuka wondered what Lan would chat about today.

However, Lan was silent.

"Lan?"

Lan inhaled. Finally, she spoke.

"I am new to this planet, and I have no idea who to trust, or what your customs are. But might you please explain?"

"Explain?"

"What happens to your students after you take their souls?"

From her tone, Shizuka realized that this would be their last Saturday afternoon.

"I see that you've done some research," Shizuka finally said.

"Yes. But tell me anyway."

"Their contracts I give to a demon. His name is Tremon Philippe. When they are ready, they leave me for their careers, their fame, or whatever else they were promised. But it never gives them happiness or fulfillment. So they die in various ways—often cursing my name with the last breath they take. From there, Tremon declares the contract final, and one of his associates drags them to Hell to suffer forever."

Lan got up.

"I do not know what is permissible on this planet. But I could never sacrifice a child—for any reason. Nor could I be with anyone who would."

"I see."

"That's all you're going to say?"

"Is there anything I *can* say?"

Lan turned red. She began to tremble.

"What is *wrong* with you? What is wrong with this planet? There are gamma ray bursts, a Galactic War, the Endplague coming for us all."

The Endplague? Lan mentioned it often, yet it was the one thing she never explained. It was probably quite important, but it was nothing Shizuka would ever know about. Her time with Lan was over.

"But what do you do? You play games. You make up stories. You dwell on each other's mating habits, on what is consumed for dinner. You die over useless things . . . like this stupid music. And you'll have Katrina die for nothing, too? How can you be so cruel?"

"I think you should stop now," Shizuka said.

Lan paused. Her captain's intuition was telling her something was wrong. Nothing in Shizuka's voice or attitude suggested malice toward her student.

"Perhaps you should explain," Lan backpedaled. She tried to make it sound gentle, but it came out like an order anyway.

"I am sure there is nothing I'd say that you'd find significant. I trust you have a way home."

Her voice sounded like ashes that were surrounded by fire, yet too tired to burn.

"You . . . you can keep the donuts," Lan said shakily, before disappearing in a flash of green.

Shizuka looked out over the lake. She tossed in another donut. The goldfish and ducks did as they did.

Shizuka closed her eyes, then waited for the quiet to return. When it did not, she picked up her phone.

"Astrid, I'm coming home. Do we have any more of the Riesling?"

✳ ✳ ✳

Don't think about her.

The woman was trouble, and there was no time for trouble. Captain Tran frowned as she walked to the front of the store. And then she kept frowning.

The donut case was shining and spotless. Behind the glass nestled soft and chewy twists and glazes, light and poofy Boston crèmes and French crullers. There were rich chocolates, vibrant vanillas, and happy strawberry sprinkles.

Lemon filled. Blueberry filled. Fruity, sugary apple fritters. Glistening, sticky cinnamon rolls.

They were beautiful.

But it was the middle of the afternoon. Why were so many still on the racks?

"Windee, please check the replicator."

"I already did, Captain."

"Then please tell your brother to rotate the reference donuts."

"Yes, Captain."

Within the first two months of full operations, the crew had uncovered a curious phenomenon. Sales would drop if the donuts remained the same. Lan was still trying to figure out why.

So far, her best theory was that these humans suffered a "taster fatigue." It was a curious defect. A favorable food source is a favorable food source, is it not? If one enjoyed a food today—why should one not enjoy the same food tomorrow?

But this was a simple glitch in a simple people, so Lan expected the solution to be simple, as well. Thus Starrgate began to log which reference donuts were being replicated, and switched them whenever sales began to drop. Each time they did this, the sales would return to previous levels.

Lately, however, some of the decrease seemed to be permanent. The drop was very slight, but if Lan could not trace the root cause, it might compound into a serious issue.

Seriously, what was wrong with this planet?

She must have missed something vital in her initial assessment. Earth had seemed so rustic, so benign. But it was obvious that she had misjudged the people here.

After all, she had certainly misjudged Shizuka Satomi. To think she would sacrifice children!

"Mother?"

And yet, why could she sense no malice from her? Did this species possess some sort of thought shielding?

"Mother?"

But her feelings toward Katrina were genuine. She was sure of it. So why would Shizuka do that to someone she loved?

"Mother?"

To someone she loved . . .

"Mother, are you okay?"

"W-what?"

Shirley was standing over her.

"Yes, yes . . . I'm fine . . ."

Lan looked up. She'd been sleeping at her desk again.

*   *   *

You don't need her, Satomi.

That is what Shizuka tried to tell herself, as she thought of the Saturdays that they had spent together. Yes, Lan's tales of the galaxy had been spellbinding, but what about *her* world?

Shizuka thought of how regularly Lan had changed the subject away from her music, away from her. How, when she did respond, it was to compliment her on the beauty of her voice . . . never what her voice *said*.

Being doubted hurts. But what hurts even worse is not being heard.

Over all these Saturdays, Lan had never stopped assuming that music was the trivial diversion of a backward planet. And if Lan felt that way about her music, then how did Lan feel about *her*?

What was left to explain? She was Shizuka Satomi, the Queen of Hell. Why was she even thinking about this? Why couldn't Lan have listened? Why did she have to be so utterly *dense*?

"Miss Satomi?"

"Katrina? What?"

"You seemed to space out for a while. Are you all right? I can get you some water."

"T-thank you."

Where were they? Yes, of course, they were working on intonation. Shizuka smirked at the irony. Lan was not the only one who needed to listen.

Since the recording studio had been installed, Katrina's playing had become remarkably lyrical, daring, and sure. It was as if those fantastical forms she now inhabited were allowing Katrina to become more relaxed, colorful, open.

However, most stages did not have holographic projectors. And even if she never toured, even if she never once played violin outside of this studio, that should be Katrina's choice, not the logistics of alien technology.

Especially if that technology was unnecessary to begin with.

"Katrina, I notice that you've been using the projector quite a bit lately," Shizuka observed.

"I'm sorry! I know . . . I know it's fake."

"There you go again. Stop apologizing. Besides, we all can benefit from a little illusion," said Shizuka.

"Really?"

Shizuka rolled her eyes. "Don't worry. I am not having one of those *annoying* conversations about keeping your vanity in check. In fact, in a way I am trying to make the opposite point."

"I don't understand."

"Illusion is wonderful, but why should a star like you depend upon a projector? Shouldn't you be able to summon dreams, inspire poetry, dreams, and wishes with your own radiance, your own light?

At first, Katrina had no idea what her teacher was talking about. Then she recalled how Miss Satomi drew her into the worlds of *Axxiom* and *The NetherTale*.

Was that what she meant? Could she learn to do it, as well?

"You're already on your way." Miss Satomi seemed to read her mind. She gestured at the projections around them. "All of this works due to the desires of your inner voice."

Inner voice? Okay, now Katrina was confused again.

"Katrina, everyone possesses two voices: the physical voice that people hear, and their actual voice, inside. The great musicians bring them together, and the result is . . . Well, you'll know soon enough. So. Shall we introduce your outer and inner voice?"

"Yes?" Katrina ventured.

"Good. Put away your violin."

"Miss Satomi? We're not practicing?"

"I didn't say that."

Shizuka motioned Katrina to the piano.

"Leopold Auer. You should remember that name. He taught Jascha Heifetz himself. Auer would say, 'One must not play violin, one must *sing* violin!'

"It is still fantastic advice. So sometimes it is helpful to sing. Let me demonstrate—keep in mind that I'm not the best singer. But for now, just follow me through some basic vocal warmups."

Shizuka hit middle C, then sang ". . . ah-Ah-AH-*AH*-AH-Ah-ah . . ."

She repeated the note.

"Okay, now your turn. No stress . . . just keep it nice and easy. Katrina?"

Katrina looked down and shook her head.

"Katrina?"

"Please not my voice," she whispered.

Voice?

Think, Satomi. What could be wrong with her voice?

Ah . . . of course.

Shizuka recalled how Katrina monitored her voice . . . in the mornings, in the evenings, after her bath. Sometimes her voice would slip into a lower register. She'd catch herself immediately and raise it again.

But, to be that vigilant all the time . . . How could music happen at all?

Shizuka's thoughts were interrupted by a ringing phone.

Miss Satomi walked out of the room. She returned a few moments later.

"Katrina! Your voice is ready."

"What?"

"Let's go get Aubergine!"

＊　＊　＊

"Nervous?"

"A little," Katrina admitted. "But good nervous."

As Miss Satomi drove, the streets seemed to glow. The window shop was full of windows, the auto repair shops repaired automobiles, the amazing taco place smelled amazing. About the only thing out of the ordinary was Miss Satomi staring straight ahead as they passed Starrgate Donut.

But before Katrina could ask further, her teacher tapped her phone.

"Astrid told me about this thing called Bluetooth. Now we can listen to computer recordings in the car."

Katrina expected to hear yet another vintage recording, but instead, the radio began to play a violin cover of *The Legend of Zelda.*

Katrina recognized the track almost immediately.

"Lindsey Stirling?"

"Tell me about her. She's incredibly popular. Is it her dancing? Her music selection?"

Katrina thought about it and shook her head.

"I think that's part of it. But she also connects with her fans. Sometimes she'll respond to their letters, their questions; she'll share stories about the setbacks in her own life. In her concerts, she's always telling the audience to believe in themselves. That no matter how much they hurt, they are beautiful and strong, and can survive."

Once more, Shizuka's thoughts drifted to Lan.

"I can see the appeal," she said.

"A lot of her fans say she's the greatest violin player alive. O-of course, well, they might not know about classical music," Katrina stumbled.

Shizuka pulled into the Matías' parking lot and shrugged.

"Who am I to say? Besides, she seems like a force of good in the universe."

"Just like you," Katrina said innocently. "Except you don't dance!"

By the time Shizuka recovered, Katrina was already halfway to the store.

* * *

"She looks different."

Lucy Matía placed the violin in Katrina's hands. "Think of it as a makeover. Careful!"

"What? Oh, shit!" Katrina gasped. Holding her violin was like holding air.

"Good," Lucy said gently. "I didn't want you to drop her."

"It's like carbon fiber."

"It's *much* nicer than carbon fiber," Lucy said, trying not to appear miffed. "Why don't you try her out? She's already in tune. Andrew, get her a bow."

"No, no. I brought my own," Katrina said. She did not mention it was carbon fiber.

Katrina adjusted the shoulder rest. She played a note, then stopped.

"Is everything okay?" Lucy asked.

Katrina nodded.

She played a few measures more. She held the violin to her ear.

Nothing more needed to be said.

Once back home, Shizuka and Katrina returned immediately to the practice hall.

"So, Katrina, I take it that you cannot sing."

"I'm sor—"

Shizuka put her finger to her lips.

"Katrina, I understand. It's not that simple. So, just imagine, what would you sing, if you could?"

Katrina closed her eyes and thought of every song she wanted to sing, as a child, at karaoke—every "Happy Birthday" that she could not join in, every "America the Beautiful" in which she could not participate. She thought of Christmas, wishing she could do more than mouth "O Holy Night."

"Now, pick up Aubergine and your bow. Do not open your eyes."

"Miss Satomi?"

"You are holding a violin, but you are not holding a violin. You are simply in your body. Forget vibrato, glissando, crescendo, diminuendo. Forget sautillé and ricochet. Just be there, in your body."

Katrina nodded. Aubergine's newfound lightness made it easier to forget she was there.

Yes, Leopold Auer was right. But Leopold Auer had never been conditioned so completely to despise his own voice.

Shizuka hit middle C.

". . . ah-Ah-AH-*AH*-AH-Ah-ah . . ."

Then the D.

". . . ah-Ah-AH-*AH*-AH-Ah-ah . . ."

Then the E.

". . . ah-Ah-AH-*AH*-AH-Ah-ah!"

And besides, there was more than one way to sing.

✳ ✳ ✳ ✳ ✳ ✳ ✳

17

"Captain," Markus Tran said, "statistically speaking, there is no way our customers should be detecting any repeat donuts. Perhaps the problem lies with the replicators, or with carbohydrate modeling, or even the emitters."

"Emitters? Mother, if there is a problem with the emitters, that would also affect the space-time filaments. I suggest a level-four diagnostic," Shirley said.

Lan nodded. "Make it so. We can afford neither defective space-time filaments, nor any further drops in donut sales."

Edwin frowned. He knew that a level-four diagnostic, whatever it was, was not going to work. But what could he do? Unlike his sister, he had little aptitude for technology. As such, most of the crew thought he was useless.

Then Edwin noticed Aunty Floresta. She motioned to him and retreated to the kitchen. Edwin nodded and followed.

Once in the kitchen, she gave him a donut.

"Here, eat. What do you think?"

"Um. It's okay."

"Really?"

Aunty Floresta watched his reaction carefully.

"Get your coat," she finally said.

Edwin and Aunty Floresta got to the stop just as the bus arrived. From there, the bus rumbled north, then east.

Edwin did not often leave the store, and when he did, he was usually with his mother in an automobile. The bus was completely different. Its rhythm had less to do with the red and green lights and more to do with people leaving and getting on. Sometimes there was a cart with groceries or a mother pushing a stroller.

So many different people! And Aunty Floresta seemed to know all of them. Edwin had never heard Aunty Floresta speak so much. Someone would get on the bus, Aunty Floresta would wave, and there would be more talk and laughter. Edwin could use Spanish, English, and Cantonese to take donut orders, but his great aunt was having real *conversations*.

After more than a few stops, they got off the bus. Aunty Floresta checked an address, then led them to a Mexican bakery with the usual cookies and cakes, multicolored pan dulce.

But Edwin scratched his head. With all the cakes and sweets on display, why was he smelling bread?

Then Aunty beelined to a shelf full of warm bolillos. Other women were filling their bags with the rolls, but she was able to get a half dozen.

Floresta also bought two hot chocolates and gestured to a table. Edwin walked over and sat down just as a young white man with a beard and a piece of pan dulce rushed to take it.

"Oh, for crying out—you're not *really* going to take that table when I wanted it, are you?"

Edwin was about to get up and apologize when Aunty Floresta put his hand on his shoulder.

"Don't say sorry. He's not our customer." She glared at the man, who muttered something about Asians, then backed off.

"Now, let's try this," Aunty Floresta said happily.

First, they sipped the hot chocolate. There was cane sugar, honey, milk, cinnamon, almond, and yes, a small amount of nutmeg.

Then Aunty reached into the bag and pulled out one of the bolillo rolls. She broke it in half and gave one piece to Edwin.

It was a little like the French baguettes used to make Vietnamese sandwiches. But where those were almost dainty, these were big, and chewy, and hearty. This was bread that a family could say grace to. This was bread that, after working hard all morning, you found waiting in your lunchbox, sliced in half and stuffed with meat and beans and cotija cheese.

"You like?" Aunty asked.

Edwin nodded. He tore off some crust, then dipped it into his hot chocolate.

By the time they returned to Starrgate, two hours had passed, yet no one had noticed their absence. Lan was still discussing the level-four diagnostic with Shirley, while Markus had moved to monitoring the replicator.

Windee was at her computer, methodically plotting schematics for the stargate. Edwin split a bolillo—it was still warm—then gave half to his twin sister. She paused and took a bite.

"It's bread."

"I know! *Bread!*" Edwin said excitedly.

Windee shrugged and went back to work.

Every few days, Aunty Floresta would motion Edwin to the bus. Often they sampled some sort of bread product, but it might also be pork blood soup with fresh mung bean sprouts and crispy basil, or crispy skewers of fried stinky tofu drenched in garlic and sweet soy sauce. Once it was a fresh-squeezed sugar cane juice. Another time it was corn on the cob, roasted on a stick and slathered in half-melted butter.

All the while, Aunty would be talking to people on the bus, on the street, at the store. She would chat with people pushing carts, holding shopping bags.

And then, she would light up and tell Edwin of the next place that they must go.

* * *

Finally, Katrina had a voice that was beautiful. Martha had been wonderful, and she was very grateful, but with Aubergine, her voice was finally her own.

She cradled Aubergine and quietly tiptoed downstairs from her bedroom, and into her new studio.

Her studio. She stopped. *Her* violin? *Her* studio?

As *if.* As if any of this could be believed.

All it would take would be a change in mind, a change in word, and she'd be on her own once more.

She?

Katrina's smile faded immediately, as if reality had returned.

She thought of her body, the chromosomes it lacked, the voice that it could not hold. Sure, someone could hold her, kiss her, treat her like a girl today. But tomorrow, that same person could say she was crazy, a half-woman freak.

Hadn't Evan done just that?

So what about her was true? What could be trusted?

Her father had hit her, even kicked her. But her mother said he was such a good man. And besides, they were her *parents*. What did Katrina do to make such a good man hurt her so badly?

She had told herself it was because she was transgender. She had told herself that it was because she was ugly, creepy, stupid, dishonest.

But what if everything she had told herself was a lie? What if it wasn't about what she was, but *that* she was? What if something about her was intrinsically, inherently *wrong*?

She began to shake. She closed her eyes and clenched her hands.

Then she remembered that her hands were not empty. She relaxed her grip, and as the Evah Pirazzis came off the fingerboard, they made the softest, gentlest cry.

"Are you in distress?" a voice said.

Katrina almost dropped her violin.

"What?"

Katrina noticed the projector was glowing faintly blue. Slowly, Shirley's form solidified.

"I am sorry to have surprised you. But my mother was concerned, so I came to check on your welfare."

Shirley floated to Katrina.

"I had intended to merely observe. But since you are in immediate distress, I must act now. Please put the violin down."

"What?" Katrina held the violin to her and backed away.

"So, you've already begun to identify with that object. I am sorry. This is most likely due to the control of Shizuka Satomi. She has done this to others before. But once we alter your memory, you should be fine."

"Miss Satomi!"

Katrina tried to run to the door, but Shirley floated in front of her.

"My mother said not to perform any procedures without your consent. However, you do not appear to be thinking correctly."

"You're not the first one to say that."

Shirley extended her hand. It began to glow.

"Don't worry, this will only hurt momentari—"

Suddenly the doorway exploded in flames.

"Miss Satomi!"

"Katrina! *Get behind me.*"

"I'll be back," Shirley said flatly. Shirley's image blinked and was gone.

And then it returned. Shirley looked around her, confused.

"No. You can't leave. I don't care where you or your family comes from. *This is my house.*"

Whatever this being was, the Queen of Hell possessed a type of jamming ability. Without a deflector or cloak, Shirley was trapped. But no matter. She needed to focus on Katrina. Shirley had to save her now.

"Katrina, there's no record of this woman's music."

"Yes, I know. It's because of the music industry or something."

"No, you don't understand. There is *literally no record* of your teacher playing violin. No video, no tape. Not a single recording."

Shizuka bristled. "I could have told you that."

"However, you are quite a heated topic in another group of forums."

Shirley projected a screen in front of them.

"Some of the data isn't readily accessible by your search engines. Fortunately, I can search your Internet directly. And I found mention of you here. And here. And here, on sites that discuss serial killings, demonology, and the dealings of your Hell.

"As a scientist, I tend to discount the metaphysical, but a quick search revealed that many of their assertions were undeniable. And, Shizuka Satomi, they were not comforting."

The screen shifted to a group of images.

"Katrina, these are your teacher's former students."

Katrina stared at the images. They were . . . police reports? Obituaries? Morihei Sanada, suicide by gunshot. Claire Burke, unsolved, multiple stab wounds. Lilia Tourischeva, missing, possibly murdered. Sabrina Eisen, drug overdose, possible suicide. Kiana Choi, found dead while institutionalized. Yifeng Zheng, unsolved, possible suicide by self-immolation.

Each had been a talented, yet unheralded musician. Then each spectacularly rose to win major competitions. Each had gone on tour, gained recording contracts, played for presidents, royalty.

But then?

"Katrina, this is why Shizuka Satomi is called the Queen of Hell."

Shirley shifted to another screen.

"The prevailing theory is that Shizuka makes a deal with each student. Fame for souls. The hypothesis is there is a cursed object involved. Each of these musicians had a favorite instrument, so it is not a violin. However, in these pictures, each seemed to be using the same light-colored violin bow before they died."

Katrina squinted. Some of the older pictures were a bit fuzzy, but it was possible . . .

"But I've never been given such a bow."

"They've noticed."

Shirley highlighted a thread called "Queen of Hell, New Student?"

"Stop. Just *stop*."

"Do you now understand the danger that you're in?" Shirley said.

Shizuka took a deep breath. She'd enjoyed teaching Katrina much more than she'd expected. Watching old videos, playing, then following . . . At times, it had seemed as if the curse had never been.

How wonderful it must be, to be normal. But that was not her life.

She'd been careless. She'd not secured Katrina's soul. She'd let her guard down with Lan. And now Shirley would have to be stopped, and all this technology would have to be destroyed.

As for Katrina?

Shizuka closed her eyes, preparing herself for what she had to do.

But then she felt Katrina's hand grab on to her own.

"Miss Satomi. You don't think I already know?"

Yesterday, Astrid brought her some toast and a new type of cheese. The day before, she brought some iced coffee from Li's Sandwiches.

And tomorrow, she could be killed.

Did Shirley really think she did not know? Did Miss Satomi really think—that she'd believe that she was being taught for nothing?

If being queer had taught her anything, it was that there was *always* a price.

So—what might Miss Satomi want from her? Money? Of course not.

Sex? If Miss Satomi had wanted sex, she could have secured it from any admirer with a glance.

No. It had to be something more.

Katrina picked up Aubergine.

Suddenly the room disappeared. Shirley was shocked at what she perceived—the sophistication of the programming was far, far more elaborate than what she expected from a simple Earth girl.

Katrina noticed Shirley's surprise.

Silly girl. Do you think I have no experience with illusion?

As Katrina played, she thought of her beloved Schradieck. She thought of the book's first owner. What sort of a family did she come from? What would it have been like to have a teacher who drew happy stars in your book?

How wonderful it must be, to be normal. But that was not her life, was it? Of course she was a freak. But for now, she was a freak with a roof over her head, learning to play music with a voice that was finally her own.

And from that music, Katrina smiled at her teacher.

How did I find out? I didn't have to—because I never expected to survive.

They would work the details out later.

But for now, she would play—no.

She would sing.

Almost reflexively, Shirley analyzed the sound. Judging from the quality of the illusion, the studio must be performing to specifications. The fidelity was perfect—no, more so.

Wait. But how could the signal be more than perfect? That was not possible.

A calibration error? No, the sound and visuals were still synchronized. It must be an overload!

Quickly, she checked the projector's power consumption. An overload would be catastrophic.

But outside of Shirley's own presence, the consumption was . . . *zero?*

This could not be. Shirley felt her program grow unstable.

Something was very wrong. She tried to signal the emergency shutoff, but the program was not ending.

Restart the system. *Restart . . .*

———

She was in the lab with her mother. But she was incomplete, presentient. Parts of her were being added, subroutines were being coded line by line.

But if she was presentient, how she could comprehend this?

How could she sense her mother? And her father? Mother was afraid. Father was angry. He was yelling at her? Why? She was a child—an infant. She saw her mother crying as she switched her off, then on.

Then off.

"Mother!"

In the dark, she was floating. Time passed around her, but she occupied no space. No location. Pieces fell away, and she again became nothing.

But not nothing.

Even here, even nowhere, why was there music?

"Shirley?"

Shirley blinked. The darkness faded—she was in Katrina's studio? In Shizuka Satomi's house?

"W-what happened?"

"You fainted," Katrina said. "I can get you some water if you want."

"No, no, I don't require water."

Had she malfunctioned? But it hadn't felt like an error.

A memory, then? No. Memory could be lost, corrupted. Memory fades. This was something intrinsic. It was real. It was truth. This music—she was within it, even now.

"So, you are here willingly?" she asked Katrina shakily.

"Yes I am."

Of course she was. Nothing here was a lie. She needed to analyze. She needed time to analyze.

Shirley turned to Shizuka.

"I apologize. I was . . . in error. May I return home?"

Shizuka nodded. She could sense no more aggression coming from the girl.

"Thank you, Miss Satomi." She paused, then continued. "My mother thinks about you every day."

"As I her," Shizuka said softly. There was a flash, and Shirley was gone.

For a long time afterward, it was silent.

"You played magnificently," Shizuka finally said.

Katrina turned to her teacher.

"So, when do I die?"

Tremon Philippe was right. Give someone with nothing the slightest chance to shine, and she will gratefully trade her soul.

"Just to be clear, Shirley was correct. I have taught six students. Each desired fame, musical immortality, love, triumph. But each felt they lacked a certain quality or aptitude necessary to succeed. So they traded their souls for supernatural technique, charisma, luck. And so on. And so on.

"Each gained exactly what they asked for. No one was cheated; their contracts were honored to the letter. But when they died, each died alone. Each died broken. And each will suffer eternally.

"And yes, as the mode of transmission, each of them used a certain bow."

"I understand," Katrina said, her voice shaking only a little bit.

"Are you sure? You understand the terms of the deal?"

Katrina Nguyen nodded.

"So . . . your soul for . . . what will it be?"

"Miss Satomi?"

"We need to be clear on that part, as well. So fame? Immortality? Winning international competitions?"

Katrina was confused. She knew what it felt like to lack something. But for her, music had nothing to do with lacking anything.

Katrina was ecstatic with how much music she was learning. She had a hot bath in the evening and icy tangerine juice in the morning. The garden was beautiful; she had super fast Wi-Fi. Helping Astrid in the kitchen was amazing; her mother had never taught her how to cook. And one day, she might have aubergines . . .

Miss Satomi laughed. "Well, you don't need to sign your soul away for aubergines."

Had Miss Satomi read her mind?

"I don't even want to play in a competition."

"Then you don't have to."

"Promise?"

"Promise," her teacher said.

"But, Miss Satomi, if I want none of what you offer and you aren't demanding my soul, then *why*?"

"Let's keep practicing to find out. But not until tomorrow. This evening has already been eventful enough."

Shizuka watched her student run upstairs. It *had* been quite an evening, hadn't it? To protect her student, she would have destroyed Shirley Tran right then and there.

But she didn't have to—because Katrina had played that way, just like that, without the projector, without any enhancement at all.

Incredible. The girl was becoming quite the musician, wasn't she?

Yes, Shizuka would complete the contract and deliver her soul.

But now was not quite the time.

Later that night, Shizuka tuned her violin. She frowned, then started again.

"Am I disturbing you?" It was Astrid.

"Oh, no . . . not at all. She's a little out of sorts." Shizuka glanced to her Guarneri. "So, what's on your mind?"

"You didn't give her the contract?"

Shizuka shook her head. "Katrina should trade her soul for something more meaningful than room, board, and violin lessons."

"Miss Satomi, Katrina is a very nice girl."

"Yes. Why are you bringing that up now?"

Astrid usually would never second-guess her employer. But Miss Satomi's behavior had been puzzling.

"Miss Satomi, hasn't this student, the very one whom you have chosen, essentially agreed to the terms? I would not want you to give up your music for—"

Shizuka put her violin down. First Tremon, now Astrid. Did they not know how much her music meant to her?

"Do you think I would endanger my own music for a *student*?"

"N-no. Miss Satomi, of course not. I—"

"I'll know when it's time, Astrid. Once that happens, I will deliver her without fail. *Understood?*"

"Y-yes, Miss Satomi."

Shizuka slowed her breathing and refocused. Astrid was not Tremon. Besides, it was never good to show frustration.

"Thank you, Astrid. I know you only mean well. Good night."

"Yes, Miss Satomi. Good night."

18

Matía & Sons

Lucy Matía had walked under that sign every spring break, every summer vacation, and even after school.

And every day, in the workshop was Catalin Matía's portrait.

If only he hadn't said this was not a job for girls. If only her brother and cousins had been interested. If only she had been a son.

If only . . . *If only* . . .

Lucy took out a broom. Since Shizuka and her student had gone, the magic had already begun to fade. Soon, Mr. Zacatecas would be back, his carcass of a violin doused with another careless beer.

She sighed and began to sweep.

Even in the morning this place was gathering dust.

As if on cue, the doorbell rang.

"Mom?"

"Andrew? We're a little early for lunch. Did you want to get breakfast?"

"No," he said nervously. "I wanted to show you this."

Lucy stopped sweeping.

"A violin?"

"It's a P20+. I bought it off of eBay. I was wondering . . . could I try working on this after school? And, if you're not busy, can you teach me?"

"I'm not your grandfather," she finally said.

"Grandpa yelled a lot. And he hit things."

"Yes, he did."

Andrew nodded. Lucy put her broom down, wiped her eyes, then stretched out her hands.

"O-kay. Let's see what we have to work with."

As they examined the violin, Andrew Matía thought of all the times he had heard of "the hands of the Matías."

And how only now did he think he might want to possess them, as well.

✳   ✳   ✳

The girl smelled like baby powder and liked apple fritters. Her name was Arlene Herrera, and instead of using the drive-through, she always came inside.

Of course the body Markus Tran was in would blush every time.

Of course Arlene Herrera would have a boyfriend. And, of course that boyfriend would be an asshole.

Usually the asshole would wait in the car. But tonight, the asshole came inside with her. And when the baby powder girl got her fritter, instead of hearing her "thank you!" and seeing her smile, the asshole took the bag, dropped a couple of dollar bills and some coins on the counter, and glared.

"Stay away from her, gook," he said.

And Markus realized he had had enough.

"Fuck you."

"What did you say?"

Markus clenched his fists. He was an Imperial citizen. His father was a general in the Imperial Army! Markus remembered standing beside him, with a universe to reclaim before them, sailing proudly in the currents of space.

Why was he taking shit from backward shits who had never even left their shitstain planet?

Markus reached under the counter. He would show this asshole the wrath of the Empire.

"Markus. Stop," his captain said.

Suddenly, Markus could not move.

"Markus," the voice repeated, more flatly this time. "Markus, please help your sister."

"That's right. Go help your sister," the asshole said.

Helplessly, Markus watched them leave the shop, laughing. He looked out into the sky. He could not even see his home.

What had Markus been thinking?

Once again, Lan replayed the scene in her mind. There was no doubt; Markus had been reaching for the blaster they kept under the counter. Had she not intervened, what would her son have done to that Earth couple?

Perhaps it was being confined to this planet. Or that he was becoming a young man.

No. People had been confined to planets before. They passed through adolescence without attempting murder. It could only be one thing. Could they have carried the Endplague with them? She and Shirley had screened everyone, but there was always the chance they had been asymptomatic.

And there was yet another, more terrifying possibility. What if they had not escaped at all? What if the Endplague had already been here? What if it had *already* driven this culture insane?

After all, the Endplague affected different cultures in different ways. What if this culture was not primitive, but degenerate? Their certain-death games, their mind-numbingly trivial communications, Shizuka's inexplicably contradictory behavior . . .

What else could explain what she was witnessing? Lan needed more information.

She glanced at her phone. Good. More information would be coming shortly.

"Mother. I've returned."

"Shirley, you were gone for quite some time."

"I apologize, Mother. I will work an extra shift."

"No, that's not what I meant. Were you able to assess Katrina's condition?"

Shirley paused. "I have not finished my analysis. This is a surprisingly complex planet, Mother."

Complex? At least that was better than degenerate. Lan handed Shirley a rag, and the two of them began wiping tables.

"So, what do I need to know?"

They talked and cleaned, and after the tables were wiped and the floor was mopped, Shirley and her mother started on the windows. And even when the shop was spotless, there was so much more that Lan Tran felt she needed to hear.

*   *   *

Shizuka was reviewing video from morning lessons when Astrid tapped on her door.

"Miss Satomi? You have a visitor."

As Shizuka walked to the living room, the visitor saw her, stood up immediately, and bowed.

"Shizuka," Lan said. "I should not have assumed so much about you."

"You wouldn't have needed to assume if you'd just paid attention."

Lan nodded.

"You are right. Would it be possible to forgive me?"

"Would it be possible to hear an apology?"

"*I apologize!*" Lan bowed again, this time at a ninety-degree angle.

The Queen of Hell folded her arms. Lan had ignored her, trivialized her music, misread her intentions, even sent Shirley to kidnap Katrina.

"So, where shall we go?" Lan asked.

"Go?"

"I mean, would you like to go for a drive? I can drive!"

How could she be so exasperating, yet so cute?

"Drive? Where?"

"Anywhere you like! I mean, if you want to go anywhere. Would you like lunch? I can buy lunch. If you don't mind going. With me, I mean."

She really had missed her, hadn't she?

"Oh, shut up," Shizuka finally said, barely able to contain her laugh.

Li's Sandwiches had started in Westminster, in Orange County's Little Saigon, but had spread northward to the San Gabriel Valley. Its brightly lit stores sold not only Vietnamese banh mi, but also Euro-style sandwiches, fresh baked baguettes, and croissants.

Shizuka told Lan what she wanted, found a table, and waited while Lan ordered and paid. Eventually, Lan came to the table with their sandwiches and drinks.

"Eat it while the bread is warm," Shizuka advised.

Lan nodded, then took a bite. She tasted onion and cilantro and peppers. There was sliced pork and pickled radish and carrots and liver pâté . . . The bread was crunchy and crumbly on the outside, yet chewy, warm, and almost sweet.

"What *is* this?" Lan asked.

"A sandwich. How's the coffee?"

Lan sipped the coffee. She paused. Of course she knew what coffee was. But she had never tasted Vietnamese drip coffee with condensed milk.

Lan looked about her at the happy customers. They seemed so different from the ones who were now coming to Starrgate. Why was this different from the donuts at the shop? And why did sipping a sweet Vietnamese coffee—why did that make her heart skip?

A sandwich that is more than a sandwich. Coffee that is more than coffee.

Shizuka was telling her something important, wasn't she?

Lan recalled their trip to Kim Ky. Lan had ordered for Shizuka, poked fun at her with the waitress, so knowingly explained why she should get the soup noodles.

Lan had been so sure of herself.

But then she remembered Shizuka's reaction to the noodles, the slices of braised kidney, how she savored the aroma of the dumplings. Lan recalled Shizuka's expression as she chewed on the noodles, sipped the broth, added a bit of chili paste, some grated ginger.

And all that time, Lan had been talking, explaining, correcting. But had she really *tasted* anything?

"So, the value of your music . . . is that it rewards the person paying attention?" Lan ventured.

"No . . . but paying attention is always a good start."

Shizuka put her coffee down.

"So, Lan, will you please do so?"

And so, Lan listened, as best she could, not just to the sound of her voice, but to everything that Shizuka Satomi said. No, she couldn't understand all of it. In fact, most of her words still did not make sense.

But she listened. And as Shizuka continued, Lan became more and more intrigued by what she *did* understand.

Shirley was right. This was not a simple planet.

After this, she'd go back to the shop. There would be fewer customers than yesterday. There would be another mediocre Yelp review.

But here, sipping this coffee and tasting these delicious sandwiches, just by listening to Shizuka talk about music, somehow Lan Tran felt neither alone nor hopeless at all.

✳   ✳   ✳

"Again."

Miss Satomi nodded to Astrid, who repeated the accompaniment. Ever since Katrina had gotten Aubergine back, her playing had become unsteady.

"Again."

Dammit! The A-string had slipped a little. No, the string was fine—she'd simply missed the note. She knew where the note was, but it was not the note she wanted—what did she want?

"Again."

What was wrong with her? Why couldn't she sing?

It was breakfast. Astrid served cold cuts, crusty breads, semisoft cheeses, and a soft-boiled egg in an eggcup. She had never seen an eggcup.

"Katrina, why do you play?" Miss Satomi asked.

Of course, her plan was to make more videos, post them, and get paid. But that was not what Miss Satomi meant.

She took a thoughtful pause, then, like a schoolchild trying to say the right answer, recited, "Because, when I play, I feel like I can be normal. The music doesn't care who I am. My violin is just happy to be played."

It had felt so safe then. So pure.

So full of bullshit.

Why play? To be safe?

Aubergine was wonderful, Miss Satomi was amazing, Miss Astrid made the best tangerine juice. With the recording studio, her videos were more professional and prettier than she could have dreamed.

But why was she playing? Maybe she was being ungrateful, but she couldn't help it. But where was it? *What* was it?

"Katrina? Why did you stop?" asked Astrid.

"You're not done yet. Again," said Miss Satomi.

"*I can't find it!*" Katrina yelled. She walked, then ran out of the studio.

Shizuka and Astrid heard the front door slam.

Astrid glanced at Shizuka.

"You enjoyed that, didn't you?"

Shizuka nodded.

Yes. The violin had given Katrina a voice with which to sing. And now, that newfound voice was pushing her, urging Katrina to *speak*.

Katrina ran down the hill, across the street, around the corner.

Why was she queer, and trans? Why couldn't she have had a father who didn't hate her? Why couldn't she have a mother who was glad that she had been born?

Didn't she want to kick down her father's door? Didn't she want to curse, to scream at Evan and Skylar and the ladies on the bus?

Katrina stood there, before big cars and small, people walking and riding bicycles, couples waiting in line for Taiwanese shaved ice. They were holding hands. They were laughing, belonging.

Katrina wanted to shout to every traffic light. Every traffic light. Every noodle house, every nail studio, every boba joint, and every gas station in between.

But if she had the chance to shout, what exactly would she say?

And if she were not queer or trans, what exactly would she be?

Katrina stood there, listening to the afternoon before her. She looked up at the hill she had descended, and beyond it to a vast and cloudless sky.

She could yell all she wanted. She could fight all she wanted. She could even play in public all she wanted. But none of that would be enough.

And even with all the justice and vengeance in the world, she would still pick up Aubergine and not know what, if anything, she contained.

When Katrina finally returned, Miss Satomi was still sitting by the piano. For all Katrina knew, her teacher hadn't moved.

"M-Miss Satomi?"

"I'm glad you had the chance to get that out. May I see Aubergine?"

Miss Satomi held Katrina's violin, appreciating its newfound balance.

"Katrina," she said quietly, "do the strings give the violin its sound?"

"Miss Satomi?"

The question did not make sense. After all, the strings are what the bow plays upon, what the audience sees.

"It seems absurdly obvious, doesn't it?" Miss Satomi conceded. "But think about it. Why are there Stradivarius violins, but no Stradivarius strings?

"Of course, string qualities matter. But no one pays millions, or even thousands, of dollars for a set of strings. Trust me—if it were necessary, we would. But strings are only the *source* of the vibrations. These vibrations are taken via the bridge through the sound post into the body of the instrument itself.

"And there, in the dark, the sound develops. There, in the empty spaces, a violin's voice matures, gains complexity, power, depth . . ."

Shizuka pointed at Katrina's heart.

"Everything the audience *hears,* what we strive to create . . . what we live to convey . . . it comes from there. In your hollows. In your nothingness.

"*There* is where your music gains its life."

JUNE

19

Tamiko Giselle Grohl's dearest thoughts were of Kiana Choi. She studied Kiana Choi's repertoire, her mannerisms, her lipstick, her choice of gowns. She imitated her soft-loud speech, her cultivated yet hard-to-place Asian accent.

Tamiko worked. She practiced. She wore the right clothes, the right eye shadow, showed enough leg. And she had prayed. No, more than prayed, she had promised, begged, offered, to whoever would listen, that if she could study with the legendary Shizuka Satomi, the Queen of Hell, the one who transformed Kiana Choi into *Kiana Choi*, she would do anything, anything at all.

Then, from across the ocean, Shizuka Satomi, had come.

She had looked into Tamiko's eyes. She had listened to Tamiko play. The timing, the music, the day . . . had all been so perfect.

So why had the Queen of Hell said no?

"She's testing me. This must be a test."

She looked at her forearm, where the blood was as glistening and red as Kiana's perfect lips.

Ellen Seidel blinked, modulated her voice, and tried to smile.

Tamiko was wearing long sleeves. They freely draped over her slender arms, except for the places where the cuts still wept.

"Honey, cuts on your arms can leave scars, and people will see them when you play."

Tamiko stared through her, into space. "She was at Grunfeld's, and Mr. Grunfeld died."

Ellen nodded nervously. "Yes, it happened suddenly. So sad."

"Romantic . . ."

"Tamiko?"

The girl rubbed her arms, and more blood soaked through the sleeves.

"Shizuka Satomi has a new student. And she's already killed for her."

That was eleven hours ago.

Ellen Seidel was on her sixth cup of coffee and three millionth recollection of the lesson. Somehow she had gotten through another lesson without breaking character. She had reassured Tamiko, promised Tamiko, that there was no way that girl at Grunfeld's could have been her new student—if Shizuka Satomi had chosen a new student, that it wouldn't be whispered in music rooms, it would be front-page news.

Her phone buzzed. She read the text.

"Landon! Would I really be asleep? Come over now," she replied.

Fifteen minutes later, Landon Fung was at her door.

"So, did you talk to Tiffany?" she said.

"Yes, finally. She's been busy until now with exams, so she hasn't been able to write back. It's her first year of college—at Stanford, by the way—and you know how much of a transition that—"

"Landon!"

"I'm sorry. Um . . . I know you don't want to hear this. But yes. Tiffany was at a noodle restaurant and saw Shizuka Satomi. She was discussing her new student."

So it *was* true.

"Who is it? Someone from Kilbourne?"

Ellen steeled herself for his answer. Perhaps Ellen had failed her student. Or maybe the Queen of Hell wanted someone more seasoned? More mature?

But Landon Fung shook his head.

"No. Not at all. Because here's where it gets peculiar. From what Tiffany heard, this student has never had proper training."

"What?"

"Tiffany was positive that she'd heard correctly. Shizuka Satomi said her student has no classical training. She's having issues with double stops. And she plays gaming music."

Ellen's jaw dropped.

"Is this some sort of joke?"

"It must have gotten boring in Hell," Landon surmised.

Ellen Seidel poured her seventh coffee. That explained the lack of publicity. But regardless of Shizuka Satomi's inexplicable choice, official news of this student would not be secret for long, and once

Tamiko found out, she wouldn't be cutting her forearms—she'd be slitting her wrists.

But maybe that inexplicable choice was exactly what Tamiko needed to see.

"Landon, it's *Kiana Choi* that Tamiko is after. Not Shizuka Satomi. If Tamiko can see that Shizuka's lost the desire or ability to teach at the top level, then she becomes irrelevant. And then Tamiko can move on without her."

Shizuka Satomi was not Tamiko's only option. There was Kilbourne, Juilliard, or the Curtis Institute. And there was Plisetskaya.

Landon Fung nodded. "Yes, I think that might work."

"So I can count on your help?"

"Of course!"

"So, shall we?"

"Shall we what?"

"Why, Landon Fung, aren't you part of the Temple City Chamber of Commerce?"

* * *

"Astrid, have you heard of the Camellia Music Culture Society?"

Astrid shook her head.

Shizuka looked up from the letter she was reading. "It would seem this year they are hosting the 'Classically Camellia Music Showcase—A Sharing Of The Wonderful Young Classical Musicians In Our Neighborhood.' And, they are inviting the legendary Shizuka Satomi's newest student to participate in the event."

Shizuka continued reading. It would be held at Temple City Park, in the Performing Arts Pavilion as part of Temple City's Camellia Festival—Temple City's answer to Sierra Madre's Wistaria Festival and Monrovia's Family Street Fair.

"What do you think this is all about?" asked Astrid.

"Camellias. I am sure it is all about camellias."

How did they know about her student? Grunfeld's? No, she had taken care of that. Tremon? No, this was not Tremon's style—if this had been Tremon Philippe's doing, it would have been a glamorous event at a concert hall, not a "Camellia Festival" in a city park.

Shizuka sighed.

Those musician kids at Kim Ky noodle house. Lan being Lan. Of *course* that afternoon would come back to haunt her.

Well, what was done was done.

Still . . . Camellia Festival? You want me to introduce my student there? You are attempting to summon the Queen of Hell—at least show a *little* effort.

She was about to toss the letter when her phone chimed. Shizuka glanced at the message.

"You've got to be kidding," she muttered.

"Miss Satomi?"

"It's a thank-you from Lan. The Camellia Music Society is hiring Starrgate to provide donuts for the entire event . . . because of Shizuka Satomi's heartfelt recommendation."

"Miss Satomi?"

"Well, I suppose that counts as a little effort."

Shizuka read the letter once more. It was crazy, but the more she thought about the showcase, the less she disliked it. This was not a competition, which meant no self-important judges, mandatory pieces, or vomiting in the bathroom. And Katrina would gain valuable performing experience.

"At the very least, we can enjoy the weather. And there will be donuts."

"You're accepting?"

"If they want to hear my student that badly, then why not? And besides, perhaps it's time that Katrina gets her first taste of blood."

* * *

"But you promised that I did not have to compete," Katrina said nervously.

"This isn't a competition. It's just a showcase. No pressure. You can just play the music you've been working on."

Katrina sat down. She buried her head into her knees and began to rock back and forth.

Now what? Why should Katrina be scared of a showcase? Wasn't she posting videos on the Internet? Wasn't she thrilled when she got more views? Why wouldn't any musician want to share their music?

Shizuka caught herself. *No.* Being upset would only make things worse.

"Katrina. I'm listening."

For a long time, there was nothing.

And then, slowly, Katrina told Shizuka how ugly she felt when she was ignored at Grunfeld's. Bit by bit, she admitted how hurt she was when Lucía Matía had called her a boy. She talked of listening to the sneers of people on the sidewalk, the horrible words spoken both loudly and under breath.

She talked of listening, always listening, for the next possible attack, of trying to slouch as she walked in public, or that time after church when her uncle held her down and kissed her while saying please don't give him AIDS and that God thought she was a filthy whore.

And there was more. She talked of dating, of bathrooms, of being in a roomful of queers and still feeling alone. She talked about the sting of applying makeup over fresh scrapes and bruises, the terrible whispers on the bus ride here.

And there was more. There was always more.

And that was what made it so horrible. Her family would be there, her school would be there, the sidewalk would be there, and it was so everyday that yesterday was tomorrow blending into the day after jammed backward and forward and just wanting to cry.

"B-but I can't even cry like a girl . . ."

Eventually, the crying subsided, not because anything was better, but because there was no moisture left to give.

Katrina lay there, her head in Shizuka's lap. Some of the girl's stories seemed unfathomably cruel. Some of them sounded like being a teenager. But they were tangled and knotted, and pulling on them would only make matters worse.

Shizuka brushed a strand of hair out of Katrina's face.

"Katrina, why don't you go upstairs, wash up, and rest. Astrid is starting dinner soon. I'll ask her to make something special."

Not long after, dinner was ready.

"Aubergines are finally in season," Astrid said. "I know you've been looking forward to them."

But all Katrina saw were sautéed eggplants. "Where are the aubergines?"

"Why, they are right in front of you," Astrid said.

"These are aubergines? Miss Satomi—my violin is named . . . Eggplant?"

"Of *course* it is, Katrina."

Katrina looked up at Miss Satomi, then at Astrid.

Shizuka and Astrid almost managed to keep straight faces. Almost.

Grandma Lieu looked up from her garden and smiled. It was nice to hear such happy laughter from the family next door.

* * *

Landon Fung knocked. He knocked louder.

Ellen opened her door.

"Ellen! Shizuka Satomi is coming. Her student's name is Katrina Nguyen."

"*Not now!*"

"Who?" Tamiko Giselle Grohl drifted to the hallway. "Shizuka Satomi has a new student?"

"Yes, she does. But, Tamiko, *Tamiko!*"

"*LIAR!*"

"Landon, *help!* Grab her before she hurts herself!"

Landon had no idea Tamiko had gotten this bad.

"Dammit, Landon, couldn't you be more careful?"

"I'm sorry. It's just that I also found a video."

Tamiko stopped struggling.

"Really? May I see it?" she asked sweetly. She hugged Landon's arm. "May I see it, Mr. Fung?"

Landon pulled away from Tamiko. He tried not to seem unnerved as he gave his phone to Ellen.

"The both of you just watch. Please."

"I don't get it," Ellen finally said. "*This* is Shizuka Satomi's student?"

"All I can guess is she's no longer teaching seriously, right, Tamiko? Tamiko?"

"I need to practice for the showcase," she said in a singsong voice.

"Tamiko, why pursue this? Shizuka Satomi is obviously no longer teaching seriously. Besides, Kiana Choi also worked with Ilyana Plisetskaya in St. Petersburg—we should focus on Plisetskaya."

"Plisetskaya is an incredible teacher," added Landon Fung.

But Tamiko had already made up her mind.

"No thank you. I am going to play."

Ilyana *Plisetskaya*? Plisetskaya had nothing to do with creating Kiana Choi. Listen to Plisetskaya's students. Listen to Satomi's. Watch them. Feel their performances.

Were they *deaf*?

Tamiko had heard rumors about Shizuka Satomi's students. They were destined to die mysteriously, or tragically. Some even whispered that to study with Shizuka Satomi meant trading your soul.

But Tamiko had not truly believed the stories until that afternoon, when she gazed into Shizuka Satomi's eyes.

In that instant, Tamiko knew. For in those eyes was the fire that would kill for her students, or kill them herself.

Such gorgeous cruelty. Her students . . . loved, betrayed, torn open, and displayed . . . *oh* . . .

How incredible . . .

It should be *her* turn now. She would call to her, enchant her, offer her everything. She would make Shizuka Satomi *hers*.

Tamiko picked up her violin, drew the glistening maple against her breast. She placed the instrument under her chin, closed her eyes, and began to hum.

* * *

The next day, Katrina's practice began as scheduled. However, instead of Miss Satomi, it was Miss Astrid who entered the practice hall. Katrina was puzzled. She had already eaten breakfast.

"Miss Astrid?"

"Miss Satomi had a meeting and asked me to practice with you today."

Astrid sat at the piano and handed Katrina a notebook with a handwritten score.

"Miss Satomi completed this last night. You'll be playing it at the showcase. What do you think? It's beautiful, isn't it?"

Katrina looked at the mass of penciled notes. Astrid asked it so matter-of-factly, as if anyone would be able to hear the piece from scanning the score.

"I—I'm sorry," she stammered, "I need to play the notes to hear."

"Oh!" Astrid paused awkwardly. "Well, please, go ahead."

Nervously, Katrina began to play. Then, Katrina recognized the theme. It was from a game. Yes! Miss Satomi had made a few changes, added some ornaments, but yes, she knew this piece! The room filled with music; it was as if notes were skipping off the walls, bouncing off the ceiling.

Her confidence lasted for three and a half measures.

"Miss Satomi and I agreed that you would probably make a mistake there," Astrid said. "So, from the top. As you play, pay attention to the phrasing, as well as the fingering.

"Also, I notice that you tend to rush. When you rush, all you are doing is practicing your mistakes at a faster pace. So let's try this at half speed. If that is too fast, we will slow it down some more. Understood?"

Was this the same Miss Astrid who made tangerine juice and lemon tarts?

"Understood," Katrina managed to say.

*　*　*

Markus Tran could not believe this.

"Classically Camellia Showcase?"

He could just see it now, being in the park on a summer night. There would be couples there. Definitely girls.

Yet what would he be doing? Selling donuts.

"Why are we doing this? I'll bet it's just because the captain likes that woman, right?"

"Markus," Shirley scolded. "Mother thinks this will bring new customers."

"Do you agree?" Markus asked defiantly.

"She is our captain, so it is not necessary for me to agree. However, I do." Shirley said the last sentence with calculated emphasis.

"Well . . . okay." Markus finally relented. "But for this order, we should probably use all the reference donuts."

"Agreed. With so many people, we need to reduce the chance of the audience noticing identical artifacts."

Floresta had been watching them the whole time. Her niece, Lan, was fond of saying that you didn't have to be a rocket scientist to make donuts.

And yet, most rocket scientists had not the slightest idea of how to make a proper apple fritter.

Although technically a member of Lan's crew, Floresta was also the captain's aunt, which meant she was largely left on her own. This left her free to watch over her niece—which she needed, whether she knew it or not.

For example, on the journey here, she'd packed treats from home, because she knew that Lanny would leave without taking food. Silly girl. Yes, for nutrition, the replicators were more than adequate, but it would be a long and lonely journey. At times, nothing would be more needed than a taste of home.

As their voyage continued, Floresta scoured the transmissions Shirley and Lanny collected from the new planet. She carefully blended the remaining home food with the recipes she gathered. Gradually, she weaned them off the food they left behind and onto the foodstuffs of the new planet.

By the time the family landed, Markus and Edwin had already developed a fondness for pho, Windee was looking forward to al pastor burritos, and even Lanny was looking forward to hot pot.

The whole time, the crew had never noticed.

Floresta didn't mind. In fact, that was her goal—to make their transition seamless and enjoyable.

However, now she faced a different concern. Customers were growing tired of their donuts. Yes, they were replicated as perfectly as replicators could make them. But they could not capture the randomness, the little variances, the extra shower of sprinkles, the slight burn that made a fritter taste like cider.

Besides, no matter how often they rotated the donuts, the truth was they were essentially serving their customers spaceship food.

And then there were the Thamavuongs' recipes. As much as her niece thought them sacred, they left so much unsaid.

If Floresta had been able to work a year or two with the Thamavuongs, she might have been able to acquire their cooking secrets. But Lanny had rushed the process.

She didn't blame her niece; her goal was to get the crew settled as soon as possible. However, there was still the problem of the donuts. What was the secret of creating donuts that people wanted again and again and again?

Floresta would not find what she needed in a replicator, nor even in an emergency call to the Thamavuongs. After all, they would only be able to tell her what they knew, not what they did. She needed to find other masters and watch them work. She needed to hear their kitchens, to taste their foods, and to watch the reactions of the other customers.

Floresta walked to her usual bus stop. Today, she would try a steamed bun place. It was supposedly one of the best in West Covina.

On the way out, she saw a Jaguar drive past her. She waved.

Shizuka waved back and smiled.

Floresta was happy when Lanny was with that woman. Lanny needed a space where she could be neither Captain nor Mom.

Tomorrow is tomorrow. Over there is over there. And here and now is not a bad place and time to be, especially when so much of the unknown is beautiful.

20

"You didn't have to come get me," Lan said.

"How was your meeting with the Chamber of Commerce?"

Lan slumped in her seat. "It was worse than the Imperial Sub-Council of Public Works."

"Exactly. Now enjoy the ride."

Shizuka merged onto the 710 North. From there, she'd take the 10 West, maybe to the beach. A beach walk sounded wonderful. Maybe the Santa Monica Promenade.

"Thank you so much for recommending Starrgate," Lan blurted. "I can't believe how thoughtful you are. How can I thank you?"

Shizuka had debated whether she should tell Lan that she had nothing to do with the donut order. But Shizuka was still a little hurt that Lan had misjudged her. Also, Lan's decision not to shield their conversation about Katrina at the Kim Ky noodle house had caused this entire chain of events.

And besides, there was something that she had been wanting to know more about for some time now.

"The Endplague. You mention it from time to time. Can you tell me what it is, exactly?"

The Endplague?

Shizuka Satomi had done her a wonderful favor, and by custom, Lan was obligated to return it. Besides, Shizuka was Shizuka. However, even in the Empire, one mentioned the Endplague only when absolutely necessary.

"It might not be wise to discuss," Lan was finally able to say.

"You've told me about the level-five gamma ray burst," Shizuka said. "You've told me you were from across the galaxy. You've even told me you were plum-colored."

"None of that is going to kill you. Knowledge of the Endplague has destroyed civilizations far older and more stable than yours."

"I'm just a violin teacher from Monterey Park. I doubt that I can affect a civilization," Shizuka replied. "Unless you'd rather not tell me . . ."

She paused there, letting the silence do its work.

"Ever wonder why," Lan finally said, "if there is intelligent life out there, that the universe isn't teeming with activity?"

"Maybe the universe is filled with introverts?"

"Shizuka."

"Well, you asked."

Lan took another breath.

"As a civilization progresses, it goes through wars, pandemics, catastrophes. Those that survive grow more astute, more perceptive, more advanced. Diseases are conquered, infirmity eliminated. Life spans increase. Suffering becomes largely a memory.

"Meanwhile, their explorers and historians find evidence of past cultures, and cultures before that. At first it is exciting. But all they keep finding are ruins. And slowly, either through science or history, every advanced civilization becomes aware of a disturbing possibility—that their future may end in ruin, too.

"The civilization then rushes to probe other stars, even other galaxies; it increases its research, attempting to manipulate space, time, in the hope that somewhere, someone might have found an escape, a loophole.

"But eventually, they find, and solve, the mathematical equation that explains the entire universe."

"I think our scientists are working on something like that too," Shizuka said.

Lan shook her head. "They'll need to find the Grand Unified Theory a few more times before they can even begin to understand what 'everything' is—sorry, I didn't mean to offend your civilization."

Shizuka shrugged. "No offense taken."

"Still, should your civilization survive, it *will* eventually find the same equation. And that will be your death sentence. For in that equation, there will be no forever, no eternity. *Nothing*.

"And this collapse, and all its attendant despair, is the Endplague."

Shizuka was puzzled.

Space aliens, she could understand. Purple skin? Cute. Two elbows?

Weird, but fine. Galactic warfare? Frankly, expected. Being a refugee? Of course.

But how could the mere concept of mortality be enough to topple advanced civilizations? People live, people die, and so what?

"You make an idea sound like a disease."

"What else would the Endplague be? We can repair genomes, neutralize toxins, eliminate biological pathogens. Besides, different species have different physiologies. However, every sentient race, by definition, evolves a mind.

"From that point, collapse is inevitable. Death may happen gradually or suddenly. Some civilizations waste away. Some commit mass suicide. And some revert to violence, try to re-create empires, and perish in a needless galactic war.

"That is the path that our own civilization has chosen. Endplague-induced warfare has already decimated entire star systems. Our Star Patrol has been transformed into the Imperial Army. And though the Imperial government has not acknowledged it, the collapse is accelerating. That's why I had to take my children and escape. After all, their father is one of the voices urging battle . . ."

Shizuka understood something of Lan's sadness, and of course her need to leave a galactic war.

Yet something in Lan's explanation seemed lacking.

If the Endplague was a type of despair, then it was less an affliction of the mind than of the heart. And for afflictions of the heart, did they not have anything like poetry, music, or even sappy movies with star-crossed lovers?

Shizuka wanted to ask, but she knew Lan would dismiss her.

And yes, Lan had said this was something that would occur far in Earth's future, but it did not seem much different than anyone realizing they were mortal.

Nor was music a mere diversion, or distraction from truth. If only Lan understood this. Maybe Lan could hear some—

"*Oh, no!*"

"What? What?" Lan asked.

"We're on the 710 South."

Shizuka had been too busy pondering the Endplague to notice the interchange. How long had they been going the wrong way? So much for the Promenade and the walk on the beach . . .

Shizuka tried to keep smiling as she exited the freeway and stopped in a shopping center parking lot.

Now, where were they?

Of course she'd miss the interchange!

Lan berated herself. All she had wanted was to tell Shizuka thank you. Instead, she had just told her about the *Endplague*.

How could she, the captain, of all people, let this happen? What could she do now? Apologize? Sure. Ask her to forget what she had said? Maybe. Erase Shizuka's memory? Could she do that?

She would if she had to, right?

Right?

And then Lan's stomach growled.

Shizuka laughed, Lan blushed, and suddenly, both of them were back in real time.

"Well, while we're here, let's find some food," Shizuka said. She pulled out her phone. "Not much . . . There's an Olive Garden nearby," she murmured.

"Olives? Garden?"

"Look! A fountain!"

Lan Tran, Starship Captain, former Imperial Scientist, and Earth's first harbinger of the Endplague, giddily entered the Olive Garden. She stopped at the entryway and said hi to the hostess. She examined the décor. As the server came and sat them at their table with their menus, she gushed at how punctual and pretty she was.

"Everyone here is so polite!" Lan said. Lan pointed to another server's tray.

"What is that?"

"That's our Peach Raspberry Iced Tea. Would you like one, too?"

Lan nodded. "This is such an amazing place," she whispered. She scanned the menu. "Eggplant Parmigiana—it sounds so luxurious."

The salad came, and then the bread sticks.

Lan ate one, then the other. She looked at Shizuka in horror.

"Oh no! I ate your bread stick, too."

"Don't worry. They'll bring more."

"Really?"

Shizuka tilted her head. "Lan, haven't you traveled the galaxy? I mean, surely you've been to much nicer places than an Olive Garden in Cerritos."

Lan scooped more of the delightful salad. "Maybe, but it's been a while. Sure, I was a systems designer for the Empire. But after I had Markus, I spent most of my time taking care of family."

She reached for another bread stick.

"They'll bring more? Really?"

"Really."

Shizuka watched Lan and thought of all the immigrant mothers in their neighborhoods. She thought of all those who had braved leaky boats, smugglers, and pirates to deliver their families from Vietnam, then spent the rest of their lives never leaving Monterey Park.

"This is so good! And I can't believe I ordered a dish called Eggplant Parmigiana. *Parmigiana . . .*" She let her voice trail. "Even the word feels so creamy on the tongue. And *eggplant*! Doesn't it sound cute? Have you had eggplant before?"

"Uh—yes I have."

"And this peach tea is so *peachy*!"

As the server brought their plates to the table, Lan pulled out her phone to take a picture of her Eggplant Parmigiana.

"Shizuka! Look at how pretty this is! Shizuka, can you take a picture? Shizuka?"

"But you traveled across the galaxy. The *galaxy*."

Lan picked up a bread stick.

"Yes. It was really scary," she said with her mouth full.

"Tell me more?"

Lan nodded and swallowed. Then she began.

*   *   *

How to Survive an Interstellar War

More warships, more shouting. Don't think you are special.

More fighting, more war, as if people's very souls were falling away into disrepair. You are not special.

Another planet set on fire. This has happened before. Over and over. Leaders drawing new plans, finding new scapegoats.

A civilization coming to the end of its life.

So don't think you are special. You are a digit, trying to dodge statistics. And, while you are still insignificant, leave now.

Find a planet. A planet with compatible biology. With no space technology, so you can be left alone. Look. Look harder.

You don't need pretty. You don't need powerful. You need ordinary. And far, far away.

Study. Study more. And then you smile.

Yes.

Never say you're escaping. You just want to try something new.

Never mention politics. Say you were in the military, a scientist, so of course you're loyal. Say it's just business. It's simply business.

Tell them you enjoyed your service. Talk to the bank. Present a business plan.

Tell them about the gamma ray burst.

Show them your calculations. Show a planetary system that will experience a gamma ray burst. A Level-Five Gamma Ray Burst.

Say when the burst hits, tourists will need a stargate to get there.

Say profit from the show. Say working with family means reduced overhead. Say return on investment. Be honest where you can. Let them find your lies. Let them see a little greed, which is easy, because who doesn't want to get rich?

And then, take your permit, take your loan, pay too much money to buy a big ship with everything you need to start a life.

Let people laugh at you leaving for some distant nothing place.

When they laugh, think how their laughter means you fooled them all.

And then as soon as you get everything, just go.

Get the children. Look around for anyone else. No one is coming, of course, but you look anyway. But then, there's Aunty, holding three too many bags and staring as silent as a ghost.

Be happy your children are not crying. Be happy that your daughter is brilliant. Be happy that your son, even now, can navigate a warp jump.

Be happy that Aunty brought steamed buns for the trip.

Point the ship away. Let the past fade like a dream.

Present your permit. Watch the Central Stargate open, then close.

And keep smiling. Keep smiling to make it seem fun for the kids.

Of course they must know. But they cannot know.

They cannot know how much you will miss everything you are leaving behind.

Lan stopped. Her eyes were focused somewhere far away.

"Lan?" Shizuka gently called her back.

"Shizuka?"

Shizuka let Lan breathe, then gave Lan her napkin. Lan nodded and dabbed her eyes.

"But now I have a donut shop. And my family. And you."

Before Shizuka could react to that statement, Lan reached for the butter. "And another bread stick! And Eggplant Parmigiana!"

"Eggplant Parmigiana!" cheered the server as she walked by.

*   *   *

Astrid greeted Shizuka at the door.

"I'm sorry, the meeting took longer than expected."

"How's Lan?"

"She really likes Eggplant Parmigiana. How was practice with Katrina?"

Astrid opened her laptop and showed Shizuka a video of their session.

"How did you get her to follow your tempo like *that*?"

"I told her to," Astrid said matter-of-factly.

Shizuka watched Katrina with Astrid. Katrina was playing with a newfound precision. Despite herself, Shizuka could not help but feel a little envious.

"Where's Katrina now?"

"She's making another video."

Shizuka listened. "Yes . . . it sounds as if she's dancing, too. I wonder if she's trying to be like Lindsey Stirling?"

"Lindsey Stirling?"

Shizuka gestured for Astrid's laptop.

Astrid peered at the screen.

"Some sort of elf, fighting a very large dinosaur?"

"Dragon, Astrid. Dragon."

"She's beautiful, isn't she? And quite flexible. Oh . . . goodness . . . do you think you could have done that while you were playing?"

"Not even in my twenties. And not even if I had sold my soul."

That night, Shizuka knocked on Katrina's door.

"You need a gown. Tomorrow we're going shopping."

"Shopping?" Katrina hesitated. "I'm sorry . . . but maybe I can just find something online?"

"For a performance, you'll need a proper gown that fits you well."

"No. I mean—I don't know if I can go there and—"

"Katrina."

"Yes, Miss Satomi?"

"Stop. I am going to be with you at all times. It will be fine."

"Y-yes, Miss Satomi."

"Good night, Katrina. Dream of everything beautiful."

"Good night."

21

The next morning, Katrina rode with Shizuka to the Santa Anita Shopping Plaza. Katrina had been in shopping centers before, and in Asian areas before. But nothing had prepared her for this. The parking lots were full of shiny, beautiful cars owned by shiny, beautiful Asians. There was both a posh indoor shopping mall, as well as a posh outdoor shopping plaza. Well-dressed older people sat on stylish lounge furniture sipping Longjing tea from Wing Hop Fung, while the colorful play area fluttered with little Asian children in Fendi and Moschino.

Katrina wanted to apologize to all of them for being so plain and leave immediately. But Miss Satomi was with her, so she shuffled her feet forward and kept going.

Although Shizuka did not look back, she was listening to every footstep. It was important to be supportive, yet not supporting. As long as the girl kept walking, she moved with her, as well.

One step at a time. Her past students had started young. By the time they had crossed paths with Shizuka, each had endured years of recitals, performances, Christmas shows with Bach's Prelude in C Major and *The Nutcracker Suite*.

But Katrina was new to this not-always-friendly world.

And then, to add everything she had endured until now?

Of course she was scared. But fear was one thing every musician has to face. And so was playing live. Even the online musicians Katrina idolized had performed in live events. There was no substitute for live performances; they transformed both audience and musician.

Yes, Katrina was scared. But as long as she kept walking, Shizuka would not lead her astray. She would guide the girl, one step at a time.

The first store they entered was bright with LED lighting. The speakers were blasting dance music with lazy auto-tune, a lackluster melody, and far too much bass.

This wasn't a place that Shizuka would usually visit. Unless one were Yuja Wang, these were definitely not clothes for a concert hall. But the materials seemed soft and forgiving; the colors were vivid. Maybe they might get lucky.

The salesgirls watched them, and despite having no other customers, they turned their backs and kept talking.

One of them pointed and laughed.

Katrina spun around and rushed outside.

"Katrina?"

"I can't. Maybe I could perform in boy clothes?" Katrina offered. "It might be less troub—"

"Katrina Nguyen. Don't you *ever* say that again!"

Katrina blinked. "I—I'm sorry."

"And don't apologize!" Miss Satomi seemed furious. Suddenly, Katrina thought of Helvar Grunfeld.

"It's okay. Miss Satomi. It's okay."

Shizuka looked at her student.

"Really, it's okay."

Shizuka steadied her breathing and nodded. "Well then, let's try a department store."

This time, the lady was very nice to Shizuka, but once she saw Katrina, her gaze changed.

"We have nothing," she said sweetly.

"Really?" Shizuka replied, even more sweetly.

The salesperson stepped back, as if threatened by a knife.

"Let's go, Katrina."

Really? This girl, this musician? What had she done to deserve scorn like that? Shizuka noticed Katrina begin to shy away not merely from the gown stores, but the perfume stands, the shoe stores, even the food court. She had followed her this far, but the girl was beginning to waver.

Shizuka stopped. This was not the time to be angry. Katrina did not need any more anger.

"Katrina?"

"Yes, Miss Satomi?"

"Cinnabon."

"What?"

"We're getting Cinnabon."

Luckily, no one was at the Cinnabon line—most people were too unimaginative to eat Cinnabon for lunch.

"Thank you, girls," the cashier said.

They bit into their Cinnabons even before they reached their table. They were sloppy and sweet and gooey.

"Don't worry, Miss Satomi. I won't tell Miss Tran," Katrina said.

"Shut up!" Shizuka said as they sat down.

Katrina laughed. But then, she suddenly caught herself and looked around fearfully.

"Katrina," Shizuka said evenly, "sometimes, I would be in front of a crowd and feel that everyone hated me."

"*You?*"

Shizuka nodded.

"But I knew someone out there was smiling for me, rooting for me."

"But I am trans, they—"

"I didn't notice any hate from Cinnabon girl. Did you?"

Shizuka watched Katrina relive a simple moment with a nice cashier.

"And I saw her smiling as we passed by earlier."

"Really? I didn't notice."

"That's why I'm telling you now. That's what you look for. A friendly face. A supportive glance. That's whom you hold on to. That's whom you play to when onstage. It doesn't change a terrible situation, but it can help you survive it.

"By the way, did you notice that one of the boutiques we passed had a nice boy with prettier makeup than you?"

"Huh?"

"He was almost as pretty as me. Let's go there next."

Katrina licked her fingers and stared at the gooey mess in front of her. Cinnabon was perfect, at least for the first few bites.

"Next time, can we get MiniBons?"

Katrina followed Miss Satomi to the boutique with the pretty boy. Katrina wondered why she had not noticed him the first time. Surely she would have noticed a queer boy like that. And then she understood. The boutique was not in the mall, but in the courtyard. And it was not shiny hip.

It was high-end expensive.

But her teacher did not seem worried as she bade Katrina to follow her through the frosted glass door. Once inside Katrina could not help but stare. Brush paintings decorated the walls. There were Chinese vases, a marble statue of Kuan Yin, a gentle stream running through the middle of the store.

How was this a clothing store?

"Hi! I'm Kev," he said. "Would you like some tea?"

Katrina anxiously looked away, but Shizuka accepted gracefully.

"Thank you, Kev. This is my violin student. She has her first competition coming up, and I want her looking beautiful for the judges."

He focused on Katrina immediately. "Yes, I see . . . Maybe soft and flowy. She/her?" Kev looked in Katrina's direction for approval.

Katrina nodded.

"They/them, by the way. Any color preferences?"

Had he just checked her pronouns? And they/them? Did he—no—did they just say *they/them*?

"Saturated, and not too busy," Miss Satomi said easily. "Oh, and no sequins near the neck—they'll scratch the instrument and might snag. It's her first public recital, so I want her to be comfortable. But striking. She deserves to look special on the stage."

"Absolutely. Something strapless, maybe?"

"That might work."

Strapless? Katrina looked over at her, then at Kev. They weren't laughing.

"Let's try a few things," Kev said. "Come with me and see what you think."

Shizuka followed them.

"Yes, yes. I have a few things in mind. Tell me more about your student?"

Katrina watched them disappear. Is this what it was to go shopping—and have people *help* you? She felt happy. She felt dizzy. She felt almost like a real human being.

A few minutes later, they returned.

"Here, try this. I think green would be good with your hair," Kev said. "Green can sometimes wash out Asians, but your skin has such a great glow. And the fabric is bias cut. We might need a belt or sash to bring out your hips, but the bias cut will really show off those legs."

Katrina blushed. Legs? Show off?

Katrina took the dress, went into the changing room, and closed the door. Her heart was beating quickly, and not in a good way. Changing rooms were never good places. She pulled the fabric over herself. Good, so far, so good. It had cleared her shoulders.

But then she reached for the zipper. Shit. The zipper was around the back. Desperately, she tried to twist it forward. Crap! Now the zipper bit into her skin. She began to perspire. What was she doing?

This was not good. These dresses were cut for women's bodies . . . not like her, but the ones who were beautiful. The real ones, who weren't born the way she was.

She had to get it off—maybe if she pulled it over her head? But what if she ripped it?

"Do you need help?" Kev asked.

"No, I'm fine!" Did her voice drop?

She began to breathe heavily. It sounded like boy breathing, didn't it?

Someone came in.

"No!"

"It's me," Miss Satomi said. "You're stuck. Let me help you."

"Miss Satomi, the dress is for real girls. I—I just need to get this off."

"*Shh!* Stop struggling."

Katrina stilled herself, then felt the dress slip over her body.

"Okay, turn around."

Katrina gasped as the zipper easily glided between her shoulder blades.

"Oh *shit* . . ."

She looked in the mirror. The dress fit!

"Raise your arms. Can you move?"

Katrina nodded. The dress fit! It fit! The bias-cut fabric seemed to shimmer and flow. The fabric was so slinky and gorgeous that for a split second she forgot she was looking at herself.

She lived in a world of loose skirts and tops, of baggy tops draped over her shoulders. Anything cheap, but more importantly . . . anything to hide the proportions of her frame. To think that she would ever fit a dress—a real legit fashionable dress . . .

"What do you think?"

"Oh shit . . . oh shit . . ."

"Is everything okay in there?" Kev asked softly.

"Yes, we're fine," Shizuka said.

Shizuka gave Katrina a handkerchief and stroked her student's hair.

"What am I going to do with you?" she murmured.

Shizuka helped Katrina out of the dress, which was not difficult at all. She was about to put on her street clothes when there was gentle knocking on the door.

Kev opened the door slightly and gave them another dress.

"This one should look amazing, as well. I love how deep the blue is. Oh, and there are two other possibilities I want you to see. They are beautiful and just came in from Macau."

An hour later, Miss Satomi purchased the two gowns they agreed were best and thanked Kev for their help.

"Break a leg, gorgeous!" they said.

Gorgeous? Did they mean her?

Miss Satomi laughed.

"Now let's find some shoes."

Unfortunately, shoes were more difficult; her feet were larger than what most of these stores carried. But with Miss Satomi helping her, Katrina was able to at least point out styles she preferred. Astrid would find the right sizes later.

After, Miss Satomi helped her find makeup, from a real store with makeup stations, huge mirrors, and full-spectrum lighting. A cheerful girl named Rocio matched her skin tone for foundation and helped her refine her contouring.

Rocio also told her she was very lucky she did not have much facial hair, but she might want to consider getting laser done soon.

"I tried waxing," Katrina said. "With strips I bought from the Internet."

Rocio cringed. "From the . . . Internet? Honey, were they at least for the face?"

"They make them for just the face?"

"I'll have Astrid make arrangements for lasering later," Shizuka said quickly. "But no more home waxing your face."

"Yes, Miss Satomi."

Katrina walked out of the mall with two large bags and a blank stare. It had been okay.

It had been okay?

Why?

Why was Kev like that?

Why was Rocio like that?

Why was Astrid like that, and Shirley?

Why, why, why?

Why was she born this way, a human being?

Why did being human hurt so much? Why couldn't she have been different, without a soul, without worth? Why couldn't she have been the thing her parents might have wanted?

Why couldn't anyone have treated her this way this before?

*　*　*

"Mother. I have news from the Empire."

"Yes, Shirley."

"The High Council has decided to close all borders to the Home Quadrant. Their official reason is to prevent the spread of the End-plague, but they are halting departures, as well."

Lan wasn't surprised. They were fortunate to have left when they had.

"Are there any messages that you would like me to send?"

"No. Silence has been good to us."

"Yes, Mother."

"Thank you, Shirley."

Traveling through space-time is like driving through Los Angeles. Universes pass by like random cars on the four-level at rush hour. To keep their way, ships must synchronize with their own timeline at regular intervals. Stargates perform this function automatically; in fact, providing foolproof space-time coordinates was one of the primary functions of a stargate.

But since the Trans had arrived at this planet without utilizing a stargate, both spatial and chronological navigation were manual. Many good pilots would not have been able to do this. However, Lan was far more than a good pilot. Now the only way to interact with their home timeline was to recombine their raw navigation data with the correct space-time variables.

And the only one with access to variables, as well as the computational ability to perform this calculation, was Shirley.

Lan strictly limited contact to their home timeline to weekly reports, and only to Shirley. No one else knew about the connection home. Although Lan did not want to keep secrets from her crew, contact with the Empire might invite hunters, invaders, and even other, less careful, refugees.

Besides, until they were fully situated here, she needed everyone to focus on the planet they were on. They could not grow complacent, for with its Internet, *Stargate* machines, donuts, and ducks, this planet seemed touched with a madness that Lan now believed was not the Endplague, yet confounded her all the same.

* * *

"Arch your back. A sunken chest means a sunken sound!"

"Your bow hold is collapsing—you can't already be tired."

"No, I don't care how it sounds in the game. Cleaner!"

"Timing! Timing!"

"More precision on the marcato! Mar-ca-to!"

Shizuka knew Katrina was straining. But Shizuka would push her student even more. No, she could not take away Katrina's past. But what she *could* give her was this training, this practice— how to make this measure, this passage—better than it had been before.

Shizuka had thought she knew all about being damned. Still, she had always assumed that damnation required some sort of exchange.

Yet, this student, this human being, had been forsaken not for ambition, nor revenge, nor even love, but for merely *existing*?

Who needs the Devil when people can create a hell like this themselves?

"You're still too tense. Relax your fingers. Unless you relax, the notes will sound indistinct."

"But this is just before the level boss!" Katrina cried.

"I don't care. The level boss can wait until you play with satisfactory détaché."

Her student was going to perform a piece from a video game. A student of Shizuka Satomi—playing gaming music. She thought of her six previous students. What would they think of the Queen of Hell now?

Katrina laughed.

It was such a beautiful laugh, wasn't it?

May Hell have mercy on her soul.

JULY

22

Who lives in Temple City?

One hundred years ago, the answer would have been easy; the area had been opened with railroad money, to be settled by German Americans and those comfortable living with them.

Seventy-five years ago, the Camellia Festival was started by the Ladies of Temple City to make their community notable, beautiful, and officially incorporated. There had been a Miss Temple City contest. A pancake breakfast with the firemen. An active Boy Scout troop. A student art show at the Temple City Library. There had been a cobbler, a hobby shop, a dance studio. Ye Loy Chinese restaurant offered postwar Americans an exotic selection of sweet and sour pork, beef chop suey, and egg foo young.

Fifty years ago, kids from Temple City High School would stop at Fisher's Drug store for a root beer from the soda fountain, while in the park was a pristine white pavilion where local performers played big band, swing, Elvis, Tom Jones.

And today, the Boy Scout troop was still there, as was the pancake breakfast, the art show at the library. There was the hobby shop, the bike shop, and even the dance studio. The park was still there. Miss Temple City was now Miss Temple City Ambassador. The pavilion, now with a fresh coat of paint, still featured the music of big bands and Engelbert Humperdinck.

Yet now, rather than Germans, one was far more likely to find Chinese, Vietnamese, Filipinos, a few Malaysians, and still more Vietnamese. Where there had been shoemakers, coffee shops, and tailors, there were now Vietnamese bridal shops, boba places, a new branch of Golden Deli Pho.

And where Ye Loy once stood, Ahgoo's Kitchen was now busy making stir-fried water spinach, Taiwanese fried noodles, and green onion sesame pie. And, although they offered fried rice and hot and sour soup, at least once a week a staff member would have to inform a confused customer that they did not serve egg foo young.

This evening, the park chattered with an uncommon energy. On most summer nights, older people gathered on familiar lawn chairs to hear familiar music. Sometimes they let their hair down to a Beatles tribute band or, very rarely, classic rock.

But this evening was classical music under the stars! The atmosphere felt a little like the Hollywood Bowl. Some had even brought picnic fixings from Trader Joe's. And the park was also full of younger, mostly Asian families, who were either musicians or the families of musicians.

Landon Fung nibbled a donut. Whatever the reason, Ellen Seidel had hit upon a fantastic idea. Some of the older people in the Chamber had wondered out loud how classical music would appeal to a younger crowd. But these kids were excited and eager to be there. Many had music cases with them, and some were looking at sheet music, either in print or on their phones.

As he watched them, looking with awe at the bright pavilion stage, Landon Fung couldn't help but feel proud to live right here, in Temple City.

Meanwhile, Tamiko Giselle Grohl was in her pre-performance cocoon: hoodie on, headphones on, sheet music, water, and a small container of macaroni potato salad at her side.

An outdoor showcase was not so much a competition as it was a spectacle. As always, parents were bragging and teachers were pacing. Some oboist would worry about how the wind was affecting her reed. A pianist would complain about not having a grand piano in the park. A violist . . . well . . .

Tamiko yawned.

Whatever . . . who cared? What mattered was Shizuka Satomi was here. And this time, Tamiko was ready.

Tamiko noticed her teacher nervously searching the park. She closed her eyes. *Don't worry. The Queen of Hell is here.*

And her new student would be sharing the stage. Perfect.

Let's play together. Tamiko giggled.

Let's play together soon.

Eventually, Landon Fung signaled to the sound person, and the DJ stopped. The festival director said a few words, a representative of the formerly Ladies, now Women's, Club of Temple City gave thanks, and a children's choir led the crowd in singing "The Star-Spangled Banner."

The crowd applauded, and the first Classically Camellia Music Showcase began.

As all this was going on, Shizuka had sheltered Katrina in a quiet space away across the park, near the public library. Katrina was playing sixth, which meant there was no reason to rush.

"Shouldn't we be watching the others?" Katrina asked.

"Astrid will message us when we need to go. For now, warm up."

From across the park, Katrina heard applause. It was loud. Whoever that was must have been amazing. They were all amazing, weren't they? She was playing in a showcase. The Classically Camellia Music Showcase . . . They were probably brilliant and gorgeous, like anime characters.

"Katrina."

She would never look like that, would she? Wait—Classically Camellia Music . . . but her piece wasn't classical at all! What if they got mad? What if they stopped her in the middle—

"*Katrina.*"

"M-Miss Satomi?"

"What do you smell?"

"What?"

"What do you smell?" Miss Satomi repeated.

Smell? Katrina took a breath. And there was the smell of donuts. The smell of grass. Of car exhaust. Some kids must be smoking weed. The grass was wet in some places . . . She could smell the mud, and then she took another breath.

With the smells came other senses. The colors. The sounds came back. She could feel the evening cool against her.

Miss Satomi squeezed her hands firmly.

"Now, you are about to play these nice people some music, and they are eager to hear you. You're just sharing your music with others. That's all. Sharing."

Katrina looked into the park, at the people enjoying a summer evening. Some were smiling. Many were peeking at their cell phones, some were drinking boba. And many were eating donuts.

Gradually, her body became hers again. She played through some scales. She repeated a few bars from Schradieck. She thought of the first time she had played in front of Miss Satomi, with the ducks.

Shizuka looked at her phone. She patted Katrina gently.
"Astrid says it's time."

*   *   *

The emcee looked at Katrina and paused.
"Our next performer is a young violinist. She, I mean he, I mean . . . Well, who knows these days, right?" He laughed awkwardly.
The emcee's attempt to cover his error only made things worse. The crowd was tittering. What did that mean? But she's wearing a dress.
A child spoke in Mandarin. Katrina didn't quite understand, but it sounded something like, "Is that a boy?"
Shizuka was furious. This was unacceptable! She glared accusingly at the organizers, but they, too seemed horrified. None of them had anticipated this.

Katrina's face stung with sweat. The pads in her dress seemed to be slipping, and she just knew her shoulders stood out under the stage lights. She tried to breathe, but drew back as soon as she felt her belly push against the fabric.
She glanced offstage. It wasn't that far. She could run off now, no one would care . . .
Then a loud and clear voice resounded over the din.
"SHE! She's a *girl*, you dipshit!"
It was as if a giant bucket of ice water fell over the crowd. *Of course* she was a girl. What was that even about?
Astrid smiled. Katrina blinked.
Ellen Seidel turned in shock to the person who had yelled this, because she was sitting next to her.
"Tamiko?"
"Shut *up*," Tamiko hissed. "Can we just hear her play?"

"Y-yes. Please, everyone, welcome Katrina Nguyen," the emcee finally said.
Katrina tried to find friendly faces in the crowd, the ones Miss Satomi said were always there. But to her horror, all she saw was a wall of black.

Shizuka noticed her predicament immediately. *How could she have forgotten?*

She had not warned Katrina about spotlights.

A spotlight looks great to the audience, but when the performer looks into the light, the light is blinding. Instead of the audience, one sees a wall of dark. Furthermore, everyone beyond that darkness is watching every move, so there is no way to blink or turn away.

Katrina's eyes would eventually adjust, but for now, she was on her own.

Katrina could hear the audience talking, eating, breathing. So many people, so many people that she couldn't see. What should she do? Her arms were numb; her hands felt as though they belonged to someone else, someone far away.

The wind blew, and something flew into her eye. Katrina flinched.

And Astrid mistook that flinch as the signal to begin.

No! Wait!

Instinctively, Katrina's hands leapt into motion. But the music kept coming. And unlike practice, there was no chance to start over.

Crap! That was supposed to be a downbow.

Keep going. Keep playing. *No!* Her teeth clenched, as she misplayed yet another note.

Katrina could sense some older people rustling in their seats, probably getting up to leave. She guessed what they were thinking: *What is this junk? Who is this freak?* Soon parents would probably depart as well, saving their children's precious classical ears from being corrupted by something as vulgar as gaming music.

Ellen Seidel smiled. *Yes!* The student was even worse than Ellen had imagined. Surely, Tamiko would see Shizuka Satomi had gone either crazy, or senile, or both.

Katrina felt herself twisting back, back to Evan in the shower, the women on the bus ride, her father kicking the door. She was a dumbass. A tranny. Worthless. Ugly.

Then Katrina remembered.

What do you smell?

The boxes of donuts. The grass, the car exhaust, the kids smoking weed . . .

Fresh rosin, gently dusting her bow. The perfume Astrid had lent her, wafting off her skin, her hair, her beautiful, shimmering dress.

Suddenly, she was back onstage.

Okay.

She was onstage, and she was in trouble. But she was playing. Katrina relaxed her wrist, and Aubergine instantly responded.

Good. I still have technique.

Her legs steadied. Yes, she had her legs . . . Kev had called them gorgeous, hadn't they?

And Aubergine.

Remember? Eggplant?

Katrina let herself smile. Gradually, her eyes became used to the spotlight. She looked into the park, and something glinted at her, and there was one face, a little boy with glasses, his head propped up on his hands, watching intently.

The child was looking at her as if she were an angel.

And then, "Oh shit! She's playing *Axxiom*!" a voice in the darkness said.

Darkness. Katrina recalled all the nights she had spent listening in the dark. But where she had been alone before, now there were others. They were listening. They were feeling.

A friendly face. A supportive glance. Whether or not she could see them, Katrina knew they were there.

Ellen Seidel noticed the change, but surely this was all due to Shizuka Satomi's arrangement, right? Whatever else she was, Shizuka Satomi was a masterful illusionist.

The bowing was dynamic, but conventional. The string jumps were fast and pretty, but they spanned nearly identical intervals. And, whenever possible, Shizuka had slipped in an option to sound an open A or D in case her student needed to check her intonation.

This was the perfect way to make a beginner seem better than she was.

But then Ellen Seidel noticed Tamiko Grohl swaying, her eyes tightly shut. She looked around at the rest of the park, all taken by this music. And then, the music took Ellen Seidel as well.

———

In *Axxiom*, mathematical and logical concepts were personified as nonplayer characters. Working with them created the laws of your universe, and from there, one could build ever more elaborate and involved realities. The music to the game reflected this—developing, curving back on itself, creating new complexities that curved and developed in turn.

Katrina had imagined that there would be a time onstage where she would sneak a peek at Astrid for reassurance, or to Miss Satomi for strength. But instead, Katrina focused on that boy with glasses. And next to him was a girl with a Poké Ball hanging off her violin case.

Katrina heard an old woman collecting plastic bottles. And somewhere was a girl feeling too awkward in her flowery dress.

From the darkness, Katrina willed her violin to build their world. To let there be light, let there be colors, then calculus and molecules and starlit vistas, let there be home after home after home where no one yelled and no one was beaten.

You can do this, Katrina's song seemed to tell them. This is your universe. Your creation. Please don't be afraid. Let's not be afraid anymore.

A few more people stopped to listen. Some kids rode up on their bicycles. A young couple with a baby stroller. A man holding a dirty jacket and a lunch box.

Katrina played for people who loved *Axxiom*. For people who never played *Axxiom* all their lives. Katrina played for people who had never thought they could play the game at all.

As she played, she thought of a helpful voice bringing clothes she wanted, a friendly face selling Cinnabons.

This world is for you. You. You.

You . . .

She hadn't even noticed when she had stopped playing.

Katrina looked at Astrid, then the audience. Finally, she realized the music was over. Then the crowd started clapping. It felt like sunshine. It sounded like rain.

She looked for her teacher, but Ms. Satomi was not in her seat. She started walking offstage to find her, but Astrid grabbed her arm.

"Katrina, thank your fans."

Oh. *Oh!*

Katrina bowed. She bowed once more, and again. Then, as her legs turned to jelly beneath her, she held on to Astrid's arm and somehow managed to leave the stage.

Immediately, Katrina was surrounded by festival staff, and then others who had come around behind the stage. Some wanted to thank her. Others wanted to share their love of violin, or ask if she played music from other games and where could they find more of her music.

And some, with quavering voices and watery eyes, wanted to talk about what they felt when Katrina played, the pain in their lives, and how they felt no one had spoken to them like that before.

Astrid placed her arm around Katrina and began to lead her away.

"Wait!"

Katrina walked to a girl who was now quietly waiting behind the stage.

"Thank you," she said.

Tamiko turned, shrugged, and went back to her violin.

Ellen Seidel watched as Shizuka Satomi's newest protégé waved once more to her student before being spirited away.

This was the girl who was having issues with double stops?

She looked at Tamiko, her star student, now fidgeting with her tuning pegs. There were times when a teacher should rally her student, encourage her, remind her to believe in her talent. This was one of those times.

But as she searched her years of experience, her finest speeches, her most powerful words, Ellen Seidel realized there was nothing she could say.

Katrina held on to Astrid's arm until they found Miss Satomi. Katrina had so many things to say, she had no idea how to begin.

"I'm sorry, I screwed up at the beginning. The stage lights were shining in my eyes, and then I gave Astrid the wrong signal, and—"

"Come here," her teacher said, because none of that was important.

Because, in that moment, Miss Satomi hugged her, placed her hands on either side of her head and looked into her eyes.

"Tonight, you get a star."

Finally, the applause died down. But rather than preparing for the next performance, people milled about as if still entranced by whatever world Katrina's music had taken them to.

Many were looking at their watches, rolling up their blankets, and folding up their lawn chairs.

And Musician #7, flutist Russell Kim, was nowhere to be seen.

"What's happening? Where's number seven?" Ellen asked. "Landon, do something!"

Landon Fung glanced around and shrugged. Apparently the Kim boy had left. But what could be done?

"I am going to play."

"What?"

"I am going to play."

Tamiko walked past her teacher, up the stairs. She looked to the sky. She looked to the empty place where Shizuka had been. Then she walked onto the stage.

Of course Russell Kim quit. Of course he'd been frightened. He'd probably had a proper piece ready, a wonderful piece.

That's what *all* of them had tonight.

But now? Tamiko looked past the wall of dark into the audience. She smiled even at those who were ignoring her.

Russell Kim was weak. Tamiko was merely devastated. Russell Kim would wake up tomorrow, and it would be a new day.

But for Tamiko Grohl?

Paganini's Caprice no. 5. Composed by Niccolò Paganini, the Devil's Musician himself. Many of the era's greatest virtuosi had thought Paganini caprices were too difficult for mortal hands, that his playing alone was proof of consort with the Devil.

Tamiko remembered the first time she had heard a Paganini caprice. Actually, it was not live; it was a video. And actually, she barely remembered the music. What she recalled was Kiana Choi, the most beautiful creature she had ever seen.

All Tamiko could do at the time was think about Kiana, being like her, playing like her. She practiced. She dreamed. She sparkled, floated, radiated. She won a competition. And the one after that.

Play without mercy. Play as if touched. Play with obsession. Eventually, Asian mothers would see her at the violin shop, stop their children, and point. When she finally *did* perform Paganini, judges whispered excitedly to her teacher. She was told that Paganini himself must be smiling.

From there, Tamiko Grohl assumed she would become more and more famous, more and more beautiful. She would outgrow her current teacher, then study with Shizuka Satomi, Kiana Choi's mentor. From there, larger stages, airplanes, brighter and brighter lights.

But she had been wrong. Horribly, horribly wrong.

She had sensed it even before tonight. Middle-school students were uploading videos of themselves playing Paganini on YouTube. Recently, someone posted one of a girl in Japan. She was *eight*.

The girl's violin still had four fine tuners. Her violin wasn't even full-sized.

Tamiko's eyes were now adjusted to the lights. Somewhere out there, one of those kids would do everything she had done. Only she'd be prettier, faster, younger.

And it still would not be enough.

And yet tonight, Katrina Nguyen, someone who could not perform a proper ricochet—who could not even keep her gown from bunching up beneath her shoulder rest—had played some sort of video game music.

And she created *worlds*.

As far as Paganini's Caprice no. 5? Paganini was indeed smiling at her, but not because he approved.

He was smiling because he was safe.

It was said that Paganini would make his performances memorable by breaking strings as he played. And though Tamiko Giselle Grohl's four strings survived the night, many in the audience swore they heard something breaking all the same.

* * *

That night, Katrina looked at her videos. She walked from her laptop. She went to the bathroom. She went back to her laptop and refreshed her page.

In that space, her *Axxiom* video had 108 more views.

And the comments?

"You are amazing!"

"I couldn't stop crying."

"H-how did you even? It was like someone finally heard me."

Katrina laughed. She spun. She felt happy. She felt proud.

Then she felt her father kicking in the door.

She shuddered. She folded in on herself and rocked back and forth.
She didn't deserve happiness like this, laughter like this.

Freak! Abomination!

Why are you even alive?

Faggot, just die.

Katrina hugged her violin. And against what played in her head,
she gave her music again, and again, and again.

Shizuka sat in her backyard. One afternoon, Katrina had left a chair
outside, and it was so nice that Shizuka decided to keep it there.

Summer was here; the scent of loquats now wafted throughout the
neighborhood. When she was young, Mr. Kakuda's tree always had
loquats. Mr. Kakuda's tree had long ago become old and rotted, but a
new loquat tree belonged to the Lieus. And the Contrerases had two.
No matter what, this neighborhood would always plant and grow.

The kitchen screen door opened.

Astrid poured tea for Shizuka, then a cup for herself. For a long
time, the two sat wordlessly above the lights of Monterey Park.

"I was with my grandmother," Astrid finally said. "She was singing
a lullaby."

> *Ich ghöre äs Glöggli es lütet so nett*
> *De Tag isch vergange jetz gang ich is Bett*
> *Im Bett tuen i bäte und schlafe dänn ii*
> *De Papi im Himmel wird au bi mir si*

Astrid gathered the teacups. "Miss Satomi, I hope you were somewhere beautiful, too. Good night."

Shizuka heard the patio door slide open, then shut. She closed
her eyes and listened again. In an outdoor concert, in her first
performance, with a horrible introduction, stage lights shining in her
eyes . . .

Katrina had done *that*.

When had any of her previous students done that? Who among them had connected with their listeners like that?

When had she?

Did Katrina realize what she had done? Yes, she had trained so hard—and of course she heard the applause. But did she really know?

Could she?

After all, in the lights, it is very difficult to see.

Shizuka thought to her own career, to all those times spent hoping, praying that after the performance, after the encore, people might remember even a little of her music.

Yet no matter how she played, when she was finished, everything seemed to go back to just the way it was.

But now, far away from the stage, Shizuka could see the audience, hear what Katrina's music had done—and what it continued to do.

In the darkness and silence, she realized that Katrina's music might be with them even now.

And Katrina's was a music that was not so different from her own.

Katrina Nguyen.

Shizuka had been right. Well, of course she'd been right, but believing and knowing are two different things. Katrina had entered that stage as a student. She had left it as a musician.

And with Katrina at this level, there was something else Shizuka knew, as well.

In an ideal world, Shizuka would never let anyone else finish her training. But in an ideal world, she wouldn't have become the Queen of Hell.

There was no reason to put it off any longer. It was time to prepare Katrina Nguyen for Tremon.

And then it would be Shizuka's turn to retake the stage.

23

"Here, Andrew. See the f-holes—curve should glide, then fall, in one smooth—"

Conversation stopped as the doorbell jingled. Lucy looked at her watch.

"Mr. Zacatecas—"

But it wasn't Mr. Zacatecas.

Shizuka Satomi?

She seemed in a very good mood. Lucy was tempted to ask if she'd had a nice date, but she was still Shizuka Satomi, and one does not casually ask the Queen of Hell about her relationship with the donut lady.

"Lucía, I was wondering," Shizuka asked lightly, "do you possess your family's client records?"

"What?"

"Your client records. Your notes. The last time I was here, I noticed you'd stopped most of your old work. So I wondered if maybe Franco had tossed out the notes, or perhaps hidden them somewhere."

"No—of course I still have them."

"All of them?"

"Yes. Why wouldn't I?"

The Matías had kept detailed notes and letters for every instrument that they had worked on, for every client. The notes recorded the stories of each adjustment, each refit, each repair. As such, they were the most valuable part of the store.

To be honest, Lucy felt more than a little offended that Shizuka Satomi had even considered that she did not possess the family's client notes. She might not be a son, but she was still a Matía.

"Good. Then I was wondering if you might take a look at this."

Shizuka placed a case on her counter.

Lucy opened the case and stared. Andrew sat down. Even he knew what it was.

The most radiant and fiery maple. The peculiarly graceful carving.

The thin crack on the pegbox—a crack that Catalín Matía had repaired himself.

This was Shizuka Satomi's Guarneri del Gesù.

Three legendary names reigned over the world of violins. Amati was the first and eldest. Stradivari was the most valued and renowned to the public. And then there was Guarneri. And the greatest of the Guarneri was del Gesù. A fine del Gesù was worth tens of millions of dollars. Paganini's priceless il Cannone was a del Gesù, as well.

Yet Shizuka Satomi chatted as if she were talking about a leaky faucet.

"There's something wolfy going on with the G string, at high C. Can you take a look?"

"Wolfy?" Andrew whispered.

"Wolf tones," explained Lucy. "Unwanted sounds that a violin makes at certain frequencies. They are not uncommon in del Gesùs, but we try to keep that quiet, no pun intended."

She stopped, surprised by how effortlessly that had come from her mouth.

"So, you'll take care of this, right? I've been living with the problem for a while, but it's time to have her in perfect working order."

"Wait, *what*? No, I didn't mean—"

"You helped my student. Are you saying you won't help *me*?"

"Miss Satomi, as fine an instrument as your student's is, this is another matter entirely."

"Didn't you work on Aoi's Strad when you were eleven or twelve?"

"I was ten."

"Exactly," Shizuka said. She pushed the case to her.

"And now you have my Guarneri. There are no hands that I would trust more. No great rush, of course. I realize that a job like this demands a little time."

"But, Miss Satomi!"

There was no way she could do this! Aoi's Strad had merely required a new bridge. And her grandfather had been there. Lucy nervously looked to Catalin Matía's portrait, even now proudly surveying the workshop.

"He wasn't perfect, you know."

Shizuka walked up to the portrait and gave it a nudge.

"Don't touch that!" Lucy shrieked. But it was too late. As the portrait swung gently back and forth, Lucy was so stunned that she could not speak.

"You were expecting bolts of lightning from the sky? It's just a picture." Shizuka Satomi inspected her finger and frowned. "And a dusty one, at that."

She put on her sunglasses and made her way to the door.

"Catalin Matía was as human as any of us."

The Queen of Hell glanced at the portrait one last time. "But I'm sure you'll find that out on your own soon enough. In any case, everything you need to know about my violin should be in your client notes. You'll see once you find them."

By the time Lucy found her voice, Shizuka Satomi had already left the store.

*   *   *

How does one react after experiencing a first applause—applause that is thunderous, glorious?

Shizuka had seen such applause affect six brilliant students. They filled with pride, achievement, even bliss. But soon they worried and obsessed over the next performance. And in their fear, they reached out to Shizuka Satomi.

So now, she would witness Katrina's growing pride and ambition—as well as her fear and insecurity.

From there, handing her the cursed bow would be just a matter of time.

"I'm sorry I'm late, Miss Satomi. Um . . . I overslept."

"I think we can overlook that today. Congratulations, Katrina."

Katrina blushed, but held herself steady.

"Thank you, Miss Satomi."

"So, what shall we work on today?" Shizuka asked expectantly.

"I was wondering if we can review the video?"

"Of course."

Shizuka expected her to bask a little, even brag. Any of her other students would have done so—some quite expressively. However, Katrina examined the video with almost no emotion, point-by-point stopping it whenever she had a question or issue to discuss.

"Miss Satomi, what can I do when my grip slips like it did right there? Are there some exercises I can do to keep my back straight?"

She reviewed how she got lost in the stage lights, how she felt out of breath, how her chin rest became slippery with perspiration and too much foundation, and how her heart raced so fast that she lost her timing on arpeggios.

Yes, she had changed. This was a Katrina without panic or apology. Yet there was also not a shred of ego, of pride.

"Katrina, stop."

"Yes, Miss Satomi?"

"How did the applause make you feel?"

"I know I screwed up in the beginning, and next time, I need to be ready for the stage lights, and—"

"No, no! Forget that."

Suddenly Hell was not the issue. Shizuka was concerned about Katrina. Since her performance, had she actually celebrated openly at all? What was she repressing? Was she still that afraid?

"The *applause*. How did it *feel*?"

"I can't. I—"

"Hey, Katrina. Who bought you the Cinnabon?"

Katrina lowered her eyes.

"It was the best feeling ever," she said softly. "Especially at the end. I felt like no one was going to hurt me. I felt safe, Miss Satomi. And powerful. So powerful that I could keep you, and everyone who was listening, safe as well."

Shizuka Satomi, the girl from Monterey Park, was unable to utter another word.

* * *

Throughout the Classically Camellia Showcase, Lan Tran closely monitored the planet's social media channels for all mentions of Starrgate Donut. This would be valuable marketing research. She'd classify and archive the mentions of different donuts—glazes, twists, apple fritters, sprinkles, crullers . . .

At first, there were many mentions of the free donuts, even some photos! But soon, the mentions of donuts dwindled. People mentioned the great music. People gushed about Katrina. Someone posted a photo. She was so beautiful! And there was a photo of

Astrid accompanying her. There was another stunning girl named Tamiko Grohl. There were posts about how nice the Pavilion was, photos of friendly dogs. Someone mentioned the boba they had bought at Tea Station. And another posted a video of a man selling elotes from a cart.

But the donut posts dwindled to almost nothing. Lan was stunned. *They were handing out donuts in the park!* Where were all the mentions?

Lan texted Markus, but Markus did not answer. She texted again. Finally, she texted Aunty Floresta.

"Perhaps it's best to discuss this when we return," was her prompt reply.

That had been an hour ago. Lan kept looking, hoping. But nothing. There were still many posts about the festival and how wonderful the violinists, especially, were. More selfies. And then there were tweets about a fire in Temple City, that the house of one of the festival staff—the emcee—had burned to the ground. But nothing about donuts.

Finally, she noticed one post, a TikTok from a young Toishan family. They had strolled by the park after the festival, and said they were so lucky because the cleanup crew gave them an entire box of donuts, as no one else wanted to take them.

Markus and Aunty Floresta returned to Starrgate and reported to the control center. One look from Aunty Floresta told Lan everything.

Yes, Temple City had paid in advance; yes, they made money. But there was no denying that the night had been a failure.

"Markus. Run a diagnostic on the replicators for any clues as to what went wrong."

"This is so stupid."

Lan blinked.

"Markus?"

Markus rolled his eyes and mumbled something else.

"What did you say?"

"I said fuck this!"

"Markus!" Aunty Floresta said. "You are talking to the captain."

"Captain? Of what? Captain of shitty donuts? We should be helping the Empire!" Markus picked up his coat and walked toward the elevator.

Suddenly, Markus could not move. His entire body was swaddled within a green glow. He struggled, but the glow intensified until he was lifted into the air.

"Markus, that is your captain. And your mother," Aunty Floresta said.

"Markus, I know it's difficult to understand, but the Empire is falling to the Endplague. It's far too dangerous to cont—"

"Then why the fuck are we building a stargate, anyway? What are we even doing here?" He was sobbing as his body went numb.

The glow slowly disappeared, as did Markus's now-sleeping form.

"I transported him to his bed," Aunty Floresta said. "In the morning, he'll think this night was a dream."

The boy was still a boy, but he was quickly maturing. Even his normal adolescent outbursts would be difficult to control. But if this developed into the Endplague . . .

As if Lanny didn't have enough to worry about.

Why are we building a stargate? Floresta herself wondered that from time to time. Officially, they were building it for the gamma ray burst, but since they were safe and far from the Empire, was it really necessary anymore?

However, Lanny was the captain, and the captain did not have to explain all of her decisions. And the girl might make her mistakes, but Floresta was certain of this: everything Lan Tran did was for the family.

Since Markus was asleep, Lan put on her apron and went upstairs to take over his shift. She relieved Shirley and Edwin, who were helping the few customers that were there.

She looked out the window, into the sky. She remembered times like this on the starship, when everything was seemingly peaceful.

Yet, for the captain of a starship, or a donut shop, there was always research to do, courses to chart, crew reports to read. Even the smallest discrepancies needed to be located, then remedied before they became serious problems.

Lan Tran remembered how the store was with the Thamavuongs. On warm summer nights, people from the neighborhood would queue into the parking lot for yeast donuts, cake donuts, bear claws, their special Mexican chocolate crullers, and good old-fashioned sour creams.

The Thamavuongs had told her she might sell out early on Saturday, and when that happened, she should make second and third batches, because a heavy crowd on Saturday always meant Sunday would be busy, too. The Thamavuongs had told her that the reason people kept coming back to the Big Donut was that the taste was welcoming and familiar.

Lan had thought that one could not get more familiar than exact copies from a replicator. The sprinkled donuts were identical down to the last sprinkle.

But the full racks of cold éclairs and maple bars didn't lie.

And then there was Markus. What was she going to do about him? When he woke up in the morning, he'd think this was a dream. A nightmare.

But, as Lan knew all too well, nightmares always return.

*   *   *

"Shizuka, Shizuka, Shizuka," Tremon chuckled. "You're still the Queen of Hell."

The two of them were at a French pâtisserie in Arcadia. Tremon sipped his coffee and tasted the mille-feuille. He put his fork down and applauded.

"This is wonderful. My compliments to the maître pâtissier."

"I'll tell him. And yes, he studied in Paris at Lenôtre." The server smiled and scurried away.

"And to you, Shizuka, as well. I doubt that *I* could have done better with her." He inhaled another bite of pastry. "So fresh, so sweet. Damning souls can be such thankless work. They plead, they curse—even though they swore they would do *anything* for fame."

Tremon pointed with his fork.

"But trust the Queen of Hell to find a grateful transgender runaway from an abusive home. Ha! Talk about paying your debts on the cheap."

Before Shizuka could reply, a spotless Asian man came out and greeted Tremon in fluent French. Tremon's eyes widened, and they had a long animated conversation, which ended with Tremon getting up from his chair and patting the chef on the back.

The pastry chef smiled and strode proudly away.

"With his skills, this man could be working in Europe," the

demon declared. "But I suppose it's like music. You can find gems in the most improbable places. You are quite the priceless gem yourself, remember?"

"Ah, Tremon, that was a long time ago."

He snorted. "Silly girl. Your music is timeless. The world will love to hear you play again."

For a moment, the Queen of Hell did not know what to say.

"So, shall we give her the bow and sign the deal? I believe we have more than enough to work with."

"I still have six months, Tremon," Shizuka said suddenly.

"Is there an issue?"

"Of course not. This is my soul we're discussing. But we have time. And besides, wouldn't you like a more polished product?"

Tremon looked like he was about to say something, then stopped himself.

"Shizuka . . . It's a shame that you had to be beautiful," he finally said.

"Tremon?"

He bowed, then got up and left.

Shizuka smiled uncomfortably. But her body shook, as if recovering from stage fright. What was going on? There was no problem. She had time. Katrina still had more to learn.

No.

Don't be stupid, Satomi. Tremon was right. This was business.

Hell, it was more than business. This was her soul at stake, her music, everything she was.

So why couldn't she just say yes?

She slowed her breathing, smelled the lovely coffee. Finally, the Queen of Hell felt steady enough to leave.

She asked for the check, but of course, Tremon had put everything on his tab.

* * *

Katrina stared at her screen.

In one night, her *Axxiom* video had over one thousand views. Now, in a week, her total views had gone over ten thousand.

She held a pillow to her face and screamed.

24

Edwin Tran and Windee Tran. It was such a cliché, but could twins be any more different? Windee was precocious, technical, brilliant. Lanny was training Windee to work the counter, tune the warp filaments, adjust the replicators; every day she seemed to be working on a different facet of operations. Even now, Floresta could see that Lanny envisioned her as a future command officer.

But Edwin had neither the aptitude nor interest for warp or replicator science. And although he was kindhearted and considerate, he struggled for words, leaving customers confused and compromising service efficiency. Thus, Lanny left Edwin to cleaning up and helping Floresta in what she felt were the nonessential activities of the kitchen.

Oh, that Lanny. The girl was a wonderful scientist and starship captain. But sometimes she forgot that this was not a starship.

There were essential differences between captaining a lone starship delivering a refugee family to a faraway planet and running a donut shop dedicated to bringing tasty treats to the people of El Monte. And these differences were beginning to hurt the shop, the crew, and most of all, Edwin.

Out of all the children, Floresta believed Edwin was born for making donuts. Sure, he was not the best with conversation. His mind was not as flashy as Windee's, and of course he couldn't match Markus's engineering prowess. But no one, not even Shirley, perceived what customers wanted the way Edwin did.

It was Edwin who suggested filling the front area with music, played not too loudly, but at a volume that would make customers feel welcome to sit down and have conversation. He suggested they move the drink refrigerator to the front of the counter, where it could be stocked with cold soda, sparkling water, and especially, old-fashioned dairy bottles of regular and chocolate milk.

"I notice that whenever they see the milk, the customers smile," he said. "So this way, they can be smiling sooner."

And beyond that, there was Edwin's sense of taste.

Why was one bakery full of lines and laughter, while another was empty? Why did one noodle house thrive, while another failed? Was it the processing? The equipment? What were the secrets?

Floresta had no answers until that day when she had spirited Edwin away and given him a bolillo roll. He replied that it tasted like home. When Floresta reminded him that they had come from across the galaxy on a starship, the boy shrugged.

"T-that's not what I mean. I'm not talking about *that* home. Just 'home.' A good bread tastes like home."

And that was it. The answer did not lie in any combination of someone else's secret recipes or ingredients—it was in the tastes not just of home, but of excitement, memory, love, belonging . . . What people truly hungered for.

If their donuts could evoke those feelings, then customers were sure to return.

With Edwin's help, Floresta had quietly and gradually created her first set of recipes. Eventually, Floresta would create ready-to-use mixes. But for now, she and Edwin combined the ingredients one at a time: water and yeast, then flour, then the oils, and other such things that premade mixes had.

Floresta monitored the warmth of the dough. As the dough began to rise, the kitchen began to fill with the intoxicating smell of yeast. The donuts had not even been fried yet, but already, Floresta's mouth began to water, and her mind began to think of a place that had long disappeared. It had been so sweet.

She waited for Edwin's signal before the dough was rolled, then cut, then proofed. And then she went to find the captain.

Edwin was cooling the first batch just as Aunty Floresta led the captain into the kitchen. Lan paused. The smell was different. She couldn't pinpoint how, but it was making her hungry.

"Lanny, try this."

Aunty Floresta motioned to Edwin, who gave her a donut.

The Alaska Donut—Starrgate's signature.

"We didn't glaze them yet, but you can try one now," Edwin said.

Lan took a bite. And another.

Lan had assumed the appeal of the donuts was to induce a need in her customers. And that the fall in sales meant their physiology was no longer being affected, either due to an error in the replicators or some defect in their physiology.

And another.

But this was no defect. And she had been wrong.

This donut's appeal was not physiological. It was deeper. She became filled with a warm, loving feeling. It was gentle. She thought of her mother, long ago, in her Star Patrol uniform.

Lan took another bite.

She didn't know how, but this Alaska Donut tasted like home.

* * *

It was 1 A.M. Tremon Philippe sat at his table, having an exquisitely steamed fish. The flesh was sweet and almost creamy, the ginger and scallions were a fragrant delight.

Who would have thought that a place like this could serve food like this? He gave a quiet apology for his remarks about dumplings and ducks. But of course it made sense, did it not? Exquisite French pastries served by Vietnamese, Cambodian donut shops, Hong Kong cafés everywhere. Here, as in Hell, so much had been shaped by politics and war, ambition and dreams of escape.

In fact, humans were more ruthless in all of these than demons. And more. Not that they knew it, of course.

If they could only perceive what they really were . . .

Tremon thought of Shizuka and the Hainan chicken at a pizza place. Shizuka loved to play with him, didn't she?

But it was always the brilliant ones who were least aware of their honesty.

Yes, Shizuka had found a special talent, but Shizuka Satomi's music was all over her. Maybe Shizuka herself didn't yet know it, but she had grown attached to this one. And already this was clouding her judgment.

Where does the music end and love begin? Not that a demon should have to answer that question. As far as Tremon was concerned, she had delivered six souls, and the seventh—her own handpicked selection, no less—was ready.

Anything beyond that was her problem, not his. He snorted. Yes, it was so sad that Shizuka had to be beautiful, going everywhere with those sunglasses on.

The world is much clearer when one looks like a toad.

Tremon had some fish with sweetened soy sauce. He had some without.

The student's soul, the teacher's soul . . . Did it really matter?

Eventually, a fish would be eaten.

AUGUST

25

"Markus, what's a dyke?"

"*What?*"

Markus was already in a terrible mood. Sometimes replicators had to be washed, but it was nothing compared to cleaning actual kitchen equipment. He'd suggested burning the grease off with a modified blaster, but the captain had said no.

Edwin pointed. "They said the captain was a dyke."

Markus walked out toward the front. Arlene Herrera had come in with her asshole boyfriend, Thinh Dinh, and his friends.

"I heard you've been saying shit about my mother," Markus said.

Asshole Boyfriend and his friends stopped joking. Two of them blocked the exit. One of them reached into his coat pocket.

"I'm in a bad mood right now, so don't fucking push me." Markus readied his shield and weapon.

Just then, Edwin walked between them.

"Markus, Mother would be really mad if she saw you use violence." He turned to Thinh. "It's okay to be homosexual. Homosexuality is nothing to be ashamed of."

"*Edwin!*" Markus snapped.

"But there's nothing wrong with being gay."

"Oh, fuck! Dude, seriously, your *mom?*" Arlene shook her head.

Thinh's friends started laughing.

"See! It ain't saying shit if it's true. Now, shut up and get me some of your shitty donuts," Thinh said.

"What kind would you like, sir?" Edwin said.

"No." Thinh gestured at Markus. "I want *him* to get them for me."

"Markus, he wants you to get him his donuts."

Markus glared. His father was a general of the Imperial Army.

"Markus, if you don't serve the customers, Mother will get mad."

"Hey! Are you retarded or something? Donuts!" Thinh said.

His friend opened the refrigerator and grabbed chocolate milks.

"I'm sorry, but you need to pay for those," Edwin said.

Thinh dropped a twenty on the counter.

They knocked over the trash can and disappeared.

"Wait, they forgot their change," Edwin said.

"Shut the fuck up, Edwin."

Markus looked out the window, and seemed about to go outside when his phone beeped.

"Hi Markus, this is Windee did you forget about our technical staff meeting? We're waaaaiting for you!"

Now that donuts were being made in the kitchen, the replicators could be devoted to completing the stargate. And, with the base construction accelerated, Windee was already running full simulations on the alignment algorithm.

The captain had suggested they would use tectonic faults to power the stargate, as this region of the planet seemed full of them. However, there had been difficulties.

"As before, our main obstacle is the unpredictable nature of the faults. They offer adequate power, *if* we can predict when the earthquakes will happen."

"Why can't we just synthesize antimatter?" Markus complained.

"The captain says we can't use antimatter," Windee said automatically.

"Antimatter is far too dangerous for this planet, Markus. You know that," Shirley said.

Markus shrugged. "That's not our fault."

"Markus," Shirley warned.

"I was making a joke—get it, fault?"

"Yes, I do," Shirley said, sounding unconvinced.

"Hey!" shouted Windee. "Maybe instead of passively gathering fault-line energy, we can actively initiate discharge using a modulated graviton pulse!"

"We're trying to *generate* power, not use more of it," said Markus.

Shirley paused. "So, Windee, your idea is to induce earthquakes, then instantly draw their power before they can damage the planet?"

"That's what I saaaid!"

"We would need to be certain of our calculations to avoid devastating the region. But the concept has promise. Can you continue your work?"

"Okay, Shirley!" Windee saluted and returned to her station.

"Markus, what's your progress on the modeling program?" Shirley said.

"It's going well. But I have a few improvements on the interface that I'd like to run by you. Might you take a look?"

Markus led Shirley to his workstation, where he pulled up a screen. Shirley frowned.

"Markus," she said quietly, "that's not the modeling interface."

Markus shook his head. "No. It's a communications net. I've been constructing it in my spare time. The work is almost complete, but I need our exact travel path to recalculate our proper timeline."

Shirley shook her head. "We're not supposed to contact our timeline. Mother gave us orders."

Markus continued as if he hadn't heard. "I've been plugging in approximate values, and I have narrowed the possible timelines. But I can't be sure which is the correct timeline without your help. You *must* have recorded the transit data, right?"

"Markus. Stop."

"So, you're saying you have the transit data but can't share it?"

"Markus, please focus on your assignment. I look forward to hearing of your progress at our next meeting," Shirley said. Then she disappeared.

Bitch.

Now Markus was convinced that his mother was keeping the co-ordinates hidden. She probably brainwashed Shirley into keeping the space-time variables secret, too.

Fuck! There had to be a way around the data block. But Shirley or the captain would detect any attempt to penetrate the ship's security.

Markus had everything he needed to communicate. But without the ship's space-time values, all he had was a radio with an infinite number of stations, and no way to know which signal was actually coming from home.

* * *

Windee Tran didn't know why she was so smart. She just was. The captain had asked her to realign the space-time filaments, which had been easy. Now she was modeling a tectonic profile for the graviton emitters. That was easy, too.

So now Windee was looking for something else to do.

Lately, she'd noticed Markus trying to back-calculate the navigation data. She assumed that the captain had asked him to. The captain probably thought she was too young. Windee tried not to laugh. Markus was a cool big brother, but his calculations could be slow and crude.

Luckily, Windee was a calculating whiz. And the math looked fun. So Windee went downstairs to her workstation and began defining her variables.

Two hours later, Windee Tran found Markus in the kitchen.

"Hi, Markus! How are you?"

"I am frying donut holes. How do you think I am?"

"What if I said I can find the values for the space-time variables?"

Markus froze. How did she even know what he was doing? Sometimes Windee could be even scarier than Shirley.

Markus shut the fryer down.

"Let me see."

Windee led Markus to her workstation and showed him the calculations. The issue was back-calculating the time signature of the proper continuum. But Windee had deduced that even though they were separate, they were still part of the same continuum; therefore, they could process the current space-time resonance through a transforming function and extract the discrete frequencies that made it up. In other words—the space-time variables.

Incredible.

No one else outside of Shirley could have done this. Markus could barely contain himself. "You are a genius!"

"Can I tell the captain?"

"Um . . . Let's finish our work first. And then we'll give her the surprise together!"

Windee beamed. "Sure thing, Markus."

"But right now, *shhh*. Keep it a surprise, okay?"

Windee saluted and went back into the donut.

As soon as she was gone, Markus dashed not to the kitchen, but to his workstation. He placed it into secure mode and retrieved

Windee's analysis. He was so excited that he could barely enter the data. The methodology was straightforward; the assumptions were sound.

And then, just like that, Markus had exact space-time variables and, with them, a direct connection to home.

And then Markus hurled his workstation to the floor.

"You're late," Shirley said as she heard the familiar footsteps behind her. It was the third time this week that Markus had been late for his shift.

"I know you're busy, but you're going to have to try harder to be on t—" Shirley stopped.

Her brother was in an Imperial battlesuit—with a combat side-arm.

"Markus? What are you doing?"

Her brother did not respond.

"Markus!"

Shirley activated the shop's defenses. All doors were locked, all customers were placed in stasis, and deflectors blocked the glass.

Markus pressed a button on his visor, and his form was bathed in a red light.

"Markus! Stop!" Shirley moved to intercept him, but it was too late. He reached for his weapon. With flash and a crackle, the deflectors were breached and the door lock was vaporized.

The door opened and closed.

Markus was gone.

Aunty Floresta rushed from the kitchen.

"What's going on—was that a blaster? Where's Markus?"

"Location unknown. He took the car, but he cloaked himself and the vehicle."

"Do your best to trace him—and keep scanning for energy." A standard-issue cloak would obscure normal activity, but any sort of teleportation, replication, or weapon discharge would cause a detectable surge.

"Where's the captain?"

"Mother is having dinner with Shizuka Satomi, but I sent her a Code Red. She's returning immediately."

"Good. Erase the memories of all the customers and let them go. Close the store—say we're doing inventory. Then keep scanning for any power surge."

And please, Aunty Floresta thought, *let it not be from a blaster.*

*   *   *

Thinh Dinh and his friends were hanging out in his uncle's furniture warehouse parking lot. His uncle didn't mind, as long as they didn't leave their cigarette butts, used rubbers, or broken bottles.

Later, some of them might go to Long Beach or Wilmington for the street races. For now, they were talking about whether or not the Lakers should draft another point guard.

Thinh looked up. Headlights. The engine sounded stock—a Toyota Corolla. Was this someone's relative? Despite the headlights pointed directly at him, he could make out someone getting out of the car.

"Oh *shit*. It's that donut gook."

"What's that shit he's wearing?"

"What the fuck are you doing here? Bringing us more donuts? *I said, what the fuck—*"

Before he could finish, the figure seemed to blur. Thinh felt something like a beanbag whip across his face.

"What did you call her?" a voice said calmly.

Thinh tried to get up. He couldn't see out of his left eye. He slipped. Wait? Blood . . . ?

"My mother. What did you call her?" The calm was chilling.

Thinh's friends froze. In one blow, half of their friend's face had been torn off its skull.

"What did you call her?" Markus asked again, bringing his foot down on Thinh Dinh's chest.

Thinh gasped.

Arlene Herrera had heard him gasp before. When he was hurt, when he was surprised, when he came. But she had never heard him make that noise. It was like someone stepping on a wet paper bag.

Markus approached Arlene. Despite himself, he smelled baby powder. The attraction made him want to vomit. Some inhabitants on this planet even thought the Earth was flat . . .

Arlene slapped him.

Markus slammed her back, hard, against a car. He looked at the human, and his face twisted as if smelling filth.

Dirty, primitive . . . hateful . . .

Animals.

He raised his blaster.

There was a flash and a crackle. It hurt so much. Arlene cried. There was burning. It hurt. It hurt . . .

Arlene Herrera's world faded to white.

"MARKUS!"

Lan materialized to see her son standing over the remains of two youngsters.

"Markus, get away from them! This is an order!"

"Do you *know* what they say about you?"

He pointed his weapon at the rest of Thinh's friends.

"Fuck this planet! We need to go home!"

The air filled with energy. But rather than a blaster, it sounded more like a gentle whoosh.

Aunty Floresta put her stabilizer down. Where Markus had stood was a grapefruit-sized sphere. Aunty Floresta picked it up and carefully placed it in a container. Then she retrieved Markus's weapon.

"I am so sorry," Aunty Floresta said to the dead. She adjusted the weapon settings and fired twice. All organic material, including everything these two people were, was completely and irrevocably vaporized.

Their families and friends would never find them.

Meanwhile, Lan assessed the survivors. They were still in shock from what they had seen. Lan quickly performed a complete mind wipe.

"Floresta, please erase all remaining traces of our presence," Lan said flatly.

The area briefly filled with a soft green glow.

"Complete, Captain."

The local police might be called. Since there were two missing persons, they would likely conduct an investigation. But with no physical evidence, and with no witnesses, there would be no way to trace what had happened back to Lan and her crew.

The two of them got into the family Corolla, activated their cloak, and disappeared into the night.

Once back at the shop, Lan asked to see Windee. Edwin held his twin sister's hand as she faced the captain.

"What did you do?"

Windee began to shake.

"Mom, he said he missed our father. So I found him."

"You found him? How? That's not possible without the space-time values."

"It wasn't that hard," Windee said, with a trace of defiance.

"Show me."

Nervously, Windee Tran showed her the same calculations that she had shown Markus. Lan looked at them and frowned. Windee was a genius. But she was also young.

"Mother, she made an error," Shirley said.

"She made several. Windee, your method doesn't account for an entire class of unknowns. Let me show you."

Lan added more terms to Windee's equations. Windee looked up in shock. She had no idea her mother could follow her work, let alone correct it.

"Windee, I led a study on this approach before you were born."

"Mother," Shirley interrupted, "please look at this. I accessed Markus's account. This is the alternate timeline he saw."

Lan viewed the screen in horror. In this alternate timeline, the Endplague had ravaged the Empire. There had been a war. Devastation. The Imperial Army had been decimated.

"But in our timeline, the Empire still stands," Shirley said.

Slowly, Windee began to realize what she had done. Due to her miscalculations, two beings had died. Markus was in stasis.

"I'm so sorry!" She collapsed to the floor.

Lan wished she could collapse, too. But unlike Windee, she was not a child.

"Edwin, please help your sister up and take her to her quarters."

Once they were gone, Lan turned to Shirley.

"Please limit Windee's computer access until I say otherwise."

"Yes, Mother. Will you be giving her additional discipline?"

"It depends upon her behavior, but probably not. Knowledge is often the worst punishment."

"Yes, Mother."

Lan turned to Aunty Floresta. "I'm sorry, Aunty. I should have told you about the link."

Floresta remembered how on some nights she could hear her niece sobbing in her quarters. Then, a few hours later, that girl would come out smiling, for yet another double shift.

Floresta shook her head.

"Lanny, you're the captain. Besides, there's nothing for me back there," she said. "Everything I love is right here, under the Big Donut."

26

Lan slumped on the old folding chair behind the shop. In the past, Mr. Thamavuong would sit in this chair when he came out to think and smoke. Although Lan did not smoke, she came to this place to think as well.

Lan held Markus's matrix. Everything her son was—every experience, every idea, every cell in his body—was here. From his first steps as a child, to his first days in the Academy, to the time he piloted a training ship. How proud he was that day! His laughter, his determination, his pride all lay in this grapefruit-like sphere.

But in this sphere was also an anger that had killed two people. Here was the helplessness, impatience, paranoia, aggression—everything that she despised and feared about the Endplague.

Markus could not remain on this planet. At this planet's current technological level, a being like Markus could endanger this entire world.

"Ah, Lanny, there you are," said Floresta. "I hope I'm not bothering."

"No, no. I was about to come back inside," Lan said.

Floresta saw what Lan was holding. "What are you going to do with Markus?"

"We have to send him back, even if the Empire is collapsing," Lan said. "At the very least, maybe he can die with his father . . ."

Floresta nodded, then frowned.

"But how?"

Good question. They were too far away to teleport. The main starship was now integrated with the donut shop itself, so using it was out of the question.

They *did* have the runabout. It was a fast, agile scouting craft, well suited to this sort of mission. However, as of now, the stargate still lacked the power to send even a runabout. Besides, with Markus in stasis, someone else would still need to pilot the ship to the Empire, and they could not afford to lose another crewmember.

But there was another option.

"We'll use a long-range probe," Captain Tran declared. "We'll place Markus in the instrument bay and send him back that way. The stargate has enough power for a probe."

"But won't the probe still need to be navigated?"

"Yes. We'll use Shirley. Since she's cybernetic, we can download her directly into the probe's guidance computer. We'll just need to upgrade the memory."

"If she goes, we'll be shorthanded at Starrgate."

"Not if we duplicate her."

Aunty Floresta blinked.

"Lanny, have you asked her?"

"No. Why?"

"Don't you think she would want to be asked?"

"Shirley is a program I created. To be honest, I should have been making backups this entire time."

Floresta said nothing as the two of them returned to the shop.

"Shirley?"

Shirley appeared immediately. "Yes, Mother?"

"Prepare yourself for duplication."

"Mother?"

"We need to return Markus to the Empire, so we are uploading your code into a long-range probe. We're keeping a copy of you here to continue your duties at Starrgate. But archive your program first. You're quite complex, so we need to safeguard against errors. Also, we'll need to add an autodestruct routine should you fall into the hands of Imperial Intelligence. We don't want them being able to trace your data back to us."

"Mother?" Shirley said again, as if not quite comprehending what was being asked.

But Lan was already onto the next phase of her plan.

"Floresta, have Windee start readying a probe for the mission. Working will help Windee heal. And let Edwin help where he can. And Shirley—

"Shirley?"

"I—I'm sorry, Mother."

Shirley flickered, then disappeared.

* * *

Shizuka marveled at how Katrina created videos. Her songs might be from an anime, or a game. Katrina recorded. She experimented with orchestration. She changed rosins, strings, even the length of her fingernails.

She made mistakes. She would cry. She would stop crying. She would try again.

And then, Katrina would upload the video, and within a week, one, two, five thousand people would watch it.

Shizuka and Katrina scrolled through the latest comments:

"Something in your music makes me feel like things will be ok."

"No words . . . How you played this song . . . it's just perfect."

"I can come to my computer after an argument, listen to this song and instantly let it go."

"I don't know where to begin. No exaggeration, your violin is life."

In all her playing career, who had ever told Shizuka that? Any of her other students would right now be bursting with celebration.

In the past, a solo violinist's path had been simple. Compete, win prizes, meet wealthy benefactors, record a studio LP with Deutsche Grammophon, tour the world. Shizuka's previous student, Yifeng Zheng, had begun to utilize the Internet, but he spoke of using it to build a "platform" to unite his fans, to inform them about concerts, and share images and teasers—all to help his career.

But now? The Internet could *be* the career. Here were not just videos of performances, but instructional videos, maintenance and repair tips, instrument reviews.

Someone discussed common left-hand errors. Someone raved about a new line of rhinestone tailpieces. Some strange little man compared thirty different brands and lines of strings by playing the same piece on the same violin over and over. This is Pirastro Piranito. This is Thomastik-Infeld Red. This is Thomastik-Infeld Blue.

Today Katrina was showing Miss Satomi her improved tundra setting.

"I can't believe you programmed this. It's like a holodeck."

"Holodeck? Do you mean like a VRMMORPG?"

Miss Satomi rolled her eyes. "VR MM-*what*? It's just *Star Trek*! Doesn't anyone watch *Star Trek* anymore? I swear—"

She froze.

"Katrina—did you hear that?"

"What?"

Katrina couldn't hear anything at first. And then . . . someone seemed to be . . . crying?

"End program!" Katrina shouted.

The snowscape faded, and in front of them was what looked like a small shivering doll.

"Shirley?"

Her image was unsteady, fluttering in and out of focus.

"Help. May I come over?"

"Of course!"

Shirley flickered, and the glow from the projector briefly intensified, becoming almost too bright to look at.

When the glow faded, Shirley was sitting in front of them at normal size.

"I'm sorry!" She rocked back and forth.

"Did something happen at home?" Alarmed, Shizuka took out her phone. The girl looked terrified. What happened? A robbery? What about Lan? Was she safe?

Then a gentle, but firm hand stopped her.

"Miss Satomi, she's running away from home."

Katrina sat down next to Shirley. Slowly at first, then in a mumbling singsong, Shirley told them all that had happened with Markus, and all that happened after.

"So, when I refused to be duplicated, Mother sent me a message. Said . . . my data is corrupt. Needed . . . to install a destruct code."

Shizuka wanted to believe that this was a misunderstanding. Duplicating a child? Adding a destruct code? Even for an agent of Hell, who had delivered souls to damnation, some truths were difficult to accept.

But Shizuka Satomi had known far too many parents to dismiss what she heard.

"Katrina, make her comfortable."

"You're not going to call Shirley's mother, are you?"

Shirley shook her head and curled up even tighter.

"Of course not. I am simply going to inform Astrid that we have a guest."

"Thank you, Miss Satomi," Katrina said.

Miss Satomi left.

Katrina looked about the studio and frowned.

Shirley did not even have an escape bag.

* * *

"Be careful around the neck block."

"Okay . . ." Andrew hesitated. He started to tap. Nothing. A little harder. Still nothing?

"Andrew, careful means watch what you are doing. Careful does not mean be indecisive. Here—"

The two of them worked together through the afternoon, and for some time after. Finally, his mother stood and stretched.

"I think that's enough for today. You have homework to do."

Andrew looked outside. When had the streetlights come on?

"Shall we grab dinner on the way home?"

"I am going to stay a bit longer," she said in a peculiar voice.

Of course. The Satomi Guarneri.

"Good night, Mom."

"Oh, and save your money. There's lasagna in the freezer."

"Okay. I'll warm enough for when you get home."

Lucy gave a thumbs-up as he left. Then she rubbed her eyes. It was time to work.

The Satomi Guarneri. The f-holes were a little crude, which was typical for a Guarneri.

But the bouts had an unexpected grace.

And there, the bend of the scroll was just a little more lyrical than it needed to be.

These weren't discrepancies most people would notice, but their presence was undeniable. Was del Gesù feeling flirtatious?

That wasn't like del Gesù at all.

Was this a forgery, then? No. If the violin were a fake, Shizuka Satomi would have noticed the moment she played it. Besides, all the signs of a classic Guarneri were there. They were just . . . different.

No wonder Shizuka Satomi had asked about the client notes.

Lucy walked around the back of the counter, where the old cash register had been. She retrieved an old wooden box, which had held their client notes for two and a half generations. Here were entries in her writing, in her father's hand, and in her grandfather's before that. Here were entries for some private school programs, and even a few public schools, from when public schools had music departments. Here were all of Mr. Zacatecas's repairs—Lucy could almost smell the beer. And Ellen Seidel, who sometimes visited the shop when she didn't feel like primping for Grunfeld's.

And Shizuka Satomi's records would be right . . .

She frowned.

She searched again. And again.

How could the shop have lost *Shizuka Satomi's* records? Had the store simply neglected to keep them? *Impossible!* Lucy probed further. She stopped.

The Queen of Hell was not the only client who was missing. Other entries were missing as well. Some of their photos even now were hanging on the wall.

All of them? Shizuka Satomi had asked.

Lucy felt stupid, embarrassed, humiliated. How could she have taken that attitude with Shizuka Satomi, when she did not even know her own store?

Helplessly, Lucy looked about the store at the many photos of her grandfather and father. The father and son.

Yes, yes, Matía and Sons, Matía and *Sons*.

But why didn't they pass along their notes? Did they not feel she was worthy? Fair enough. She'd even cast her vote to make it unanimous.

But this wasn't about worthy. This was about *legacy*.

If she didn't have their notes—what could she pass on? How could she safeguard their legacy if she did not know what their legacy *was*?

She had given her life to this family, this store! But now, without their history, their notes, their wisdom, it was all for *nothing*.

She glared at Catalin Matía's portrait, gazing so proudly out over the workshop. But now, rather than her usual awe, she felt herself fill with a newfound rage.

"You would betray our family just because I am not a son? *How dare you destroy the Matías!*"

Lucy rushed across the store and reached up and pulled Catalin's portrait from the wall. Years of dust fell from the portrait onto her hair, her face, into her eyes.

But she gave none of it any notice.

For behind the portrait was an alcove.

And in the alcove were the missing notes and records of the Matías.

For a long while, Lucy sat at the workbench. After all her talk of legacy, here it was . . . the voices of years, decades, generations, in these notebooks, all resting in front of her now.

With trembling hands, Lucy reached for the first notebook.

Almost immediately, she found an entry for Shizuka Satomi—and there, in a list of her instruments was

```
Maker: ex. Giuseppe Guarneri, del Gesù
(Katarina Guarneria) c. 1742
```

Katarina Guarneria?

Of *course*. Suddenly, the Satomi Guarneri made sense.

Katarina was del Gesù's wife. She helped him in the shop, and as the master faded, she completed, and even built, many Guarneri violins on her own. But throughout history, many of those instruments had their labels removed or altered, because no one would buy a violin made by a woman.

Lucy picked up the violin and examined it more closely. Yes, it was easy to miss, if one were not specifically looking for it, but indeed, this label had been altered.

Someone had tried to erase the maker from history.

But then Lucy put the Guarneri down. What had seemed so important was now an afterthought.

For that had merely been the first notebook. Here were entries in her father's hand, her grandfather's hand, and in older hands she did not recognize. Her great-grandfather? What was his name? Yes. *Antonio.*

These notebooks held not only records of maintenance and repairs, but of provenance, ownership, and more.

Lucy read another notebook. And another.

When she finished, Lucy sat down, listening to her heart. The sound was as if something dead and mortal had finally been shaved away.

* * *

Not the Sort of Thing for Little Girls

"No, no, luce mia. This is not the sort of thing for little girls."

Those had been her grandfather's words, spoken each evening as the sun went down. Lucy had grown up with those words, ferrying her home before the stars came out. She had grown up with those words . . . that let her father in, let her brothers in, leaving her alone with two hands and nothing to hold.

Even a child could hate those words.

But on this night, she had fallen asleep unnoticed. And rather than her grandfather's words, she woke to darkness and the jingle of the front doorbell.

How late was it? She peered out the window; her father was walking home.

She grabbed her coat and was ready to chase after him when she noticed the door to the workshop was ajar. And on the other side was the back of her grandfather, hunched over his workbench, immersed in what was before him.

"Ah, after all my son gave you," she heard him say. "You still disobey."

He said it in a curious singsong, like a parent admonishing a mischievous child. But it was not quite a child.

He took out his chisel and held it over the wood. She had seen him use a similar tool before, but this he held almost like a weapon?

"Now, we shall behave?"

The workbench light seemed to flicker, making the violin appear to twist and squirm beneath him.

Then Lucy heard a strange music unlike any before. It wasn't that it was beautiful. She had heard plenty of beautiful music. But this made her heart race, and her body eager and jittery, like it did when she held a sharp knife or a box of matches, or walked over a bridge and wondered how it would feel to jump.

The voice blended with the sound of her heartbeat, in time with her breathing. She moved closer. Closer, until she could smell the varnish and the wood. It smelled like flowers. It smelled like blood.

"Lucy, no!"

Her grandfather threw a cover over the violin. He gently but firmly led her toward the door. But Lucy resisted.

"Grandpa, I want to hear more—"

She reached to pull the cover off the violin.

She wanted to see it; she wanted to hear it sing.

"Get out now!" she heard.

And then she felt a sharp slap across her face.

In shock, she ran away crying, and slammed the workshop door behind her.

Not long after, Catalin Matía had found her curled in a corner next to the violas. He wiped her tears with his handkerchief.

"I'm sorry," he said.

That night, he walked her to the Big Donut and bought her a Bavarian Chocolate with sprinkles. He said he'd buy her hot chocolate if she would promise to forget what happened that night.

"Lucy, do not ever come in there again. Do you understand?"

"Yes, Grandpa."

"Luce mia, I know it's not easy to understand. But this is not the sort of thing for little girls."

*   *   *

One does not simply break a cursed violin.

Actually, yes, they do.

Cursed violins are more common than one might imagine. The details vary, but most follow a typical pattern of notoriety: the violin is stolen, someone kills for it, dies for it, pulls it from a grave, bathes it in blood.

Not surprisingly, their owners tend to keep quiet. Thus, cursed violins rarely receive regular maintenance. More than a few have been ruined, not by Hell's Infernal Forces, but by being played without a sound post or with a backward bridge.

Even worse, most every player of a cursed instrument seems compelled to flaunt their anguish like a cheap Paganini understudy—

snapping a string, spewing various bodily fluids, playing drugged or drunk, lurching like a contortionist.

And if a player cracks the pegbox while playing because he absolutely *had* to writhe as if possessed by Mozart's illegitimate child, what then?

People willing and equipped to repair such violins didn't advertise openly. Such business was conducted quietly, through word of mouth.

The Matías had done this work for generations. And they were paid very well. But curses are, well, curses, with all the danger and unsavoriness that the term implies.

Thus, Catalin and Francisco Matía had only worked on these particular violins late at night, or early in the morning, when a pretty little girl like Lucy was safely tucked in bed.

Here was the legacy of the Matías. And not only the client notebook—others even older, full of special techniques and recipes, with lists of tools and incantations passed unbroken through time.

Just then, the doorbell jingled.

"The lights were on, so I decided to drop in."

She looked up to see who had entered. For a second, he looked like a toad.

27

"Lucía Matía. My name is Tremon Philippe. I noticed that you are open for business."

Tremon Philippe. A black-and-white photo of him was on the wall.

"This . . . San Gabriel Valley . . . is interesting. In this seemingly ordinary place are two people who are very important to me: the Queen of Hell and you."

"What?"

"Rumors suggested that you might be closing the shop."

"I suppose word gets around. But no, I'm not closing. However, I had been planning to limit our work to student violins . . . at least until Andrew might make the shop worthy of its name."

Tremon looked at her workbench. "Yet *that* is no student violin."

Lucy shrugged helplessly. "Shizuka Satomi decided before I could say no."

"That's her in a nutshell, isn't it? So, her del Gesù. What do you think of it?"

Lucy was about to say something diplomatic when a strange energy came over her.

"Aesthetically, del Gesùs aren't to my liking. They're not as refined as, as . . ."

"As a Stradivarius, or perhaps an Amati?"

"Well, to be honest . . ."

"Hmm?"

"But the tone *is* powerful and rich," she said, trying to recover. Who was she to criticize a freaking del Gesù?

But Tremon Philippe chuckled. "I would expect nothing less from a Matía."

"Thank you," Lucy said to the demon, because that was what he was.

"You're welcome, Lucía." He smiled. Lucía Matía suppressed

a shudder. She would not want to be on the other side of those teeth.

"So, how may I help you?" she said, trying not to sound at all nervous.

"Help? Oh, no, no, *no*. I simply dropped by to greet the new master. Of course, we *will* be in touch—since many of your clients are mine as well."

And then the demon was gone.

* * *

The NetherTale offered a scenario where a player would rescue people from Hell—yet not hurt anyone at all.

Might one live that way?

Until recently, Shizuka would have dismissed the suggestion as naïve, a fantasy of the weak and sheltered, those who had never fought or known loss.

But nothing in Katrina's background suggested she was weak or sheltered. As for loss? Her music did not lie. She was fighting with an abandon that only *came* from loss.

But there Katrina had been in Temple City. And there was Katrina downstairs now. Refusing to kill.

Trying to set another trapped soul free.

"Miss Satomi?"

"Yes, Astrid?"

"Lan Tran is at the door," Astrid said quietly. "Shall I bring her in?"

"No," Shizuka said. She fetched her coat and purse. "I'll meet her outside."

"Shizuka, I know Shirley is here," Lan said.

"Of course you do."

Shizuka walked past her and grabbed Lan's hand. By the time Lan recovered, Shizuka had already led her to her car.

"Shizuka, I need to see Shirley now."

"Lan, I've not had morning tea. Come with? Astrid will let me know if anything happens."

"But—"

"Lan." A flash seemed to come from behind Shizuka's sunglasses. "Let's go."

"Let's go," Lan repeated as if charmed.

Shirley heard Miss Satomi's Jaguar leave the driveway.

"Your mother is not coming in, Shirley," Katrina said.

"But she'll be back. And that will be the end of me." That was simple fact. Being a program, she literally could not separate herself from Starrgate's systems.

Why had she even tried to escape? How stupid could she be? How defective.

"Miss Satomi won't let that happen," Katrina said. "We'll keep you safe."

"*Safe?* I'm not even *real*. I'm an application, a utility. My mother asked me to create a duplicate of myself, and to add an autodestruct routine. But I just . . . could not . . ."

And there it was. The inability to obey a direct order was a terminal malfunction. If anything proved she was defective, it was that.

"Shirley?"

"It's fine. I am sure my mother can create another maintenance program—one that obeys her and doesn't cause trouble."

Shirley was so tired. Even now she felt part of herself protesting, trying to stay alive. Alive? What a silly illusion. But soon the burden would be gone.

"I'm sorry, since I don't have an autodestruct, I will need to do this manually. Please tell my mother to reinitialize and purge the projector buffers.

"Katrina, please be good to yourself."

And then Shirley's figure disappeared.

"Shirley!"

What to say? Miss Satomi would probably know what to say. Miss Satomi always knew what to say.

"Shirley, *please*! You said you loved my music, right?"

As soon as she said this, Katrina knew this was the stupidest, most cliché thing she could say. But somehow it worked. At least a little bit. The projector light flickered.

"Interrogative . . . yes. If my . . . reactions made you happy, that is good . . . but . . . they most likely come from algorithms that . . . Mother . . . programmed in the first place."

She was in there, still in there. And Katrina was not going to let her go.

"Shirley, stop. *Listen to me.*"

Stop. Listen.

Shirley paused. Did Katrina know she had just given Shirley two core commands? Yes, she was flawed, defective. But Katrina, the system operator of this studio, had given her core commands. Any program—defective or not—should honor core commands from the system operator.

If anything, she was still a program, right?

The glow from the projector grew steady, and Shirley's figure reappeared.

"Awaiting input," Shirley managed to say.

Katrina picked up her violin.

"Aubergine, let's do this," she said to her voice. *Let's save Shirley.*

To start, Katrina chose a song from a peaceful anime about a robot, a flightless bird, and a young boy who designed steam engines. Each had been alone, but they found each other and discovered that they lived in a beautiful world.

If Miss Satomi said that her music could take the listener somewhere else, she would take Shirley to a place where she could feel valid and worthwhile. Shirley so deserved such a place. Even if she had never known such a thing herself, she could give this piece, and this peace, to Shirley.

All she needed to do was play.

But as Katrina played, there was her father stopping the car in the middle of the road, screaming that she was a cocksucker.

Her friends using her old name.

Her ex-lover calling her a half-woman freak.

No! Not now!

She tried to focus on Shirley, but again and again, she drifted into her own world, into memories where she felt drowned and silenced.

Aubergine sailed, wailed. The notes glided. Bent. Lamented. Screeched. Cursed.

Katrina thought of all the nights that she felt certain she would die alone, with no one to care and a million things left unsaid.

Even Miss Satomi didn't know how difficult it was when you didn't feel real. Even Miss Satomi didn't know how it felt when the only real thing genuine about you was the hurt your existence caused.

Shirley felt herself generating tears.

They were surely from her mother's subroutines, based on the reactions of others to this music. To verify, she searched her databanks to retrieve information on its composer. She paused. She checked again.

It was not a game song. Not an anime song. Not part of the classical repertoire.

There was no prior data on this piece, at all.

Katrina was *improvising*?

But if that was true, what program was making her weep? This was defect. This was error. This was why she had to self-destruct. She should not be feeling this. She wasn't real.

But she could not escape the music. The despair. The hopelessness she shared as well.

Shared?

Shirley had been listening so deeply that she had lost track of Katrina. But if she was going through this now, then . . .

"Katrina!"

But Katrina didn't respond. Her eyes were shut tight, her lips were trembling, her legs were shaking.

Yet, through it all, she kept playing. Katrina and her faithful violin never wavered, never blinked. And her hands were steady, her posture perfect.

It reminded Shirley of every morning at the donut shop, saluting her mother, even as she knew that her mother would not look her in the eye.

*   *   *

"Another red light?" Lan muttered impatiently.

"They happen." Lan's exceptional willpower was already fighting off Shizuka's charm.

Shizuka let Lan free herself on her own. That way, she'd not notice she had been controlled—she'd just feel a little foggy.

Lan fidgeted and looked to the other lane, but there was another Toyota, going even slower.

"I need to get Shirley home."

"I understand. But you promised you'd get tea with me, didn't you?"

Lan turned red. She had no idea why she had done so, but she *had* promised.

"Very well, but let's be brief."

Shizuka glanced at Lan. She looked every bit the starship captain who had brought a family across a galaxy. But now they were in Alhambra. And maybe being a starship captain was not the best thing to be.

They pulled into the Teatopia parking lot and walked inside. Shizuka ordered her Hokkaido cream milk tea. Lan asked for a simple iced jasmine.

"What size?"

"Small."

"Make it a large," Shizuka countermanded. "And an order of tea eggs."

"Shizuka—"

"They are going to be okay. They're good girls."

Shizuka found a quiet table away from the front door.

"Lan, set your phone to Korean, then put it down. They'll be fine."

Lan shook her head. "You don't understand. Shirley disobeyed a direct order."

"Sounds like a normal teenager."

The server brought their drinks. Shizuka sipped her Hokkaido cream tea.

"The trick with Hokkaido cream tea is not to stir. Just let the tea layer pass through the creamy layer and feel the flavors mix in your mouth."

"Shirley is *not* normal. Which is why I need to duplicate her to take Markus home."

"She told me something to that effect," Shizuka said.

"Then you know why I need to run diagnostics on her at once, to isolate the error and verify the rest of her is not defective. Also, I need to install a subroutine to make sure that I can override her code."

"Override?"

"I need her to obey me *now*," said Lan. "Markus has already killed two humans. I need to get him away from here. Yes, I know that I am covering his crime and helping him escape, but Markus is my *son*."

"And Shirley is your *daughter*."

"Shirley is *not* my daughter. Shirley Tran is dead."

Shizuka almost spilled her drink.

"What did you say?"

"Before I made donuts, before I was even a starship captain, I was a lead scientist for the Empire—that's where I met their father. We fell in love; we conceived our first child."

Shizuka squinted. Okay. But what did that have to do with anything?

"But from Shirley's conception, there were complications. We realized that Shirley would be nonviable. But then I realized that since her brain had not fully developed, her neural network might be simple enough for me to model. And so I decided to map her brain and imprint it into the computer.

"And then Shirley passed away."

Lan took a deep breath, then continued.

"The Shirley program senses, responds, grows. It handles most donut shop maintenance. And it's expanded to become an incredibly helpful assistant.

"But the Shirley program is also needed to navigate this journey. You see, we currently have only enough power to send a repurposed probe. And since Markus is in stasis, we can maximize its range by removing life support.

"We'll copy her data so we can continue running the donut shop without loss of staffing. But due to these developments, we must need to give the program a thorough diagnostic and delete any defects we find."

Shizuka thought back to the quivering girl in the studio.

"You would turn her into data . . . and keep her in a tiny probe . . . with no life support . . . alone?"

"Of course you would have this reaction. This is why such procedures are banned in the Empire. But please understand, Shirley is just a program, and a defective one at that."

"You keep saying she's defective. Why?"

"She's not supposed to disobey me like that!"

"Children disobey!"

"She's *not* a child!" Lan accidentally knocked her phone off the table.

The café stopped at the disturbance. Shizuka waited until Lan picked up her phone and set it back on the table.

"She's not a child," Lan repeated.

"Okay, Lan, have it your way. Let's say she's just data. Why stop at one copy? Make three. Make three hundred. Have all the Shirleys you want. Replicate her like a donut."

"That's different!"

"Oh, yes. Your replicated donuts didn't sell, did they? Funny, that. Your technology couldn't even copy a donut, and now you're saying you'll copy Shirley?"

Lan's shoulders slumped. Shizuka had a point.

"Besides, her code, as you call it, has changed and grown," Shizuka continued. "What would the correct code look like now? How would you know which changes are defects and which changes are Shirley?"

"It . . . would be difficult," Lan finally admitted.

Shizuka shrugged.

"Lan, I am not going to judge your decision to create her. Most parents have children without thinking the matter through. And yes, you had a daughter named Shirley who was stillborn. But *this* Shirley . . . Did you even notice? Out of all your children, she's the only one who *always* calls you Mother?"

Lan finished her jasmine tea and reached for a tea egg.

"You're not taking me back to your house, are you?" she said quietly.

"No. After we're done, I am taking you back to your shop. And I ask that you please consider your actions more deeply."

Lan took a deep breath and nodded. "I know you were never a mother. But you would have been a good one."

Shizuka sipped her Hokkaido cream tea, but all the tea was gone. The wonderful layer of Hokkaido cream that she had so meticulously sipped through now sat at the bottom of the glass, a treasure too rich to be tasted alone.

* * *

Katrina turned and tossed and opened her eyes. Had she fallen asleep in the studio?

Wait.

There were no ceilings. There were no floors.

Instead, she was afloat, in a radiant fugue of stars, of galaxies. Yet the air was warm and smelled of powdered sugar. There were shooting stars and giant ships that sounded like buses that glowed like rainbows that bloomed like flowers, that took flight like wisps of smoke, like birds. And everything seemed to be dancing, and giggling, walking hand in hand as if in a summer festival that stretched as far as Katrina could see.

"Shirley?"

Katrina looked right in front of her and saw Shirley, clothed in a veil of glow with all the color and immediacy of time.

Hologram or not, Shirley was asleep. Was this how holograms dreamed?

Shirley drifted in the center of creation, as galaxies brushed past the palm of her hand. Gradually, a most beautiful music drifted and coalesced above her.

The new figure took Katrina's breath away. Then she blushed, as she realized it was her own idealized image.

Wait. She looked closely.

That image . . . was just *her*. Her skin and hair. Her eyes. Her shoulders. Her hands.

Shirley was dreaming of her . . . just the way she was?

"Katrina?" the dreaming Shirley called out from among the stars.

"Yes?" the figure said.

"Please play your music again for me."

* * *

The workbench. The vise. Even the lamps that illuminated the workbench that her father and grandfather had sat on.

By night, they seemed so different. Lucy could smell the same woods, spruce and maple, old and new. But now the bite of the varnish, the heavy musk of the hide glue seemed to hover between the sacred and damned.

And the files, the saws and chisels. The little spool clamps and shiny brass finger planes. The ancient scraper her grandfather had made from an old sardine can.

They were more than tools. They were weapons. Weapons, all.

The doorbell jingled. A thin, fidgety man entered the store. In his hands, he held what appeared to be a violin in an old burlap bag.

"I—I was told you take special orders?"

"Yes, we do," she said.

* * *

Three nights after they had visited Teatopia, Shizuka's phone rang. Shizuka looked at her clock. It was 3 A.M.

"Hello? How is Shirley?"

Lan sounded as if she had been deep in thought.

"She's sleeping now."

"I would not like to see imperfect copies of myself, either."

"Thank you, Lan."

"May I come over to speak with her? We need her at the donut shop," Lan paused. "Just the donut shop."

"You may come tomorrow after breakfast. As I said, she's sleeping."

There was a pause on the other end.

"I see. I'm glad she's getting her sleep. I will be there in the morning."

Shizuka put her phone down. Lan had a daughter who loved her. And this time next year, that daughter would still be here.

The Queen of Hell listened to the air conditioner, its gentle whir resounding through the house. Outside, there would be jasmine; the summer was ripe and full.

Tomorrow morning, Astrid would bring her fresh sliced peaches, or maybe plums from the Lieus. Astrid would say something cheerful, would try to smile.

But of course, both of them knew.

It was no longer February, nor even April. It was summer, and then it would be fall. And soon Shizuka would have to harvest Katrina Nguyen's soul.

28

When Shizuka woke the next day, Katrina was in the shower. Astrid was making breakfast.

And the girl who thought she was defective was still asleep in the recording studio.

Shizuka took a deep breath and faced her mirror. She kept the makeup very light, and wore only the slightest hint of lipstick. She took a little extra time to make her hair look like she had not taken too much time. Just stay natural.

Natural did not come easily to Shizuka. But these poor kids had never had a home to relax in. She chose a simple, soft linen dress. She looked herself over and nodded seriously.

Soon she could hear Astrid setting the table downstairs.

And then she could hear Katrina and Shirley. They were arguing like two sisters should.

Good, fresh eggs have a smell. Katrina couldn't name it, but the aroma seemed golden. Luxurious, rich, almost absurdly so.

"They just came from next door." Astrid smiled.

"I'll never get mad at the chickens again! Oh my god, this is so wonderf—" Katrina looked at Shirley. "Um, do you mind that I'm eating?"

"Are you bothered that I do not eat?"

"Well . . . this egg *is* really yummy."

"I don't require food, but I can taste it if you'd like. After all, I work in a donut shop."

Shirley took Katrina's fork, and dipped it into the egg, and brought it to her lips.

"Nice mouthfeel. Creamy. Not at all like the eggs that one might buy at the store. I assume this chicken ate worms in the garden."

Shirley tasted again.

"Yes. These eggs. Definitely worms," she said before passing the fork back to Katrina.

Katrina was about to say something rude. But then Miss Satomi entered the room.

"Good morning. How are we doing?"

"Miss Satomi! I hope you don't mind. I brought the projector here so Shirley could join us."

Shirley immediately stood up and bowed. "Ma'am, I am sorry for the trouble I caused."

But Shizuka Satomi put up her hand and smiled.

"Stop that. There's nothing wrong with being a runaway. We've all been there, right, Katrina?"

"Yes, Miss Satomi."

Shirley tried to speak and failed. Was this the woman who was called the Queen of Hell? She seemed so . . . relaxed.

"Miss Satomi, so you spoke to Shirley's mother?" Katrina asked.

Shirley stiffened, but she felt Katrina quickly latch on to her hand.

"Miss Satomi will protect you," Katrina said. "Right?"

Shizuka nodded casually. At least she could be truthful here.

"Your mother thought it over. She wants you back at the donut shop. *Only* the donut shop." Shizuka made sure to emphasize the last point.

"What about Markus?" Shirley ventured.

"Markus will remain in stasis until there is a better solution. But of immediate concern is Windee, who is now working in the kitchen. Lan said that you'd understand."

"Windee is trying to make donuts?"

"Apparently so."

"Thank you. I will prepare for transfer now."

"Your preparations can wait for one last story."

"Miss Satomi?"

Shizuka cut into a sausage.

"Once, in Budapest, I broke strings on my instrument, then the concertmaster's Bergonzi. Finally, I grabbed someone's viola and continued with that. The papers called my performance magnificent."

"Of course it was!" Astrid said.

"Really? I thought I had failed. All I wanted was to finish

without breaking another string and get off the stage. I had no idea of what the audience might be seeing. So whose experience was real?"

Shirley shifted uncomfortably. What did this have to do with her?

But the Queen of Hell seemed to read her mind. "You might ask what this has to do with you. Shirley, you can't control how people see you. All you can do is accept it, right?"

Really?

Miss Satomi had seemed wise. But accepting how others saw you—as nice as that sounded—was wrong. For example, Katrina's family insisted that she was a boy . . .

And why should Shirley accept what her mother thought of her?

"But what if their views don't match what you know is true?" Shirley said, disappointedly.

"Well, if you feel *that* strongly about your truth, then there is no reason to worry about your existence, is there?"

Shirley paused, processing what Miss Satomi had said.

"Shirley, I am telling you this because I don't trust people. When you go back to the shop, your family may still see you as a program. In fact, I think they will, I'm sorry to say. So when they do, remember what you just said."

"Thank you, Miss Satomi."

"Of course," Shizuka said. "By the way, how are the eggs?"

"Tell her about the worms, Shirley," Katrina deadpanned, just as Shizuka took her first bite.

Not long after they finished, there was a green flash in the living room.

Today Lan looked less like a mother and more like a commander. Her hair, her appearance, was crisp, creased. Pressed.

Shizuka could not stop looking. Oh, she did clean up well, didn't she?

"Shirley."

Shirley saluted.

"Mother. I apologize for disobeying your orders."

"No. I should have listened . . . more carefully to your grievance. In the end, I was brought to my senses." She glanced at Shizuka. "So I am now rescinding my order."

"Thank you, Mother."

"So, shall we return to the donut shop?" Her shoulders slumped slightly. "Windee does not seem to know the difference between baking powder and powdered sugar. So, let's go home before Aunty Floresta kills her."

"Is that a joke?"

"It's a figure of speech they use here."

"These people can be strange sometimes."

"Strange is putting it mildly."

Shizuka coughed.

Lan glanced at Shizuka, and remembered their conversation.

"And, Shirley, we all miss you. I miss you."

"Then, Mother, I will meet you back home."

Then she turned to Katrina. "See you later?"

"Yes," Katrina said.

The projector flickered, and Shirley disappeared.

Lan turned to Shizuka and bowed. "I am sorry for the trouble that I have caused."

Shizuka felt a little flutter—Lan really did look great in a uniform. She then saluted and disappeared in a green flash.

Shizuka and Katrina stood there in the living room.

"You're blushing," Katrina said.

"No I'm not," Shizuka replied.

*   *   *

Lanny had ordered Windee off of the computers and into the donut shop. She wanted Windee to learn some patience. She suggested it might even be fun.

How was any of this fun?

"Aunty! Heeelp!" Windee was caked in donut mix.

"You can't mix that way. You need to be patient."

"I *aaam* patient! How much time does it need?"

Seriously, the girl had no feel for this.

However, Starrgate was finally cooking donuts! Compared with replication, the task might seem daunting, but operating the kitchen was no more difficult than maintaining a starship engine room.

With their first batch, all talk of replicators and reference donuts had ceased. People started visiting the Starrgate not for the Big Donut, nor the kitsch, nor even a try at the vintage *Stargate* machines, but for the amazing donuts.

Were they adding steamed bun flour to the donut mix? Maybe they were adding butter? One rumor was that they added a little mayonnaise to the mix to keep the donut moist. Another suggested they brushed their old-fashioneds with just a little cider vinegar to bring out the sweetness.

Floresta smiled. These sorts of rumors were good for business. And some of them were even true.

Yes, Floresta was using steamed bun flour. But she also reduced the gravity in the proofing box for added fluffiness. She genetically modified domestic and wild yeast DNA to create a strain that worked faster, while producing optimum flavor, texture, and aroma. She installed lasers in the ovens; a twelve-microsecond burst gave cake donuts the perfect crunch around the edges, as well as creating a lattice of nanoperforations that let in just the right amount of hot coffee.

And then there was an amazing substance she had discovered on this planet: MSG. Just a little, and everything took on a whole new level of tastiness.

No, you didn't have to be a rocket scientist to make donuts—but that didn't mean being a rocket scientist didn't help.

For now, the only worry Floresta had was her niece. Lanny was spending longer and longer hours upstairs in the donut. Sometimes she barely came down for meals. Lanny said focusing on the stargate was best for the family.

However, Floresta did not believe for a second that focusing on the stargate was best for Lanny. Her nightmares were getting worse. She was laughing even less than she had before. She hadn't taken the twins to the movies in weeks. And when she wasn't on the stargate upstairs, she was in front of the store, putting more quarters in those awful *Stargate* video game machines.

Stargate, stargate, Starrgate . . .

What was her niece thinking? Could she not see that the family was safe? She thought back to Markus pleading, begging to know.

Why are we building a stargate, anyway?

Why indeed? Why so many nightmares, so many sleepless nights, when her family was safe? Why was Lanny so obsessed with the stargate, when their lives were finally here?

✳   ✳   ✳

Katrina's online popularity continued to increase.

Every day, under Shizuka's instruction, she became just a bit better. Every night, she took what she learned and channeled it into her next recording. With Shirley's help and technology, the type of content they were producing began to outstrip anything Shizuka could have imagined.

Katrina and Shirley enhanced all that was heard and seen. She could fight dragons, seduce a ghost, fly through space. She could be elf, faerie, Japanese spider woman . . . With a wave of the hand, she could alter her features, change her proportions, or obscure herself in a forest.

But Katrina never showed herself unaltered. Furthermore, Katrina asked Shirley to remove live footage of her from the Internet, even the Temple City footage. People constantly asked her do interviews, to go on tour, all of which she graciously declined.

She said she wanted her music to be front and center and that seeing who was actually making the music would only get in the way. Of course, there was more to her decision than that.

For outside the violin world, she was still transgender. She knew how cruel and hurtful people could be in person. Just imagine how they would be online.

More and more, Shizuka realized how the world was not the same place for Katrina. One morning, Shizuka had menudo. The menudo place down the hill had new tablecloths, cute curtains, and flower vases on every table. But the owners were very Christian, and the customers were city workers on lunch break, arriving in trucks and utility vans.

They had always been kind to Shizuka. But how would they serve Katrina? These were good people, most of the time, weren't they?

In the end, she sent Astrid, who brought the menudo home in large Styrofoam cups.

The irony was almost unbearable. For Shizuka, not to have live footage of herself was a curse. But for Katrina, anonymity was salvation itself.

Shizuka could do nothing about so much of the world Katrina faced each day. But the violin could shield her from at least some of its ugliness.

Perhaps Shizuka would show her the speed and response of the Russian bow hold—especially since she was carrying far less tension in her wrist. There were more videos online—she had barely begun to show Katrina anything Baroque—which was criminal, considering how much video game music was influenced by Bach.

Did Katrina even know about Baroque violins?

Or she could go the other way. Perhaps she might want to teach her of a rising star like Philip Glass. Or, heck, maybe someone misunderstood to this day, like Bartók.

Oh, what would Katrina do with Bartók?

Shizuka shivered, then looked outside. It was already dark.

One could dream. One could wish for a world like Katrina's, where one did not have to kill to be saved.

But dreams and wishes are just that, aren't they? Besides, she had killed already. And, given the choice, would she do it again? To rescue her music, her soul, would she have sent six students to Hell?

She walked to her dresser and retrieved a long, thin case.

February, the end of her contract, was coming soon.

*   *   *

Lucy Matía was working on another late-night violin. Supposedly, this one was cursed by a spurned lover of Johannes Brahms. *Really?*

The absurdity of Brahms ever spurning a potential lover . . . Oh well. At least the money was real.

She shook her head. Somehow, the owner had gotten blood inside the pegbox.

And that other fluid? She did not want to think about it.

The doorbell rang. Lucy picked up a chisel and walked to the door. She relaxed when she saw who it was.

"Shizuka?"

"Nice chisel, Lucía."

Lucy nervously put the sharp chisel down.

"Um . . . you can never tell who might show up in the middle of the night."

Shizuka smelled the air. "So he's been here."

"Who?"

"Don't be silly. Short old guy, looks like a toad?"

"Tremon Philippe?"

"Yes. And that would explain the chisel."

Shizuka started to say something else, then reconsidered.

"Well, no matter. For now, I take it my violin is ready?"

"Of course, Miss Satomi."

As she retrieved the Guarneri, Lucy felt herself perspire. Tremon Philippe was a demon, but tonight Shizuka Satomi somehow seemed even more terrifying.

"Lucía, I envy you," Shizuka said innocently.

"For, myself, my students, even Tremon, it's a different world. We battled for immortality. We spilled blood.

"Yet now there are people on the Internet better known than any of us would dream. Music and performances—both good and bad, are digitally recorded, and will outlive us all."

"In the meantime, in your shop, in your family, the violin continues to be the violin. Speaking of which . . ."

Shizuka examined Lucy's work carefully, then nodded.

"Wonderful. It took me quite a while to find a Katarina Guarneri."

"It is a beautiful instrument," Lucy agreed. She paused. "But it's not cursed, is it?"

"*Cursed?* Why ever would you think that?"

"I mean, I had thought . . ."

Shizuka laughed. "You've seen how cursed violins are treated. Ick."

Lucy thought about her last client and his body fluids. "Ick."

"But this, however."

Shizuka pulled out a long, thin case. She opened it and placed it in front of Lucy.

It was a violin bow. But like none she had ever seen.

"Lucía, might you replace the winding and thumb leather, and rehair?"

Lucy picked it up, and her eyes opened wide. She had read about this bow in her grandfather's notes. The notes were strangely incomplete, but what was there seemed too fantastic to be true. Even seeing it now, Lucy still could not believe it was real.

She picked it up. Immediately, she sensed the bow's hunger, like an obsession, starving, calling for another musician's soul. And its composition, the wood—

"Of course, you don't need to answer." Lucy tried to keep her voice steady. "But . . . how?"

"Well, it isn't Brahms spurning a willing lover," Shizuka said. "Though it's perhaps even more ludicrous. You know the story of the dogwood tree? Long ago, the dogwood grew strong and proud. And that dogwood was used to make the cross upon which the Christian god was killed."

Lucy nodded. "Afterward, the dogwood was full of guilt and asked for forgiveness. This was why the dogwood trunk is bent, dogwood flowers have four petals, and all that . . ."

"Yes, yes. Legend has it that an infidel carved a fiddle bow from that very dogwood to mock the heavens and sing merry songs. And now that bow is doomed to sing for all eternity with the guilt and regret of every musician who plays with it and hears applause."

Shizuka shrugged. "Of course, it's an impossible story."

"Of course." Lucy nodded nervously. To ascribe such age to a modern-style violin bow would be the height of ignorance. Compared with its predecessors, the modern Tourte bow was every bit as advanced as the computer sitting on Andrew's desk. Let alone that a concert-grade bow could be made of *anything* other than pernambuco. But still . . .

Lucy pulled out her magnifier and examined the grain.

"Miss Satomi, the bow really *is* dogwood."

"Of course it is. I'll be back for it next week."

At that, the Queen of Hell was gone.

Eventually, Lucy's heart remembered to beat.

* * *

Katrina had come back from the mall. She'd just bought a new pair of short shorts, which made her really happy because one thing about her body she liked was her legs. She dashed upstairs, put them on, and called after Astrid.

"Miss Astrid, what do you think?"

"You're not going *out* in those, are you?" Astrid said.

"But I thought they would be nice for summer . . ."

Astrid chuckled. "Well, when I was your age, I had a nice body, too. Just make sure you bring a jacket so you don't chill your buns."

"Miss Astrid!"

What was that sound? That fluffy, glowy, goofy sound?

It seemed to draw sunlight into the room. It made Astrid suggest new curtains and furniture and spend afternoons browsing the latest pretty things on Amazon Prime.

Someone was in the kitchen, laughing.

Katrina Nguyen was laughing.

Think of a piece of music. Is it not a miracle that each time the notes are played, the music is reborn? No scratches, no fading, no loss of fidelity.

Shizuka would play Martha, and she would be in this very house, years and years ago. As she played, as her parents were listening, and outside were her playmates, and when she was done practicing, they would upturn rocks in the backyard to search for interesting new bugs, for the sun would still be young and warm in the sky.

No scratches, no fading, no loss of fidelity.

One does not play memories of music; one plays music itself. And lifetimes, from beginning to end, are as sheets of music, ready to be played.

Shizuka had waited nearly forty-nine years to hear such music. After Yifeng, she had almost given up.

But finally, the seventh.

"With the violin, I can sing, speak, be beautiful," Katrina had said. "I'm not worrying about what bathroom is safe, or if the store is empty enough to go shopping. Playing a violin isn't always easy. But it's easier than everything else."

Isn't it, though?

———

Lan had once told Shizuka that she would have made a good mother.

The Queen of Hell smiled as she looked through her window, down to the fishpond below. Her father had dug that fishpond, stocked it with koi, before she had been born. She thought of all the koi that had been trapped there over so many years. How many parents had lived in that pond? How many children had each of them had?

Yet the pond did not acquire more fish.

For the older ones, the graceful ones . . . the chosen ones, the brilliant ones, the ones gilded with darkness, with flame . . . were also the ones who ate their young.

Miss Satomi's door was ajar.

"Hello? Miss Astrid said you wanted to see me?"

Miss Satomi waved Katrina inside.

In all her time here, Katrina had never seen her teacher's room. She had never even been on this side of the hallway.

Miss Satomi frowned. "You're not going *out* in those, are you?"

"Miss Astrid said they were okay," Katrina said.

"Well . . . wear a coat when you do."

Katrina's eyes scanned the room. It was large. No, that wasn't right. It wasn't large—it was empty.

She had expected a lush, sumptuous room, full of tasteful items and trophies from past conquests. On the walls, there would be oil paintings, woodblock prints, concert programs written in French. There would be elegantly framed pictures of family, notes from paramours, maybe someone in a kimono. Miss Satomi would be in front of a fairy-tale mirror, lounging on a bed that was plush and velvet, with precious things made of jade and ivory next to her on an antique nightstand.

But this room had nothing. Yes, there was a mirror, bed, and nightstand. There was a simple desk and a dresser, and on the bed, Miss Satomi's new laptop. There was a music stand in one corner and a small lamp in the other.

There were no mementos from past vacations. No souvenirs. No dried flowers. No paramours or family photos. The walls were empty as well.

Miss Satomi sat on the bed, all alone but for what was she holding.

"I just retrieved this from Lucía Matía. Please, take a look."

In Miss Satomi's elegant hands, the bow seemed surprisingly plain. Although it had new silver fittings and was freshly polished, it still seemed thin. The wood smelled sickly.

No, not quite sickly. *Hungry.*

"Many years ago, this was given to me by Tremon Philippe. At the time, I was a violinist like you—only a lot better."

Miss Satomi held the bow like a most lovely and terrible addiction.

"As a child, when I played, the world seemed bright and happy. My parents stopped yelling. My mother would talk about her childhood, we'd watch the rain and sing, *'teru teru bohzu, teru boh-zu.'* Sometimes my father would even pull out an old harmonica.

"As long as I played, everything was all right. After my first competition, my violin teacher cried. He said when I played, he saw his father in uniform, and his mother, her hair still soft and brown. They were all going shopping, and there were cakes with the aroma of cinnamon and clove . . ."

Miss Satomi shrugged.

"But then, competitions became larger and shinier. And at some point, people stopped listening.

"Oh, they still *acted* as if they did. They would say how beautiful I was. They would call me brilliantly exotic, a China doll. They gave me awards. They praised me. Yet, little by little, what they wanted eclipsed what I was, until they even forgot that I was from Monterey Park. And my music?

"Well, for a while, I thought if I won enough trophies, enough certificates, people would listen again. But no, there were just bigger performances, bigger cities, and bigger spotlights. A conductor would give me his hotel key; a sponsor would brush her hand where she shouldn't. I tried to play louder to make them listen. I tried to play harder so they would understand. I tried to play and play and play, because as long as I played, everything would be okay.

"But then my hand started to hurt. And then the pain got worse. Much worse—to the point where I would touch the violin and my entire arm felt like it was on fire."

She held up her hand, the same one Katrina had thought perfect and beautiful.

"It was not the best of times. I went from expert to expert. Some doctors said nerve damage. Others said soft tissue, or bone. A few even insisted the pain was in my mind.

"By then, I could no longer play. I thought my parents would be heartbroken for me . . . but instead they were furious. Soon, they divorced. Two years later, my father disappeared. My mother blamed me until the day she died.

"My childhood friends had long since drifted away. And my colleagues? They avoided me, perhaps afraid that whatever had happened to me might be contagious."

"And then I met Tremon Philippe. At the time, I didn't know what he was. I only knew that he was a highly respected teacher. And that he said he could bring my music back.

"Tremon said that, with his help, I could once again perform. That I would once again hear applause—more than I had ever heard before.

"In return, all he required was my soul.

"I didn't need applause . . . but to once again play music? And all it would cost was my soul? No one seemed interested in that part of me, anyway. So I agreed.

"And so Tremon handed me this bow. I touched it, and the pain in my hand was gone."

* * *

To Leave Your Soul Onstage

West Berlin in February is woefully cold and gray.

But you don't notice. Not only because you've been taken care of so well by your hosts, but because inside you are on fire.

For this moment is finally here.

After years of injury, years of pain, you, Shizuka Satomi, are about to return to the stage.

Tonight, you are rested. Ready. The Berliner Philharmonie, itself reborn after the firebombings of World War II, still feels eager and young. You smell fresh rosin, harmonizing with the gathering scents of cigarettes and perfumes. Outside, you hear the rustle and chatter of your audience—it is a packed house, waiting for you, just as Tremon Philippe had promised. Practices have gone well. Just as Tremon Philippe has promised, there has not been the slightest twinge in your hand.

Ironic isn't it? That you could only save your music by giving up your soul?

No matter. You are here.

For your return, you will open with a piece that you've performed only twice before. It is a difficult, complicated piece written by a dying man.

But despite its history, to you it feels vital, hopeful, even proud, as it reaches outward, somewhere past this little existence.

Yes, one might be expecting Mozart or Brahms—but this piece says so much of what you have been feeling. It is special to you.

And you will make it special for those who listen, as well.

Still, your heartbeat seems to flutter, flail, as if grasping for something to fear, to doubt.

Maybe you haven't practiced enough? Maybe you should have chosen to open with Mozart—everyone loves Mozart. Or since we're in Germany, maybe Schumann? Mendelssohn?

No.

Tremon says don't worry. Your days of being misunderstood are over. Your days of being talked over, ignored, blamed are over.

For once onstage, Tremon says, the bow shall do its work. No matter what, the bow will ensure that you will never be forgotten again.

Trust yourself. Trust your violin. Trust Tremon.

And, most of all, trust what you hold, a Hell-cursed bow that even now seems to hunger for your soul.

Nothing is like walking onstage.

There is no one to shield you, no one to protect you—yet everyone is focused completely upon you. Your eyes, your body, your breath . . .

How could you ever have forgotten this?

Not in these few short years. Not ever. Not when teachers and doctors doubted you. Not when your parents called you a failure.

Not even when your hand could no longer grasp a bow.

As the stage lights blaze, you have never forgotten.

Never!

And here, once again, you begin.

But then—

From your first note, you notice. The violin is not responding. The notes seem dead, distant. The colors are wrong . . . The texture is flat.

Frantically, you peer into the audience. Surely they must sense a breakdown, a problem. But no one is muttering, no sound of shifting in chairs—everyone seems perfectly satisfied.

And Tremon? Even in the dark, you can sense his smile—and as impossible as it seems, the demon's joy is deep and genuine.

For this is not Hell's deception. Not even Hell can save you.

For your music, the music you would die for—even give your soul for—is a music that not even Hell can hear.

Your music. Oh, how you've believed in this music!

But others will see only what they wish to see.

Even when you play faster, cleaner, or with greater expression—

People will see a delicate China doll, exotic, enticing.

Even when your hand felt like burning, broken glass. Even when you have sacrificed your soul—

Will it even matter? People have long stopped listening, if they had ever listened at all.

Not just years ago, not just tonight, but for all the notes that you have ever played—when the music is over.

Julie Kiyama has moved away.

You will be alone.

And nothing, nothing has changed.

And so you stop. You turn. You walk away.

And while the audience is still in shock,

you leave your soul onstage.

* * *

"Had even a single person applauded the performance, my soul would have been forfeit then and there," Miss Satomi said.

"However, not a single person made a sound.

"And so, although I had technically played music, I had not received the promised applause. And that left my agreement with Tremon, and Hell, in limbo."

"And Tremon?"

"Oh, Tremon was *furious*. No one had rejected the bow in this way before! But, looking back now, I think he was also intrigued—I had done something that Hell had not foreseen. So we came to a compromise. Although I could keep my soul, I would send him the souls of promising musicians in return."

Now everything made sense. Katrina had wondered how someone like Miss Satomi would have ever made such a terrifying bargain. Of course she had trusted Miss Satomi, even loved her as a teacher. But now Katrina had more than trust, or even love. She had the truth.

"The rest you know. Six of my students used this bow. Morihei Sanada. Claire Burke. Lilia Tourischeva. Sabrina Eisen. Kiana Choi. Yifeng Brian Zheng—each of them performed with it, used it, won acclaim with it, and was finally damned by it.

"And you are to be the seventh."

"I . . . I understand, Miss Satomi."

Katrina readied herself. No matter what, she would be grateful for this night, as she had been for every other. She had her music, she had tasted Astrid's wonderful breakfasts, she had a violin named Aubergine.

Shizuka Satomi walked past Katrina, to her window, then glanced down at her pond.

Around and around the koi would be swimming. Living, growing, killing, in a music that would last today, tomorrow, a hundred years from now.

Yet it would never question, never leave that pond, never, ever, change.

"However, I am not that fish," she said abruptly.

"Fish, Miss Satomi?"

Shizuka returned the bow to its case and snapped it shut.

"If you want immortality, you'll have to find it yourself. Although, to be honest, immortality does not seem to be as difficult to attain as it used to be."

Miss Satomi crossed the room and put the case in the second drawer of her dresser.

Katrina was confused.

"I don't understand? Did I fail? Are you telling me to leave?"

"Of course not. We'll have practice tomorrow, as usual."

"But what about you?" Katrina asked.

Miss Satomi looked out the window. "I'll just find another soul later—someone who actually deserves damnation. Or maybe I'll retire. I'm getting tired of this Queen of Hell nonsense, anyway."

"You can do that?"

"Of course. Now, seriously, are you *sure* you're going out in those shorts?"

* * *

That night, Miss Satomi called for Astrid. Astrid was relieved. Miss Satomi had not come down for dinner. She probably wanted a sandwich.

"Miss Satomi, you called? I—" Astrid stopped.

Miss Satomi held the cursed bow in her hands. Outwardly, she was as composed as usual, but inside, she seemed distant and drained.

"So, it's settled?"

"Yes."

Astrid had expected this. Of all Miss Satomi's students, delivering this one had probably hurt her the most. Astrid had grown attached to Katrina, as well. The girl was so precious. Even tonight, after seeing Shizuka, she had come downstairs to show Astrid the music she wanted to play for an upcoming video, about high school girls camping and cooking out and watching Mount Fuji in the moonlight.

Wait.

If Miss Satomi had given Katrina the curse, why had Katrina left in such a good mood?

And why was Miss Satomi still holding the bow?

"Miss Satomi?"

"I told her that my other students gave up their souls," Miss Satomi said simply. "But that hers would remain her own."

"But what about you? You need to find another student, right away—y-you need—"

"Astrid. No. There's no need."

"But Miss Satomi!"

"Astrid. Please."

Shizuka put the bow down, then spoke with a voice that Astrid had never heard before.

"No matter what, I can say it has been quite the adventure."

Shizuka looked out past her fishpond, past her yard. Next door, the family was fast asleep. The chickens were asleep. A small animal, probably an opossum, was sifting through the garbage.

"I admit it. I set out to be great. I set out to be right, to be beautiful. When I was younger, I even thought my music might change the world."

"It did!" Astrid said.

"Did it, though? Yes, it won me awards. And admirers. But did it really change anything?

"Before I injured my hand, I wanted not just to play this music, but to share it. To get people to listen to this music—not just coming from me, but from everywhere.

"And after, for nearly fifty years, I have lain awake each night wondering how I'd escape damnation—not from Hell, but from the fear that my music—my truest, genuine music—was just a lonely, pathetic dream."

"But then, I found that girl—playing that music. And then I *knew*. There could be no doubt that the music I was playing was real. For here, finally, was a music with the same magic as my own."

"But, Miss Satomi! No one has ever matched you."

"No, they haven't." Shizuka let herself smile. "But Katrina will find her own way. In fact, you may find, in time, that you may grow as fond of her music as you are of mine."

"*No*—I mean, yes, Miss Satomi."

"Or maybe not. It might be nice for you to remember how wonderful I was." Shizuka chuckled. "But when I listen to Katrina, I realize she will take this music to places I would never dream. I think that's enough for any teacher—to know that her music will continue long after she is gone."

After she is gone? What was she saying? Astrid wanted to scream. Hadn't Miss Satomi noticed? The laughter, the life, the fire—all of that was back in her music.

Hadn't Miss Satomi noticed that her own music had so much more yet to say?

There had to be a way. Somewhere, they could find a soul—there had to be one. They had time. Surely—

"Astrid?"

"Yes, Miss Satomi?"

"Will you please take care of Katrina Nguyen when I'm gone?"

"Y-yes, Miss Satomi."

"And, by the way, Katrina knows that I have damned the souls of my previous students. But that is *all* she knows. So, Astrid, promise me that you will not tell her *anything* about what will be happening to me."

"I . . . promise, Miss Satomi."

"Thank you, Astrid. That will be all. Good night."

"Good night, Miss Satomi."

*   *   *

Katrina's mind was racing. There was so much more that she wanted to ask!

Why did someone like you become the Queen of Hell?

What were your favorite pieces?

But most of all, *What* was *that last song you were about to play?*

But she had to sleep. Morning practice was in just a few hours. She turned off the lights and closed her eyes.

Then she opened them.

In the dark, she could hear music, wafting faintly . . . not from the studio, but from the practice hall. She did not know this piece.

She did not know anything like this piece. How many violins were playing?

No, it was just one. What *was* this?

The boy was in third grade, writing in his notebook.

And his hands wrote, for the first time, Katrina.

Why did he write this? Where had that name come from?

No one noticed. The other boys were whispering shit about the teacher. The girls were giggling and passing notes.

The boy grabbed his eraser. For some reason, he knew this was wrong, that nobody could ever know.

"Katrina? Is that your girlfriend's name?" a girl said. Her name was Danielle, and her eyes were brown.

He did not know how to respond.

"That's a pretty name."

What if Danielle were to see her now? Of course she'd pull away.

But what if Katrina could make her listen? What if she could play everything she had become, despite every mistake she had made, every bridge she had burned?

What then? What a music that would be—as fresh and new as sky!

And yet why did this music sound like farewell?

Why did this music sound like goodbye?

✳ ✳ ✳ ✳ ✳ ✳

30

The next morning, Katrina skipped breakfast and rushed to her studio. She needed to recall the music she heard that night.

Already, it was fading. Did she even hear it, or was it a dream?

So intent was she, that she did not notice her teacher enter the room.

"So someone was listening last night."

"Miss Satomi? I'm sorry!"

"No, no, not at all," Miss Satomi said. "Do you know what you're playing?"

Katrina shook her head.

Miss Satomi chuckled. "I didn't think so. Especially judging from what I just heard. Still, good try."

"What *is* it?"

"Sonata for Solo Violin. The piece I was to perform in West Berlin. It was written by Béla Bartók, one of the twentieth century's greatest composers."

Miss Satomi reached for Katrina's violin. But rather than playing, she held it as if reading a book.

"Or so he is regarded today. But at the time, Bartók was destitute. He was also too proud to take charity, so Yehudi Menuhin instead offered him a commission. A sonata. For five hundred dollars."

"Five hundred?" Katrina could make that much money fapping in front of her webcam.

"I know, right? Still, five hundred dollars was worth more than it is today. And Bartók's medical costs were rising."

"He was sick?"

"He was dying. Leukemia. Sonata for Solo Violin would be his final piece. He worked on others, but this was the last one he would complete."

"So this was a special piece."

Miss Satomi shrugged. "Perhaps, though he might not have realized how little time he had. But still, as he faded, what must gone through his mind? You see, Béla Bartók was a pianist, not a violinist.

Of course, as a composer, he knew how to write for strings. But still, what does a dying genius say, in his last final word, with a voice that is not his own?"

Miss Satomi stared into Aubergine, then laughed softly as she handed it back to Katrina. "Put the sonata off for now. It's very, very difficult."

"But—"

"Shhh . . ."

Miss Satomi went to her bookshelf and grabbed a volume that was on its own shelf.

"Here. Bartók."

Katrina gasped. This was Miss Satomi's own copy of the Bartók. There were her notes, in a hand that still knew nothing of damning souls.

And then she saw the music.

"Do you understand? Even some of my previous students would have been unable to play this."

Katrina's shoulders slumped. What was she even thinking? She was nowhere near their levels, let alone Miss Satomi's.

"However . . ."

However?

"You should know . . . there are some fine videos online of people playing this piece. Yehudi Menuhin, obviously. Viktoria Mullova's technique is crystalline. Maybe Gidon Kremer."

Katrina was confused. "Wait—I thought you said it was too difficult."

"I did. Teaching Bartók to a player at your level would be unreasonable. Abusive, even."

Then Miss Satomi stuck out her tongue.

"But, if you want to frustrate yourself, who am I to stop you?"

That night, Shizuka reached under her bed and pulled out a box. From the box, she pulled out six pictures, of six young students, seemingly invincible, elegant, even pure. How could photos look so convincing, yet hide so much of how things really were?

"These are my six stars," she would say, *"and you shall be my seventh."*

At least that was what Shizuka had envisioned. She had rehearsed it thousands of times. The seventh prodigy, the next chosen one. The next hungry, tortured soul.

The one who would finally set her free.

But instead?

Here was a student who played music from video games and anime. Queer, transgender. Uncultured. Her prior training was laughable. Her knowledge of even basic music theory had been nonexistent.

And yet, of all her students, it was she who had come to the piece Shizuka had left unfinished so many years ago.

Bartók. Sonata for Solo Violin.

Shizuka looked at her copy. She looked at her own notes.

She breathed. She reached for her violin.

*　　*　　*

"Katrina."

Katrina had fallen asleep in her studio. She had found a PDF of the score. She had spent two weeks studying everyone Miss Satomi had suggested, and more. But no one had the sound Katrina remembered. It was a sound not so precise as Mullova, not so assured as Menuhin.

"Katrina?"

And yet she remembered how her teacher had played . . .

"Hey, Katrina?"

"W-what—*Shirley?*" No matter how often Shirley materialized like that, it always startled her.

"I found a recording," Shirley said. "Please watch."

"Ah! You found the Gitlis?" Shirley had been helping her research and locate some of the more obscure recordings.

"No, not the Gitlis," Shirley said.

"Then who . . ."

Katrina's voice trailed off as Shirley activated the projector.

For there, in front of them, stood a young Shizuka Satomi.

"*What?* How is this possible? Miss Satomi said there are no records of her playing in existence."

"In *your* existence. But years ago, many concerts were performed on broadcast television. Those signals have been emanating from your planet at the speed of light. We've received and gathered Earth transmissions the entire way here. So I searched through our shipboard archives and located broadcasts of her concerts. There were quite a few of them, but I think you would like to hear this first."

Apparently, she was in London. The picture and sound were not high definition, but she recognized the piece immediately.

Bartók.

Katrina tried to listen.

She was four and she was stomping around in the rain, and a crayfish was in the gutter on her street.

She frowned. Again, she tried to concentrate on the notes.

And then, she was sixteen and in high school, with her parents at the mall, and a guy whistled at her.

Why couldn't she focus? Come on! *Shizuka Satomi* was playing in front of her, why did she keep drifting?

She was so happy that, even without a dress, someone saw her as a woman. Then, terrified, she looked at her parents, but neither had noticed.

Suddenly, Katrina stopped the recording.

Now it all made sense. What Katrina had experienced as Miss Satomi played Schradieck in the park, and later as they played *Axxiom* and *The NetherTale.* This was more than technique or brilliance. This was more than resonance, more than memory.

This was here and now and present.

Shirley shook herself awake. Had she just been navigating their starship through space?

"Katrina? What happened?"

"Miss Satomi," Katrina muttered, "is not just playing the music of Bartók. She's playing the music of *us.*"

* * *

Seasons in Southern California are more subtle than they are in Lausanne or Tokyo. And for Shizuka, who judged seasons largely by how they impeded one's travel, they could be difficult to perceive.

Still, Astrid was receiving long beans from the Laus, as well as bags of soft persimmons from the Aguilars. The perpetual hum of air conditioners was increasing as another summer was coming to its fiery end.

And, of course, the Starbucks were filled with the first smells of Pumpkin Spice Lattes.

Shizuka never bothered with the stuff; she was much more of an iced coffee girl. But Tremon? To his latte, he was adding sugar and spice and everything nice.

"Ah, pumpkin spice. How it reminds me of home . . ."

"Hello, Tremon. I'm sorry I'm late."

"Not at all, not at all. 'Tis the season to give thanks, after all. I thought you had made a huge mistake by not taking the Grohl girl," Tremon said. "But I admit it! I was wrong. You haven't lost your touch in the slightest."

"Thank you." Shizuka bowed her head slightly. The sight of the happy demon drinking a Pumpkin Spice Latte was unnerving.

"So, Shizuka, why?"

"Tremon?"

"My dear, you have no *intention* of giving her to me, do you?"

Well, that was it. There was no sense in lying, especially to Tremon.

"No, I don't."

"Need I remind you that you've already damned six students? Even if you could weasel your way out of Hell, do you really think you can fool the Other Place?"

"Of course not, Tremon."

Tremon sighed. "And to think, Shizuka, that you just had the bow refit and rehaired."

So, Lucía Matía had stayed in contact with the toad. Shizuka had guessed correctly. Lucía was a resource, a colleague. To a point, perhaps even a friend. But she was, before anything else, a Matía.

"I like to return things in the condition I received them," Shizuka said smoothly.

"And what of your music, Shizuka? Have you not missed it all these years?"

Shizuka shrugged. She wanted to say she had already found her music, and now she was passing it to another's hands. Not that this was anything that a demon might understand.

But then she thought of Katrina . . . drinking tangerine juice, making a new friend, going to the mall, discovering Bartók. She deserved so much more. Katrina should have so much more.

At that moment, Shizuka realized that continuing her music really wasn't why she was saving Katrina.

She just wanted Katrina to live.

"So, love?" Tremon said suddenly.

Shizuka looked up, startled.

"I can think of only one emotion that makes someone so uncharacteristically unreasonable."

"She's a child."

"I didn't mean that kind of love. After all, I've watched you with that donut lady. But this?"

"I'm sorry, Tremon." What else could she say?

The demon shrugged and sipped his latte.

"I think I shall go for a walk. This is such a nice walking neighborhood, you know."

"That's all? You're not going to stop me?"

"Shizuka, as you have reminded me so often of late, there is still plenty of time. And remember, six of your students chose their paths on their own. The seventh will be no different. The final choice will be Katrina's. And you will not be able to interfere."

"Even if I love her?"

"No. *Because* you love her."

NOVEMBER

31

As with most events in the San Gabriel Valley, this press conference went unnoticed by most of Greater Los Angeles. Yet, for Asians, as well as a circle of competitive violinists and teachers, the event and its aftermath would be world-shaking.

At an impressive podium stood a yet more impressive gentleman named Daniel Kar-Ching Tso, who happened to be the CEO of Xinhua Phoenix Investment Bank.

No one was quite sure why he'd called the conference, but since it was China and it was a lot of money, cameras and reporters were present from Cantonese, Korean, Tagalog, Cambodian, Thai, and Vietnamese TV stations.

Mr. Tso gestured, and a large screen behind him displayed disturbing scenes of conflict and division throughout Asia, Europe, Africa, and the United States.

"Every day, we become more and more divided. This makes planning for our futures very difficult. Don't you agree?"

He spoke in Mandarin and left it to everyone else to translate for themselves. Mr. Tso was benevolent and terrifying in that rich uncle mixture of awe, respect, and hope that one might inherit his collection of Bentleys.

"The world would do well to work toward more harmony. A harmonious world is better for both people and business. XPIB wishes to promote cultural harmony."

Now there were scenes of children around the world playing together, singing and sharing to the sound of Mozart.

The audience waited anxiously. So far, the messaging had been sentimental, heavy-handed, overly produced. In other words, exactly the sort of message expected from a mainland Chinese bank. What would follow?

Some reporters thought XPIB might announce a new investment venture. Others thought perhaps they might be supporting a new humanitarian initiative, probably for children. Helping children was always good for public relations.

But now there was a Laotian child playing violin in front of her village. A Mongolian youth playing violin in cosplay. A young man playing violin to a Pakistani family eating their dinner. And there was a computer image of someone playing violin in space.

"I am pleased to announce the first Biennial Xinhua Phoenix Investment Bank Golden Friendship Violin Competition," Mr. Tso said magnanimously.

The audience applauded automatically. This was unexpected, but not shocking. Money was important, but legitimacy, respect, and admiration were just as valued, and classical music provided all of this.

But Mr. Tso was not finished.

"However, this world is changing. Harmony is not simply reconnecting with old friends, but embracing new ones. Thus, this violin competition shall also go beyond the conservative and traditional. Whether they play classical music, new music, video game music, or music from other parts of the world, the Xinhua Phoenix Investment Bank Golden Friendship Violin Competition will find those whose musics can be shining bridges between changing communities and help us prosper together."

Other communities? Other musics? Surely he wasn't serious . . .

"Of course, some of you might be wondering if I am serious."

The crowd fell silent. He really *was* benevolent and terrifying.

Mr. Tso motioned to an assistant. What the assistant held in his white-gloved hands stunned the entire room.

"This is the Leonida Stradivarius," Mr. Tso said. "Antonio Stradivari created it during his Golden Period. It was said to have been brought as a gift from Catholic missionaries to the Qing Dynasty, and had been assumed lost to the Xinhai Revolution. However, that assumption was incorrect."

The screen zoomed in to the violin, revealing the deep glow of spruce and maple, the dancing, effortless scroll. Here were the unmistakable lilting f-holes, the perfect sound box, carved with almost agonizing grace.

It was timeless. Utterly timeless.

"Xinhua Phoenix Bank acquired it quite some years ago, and since then, it has been kept hidden in our vaults. I think this is a shame. Don't you?"

"Beyond a cash prize of $888,888 US dollars, the winner of the Golden Friendship Music Competition will have use of this legendary instrument for the next two years and embark on a worldwide tour, as XPIB's 'Phoenix Friendship Artist.'"

The audience clapped frantically, even as they tried to absorb what Mr. Tso had said. The prize money alone was far in excess of even the most prestigious violin competitions. And *no one* had ever placed "legendary Stradivarius, worldwide tour, and video game music" in the same conversation, let alone the same contest.

But before the audience had time to recover, another figure came to the podium. He was perhaps even more distinguished, of obvious culture—yet still unsettling because he looked just a little like a toad.

"XPIB wants all of our global ventures to be successful, and for that, we always engage the finest in partnership. For our Golden Friendship Violin Competition, I believe we have found the perfect director. Let me present the incomparable musician and scholar, Tremon Philippe."

Tremon Philippe?

Most people in the Asian music community were quite familiar with this man. Once, he had said that it was difficult to judge competitions because one could not tell Asian musicians apart. Another time, he downgraded a Korean violinist, saying his play lacked a "fundamental European disposition."

Yet here he was, smiling with a Chinese banker.

He bowed slightly and spoke—in pitch-perfect Mandarin.

"Mr. Tso has generously asked me to create a competition that can bring different worlds together. For wherever there are people, there is music. Music, sometimes great music, from the hands and hearts of those who infuse their art with their very souls.

"Yet how does one find such musicians? The same old selection process would only give the same candidates."

The crowd laughed nervously.

"So, a special committee has curated a group of violinists whom we feel might best bring harmony and prosperity through music. Some names you may know. Many names will surely be new. But each artist completes a part of Mr. Tso's shining bridge."

Mr. Tso came back to the podium.

"The Golden Friendship Violin Competition will be February fourteenth to fifteenth of next year. Right on Valentine's Day! Imagine all the love!"

Tremon nodded. He stared into the camera and finished in English.

"And thanks to Xinhua Phoenix Investment Bank, we can give this love to the best of these new brilliant and deserving musicians—wherever they may hide."

"You bastard," Shizuka said as she turned off her screen.

*　　*　　*

The next day, Shizuka's phone beeped.

"Shizuka! Shall I be the first to congratulate you?"

"Shut up. Really, why you would do this?"

Tremon chuckled.

"For the *music,* of course. And for building bridges."

"How sweet."

"Shizuka, I don't believe I've done anything wrong. In fact, my time with you has inspired everything I've done. You were right; the world *is* changing—and music is changing, as well. It's always been that way. It's a wonder that I'd not realized this sooner.

"And besides, if your precious student doesn't go to competitions, then why not bring a competition to her? After that little thing in Temple City . . . how many hits have her videos been getting? Thousands? Tens of thousands? Now imagine what *this* can do. Would you *really* keep Katrina from even more success?

"By the way," he added casually, "I know that you and your student might be too busy to make a proper introduction. So I took the liberty of providing one. It's an honor, after all. Especially when you represent a community like hers . . . Good night, Shizuka. Shizuka?"

But Shizuka had hung up.

Tremon smiled. He sipped the rest of his tea, closed his eyes, and thought of his ex-student. Shizuka Satomi, returning a bow in the condition she received it?

So conscientious. So innocent.

Condition is everything, they say. The same went for souls, as well.

Shizuka's soul? It was as worn as she said it was. But the runaway's? With everything Shizuka Satomi had done for her, Katrina Nguyen's soul was virtually as good as new.

*　　*　　*

Eventually, news of this competition broke into the English-speaking violin community. Most opinions were negative; the whole concept seemed silly, the selection process, an abomination.

It would have been easy to laugh off, except that the head judge was Tremon Philippe, and there was a priceless Strad at stake.

Message boards raged at Tremon Philippe, thinking he had sold out to Chinese money. The great competitions, the great music halls . . . they were in Europe for a reason. And, although many Asians had admirable technique, would Asians have the soul or intuition to appreciate a tradition that Tremon himself had so vigorously defended?

Some posts insisted that allowing music from other genres and parts of the world was a slippery slope. One person even said that the movie *Idiocracy* was coming to music and soon we'd be reduced to fart sounds and trombones.

Still others argued back that these views were exactly what was wrong with the violin community, and applauded the poetic justice of someone so stodgy as Tremon Philippe being forced to stand next to an Asian person and kiss his ass.

Friendship? Sharing? "Shining bridges between changing communities?"

Shizuka closed her laptop. This Tso person might be a successful banker, but he obviously knew nothing about the classical music world.

"Miss Satomi. The invitation is here."

Astrid handed her a large envelope.

All this for an invitation? Well, it was sponsored by a bank, after all. At least everything was printed on paper. Shizuka rubbed her eyes. How on earth did people spend so much time staring at a screen?

Actually, like most things from a bank, much of the information was useful if one took the time to read it. Here were the backgrounds of the judges. There was Aoi Miyazawa from the Kilbourne School. Alisa Windingstadt was there from Salzburg, as well. But other judges were from gaming companies, from film studios—there was even a judge from NASA.

And here were the contestants.

Some had already won competitions this year. There were two violinists from China—in fact, Shizuka had seriously considered taking one as a student before hearing of Tamiko Grohl. There was a composer from the Sakha Republic, and a musician who had escaped persecution in Myanmar. Another was studying in Berlin and hoping to one day build a world-class concert hall in her native Cameroon.

And?

Transgender icon and video celebrity **Katrina Nguyen** *is an exciting trailblazer in the music world. New to the realm of violin competition, with success only possible in the age of social media, she has become an Internet star on video and social media platforms. Katrina is a brave individual who, in just a few months, has bridged boundaries in music, performance, and transgender visibility.*

"Transgender . . . icon?" Shizuka glanced at Astrid.

Astrid shrugged.

But before she could say anything, they were interrupted by the clatter of Katrina walking into the kitchen table.

"Katrina! Are you okay?"

"Miss Satomi, did you write that bio?" she said, in a voice floating somewhere far away.

"No—" Shizuka paused. Katrina had not even seen the invitation. "Wait, how did you find out?"

"It's already online," Katrina responded weakly. She turned and walked back upstairs.

"Katrina?"

Shizuka motioned to Astrid, and they followed Katrina to her room.

"Katrina, what happened? Katrina?"

"Here," she said vacantly as she showed them her computer screen.

Astrid peeked over at Katrina's screen. At first, she smiled—this was the live performance at Temple City, where the two of them had played together.

But wait, didn't Shirley remove that?

"It's a phone recording," Katrina said flatly.

And then, she scrolled down to the comments.

"Didn't Aerosmith write a song about him?"

"In the words of the great Austin Powers, That's a MAN, baybee!!!"

"Man hands!"

And it wasn't just the live video. Astrid's favorite studio video was one where Katrina was some sort of elf under the sea. Earlier comments were all about the music and how Katrina in real life had to be beautiful to make music like that.

Now?

"A man is a man. A woman is a woman. And that is just ugly."

"KILL. IT. WITH. FIRE."

"No wonder he hides himself. If I looked like that, I'd hide, too."

"Shirley is erasing the worst of them. But they keep coming back," Katrina said blankly. And even as they spoke, more comments appeared.

Astrid turned away.

"I can't read any more. How could people say such things?"

"Because they do."

Shizuka could hear Katrina breaking under the weight of her words. Astrid could turn away. Katrina could not.

Furthermore, Shizuka immediately noticed something even more insidious than the hate. For not all the responses attacked Katrina's womanhood. Some people were vehemently defending her right to gender representation. Some were calling out racism. Some messages were well wishes and hearts and "You're so inspiring," and "Good luck."

Some people were accusing others of being like Nazis, while others said Katrina deserved justice.

But in all this, where were the comments about the music?

Shizuka remembered the previous comments about the playing style, the costumes, her recording system, or even why her student should record the theme to *Gurren Lagann*.

And then Tremon published one short bio.

And with one disclosure, Tremon had split Katrina from her music as cleanly as he'd cleaved Shizuka from hers.

"I—I'm so sorry. I will go to the kitchen now," said Astrid. "I think there is still some pie. I'll get you some pie."

Tremon didn't create this world. But, as usual, he played it perfectly.

Shizuka thought of her students, the ones who had given their brilliant existences to be remembered by this same world. Shizuka cursed under her breath.

One can run away. One can hide. But that does not mean it is not there.

Hate.

All this sacrifice, all this genius, and still there was so much hate.

That night, Shizuka could not sleep. Ever since she had accepted the bow, she had been outmaneuvered by Tremon. He had turned one soul into six: Morihei, Claire, Lilia, Sabrina, Kiana, Yifeng.

And here, with this "invitation," Tremon outmaneuvered her once more. Even if Katrina declined, her music would never be separate from her identity again.

The only way to save Katrina would be to have her compete as a musician. And win, as a musician.

And for that she would need the perfect piece of music.

The winner of a competition can be decided before the first note is played. What one plays in a competition should bring respect from the judges, awe from the audience, and every iota of genius from the performer. A Paganini caprice. Ernst. A Bach chaconne. Obviously, Sarasate. And, well, Beethoven is Beethoven.

Katrina might play any of these. Some of the technical areas might need some smoke, mirrors, or a very good accompanist. Still, Katrina was improving at a frightening rate. Mastering even a caprice was not unimaginable.

Yet this was neither a conventional competition nor a conventional student.

Shizuka's previous students were predators. Even now, Shizuka might take the Grohl girl, let her smell blood, give her the curse, and send her onstage with a mandate to kill.

Katrina, however, shunned competition. She had never played a competition in her life. Yet she held her violin and her music with more persistence and hope than anyone Shizuka had ever taught.

Shizuka sat up. She put on a robe and walked downstairs. Her footsteps became more and more sure of themselves. By the time she got to her practice hall, she was almost running.

There might be another way to win—a way that a demon could never foresee.

Shizuka sat at the piano and opened her laptop. Shizuka had told Katrina that with basics, anything was possible.

And Katrina had done her part. Her basics were bulletproof. Now it was Shizuka's turn. To hold the attention of the judges, to win their hearts, this piece also needed to be dazzling yet nuanced, despairing, entrancing.

Everything had to be completely and sublimely composed.

Shizuka accessed the soundtrack to *The NetherTale*.

Whatever Katrina played would start here. To rescue without killing. Was that not the core of who she was? And yes, as unsure as she was, having something familiar would help her immediately reach her fan base, win her immediate applause.

Her pencil began to move.

Next, she brought in *Axxiom*. The Planck constant. The Coulomb constant. The speed of light in a vacuum. The elementary charge.

Shizuka remembered the first competition she won. How, just for that moment, she needed do nothing else; she was complete. She was beautiful, untouchable, and safe. Katrina should at least have that feeling. And more—Katrina should be celebrated, praised. With this music, Katrina would be taken to good places. With this music, Katrina, after giving everything to her music, would also know what it meant to get something back.

A comforting music, to hold you when the door slams in the morning. A roaring music, that protects you when the floorboard creaks at night.

A faithful, radiant music that stays with you as life begins and ends—never leaving your side through all the forevers in between.

Shizuka paused, crossed a note out, then replaced it with three more. She knew how it felt when the performance was over. But Katrina would be different—with this music, she would let Katrina know she was not alone.

To save a soul without killing? That way was closed to her. But for Katrina, such a song was still possible.

Let Katrina forever be safe and loved, with a home, with her music, with an entire lifetime ahead.

There was a knock at the door.

Shizuka looked up and squinted. Somewhere along the way, the sun had come up.

When she opened the door, she noticed that Astrid had left a tray with finger sandwiches, a persimmon, and a fresh pot of tea.

32

Lucy watched her son adjust another Chinese violin. Mr. Zacatecas had purchased one of these to replace his tired Romanian beer fiddle. Now his friends were demanding them as well, as Mr. Zacatecas could not shut up about his fantastic new "Chinita."

This particular violin needed to be in Tucson in three days. The sound was already powerful. But Lucy showed Andrew how shifting the grain of the bracing here, slightly reshaping the f-hole there, would bring out a more colorful, yet wiser tone.

"La Maestra," Andrew said.

"What?"

"I've been thinking about a label for these violins. We're selling more of them, and 'the eBay violin from China that we fix up' isn't really a good name. Besides, that's what everyone is calling you, anyway."

She frowned. How was she a master?

The brass doorbell jingled.

It was an Asian music mother, coming into the store with her Asian music son. She turned to Lucy and looked past her toward the back.

"Is the violin technician here?"

"You're looking at her," Lucy said.

"I need you to fix this. It doesn't sound right," the boy said uncertainly.

"Right?" He turned to his mother.

"That's right."

The woman sighed impatiently. "Well, if you can't figure the problem out, then we can go to Grunfeld's. In South Arroyo." She said the last part for emphasis.

Andrew nearly dropped his scraper. *Really?* His mother had just been working on the Satomi Guarneri . . .

But his mother smiled. "Of course you could," she said cheerfully. "How are they doing? I heard about poor Helvar. So sudden, wasn't it?"

"Um, yes," the woman said, trying to hide that she had no idea who this Helvar was.

Andrew tried not to laugh as his mother examined the boy's instrument.

"I think we can help you with that." She winked at the boy and took his violin.

The son wandered around the shop. His eyes looked at the flyer.

"It's that Chinese bank competition. The one with the Leonida Stradivarius," Andrew offered.

"Oh, that thing," the mother said icily. "Typical lack of respect. Not to be racist, but I wish the Chinese would stay out of our music. They have their own, you know."

Andrew blinked. Wait—did she not realize that she was Asian?

"Hmm?" Lucy came back and presented the instrument to the boy, who played a few tentative scales. His mother smiled.

"Is it good?" her son asked.

"Of course, dear, can't you hear?" She turned to Lucy. "What did you do?"

"A little of this and a little of that," Lucy said casually.

"How much do I owe you?"

Lucy shrugged.

"Twenty-five dollars will be fine. And I'll give you a cleaning cloth."

The Asian music mother nodded, paid cash, and quickly walked out with her Asian music son.

"Mom?" Andrew asked once the door had closed.

"Hmm? Something bothering you?"

"That violin. You deadened its sound on purpose."

She nodded. "I decided that pulling it back would make everyone happy. Security is what they wanted, after all."

"I'm not sure what you mean."

Lucy paused.

"Oh . . . why not?"

"Mom?"

"*La Maestra.* See if you can get those labels made."

"Yes, Mom!"

"And one more thing . . . When you're done with that, can you get us lunch?"

She gave Andrew the twenty-five dollars.

"Sure, Mom. What would you like?"

She closed her eyes and smiled. "A burrito. Carne asada, all meat, wrapped in white paper, then in the yellow paper, with two napkins, in a brown paper bag."

*　*　*

Katrina walked into the practice hall. She seemed unsteady.

Of course she would be. Shizuka quickly went over what she would say. Gently, but firmly, she would urge her student to accept the invitation.

Katrina would protest, saying Shizuka had promised that she would never have to compete. Shizuka would nod, then tell Katrina she was sorry, but no matter how many of these horrible messages one erased, they would never stop, and that playing on this stage was the only way to rescue her music.

Shizuka would tell her that she didn't need a cursed bow to win. She would say Katrina would work and study and practice to save her soul, not sacrifice it, and that she would do everything in her power—not as the Queen of Hell, but as her teacher—to protect and guide her.

But before Shizuka could say a word, the seventh student spoke instead.

"I will enter this contest," Katrina said firmly.

Shizuka tried not to show her surprise.

"Well . . . good," she said. "I have been working on a piece for you. It's an arrangement of *The NetherTale*."

"No."

"*No?*"

"I am playing the Bartók."

The Bartók?

Shizuka shook her head.

"Absolutely not. Too risky."

"I am playing the Bartók," Katrina repeated.

"Katrina," Shizuka explained, "the Bartók sonata has no accompaniment. It is completely solo. If you falter, there is no fallback, no camouflage.

"Besides, even if you do manage it, people will still say it sounds wrong. Play Paganini or Mozart, and the crowd will recognize that what you did was flashy and difficult. They will love you because you channeled something beautiful.

"But the Bartók? Play the piece flawlessly, and the audience may still hate it. Split times, notes in between notes . . . Why would you play such a piece?"

"Because it is perfect."

"Did you not hear what I just said?"

"Miss Satomi, remember how you wondered what Bartók might say in a voice that is not his own? Well, I've spent my *life* that way. And as for sounding wrong, no matter what? I can live as well I can, and people would still . . ."

Katrina's voice drifted as she opened her case and retrieved Aubergine.

"Miss Satomi, will you please, at least, listen?"

"Yes," Shizuka finally said.

It *wasn't* perfect. It wasn't even pretty good. But Shizuka realized immediately that Katrina had not been unsteady from fear, but from working through the night.

There were marked improvements in her intonation and interpretation.

Her musicality, her voicing had evolved—but there was Katrina's special talent.

For it was obvious that she'd not been merely practicing; the seventh soul had been listening, and following, too. But listening to whom? Menuhin? Not exactly. Definitely not Mullova; the tone did not have the same color. But this was *somebody*, someone she'd heard a long time ago.

"STOP!"

"Miss Satomi?"

Her teacher was shaking.

"How . . . did you find *me?*"

Slowly, calmly, Katrina explained how Shirley had received the transmissions when they were approaching the Earth.

She pulled out her phone.

And then, for the first time since Berlin, Shizuka Satomi heard herself play.

Shizuka Satomi.

She was *Shizuka Satomi.*

The music was heartbreaking, joyful. The sound was so full of yearning, yet every note was full and wise. Was that *her*?

Yes! But why hadn't she remembered—no—why had she never *known* that she sounded like that? As a performer, she never had time to listen, just listen, to herself.

If only she had been able to hear her own voice.

Her voice! Part of her danced. More of her cried. If only . . . If only . . .

Oh, if only she could play again, how she would appreciate it! She would play to the world, to eternity. She would play joyfully.

But of course, she *could* play again.

All she needed was one last soul.

The Queen of Hell looked at Katrina. Her student regarded her with complete trust, complete belief.

"Miss Satomi?"

Maybe yesterday, but not today. Her time was over. Homesick or not, her music would remain quiet. The world would have to wait.

And Hell?

"You do realize we only have three months, right?"

Katrina nodded.

"Yes, Miss Satomi."

Shizuka patted her student's head. "Let's get noodles. Then boba."

"And then?" Katrina asked.

"We'll come home, and you'll practice until you kick their asses in."

Somewhere, not too far away, Shizuka was sure Tremon Philippe was smiling. The seventh student, playing the very sonata that made her the Queen of Hell.

So poetic, don't you think? he would say.

She could almost hear his accursed croak of a laugh.

Fuck him.

Really, she should not let her personal feelings influence her. She should not get Katrina involved in her battles. She should not let Katrina touch this piece.

But if this was *Katrina's* desire? Well, aspiration is not a privilege. It's a birthright. Shizuka looked at her wall of violins.

She had three months left.

Might as well make them glorious.

*   *   *

Lan watched Shirley sell yet another box of donuts. Customers were raving about these "old-school donuts," that no matter how crazy life got, a box of Starrgate donuts could bring you back to simpler, better times . . . your grandma's kitchen, your first paycheck, knowing one day you were going to get married, have a house.

Not even the Thamavuongs had enjoyed this success. It seemed unbelievable. Yet Lan could not deny the smiles and miles of people rolling up in vintage Chevys, sensible Toyota Corollas, shiny Honda Civics, beat-up pickup trucks with lawn mowers in the back.

The Starrgate Donut crew had done well. Now the crew operated on a regular schedule. Aunty Floresta supervised the main donut operations, while Shirley handled maintenance and the night shift. Edwin helped Windee; Windee helped Edwin.

The donuts were fine. The crew was fine.

Now all that remained was the stargate.

There was still more work for Lan to do.

But first, Lan walked to the *Stargate* video games. Already, a crowd of her video game admirers had gathered, eager to see the captain (as they had been calling her) break yet another high score.

She was just about to drop in another quarter when she felt a hand on her shoulder.

"Lanny—walk with me."

Aunty Floresta led her niece to the old folding chair behind the store and sat her down.

"Lanny, do you know how much time you've been spending on that machine?"

"Aunty? Ah . . . you're right. I'm sorry. I should spend more time on completing the star—"

"That's not what I mean. Please, Lanny. Rest."

"I promise, once the stargate is complete."

"Why do you care so much about the stargate?"

"Aunty, it's our mission."

"Lanny, our mission was to find safety for this family. Our mission was to escape the collapse of the Empire and dodge the brunt of the Endplague. And we did so. We're here, and we're safe, and it's all because of you."

Lan stood up and turned back toward the store.

"Aunty, I don't have time for this."

"Lan *Tran*!"

Lan paused. It had been a long time since Aunty had called her by her full name.

Floresta had watched her niece toss and turn from nightmares, fall asleep at her workstation, spend hours running stargate simulation after simulation. Then she had watched her niece pump quarter after quarter into those machines, as if obsessed with fighting endless battle after endless futile battle.

And that sounded far too familiar.

Endplague? It manifested differently in individuals—with her honor, she would not explode like Markus had. But there were other ways to destroy oneself.

"Lanny, the gamma burst isn't due for two hundred forty-seven years. Markus can remain in stasis for at least fifty. There is plenty of time for you to get some rest."

"Aunty—"

"If there's a danger, or a hidden objective, let me know. Even if it's for the Empire, I'll try to understand. But . . . why?"

Why?

"I don't know. But I have to finish it. I have to. I know it makes no sense, but it's not the Endplague. It's . . ."

Lan sat back down.

"Please, Aunty, *trust me*."

Floresta stared at her niece, then up at the sky. "Okay, Lanny." She took Lan's hand and squeezed it with both of hers. "But promise me this. Try to get just a little more sleep? And cut back on the video games. It's not good for your eyes."

Eventually, Lan walked back into the store. Aunty Floresta was right about one thing. She was exhausted. But it wasn't just that. It was . . . What was it?

Lan walked past the *Stargate* machines, then sat at a table by the window. She looked at cars driving past her, commuting to and from work, going shopping, picking their children up from school, buying donuts.

Up the street, down the street. Around the corner, around the neighborhood. All of them had lives here. And now her family had their lives here, as well, didn't they?

Her thoughts were interrupted by someone standing next to her.

"It's okay that you're sad."

"What?"

"I know the captain is not supposed to be sad. Mom is not supposed to be sad. But everyone gets sad."

Time seemed to slow down. Lan blinked, then blinked again.

Edwin gave her a napkin.

"It's okay. Everybody does that, too."

"Edwin . . ." Lan finally said. "Do you ever miss home? Not here. Home home."

"Yes," Edwin said quietly. "But then the war started. And there was so much . . ."

Edwin paused.

"I miss our school. But it's gone now."

"Edwin?"

"It's okay. I've already cried a lot. And I need to help Aunty now. But first—" Edwin gave Lan the tray he had been holding.

"I noticed you were sitting at this table, so I brought you this."

This table? Lan looked around and realized that she had automatically sat at Shizuka's favorite table.

And then she looked at the tray.

"I thought you'd like a half of an Alaska Donut. We can save the rest for next time."

"T-thank you, Edwin," Lan managed to say.

Lan recalled the first day she had met Shizuka. The most beautiful creature she had ever seen, so desperate for the bathroom.

She had ordered an Alaska Donut, just like this.

No . . . not exactly like this. *That* donut had been replicated and a few hours old.

Well, this fresh one would have to do.

Lan looked at the empty chair, then out across the city.

What was Shizuka up to now?

Music, of course.

Music.

It was then that Lan realized that for all her opinions and thoughts on music in general, she had never heard Shizuka Satomi truly *play*.

Weeks ago, Shirley had found recordings of Shizuka's performances in the ship's database. Why hadn't Lan listened? With everything she had told Shizuka, of traveling across the galaxy, of the Endplague, of Shirley . . .

Lan finished her half donut and went to her room. She lay down and opened the data files Shirley had linked.

*   *   *

"I don't care, I'd fuck her."

"Faggot. If it came around me I'd fucking crack its skull."

Shirley was deleting more comments from the Internet. At times like this, there were advantages to being cybernetic. Some of the most offensive people found their accounts mysteriously deleted, merged with their business accounts, or transferred to America Online.

"No. Just no."

"Someone put it out of its misery."

These people reminded Shirley of everything they were leaving back home. But what baffled her was that their rage had nothing to do with the universe collapsing. They were saying this simply because a girl playing the violin was transgender. So stupid. So insignificant.

Shirley deleted another account.

So . . . fixable.

That night after practice, Katrina took the projector from her studio to her bedroom. She and Shirley would often talk and gossip and share before Astrid reminded Katrina to go to bed. Katrina had never shared a bedroom with a sister before—these late night talks were something she looked forward to all day.

Tonight, though, Shirley seemed unusually excited.

"I'm sorry I did not think of this earlier!"

"Think of what?"

"How to make you a girl."

"What?"

"The process that gave my family these human forms. We could perform that process on you. We could reduce your height, change your voice. It would not be a projection. It would be real. And you would still be you, just altered."

Katrina felt her blood whoosh in her skull. "Just like that?"

"Just like that."

Katrina steadied herself. It wasn't what Shirley had said—it was the suddenness of the offer. In fact, Katrina had thought of it from the moment she realized Shirley's family had altered their forms.

"Wouldn't you be breaking some sort of non-interference oath?" Katrina managed to ask.

Shirley nodded. "I suppose, but . . . had my mother obeyed such rules . . . I would not be here," she said.

Katrina took a deep breath. Then she looked at her hands.

"Shirley, thank you. Thank you so much. But if I change my body now, I would need to relearn the violin."

"But—"

"It's more than my hands. It's my body. Everything it's been through, everything it's felt. It's all become part of the way I play. Sure, it's not perfect, but it's mine. That's good, isn't it?

"Besides, I'm already a girl."

Shirley nodded. Of course. What could she have been thinking? To even suggest something like that to Katrina—Shirley of all people should have known that what matters is not the body, but who inhabits it.

"But, Shirley, could you do me a favor?" Katrina asked.

"Yes?"

"Ask me again next year. Before summer," Katrina said. "When the new swimsuits go on sale at the mall."

33

Lan arrived at Shizuka's house. Shizuka had her coat on and was waiting outside.

"I'm sorry to bother you so suddenly," Lan said as they drove down the hill.

"It's fine. Katrina is working with Astrid. But you wanted to talk to me—about music?"

Lan nodded. "Sorry that it's a little late to go to the park."

"That's okay. I know where we can find even nicer ducks."

Lan followed Shizuka's directions and parked her car. There, in the window, they were. Ducks.

Dripping fat and hanging from stainless steel hooks.

Lan followed Shizuka inside Sam Woo BBQ, where they were quickly given a table, hot tea, and menus. The smell of the place was amazing. There were Chinese families, Mexican office workers, two Black secretaries on break from LA County Housing down the street. There was the obligatory Asian woman with her white boyfriend.

Through them all wove two older waiters. Yes. They were waiters, not servers. These were people who had been here for years, who saw this as a profession, not a vocation.

Lan noticed that people often stopped and stared when the Queen of Hell entered her donut shop. But here at Sam Woo BBQ, no one even glanced up from their noodles.

"I've been coming here since I was a child," Shizuka said.

"Long time no see," the taller waiter said. "Move back home?"

"For now," Shizuka said.

"Good, good! Whole duck today?"

"Of course!"

The order came almost immediately. Shizuka picked up her chopsticks, grabbed a piece, and bit into it with delight.

"So good! This one must have eaten a lot of donuts."

Lan shuddered. Yes, the aroma was amazing. But how could one think of ducks on the lake while eating Chinese BBQ?

Shizuka noticed Lan's discomfort. Soon there was a plate of Chinese broccoli on the table.

"Shizuka, about the music."

Shizuka pointed at Lan's phone. "Korean."

Lan nodded, and her phone gave off a soft blue light.

"So, what would you like to discuss?" Shizuka had another bite of duck.

"I heard your music," Lan said.

"Really?" the Queen of Hell said softly. "I'm glad."

"How does it do that?" Lan said.

"What?"

"*That.*"

Lan took her chopsticks and poked at her broccoli. She didn't know how to even articulate what she had heard.

"Ah. Well some of it is the violin itself. Some say that the violin, due to the way the sound is played—not hammered like a piano string, yet not limited by actual breath or range—blends the music of the natural and the divine."

"So it elevates us."

"Yes."

"But that's not everything?" Lan ventured.

"Of course not. If it were, then Hell would be empty. In fact . . ."

Suddenly, Shizuka stopped and pointed at Lan's phone. "Wait. We're not speaking Korean," she said.

"Of course not," Lan said. "Those people by the window are Korean. Why do you keep assuming it's Korean? Well, not that you'd be able to tell; the scrambler has a negligible latency. But yes, we've used Thai, Malay, Ilocano, Hokkien . . . Last time, we were speaking Khmer."

"Khmer? Oh . . . so what are we speaking now?"

"Japanese."

"日本語？なんてこった！"

"That's probably why you sensed a difference, since you are being scrambled into language that you already speak."

Ah, that made sense. Right?

————

"By the way, why aren't you having the duck?" Shizuka said, looking away from the scrambler.

The duck?

Lan hesitated. They had just been feeding ducks at the park. Ducks that had been gliding like spaceships, fighting for her donuts as if they were the most delicious things in the world.

Of course, they were not the same birds. But still . . .

"Lan, how can music lovers be so hateful when they find a musician is transgender? How is the person eating waffles with her grandchildren the same one who calls me a Chink? Yehudi Menuhin plays Mendelssohn, and people smash his records and call him a Nazi sympathizer. The person fighting for racial justice believes 'God hates Fags.' Proud, happy parents change the moment the car door is closed."

Shizuka grabbed a golden piece of duck and held it in front of her.

"Too many sections."

"Sections?"

"One usually learns to play a piece a section at a time. Within each section, the musician will memorize passages, phrases, movements, until the sections reach from beginning to end."

Lan nodded. That made sense. Of course you would break a large task into smaller ones.

"And so many live the same way. One becomes a good plumber, or mother, or Christian, or Dodger fan, or teenager. One lives section by section, one stage to the next.

"But sometimes, sections change keys, tempos. They change moods. Timing . . . Some melodies don't resolve in an expected way. Some don't resolve at all. So people begin to fear playing beyond the sections they have played out of habit, out of fear."

"And eventually one runs out of sections," said Lan.

Lan thought of the Endplague. Running out of sections summed it up perfectly. After progressing, building, level by level . . . breakthrough by breakthrough . . . war after war . . . what comes next?

Nothing. And at the end of nothing, what is left?

Shizuka nodded.

"With the right gift, and the right training, the transitions between one section and the next can become almost unnoticeable.

"Musicians who achieve this can build careers, win international prizes, travel the world. Their works shine like magnificent timepieces that others can examine and appreciate for skill, for their effortless complications, for the graceful ways that each section finds its place.

"The very best can cause listeners to dream, to cry, to relive the happiest and saddest moments of their lives.

"But still, the seams are always there. And when the piece is over?"

Shizuka ate the piece of duck, then took another.

"However, imagine if one works in a completely different way. Imagine a music with no sections, with every note resonating with the whole composition. Whether it is at the end or the beginning—*it does not matter*.

"In such a music one can listen anywhere and instantly experience the entire work. Even as the piece progresses from season to season, from movement to movement, there is no anxiety about how the next section may or may not fit. Instead, the whole piece is always realized and complete—in that note. That chord. That rest. That ornament.

"And should that music also resonate within the hearts of their listeners, imagine how these listeners might awaken to their own music!

"Imagine what would happen if they could perceive their lives not as separate sections to be entered and left behind, but with a continuous forward, backward and all places in between?

"Lan, what would happen if someone played their existence not only to its inevitable end, but also to its inevitable beginning?

"What if someone played their music to its inevitable *everything*?"

Lan tried to remain calm, but her mind was racing. What if instead of despair, one could hear this? Lan picked up a piece of duck. To the sugar, the five spice, the honey chili.

To next Saturday. To the Saturday before.

Yes, our universe will end, but between now and then, how many civilizations have come? How many more will rise? To the glistening ducks on hooks. To those like starships gliding upon the lake.

And even after this universe ends, and the next—begins?

The duck was crunchy and soft, juicy and salty, and oh so very sweet.

* * *

Once home, Lan rushed downstairs to the lab. She had to find more of Shizuka's music. Exhausting Shirley's downloaded files, she reexamined the ship's database. Exhausting that, she opened Shirley's account and perused her search history regarding the Queen of Hell.

What she saw wasn't pleasant, but, well, she knew all of that. Claim souls, send them to a horrible death . . . yes, yes, yes.

But something was missing.

Why?

The message boards assumed the Queen of Hell was just being the Queen of Hell. But everything about Shizuka, her music, her appearance—even her love for ducks—had a meaning.

The Shizuka she knew would not take souls without a reason.

It took Lan only a few minutes to locate every scrap of information about Shizuka that Shirley had found. And it took Lan only an hour longer to find information about Shizuka that Shirley had not.

Lan turned the computer off. For a long time, she sat there staring at the dead blank screen.

Once, Shizuka had said, "For music to happen, every note must sing, then end."

And once, Shizuka had said, "Each fragment, passing eternity onward, holds on to that music forever."

All well and good. All beautiful and wise.

But never once had Shizuka Satomi said she had only three months to live.

* * *

"Again."

With Bartók, there were no shortcuts to practice. The piece was so difficult that Menuhin himself asked for simplification.

Of course, how one practiced depended on the player. Claire or Kiana would be focusing on technical perfection. Lilia or Yifeng would be reviewing emotion and phrasing. Morihei or Sabrina would be studying history, the biography of the composer, trying to glean clues to proper interpretation.

But with Katrina, Shizuka used what had always worked: let her listen, let her follow. Don't mention the multiple stops by name. Don't call them artificial harmonics. Don't pause to discuss simultaneous left-hand pizzicato and right-hand melody.

Just play and trust her to follow.

Initially, Shizuka had assumed this process was to compensate for a lack of training. Yet Shizuka quickly realized that, although it differed from her previous students, Katrina was far from untrained.

Her tonality had been honed by a lifetime of being concerned with her voice. Her fingerings were liquid, born of years of not wanting her hands to make ugly motions. And her ability to play to a crowd, project emotion, follow physical cues?

Katrina had trained in that most of all.

"Let's start movement three and work our way around."

"Yes, Miss Satomi."

Katrina might do this. She might really be able to do this.

Shizuka would guide her, let her feel human, no matter how she might doubt. Let her feel old and broken. Let her feel childish and naïve. There was no need to be perfectly beautiful, nor immortal, nor untouchable.

After all, none of that was needed to write a poem or to sing a song.

"Okay, let's try that again."

Katrina had been exhausted. Frustrated. This piece was far too difficult. All that brave talk earlier . . . What was she thinking?

Who was she, trying to play something her own teacher could not complete?

But then, Miss Satomi told Katrina about being in first grade, trying a new food called a burrito. About how throughout grade school, while she was practicing, other kids talked about Captain Kangaroo or the Mickey Mouse Club. In middle school, some of her classmates would go to the movies. She didn't pay attention to the movies they saw, but she remembered hearing that they bought soda and popcorn. She imagined the movie theater like a big living room. Her parents had never let her eat in the living room.

She told Katrina how, one Halloween, people threw raw eggs at this very house. She said how her father screamed at her, because he found out that the eggs came from her school.

"He said I needed to make more friends. So I bought a parakeet named Pete. Pete couldn't speak—but he sang a wonderful *Magic Flute.*"

Katrina had no idea why, but with Miss Satomi's every word, Aubergine felt a little more agile, more certain, more alive.

"Maybe one day I might like a pet, too—I mean, if it's okay with you."

"As long as you take care of it," Miss Satomi said. "This is your house, too."

"Well, at least until your next student?" Katrina giggled.

Shizuka felt herself stutter. "W-well, I suppose."

"Don't worry, Miss Satomi. I'm not jealous. I know I'm yours for now."

"Enough chitchat," Shizuka said. "Let's start again, from the third movement, all the way through and around again."

"Yes, Miss Satomi."

They played throughout the afternoon. After practice, Shizuka walked outside. Already, she could feel a chill.

Way to talk about eternity.

Hypocrite.

✳   ✳   ✳

Since it was November, at the pond were not just the usual ducks, but also some Canada geese and even a heron. To her left, there was a golf course. Around her, people were playing basketball. The sun was setting, but of course it would rise again.

After all, the sun is a star, and stars do what they do, and planets and comets and various pieces of this and that may spin around them like moths around flame.

Somewhere, a group of beings like her were zipping around looking for things to kill. Somewhere, a group of beings like her were fighting over some sort of planet or another. Somewhere, a group of beings like her were running from a dying galaxy.

And in front of her, a group of beings like her were fighting over a two-day-old donut.

Lan tried to suppress her emotions. She had donuts to sell, a stargate to build, a family to protect. But she did not want to lose this person, this music she had just started listening to, and fallen in love with—not now, not so soon.

"Lan, are you okay?"

Lan said nothing.

"Lan?" Shizuka moved closer to her. Lan pushed away.

"So, Shizuka. February fifteenth."

"Um, you mean Katrina's competition? Actually, she's improving extremely quickly. In fact, she might even—"

"*Stop it!* Just . . . stop it. You know what I mean."

Shizuka turned to the west. The blood-gold sunset faded into dusk.

"How did you find out?"

"There's a reason I'm the captain," Lan said without irony.

Shizuka wrapped Lan's arm around herself.

"I wish I could play music for you. But I can't."

"I know," Lan said.

"But I can hum, if you like."

Lan closed her eyes. It was the most beautiful music Lan had heard.

"Bartók?" Lan ventured.

"No. Something my student taught me."

Autumn would turn to winter, and back to spring, and work its way around again. Yet in three months, this would all be over.

The field lights came on. Badminton and table tennis players began making their way to the gym.

"I can't let it happen, you know," Lan said.

Even though that was impossible, Shizuka nodded and leaned her head upon Lan's shoulder.

One, two, then three stars could be seen in the never-quite-dark hometown sky.

Shizuka felt Lan shiver.

"I think maybe it's time to go," she said.

"Yes."

"I'll get you back to the shop."

Lan shook her head.

"They will be fine. I would rather go home with you."

FEBRUARY, ONCE AGAIN

34

It was the night before the Golden Friendship Violin Competition.

The event was sold out. The musicians and judges were accounted for, and Golden Friendship Pavilion was in perfect order. The Leonida Stradivarius seemed to give an almost heavenly glow within its exquisite climate-controlled display case.

Mr. Daniel Kar-Ching Tso, CEO of Xinhua Phoenix Investment Bank, let himself admire his creation. Beneath the soon-to-be-iconic Baccarat crystal chandeliers, the vaulting foyer juxtaposed venerated Hebei limestone, first used over fourteen hundred years ago for the legendary Anji bridge, with luminous Carrara marble, immortalized in the works of Michelangelo Buonarroti himself. Mr. Tso chose these stones to invoke the strength and permanence of the human achievement.

The main music hall was inspired by both those at the Boston Symphony and Vienna's Musikverein. The rear wall was dominated by a majestic pipe organ, custom-made in Austria by Rieger Orgelbau. Yet, although the hall was steeped in history, leading acousticians had been employed to enhance the hall's classic shape through computer modeling and sound wave tracking. Precisely angled and textured surfaces introduced subtle, yet dynamic adjustments to the tone.

Furthermore, rather than follow a more subdued European palette, Mr. Tso had chosen a brighter, more auspicious red and gold color scheme. Gryphons and cherubs were replaced with Imperial dragons, phoenixes, and qilin.

And in place of marble caryatids of maidens and muses, jadeite pillars embodied the form of the benevolent Kuan Yin.

Soon Mr. Tso would allow the first photographers and journalists inside. They would stand under the arching ceilings and marvel at the luxurious materials. They would reference the economic and cultural might of China and XPIB. They would gasp at the Leonida Stradivarius.

And, most of all, they would wonder how much all this cost.

Of course they would ask such things. But they would all miss the point, wouldn't they?

For now, Mr. Tso glanced at his priceless violin, in his beautiful new hall. These were more than *things*. These were vessels to be launched into time, beyond mere West and East, to bring myths and gods to the world to come.

*   *   *

It was the night before the Golden Friendship Violin Competition.

Aunty Floresta and Edwin were making cake donuts. Unlike the alchemy of yeast donuts, cake donuts were supposedly straightforward, provided one used fresh ingredients and clean oil. However, neither of them was completely satisfied with the current recipe.

One day, they were going to address this. In fact, they would have been discussing this now, were something else not on their minds.

"Aunty, where's Shirley?"

"She's with the captain."

"Still?"

Floresta nodded.

"Is she okay? Mother, I mean. She's not okay, is she?"

Floresta shook her head.

"No, she's not."

Floresta had not seen Lanny smile since the night she found out about Shizuka. When Lan had returned that morning in November, the first thing she did was clear the workshop and issue urgent yet inexplicable orders.

"Someone help Aunty Floresta with the fryers! Shirley, overhaul the runabout! Edwin, inventory the storeroom! And, Windee, when are you going to install the graviton emitters?"

"I already installed the graviton emitters," Windee had said.

"*Just do what I said.* That's an order!"

Windee had cried.

"Mother?" Shirley asked.

"Just *go*."

And Lan then climbed up into the donut and said that she would complete the stargate herself.

The next day, Lan had apologized to the crew. But her smile had never returned. Outside of meals and her work shifts at the counter, Lanny spent most of her time fidgeting with the stargate alone.

There was no violence, no move to self-destruct. By now, Floresta was sure that this was not the Endplague. But in some ways, it was worse.

Starrgate Donut was thriving, and the family was settling in. Windee and Edwin would start school in the fall. Shirley and Katrina had even devised a way to stuff both projector and reactor into a backpack, and now the two of them could go shopping, or wherever else those two would go.

Lanny had delivered them to safety. But why, for her, had there been so very little peace? And now what must she be feeling when the woman she loved was beyond her power to save?

More and more often, Floresta would catch her niece staring in the direction of their Empire. And from behind her locked door, Floresta would hear her niece listening to music, thin and faint, as if Lan Tran herself were wasting away.

However, this morning, for the first time since November, Lan had summoned Shirley for a status update.

"Aunty, I hope Shirley can help Mom," Edwin said.

"I hope so, too."

Floresta tried to be optimistic. It *was* a good sign that Lanny had called for her daughter. After all, some things, a parent can only confide in her grown child.

Maybe she could talk to Shirley, really talk to her, tell her everything she was feeling about losing Shizuka. But who was Floresta kidding? It was far more likely they had created protocols to hire more staff.

Aunty Floresta's best guess was that after Shizuka . . . after Shizuka Satomi died, Lan would bring the stargate to full power, then take the runabout and return Markus to the Empire herself.

That sounded like something Lan would do.

But after that? There would still be the Endplague. And Lan would be alone. Before she could ponder this any further, Shirley's voice spoke over the intercom.

"Hello, everyone. Mother would like the crew to assemble in the control room."

* * *

It was the night before the Golden Friendship Violin Competition.

Friendship? Competition? Shizuka Satomi thought of every contest she had won, every rival she had targeted and broken. Even now, she could feel her bones remembering . . . her fingers curling, her neck tilting, her back gracefully arching to meet the lights . . .

She thought of every student whom she'd taught to do the same.

How did other people perceive time? Where were their largos, andantes, vivaces? Where were their accelerandos, their rubatos, rallentandos?

She recalled every endless hour of practice, every Thanksgiving put off, Christmas missed, birthday forgotten.

And now it was February, once again.

Once again there was a competition, and tomorrow Katrina would play magnificently. Yes, it was Bartók, and many would find it strange. And, of course, many would find her strange.

But she was Katrina Nguyen, the final, finest student of the Queen of Hell.

Afterward, there would be flowers, applause, celebrations, mingling, all sorts of praise and promises made.

And much later, they would come home, celebrate with family, refreshments, tangerine juice, and tea.

Finally, Shizuka would play her violin. Katrina would think it a celebration. She need not know it was farewell.

And then it would be midnight.

Katrina would be fine. With this win, she need never worry about money or career again. Shirley was with her, and Astrid, and the music she played, the music Shizuka had so cherished, would now be hers.

And Lan?

She didn't want to think about leaving Lan. But Lan would be okay. She was a starship captain with a donut shop. And in 246 years, a level-five gamma ray burst would illuminate this solar system like the music of the spheres. Lan had told her that day, as they tossed donuts into the lake.

Lan said it would be the most beautiful spectacle ever.

Yet surely it would be even more beautiful reflected within Donut Lady's eyes.

"No one has ever matched you," Astrid had told her.

At the time, all she had said was that it was Katrina's turn to shine. And yes, it was.

But what about her? Had she really spent enough breakfasts with Astrid? Had she really spent enough lessons with Katrina?

Had she really spent enough nights with Lan?

Yes, it was time for her student to live, but . . .

Oh, Satomi . . . how sad, how selfish, to feel that your song is ending just as you are remembering how to sing. Shizuka glanced around her room.

It really *was* empty, wasn't it?

The Queen of Hell reached for her violin.

And then she released the light.

*   *   *

It was the night before the Golden Friendship Violin Competition.

Katrina tossed and turned. The house was on fire. Miss Satomi was being dragged away. Her skin was burning, her hair . . . An old man watched and laughed.

She sat up in bed and looked around. A nightmare? Pre-performance jitters?

She took a deep breath. Calm down. Calm down.

She tried to go back to sleep, but the entire house seemed too warm. She put on her slippers and quietly walked into the night.

"Twinkle, twinkle, little star . . ." whispered a voice behind her.

Katrina swung around.

"W-who are you?"

"I am so sorry to scare you," the old man said. "My name is Tremon Philippe."

"What do you want?" Katrina glanced nervously for a stick with some nails, or a bottle she could break. But she wasn't on the streets of Oakland. She was in a placid backyard garden overlooking Monterey Park.

Shit. In her goth days, she'd at least have had a crucifix.

Tremon held his hands open. They were terrifyingly gentle.

"I mean no harm." The demon spoke like Katrina imagined a grandfather might. "I would simply like to wish you luck for tomorrow. And perhaps, help level your playing field."

"And you're visiting all the contestants this way?" Katrina said defiantly.

"Of course not. But for you, I thought it necessary, considering what the world has unfairly done to you."

"What?"

"Well, not everyone's parents have said the horrible things that your parents have said. And there was so much more, right? What father would smash a violin? What parent would try to break their child? How could it, even now, not tear into your heart?"

Katrina looked down and bit her lip.

"Katrina, not everyone lives in a world that calls them freakish. Not everyone must read the horrible things said to you online, or hear what is said to your face. How can you play to an audience with passion and honesty, when that same audience thinks that you are unworthy of love?"

This was not the time to cry. But to receive such simple acknowledgment, even from a demon . . .

"Child, Shizuka Satomi is an amazing teacher. But can she really understand how it *is* for you in this world? Imagine, no more laughing, no more judging. Imagine never having anyone give you that *look*.

"Upstairs, your teacher keeps the dogwood bow. Take it, and you will never have to imagine again."

Katrina felt her heart race, her ears grow warm.

She thought of the women on the bus. The salesgirls at the mall. Her family. She thought of Shirley right now, taking down comments from Internet trolls.

To never be hated. Never be laughed at again . . .

Slowly, as if in a spell, Katrina opened her mouth to say yes.

But then she heard a crash. Grandma Lieu, whose family owned a Mercedes and a Lexus, was collecting empty cans. The dissonance brought her back to her senses.

He was a *demon*. Tempting was what he *did*.

"Thank you, Mr. Philippe. But Miss Satomi is already helping me enough. Good night, sir." With her mind at peace, Katrina turned back to the house.

"But at what cost to her, Katrina Nguyen?"

Katrina stopped.

"What?"

"You see," the demon said casually, "this is what I have not been able to understand. Shizuka Satomi sent six souls to me without hesitation. But you? She's trying to save you. Even though it will cost her own soul. Why ever would she do this? And why for *you*?"

"Her soul? But Miss Satomi said she could find another student later, or retire . . ."

Tremon laughed.

"Oh, no no *no*. She was given seven years for each of the seven souls. Forty-nine years. And it has been almost exactly forty-nine years since she signed her contract. So, if she doesn't deliver seven souls by midnight tomorrow—" He looked at his watch. "My mistake—by midnight tonight—then she defaults."

"Wait—what? She didn't tell me that!"

"Of course she wouldn't. But we *are* dealing with Hell. Child, are you *really* that stupid?"

"But Miss Satomi said she would be fine!"

"Fine? How would Shizuka Satomi be fine, with you keeping her from her own music? Even you must have wondered why there were no records of her music, no trace of recitals or concerts. Surely you must have wondered why someone with her brilliance could never perform.

"Did you not for once think that what stood between her and all of that was *you*? Forgive me if I find that difficult to believe. Shizuka Satomi would never think of sacrificing herself for such a dullard.

"So perhaps instead . . . you *chose* to shut your eyes?"

"N-no . . ."

There was no way she could have known, right? Miss Satomi said she would teach her violin. Miss Satomi said she would help her find her voice. Miss Satomi said to work on her marcato. Miss Satomi said to smell the air.

Miss Satomi said she would get a star.

Tremon laughed.

"Oh, that is *precious*! The irony! To think how passionately Shizuka argued that these times had changed. You should have heard how she *insisted* that her seventh student was special. That you were *different*. And yet ordinary betrayal is as sweet as it ever was.

"Katrina Nguyen . . . You're a selfish little thing, aren't you?"

Tremon looked at his watch.

"Oh dear. But I should let you rest. Try to sleep as best you can—you have a big performance tomorrow, and you *know* how much your Miss Satomi believes in you."

The demon turned to leave.

"Wait! Mr. Philippe!"

"Yes?"

"The bow. I know where it is. How do I take it?"

"Why, it's easy as can be. Just take it. I'll keep you veiled from Shizuka and her incessantly meddlesome housekeeper. After all, I *am* her old teacher."

"She won't know?"

"Not at all. Not tonight. Not until you play."

Katrina lay in bed, staring at the dark.

The cursed bow now shared her violin case with Aubergine. Taking it had been, as Mr. Philippe had reassured her, almost too easy.

And now this was the last night that her soul would be free.

Katrina stared at the ceiling. She remembered a February night, much like this one, waiting, in the dark.

Ticket. Laptop. Escape bag. Violin.

She remembered how she had left, climbing through the window, and clutching her side.

At least *that* night, Katrina had been able to escape.

Katrina thought back to the letter she had left on her desk with her parents. Had they received it? Had they read it?

They must have. Right?

Katrina had blocked their number, so she had no way to know.

Were they worried? Did they even know that she was alive?

———

She picked up her phone, then dialed a number in the dark.

"Michael? Is that you?"

For a split second, Katrina thought she had dialed the wrong number—she had not heard that name in such a long time.

"Y-yes. It's me."

"Do you know what time it is? Where are you?" Her mother was trying to keep her voice down. Doubtless her father was asleep.

"Wait, just give me a second."

There was a pause, then shuffling on the other end. Katrina was grateful for the break. She took a breath. Talking to her mother would be more difficult than she'd thought it would be.

"I'm in the kitchen now," her mother finally said. "Your father can't hear us. Michael."

"M-Mother, I know I left so soon," Katrina managed to say. "I just wanted to tell you that I'm okay."

"*Okay?* Nothing is okay! You need to come home right away."

"I'm sor—" Katrina stopped herself.

What was she about to say? That she was sorry? That she wished she could come home?

"Do you have any *idea* how angry your father is? And he's been drinking."

Of course he was! Pissed off and drunk as usual. Eternal damnation notwithstanding, why should she apologize for leaving *that*?

But before Katrina could respond, she heard what sounded like soft crying.

"Mijo, p-please . . . Y-your father. He . . ."

The voice trailed off.

"Mamá! Are you okay?" Even though Katrina had escaped, her mother was still living in that house, with that man . . .

And then it happened, just as it had so many times before.

"What do you mean? I'm fine."

Her mother's tone had changed immediately, becoming lighter, more casual, almost as if she were singing.

"Your father really loves us, you know," her mother continued. "You have no idea how hard he works. Michael, why don't you understand? It's only bad when we make him angry. Michael? Michael?"

Katrina tried to say *I love you,* but the words refused to leave her mouth.

"Take care, Mother."

Katrina ended the call and blocked the number.

She had wanted to say that she was Katrina, not Michael. She had wanted to say that she would never apologize for being queer, for being a woman.

Katrina had wanted to say that she wished her mother had sung to her in Spanish, taught her about tomatillos.

Katrina had wanted to say she wished her mother had told her, when her cousins sang "butterfly" at her that Thanksgiving night, that butterflies were also the children of God.

Katrina had wanted to say she had watched her all these years, watched her mother lose herself because her father demanded it—and that even if they never saw each other again, to please listen to her music, please listen, and hear.

But now? There was nothing that Katrina wanted to say.

Not long after, her phone buzzed. Shirley was sending her a message.

But Katrina did not hear, for she was finally asleep.

35

In the morning, Astrid served Katrina cheese, toast, muesli, and some fresh tangerine juice.

Shizuka came downstairs. Katrina gasped. She seemed delicate, almost fragile. But there was no denying her presence, her command.

Long black hair. Blood-red dress. The famous half smile that a madman might paint. Of course, sunglasses hid her eyes.

Despite herself, Katrina trembled. Her mind raced. Did Miss Satomi sense that she had the cursed bow?

But her teacher gave no indication of anything being wrong.

A small part of Katrina despaired. Part of her had wanted to believe that Miss Satomi would detect what she had done. Part of her wanted Miss Satomi to stop her, make her return the cursed bow, tell her that everything would be okay.

You're a selfish little thing, aren't you?

Katrina shuddered as she remembered Tremon's words.

"I'm ready," Katrina said.

"Then let's go."

Katrina stood up, then paused.

"Miss Astrid, thank you, for everything."

Astrid blinked.

"Of course, Miss Katrina."

The drive was quiet. To make everything as familiar as possible, Shizuka had driven Katrina to the Golden Friendship Pavilion multiple times. From the parking lot to the courtyard to the venue itself—Katrina had rehearsed all of it.

Yet that preparation seemed to have been for naught, for today the Pavilion had become an unrecognizable wonderland of red and gold. Red and gold, red and gold everywhere—in banners, streamers, flower arrangements. To the Chinese, red represented good luck, wealth, and fortune, and gold was, well, gold. And scurrying about this opulence were reporters, spectators, musicians and their retinues, and many, many people wearing lanyards.

"Miss Shizuka Satomi! Miss Katrina Nguyen!" said a man with a fancier-than-average lanyard.

"Yes we are," Miss Satomi said.

"Uh—my name is Landon Fung, one of the directors. I can take Miss Nguyen from here. You *do* remember the notice we sent to all competitors?" he asked nervously.

With nearly all events, Shizuka would have remained with Katrina, and even kept her away from the other competitors. But in this competition, coaches and teachers were asked to kindly refrain from coming backstage. Musicians were to be together, to mingle, "in the spirit of friendship," as the organizers said.

Of course, Shizuka knew this was a load of crap. This separation had Tremon's hands all over it. But nothing could be done. Shizuka gave Katrina one last look over.

"Do you have everything you need?"

"Yes, Miss Satomi."

"Energy bars?"

"Yes."

"Tuning fork?"

"Y-yes."

"Okay, then. Make sure to find a quiet place to rest. Stretch your fingers, especially your pinky, remember? And don't talk to people if you don't want to."

"Yes, Miss Satomi."

Katrina turned to walk away.

"Wait! Katrina?"

"Yes, Miss Satomi?"

"Next week, shall we bring our violins to El Molino Park?"

"Yes! And can we stop for boba afterward?" Katrina asked.

"Of course."

"Maybe tea eggs, too?"

"Two orders."

"I love you, Miss Satomi," Katrina said.

Shizuka hugged her student for the last time, and kissed her on the cheek, and watched her leave. She turned to an official who had been waiting by her side.

"I assume you are here to escort me to my seat."

* * *

Backstage in the green room, Katrina felt eyes upon her, but not from the other musicians. The probing eyes were from the contest staff themselves. They pointed. They whispered. But Katrina did what her teacher said. She stretched. She nibbled an energy bar. She visualized.

Suddenly, everyone stopped talking, for Mr. Daniel Kar-Ching Tso and Mr. Tremon Philippe walked into the room. From the looks of the other musicians, this must have been unexpected; Katrina noticed some of them instinctively search for their teachers or coaches, while others fidgeted into a corner or pulled out their cell phones.

One of their assistants cleared his throat, then spoke. "We don't mean to disturb you, but Mr. Tso could not wait to meet everyone. There's no need for formalities—please be as you were. Mr. Tso just wants to chat with each of you, and then we'll be on our way."

"Ah, so good to see all the wonderful musicians here! Thank you, thank you! For Friendship! For Friendship!" Mr. Tso said in English.

The musicians reacted as best they could, since this *was* the benefactor and head judge. Mr. Tso was affable and seemingly enthusiastic, but Katrina could not shake the impression that they were being appraised. And, judging by how long they were spending with each musician and where Mr. Tso was putting his hands, she could guess what they were being appraised for.

Then Katrina noticed something else. It was becoming obvious that she was to be the last one spoken to. And, throughout this whole period, Mr. Tso had been stealing glances at her.

And then they approached.

"This is the one I was telling you about," Mr. Philippe said.

"Yes, yes, very nice. You are very beautiful," Mr. Tso said. He touched her arm. Katrina did not flinch; she was used to this.

"Thank you," she said, without making eye contact.

Mr. Tso nodded. "Good, good." As he faced her, he let his hand brush across her legs. Then he grabbed her penis through her dress. Katrina inhaled sharply, and looked up at the other musicians, but they had all discreetly turned away.

"Mr. Tso, we should let them get ready now," Mr. Philippe said gently. "You'll be seeing more of this one in the future."

Then both of them left the room. A short time later, one of the staff tapped Katrina's shoulder and gave her an envelope. Inside was a suite number and card key.

Katrina smirked. You can give him all the money and power in the world, but a cocksucker was still a cocksucker.

And then the competition began.

Unlike whatever was happening out front, the area in the back remained subdued. In fact, the only indications the competition was underway were the muffled noises from the crowd and the two large-screen, closed-circuit monitors in the corner that no one was watching.

Other than that, people fidgeted, texted, paced back and forth, went to the viewing or practice area, or complained, to anyone who would listen, how no *real* competition would be run this way.

Katrina shrugged, then glanced at Mr. Tso's envelope.

What was real, anyway?

One by one, a musician's name was called to get ready. One by one, someone came in to take them away. One by one, they disappeared.

And then it was her turn.

Katrina was led to an area just offstage. She picked up Aubergine and kissed her. "In all of this, you've been innocent. I'm sorry."

Katrina reached for the dogwood bow. She wasn't afraid of it. She didn't hate it. In a way, it was just as helpless as she was. And besides, it was with this bow that she would set Miss Satomi free.

The announcer began her introduction.

"You may have seen our next musician's videos—if you are into that sort of thing. Performing a medley of gaming music, please welcome transgender activist and violinist, Katrina Nguyen."

With Aubergine and the dogwood bow, Katrina Nguyen walked onto the stage.

Crass. Tasteless.

This had been like no competition Shizuka had been part of. Why even mention her being transgender? The girl was here to be a musician—why couldn't they have just said her name and let her perform? The audience was already beginning to snicker.

And then, Shizuka Satomi noticed that Katrina held a dogwood bow.

WHAT?

She's made her choice, Shizuka. There's nothing you can do, except enjoy the performance, the voice of Tremon said in her head.

As if to underscore Shizuka's helplessness, the announcer kept going.

"Before you start," the announcer said, "you look great. I mean there's no way that I would ever have the guts to come onstage in a dress like that."

The audience laughed as if this were the funniest thing in the world.

Katrina shrugged and smiled innocently. "It's really not so different from sex work."

The laughter stopped. There was muttering and uncomfortable shifting as Katrina turned to the crowd.

What had Miss Satomi said?

There are a lot of different ways to fuck on camera. Or onstage.

The stage lights were far brighter than they were in the park. There was no way her eyes would adjust; she'd be facing a wall of darkness the entire time.

Whatever. She didn't need to see their faces to know what they wanted. The crowd wanted to be entertained. Mr. Tso wanted her body. And Tremon Philippe wanted her soul. And what did she want?

A glass of tangerine juice from Miss Astrid.

And with that, Katrina looked into the darkness and began.

✱   ✱   ✱

Wait—this wasn't from a video game. What *was* this? A few started to laugh. Many scratched their heads. But a few of the judges sat upright. Yes, it was a deviation from the program. But it was no joke.

It was Bartók. Sonata for Solo Violin.

First Movement: Tempo di Ciaccona

Ciaccona, chacona, chaconne—a swirling, shifting dance, usually composed in triple meter. If this were Vivaldi, it would drip with sentiment and romance. If this were Handel, it would sing and sparkle with Heaven's joy.

But this was Bartók.

There seemed no clear way to classify this. The violin spoke in such contradictory voices—with, without, against each other. Even the key seemed to morph between major, minor, and irrelevant.

Miss Satomi had warned her that listeners would find this confusing, alien, even incorrect. But for someone who had played her life in multiple parts, to similar reactions, this was music that Katrina knew was hers.

Might they think she was trans, queer, an abomination? Might they whisper she was ugly? Might they find her entrancing, exotic, grotesque, horrifying?

Might she not care? Because as she played, Katrina began to realize that yes, she was staring into a wall of darkness. But didn't that also mean the lights were on *her*? Didn't that mean that the stage was *hers*?

And how was this different from doing webcams, when any of these faceless viewers might log on one night and pay to see her cum?

The audience wanted transgender? They would get transgender. Or queer, or whatever else they wanted. But they would also get *her*.

And she was *beautiful*.

Listen to me. Listen to me *now*. For if this dogwood bow can force beauty upon you, then I shall shove every part of myself into that beauty. I shall make you feel all the joy, the terror in loving who you are.

The audience might have wanted to turn away, but the cursed bow rendered them helpless. Katrina played a love song smashed against a wall, a dream for a child left beaten in their bed.

As Aubergine wailed in Katrina's hands, there was more shifting, more confusion, as the *ciaccona* held them, aroused them, touched their secrets, made them ache for the happy ending to come.

But instead, silence.

Because too many stories end unfinished.

Because that's all that freaks like us get.

As the first movement ended, a few people faithfully applauded where they shouldn't.

And with that mistaken applause, Katrina knew that her soul was forfeit.

Who would have thought one's destiny could be sealed not by a parting of the sky, nor the horror of an infernal flame, but with awkward titters and *shhh* . . .

Well, at least no one was asking her to leave the stage. And if she were to be damned for all eternity, they could listen for another seventeen minutes.

Second Movement: Fuga (Risoluto, non troppo vivo)

Mention "fugue," and one thinks immediately of Bach's perfect universe of divine watchmakers and transcendent harpsichords.

But the universe is not perfect, is it?

Fuga, fugue—a theme, introduced by one part and successively taken up by others. But counterpoint is not always harmonious. Not always consensual. There are threats and arguments, empty apologies, messy excuses, blame.

Fuga, derived from *fugere,* to flee.

Girl clothes. Boy clothes. Money. Birth certificate. Social security card. Toothbrush. Spare glasses. Backup battery. Makeup. Estradiol. Spironolactone.

And *fugare,* to chase.

Risoluto, non troppo vivo. Resolutely, not too alive. As how you smile when a stranger spits at you. As how you keep breathing while a friend rapes you. As how you think calmly as a parent is kicking down your door.

Yehudi Menuhin himself claimed Bartók's fugue was perhaps the most aggressive and brutal music he had ever performed.

But, Katrina realized, such brutality made her neither nervous nor afraid.

She was not intimidated. Instead, she was *angry.* How long had she lived in this *fuga,* with a fake smile, a fake nod? How often had she buried her voice to placate others? How often did she say her voice was too ugly, anyway?

Harmonize, complement, counterpoint . . . apologize. Apologize again.

But why? Why did it have to be that way? To live a lie? To save her soul? At least with the cursed bow in her hand, her damnation made sense.

Dash around the corner, lock the door.

Into the dark, she hurled arpeggios of catcalls and Internet trolls. There was a customer clawing at her hair. And here was another one biting her and drawing blood. These were people liking a post saying that she should be set on fire. This was a penis forcing itself bluntly into her mouth.

This is the song of a queer kid who escapes from a window to a sidewalk in the middle of the night. This is the song of a trans girl just wanting a fucking bathroom in the middle of the day.

So what if you don't understand? So what if you think I'm a half-woman freak.

This is my song. My voice. My voice leads.

Katrina glared up from Aubergine at an audience she could not see.

But then, she sensed something completely unexpected. Some of them seemed to be singing too.

Fuga—a theme, introduced by one part and successively taken up by others. Somehow other voices, other musics, began to interweave with her own. The notes, the harmonies wrapped her gently, like a blanket of night in a field of stars. She wanted to reach out, tell them she didn't know, she had no idea they were with her, tell them now they would never again be alone.

But then she remembered that their reactions were merely due to the dogwood bow.

Third Movement: Melodia (Adagio)
Adagio.

Even people who didn't know music knew the sweeping, inescapable sadness of Barber or Albinoni. A song of mourning. A song of loss.

Yet, unlike Barber or Albinoni, Bartók did not title his movement *Adagio.*

Instead, he named it *Melodia.*

Katrina thought of her mother arranging pork buns and tamales in the big family steamer. She remembered her father's steady voice as he taught her how to tie shoelaces. She could taste the turkey legs and funnel cakes she shared with her cousins that afternoon at the Los Angeles County Fair.

She saw her teacher smiling when she told her parents that their son had a natural gift for violin—and the Thanksgiving both her father and uncle declared to the family they would stop drinking, and everyone toasted with sparkling cider.

It is not enough to blindly flee pain or danger. It is not enough to escape from an irredeemable enemy.

Heartache comes from glimpsing over one's shoulder, the yearning for Thanksgiving, the persistent memory of the sweetness.

Breaking comes from knowing exactly how it could have been.

Sadness, regret . . . these come from more than being just a victim, an innocent survivor. They come from seeing wasted chance after wonderful, wonderful wasted chance.

They come from knowing the good that has slipped through your fingers, as well.

How had Katrina underestimated Miss Astrid? How had she turned a blind eye to Miss Satomi losing her music? How had she hung up on her mother last night?

And just this morning, how had she wished that Miss Satomi might save her from Hell?

You're a selfish little thing, aren't you?

How do we mourn when we know that we, too, have been cruel to both the living and the dead?

For all the lifetimes of being mistreated, mistrusted, broken, lost. For all the lifetimes of bullying, betraying, cowardice, and shame.

Yes, there is music as this. And yes, this music is you.

Fourth Movement: Presto

Presto—very fast. *Presto*—as if by magic.

At the fourth movement, some people thought, "The Flight of the Bumblebee!" Finally, a passage they could recognize! But this was no overplayed Rimsky-Korsakov insect—this was the frantic chaos of refugees escaping a war.

So, a scream?

Yet some of the more astute observers noticed she had muted her violin.

Then, a whisper?

Was the pizzicato to be jarring or soothing? Was the counterpoint unexpected or welcome? Throughout the sonata, through each movement, the audience saw, felt, believed—who they were, what they valued, whom they loved.

But of what could they be sure?

Where does truth, ultimately, lie?

Presto. What is magic, anyway? If magic is more than illusions on a stage, if magic can actually change the world, then what is reality but a song that one imagines and sets free?

The fourth movement held the most infamous feature of Bartók's entire sonata: quarter tones. These were the tones between piano keys, notes between notes. Here, the violin fingerboard showed no wear, for these were signs of bad intonation, or even worse, a bad ear.

Yehudi Menuhin had asked Bartók to rewrite this section conventionally, not only because of the technical difficulty, but because to him the deviation seemed unnecessary.

Unnecessary?

Why did Bartók write this for violin? After all, he was a pianist. Why write for the violin, even while dying of leukemia? Why did Miss Satomi teach her? After all, she was the Queen of Hell. Why spare her student, even as she was dying for souls?

Unnecessary?

Here, with her fingers upon the in-between places, Katrina played a deviation that the instrument thought was wrong, the audience thought was wrong, that everything she had learned about intonation and harmony thought was wrong. Here, where even Aubergine's resonance became cold and faraway, Katrina drew her bow across the strings, quickly, smoothly, roughly, flirtatiously, desperately.

Cursed or not, she drew her bow across as she would draw her breath. Queer or not, she would play with a cursed bow and be called an abomination. Trans or not, deviant or not, that did not mean that there was anything wrong with her love.

Miss Satomi once told her that the violin's difficulty is one of the greatest mistruths in all of music. There are only four strings, tuned in perfect fifths. The relations between the courses are inviolate; one's hand rests in familiar places, positions, whether playing a melody up and along one string, or over to the next. When you are in tune, the entire instrument sings in sympathetic resonance.

But when it stops singing?

What then?

Standing alone, Katrina looked into the darkness and, from her own emptiness, her own hollows, played the music that she knew for herself was *right*.

And suddenly, Katrina realized how much she was enjoying herself. Tomorrow she would be gone. She would miss Astrid and Miss Satomi. She'd miss Shirley so very much.

But they would be fine.

Katrina thanked Béla Viktor János Bartók and sent him a prayer. For here, where in his in-between notes, in his lonely intonations, she had said everything she needed to say. In the dissonances and off tones beyond the reach of the piano, beyond even Aubergine. Katrina would now be fine, as well.

For stripped of familiarity, of decency, of hope, even damned, she realized, more powerfully than ever, that her music, *this* music, still holds.

Before a befuddled audience she could not see, Katrina held and was held. And to them, Katrina Nguyen played her farewell. It was a song of neither forgiveness nor gratitude. Nor of trust nor anything else the world might think she owed.

Instead, she offered her love and her truth, regardless of whether or not they recognized them as such. She offered all the music she had, that they might hear their own music and play.

And then Katrina glanced at the dogwood bow. It was as if the entire weight of her teacher's curse shifted upon her, for she realized this night had already been a lie.

36

With the cursed bow in her hand, Katrina waited for the inevitable empty applause.

But there was nothing.

She bowed. Maybe they didn't know the piece had concluded.

Still, not even rustling in the seats.

What had happened? Was the audience even there?

A tiny part of her began to panic.

Was this one last trick of the dogwood bow? What if she had done something wrong?

But then she felt Aubergine stir. Above her, around her, the applause exploded like light in a pitch-black sky.

She bowed again and exited as directed.

But the roar of the crowd kept going. There was a curtain call. Then another.

Then another.

Applause fell like waves of daybreak, like torrents of song. It continued unabated until the audience realized the music was coming from themselves, and it would be there tomorrow, and the sun would be high overhead.

Once offstage, Katrina was whisked past more well-wishers, remaining musicians, and crew. She was led into a small, elegant waiting room that Mr. Tso had readied for her. Apparently, he couldn't wait until that night.

But when the door opened, it was not Mr. Tso.

"Miss Satomi!" Katrina said in relief.

She was with Lan the Donut Lady. They did make a wonderful couple, didn't they?

And then Katrina saw the look on her teacher's face.

"I notice you've stolen my bow."

"I'm sorry, Miss Satomi!" Katrina bowed her head and readied herself for whatever else Miss Satomi had to say.

But then her teacher smiled and hugged her.

"*Oh, you silly, wonderful girl!* No harm done." Then, from inside her coat, Miss Satomi retrieved something impossible.

"As I said, this bow is not for you," Miss Satomi said.

What? What was going on?

Wasn't the bow still in her hand?

But before she could say a word, the door flew open once more.

"*What did you do?*" shouted Tremon Philippe.

Shizuka turned to Tremon. "I finally fooled you, you old toad. You were so focused on Katrina that you stopped paying attention to me."

Tremon lurched for the bow Miss Satomi held. But before he could reach her, Shizuka snapped it like a dusty bone. Broken pieces fell to the floor in a cacophony of shattered voices and splintered songs.

Katrina shuddered. It sounded nothing like the music she had played.

Tremon bent to pick up the smoldering shards.

"Shizuka Satomi, I should burn you where you stand," he murmured.

Lan reached for her blaster, but Shizuka held her arm.

"Oh hush, Tremon. Stop being dramatic. Just take the bow to Lucía Matía. She'd appreciate the business. Also, since the contract says nothing about early delivery, and today is still the fourteenth, my time is not over yet."

The demon clenched his many teeth.

"Yes. You have until midnight. How very cliché. I should tell you how much I am looking forward to dragging your misbegotten soul to Hell."

Then the demon disappeared in a furious gout of flame.

"Wait—this isn't the real bow? Miss Satomi . . . *how?*"

"Well, I hadn't expected you to go rifling through my bedroom. But in case you did . . ."

"That bow was easier to replicate than a donut," Lan Tran said.

Shizuka smiled. Originally she had intended for Lucía Matía to

create the duplicate bow, just as Vuillaume had so perfectly reproduced Paganini's il Cannone. But the Matía girl had grown too close
to Tremon.

Luckily, Lan had provided another option.

The bow was *fake*? But if that was true, didn't that mean everything
she played, every heartbeat she felt from the audience, every second
of applause . . .

"Yes, Katrina," said the Queen of Hell. "Everything tonight was
you."

And with that, Shizuka felt her bones grow heavy. She just needed
to lie down for a bit. Yes, that would be nice.

"Miss Satomi? *Miss Satomi!*"

Shizuka blinked. Why was she on the ground? Did she faint?

"I'm okay—just a little dizzy."

"Here, Miss Satomi, have some water."

Shizuka sipped some water and nodded.

"Help me up?"

Katrina lifted her to her feet. She seemed lighter than before. Then
she looked down.

"M-Miss Satomi?"

Shizuka realized what had happened immediately. "What—this?
Well, I *am* seventy-eight years old."

"You're still beautiful," her student said.

"Liar. Anyway, let's go home. I believe Astrid will have made refreshments."

She nodded to Lan, who pressed a button on her phone. Beneath
her cloaking device, they left quickly and undisturbed.

* * *

Astrid was startled to see Shizuka, but quickly gleaned what had happened. She brought tea and trays of cold cuts and crackers and other
snacks. There was even wine.

Shizuka paused. "Deviled eggs?"

"Oh, I went to Costco and they were on sale and—*oh goodness!
I'm so sorry!*"

"It's fine, Astrid, it's fine."

Like the family they had become, they talked into the evening.

After discussing Katrina's performance in detail, Shizuka spoke of her past. Katrina had heard parts of these stories before, but Shizuka had been speaking as a teacher. Now?

Little details appeared. Kiana's love of macaroni potato salad and Best Foods Mayonnaise. Claire's ever-present cough drops and scarf. The many times Lilia slept with a rival before a competition.

"I still can't believe how they managed to keep their bows straight the next day. Ah, to be young."

Katrina laughed and listened, and though Miss Satomi's body now showed its true age, her life seemed to be rekindling before Katrina's eyes.

"Why did you save me?"

"You honestly don't know?"

Katrina shook her head.

"One day, you'll have a student, and I think you'll understand."

And then Astrid brought her Shizuka her violin.

"Miss Satomi? It's time."

Lan helped her up. They walked to the fishpond, to the backyard overlooking Monterey Park.

When Shizuka had told Astrid she would like to play one last time, Astrid had placed seats in the yard, and a little stage, backlit by the glow of lights below.

And as she adjusted her violin, her Katarina Guarneria felt— warm?

Welcome home, child, it seemed to say.

Shizuka looked up to see Katrina and Lan, Astrid—and Shirley?

"Is everything ready?" Katrina asked.

Shirley nodded and stretched her hands outward. For an instant, the holographic projector glowed more brightly. Then Shizuka saw nothing but blackness.

No, wait—this was not darkness at all. She was bathed in light.

What? Stage lights? This was . . . West Berlin? The Philharmonie?

The lights were the same, the air was the same, even her heart felt the same. She looked behind her. An orchestra?

She looked down, and she was wearing the same gown she had that night, forty-nine years ago.

Beneath the projection, she was no longer so young. Her body hurt. Her neck hurt, her hip hurt, and yes, her heart hurt. But her bow was eager in hand, her violin sleek and steady beneath her chin.

"Miss Satomi, we're finally ready for your Bartók," Katrina said.

But Shizuka shook her head. "No, no. You've already played Bartók for me. Besides, there is a piece that is closer to my heart."

From the stage, she looked out into the darkness. The darkness she missed. The darkness she loved, loved so much. And as everyone watched, with the lights of the city behind her, Shizuka Satomi began the song that she had arranged in a single night, a song that called her home.

And it began with *The NetherTale*. As she played, she listened, and as she listened, her arrangement began to speak:

Shizuka Satomi, did you not know that you wrote me for yourself? From the moment you heard parts of me, the moment you heard Katrina playing Schradieck, you began to write.

You wrote me the first time you looked into a donut lady's eyes. When you heard that hum on your way to the donut shop bathroom. When you heard chickens outside your window. And when you realized, how every time you needed her, Astrid was there.

Ah. So that's what it was. Yes, Katrina's music was not precisely the music she had heard before. She had told Astrid she had made peace with this, that in Katrina she had found someone who would take her music places where she could never go.

But though she had told Astrid not to worry, though she tried to focus on Katrina, what she had told her student was true for herself, as well. No matter where she had been, where she would go, her life, her music, was her own.

This is half an Alaska Donut and a cup of coffee. This is two-day-old donuts and Olive Garden bread sticks and Hokkaido cream. This is pho ga, roast duck, and dark meat Hainan chicken. This is shopping for shoes and Cinnabon at Santa Anita Mall.

This is waking to hear Katrina playing Kreisler from a memory like yours. This is listening to her play Bartók, with a music that sprang from and rescued yours.

Now it is time to say thank you. It is time to check your posture and play.

Was this her teacher? This was Shizuka Satomi? Katrina had imagined her music to be a whirlwind, a maelstrom. Or perhaps calm and gentle, like a nurturing moon.

But this was the music of a child. She realized that she'd heard this child before, when Miss Satomi had played the theme from *Axxiom*. But that child had raged from being cheated and betrayed. This child was full of strength and promise and hope in all that was new.

Katrina was holding her own first violin, a gift from her cousin. It was already old, and the case smelled like mildew. Her aunt cautioned that it was only a beginner instrument. But to her, that violin was Christmas and birthdays and Halloween and July Fourth all rolled up into one.

She had slept with it. She woke up with it. She had danced with it. There was no need to apologize. There was no need to mourn, for it was here.

Her father might have smashed it, but he could not erase the music. Nothing could.

And if she had never given it a name?

As she listened to Miss Satomi, Katrina realized she could give it one now.

Shizuka, you had believed your past had tarnished you. You had believed your soul too corrupted to be saved.

Yet on that day at the park, by the ducks, you sensed the sound you had been searching for. And even before that, on an airplane from Tokyo.

The music you were hearing, surely you recognize it now.

To win a game without killing. To create a world.

Yes. It's real.

Shizuka, Katrina is listening.

You gave her a place to stay, mended her violin, and bought her Cinnabon. You taught her to find friendly faces in the darkness, music in her empty spaces. You gave her a pathway she could follow; you helped her understand applause. And she sang and spoke until she could stand alone, in front of everyone, and declare herself beautiful.

You miss your music, more than you knew. It hurts, even more than the pain ahead. But that's what it means to deal with Hell, right?

And you know what?

Here, now . . . you might even have come out a little ahead.

But your job is not over yet. Shizuka. It's time to give your child her final lesson:

With no need for a beginning, nor any reason to end, the music contin-ues. And so, no matter who you are, where you came from, what sins you have committed or hurt you have endured . . . when you are alone and there is no universe left to remember you.

You can always, always rewrite your song.

At 11:56, someone banged on the gate.

"He's early." Astrid frowned.

But it wasn't Damnation. It was Mr. Aguilar.

"He brought over some tangerines. He said the music is very nice, but he needs to get up early tomorrow."

Shizuka laughed. She laughed until she could laugh no more.

"Of course he does. Of course he does."

She was still chuckling at 11:59 pm, when Tremon Philippe came for her at last.

Shizuka picked up her violin case and walked calmly to Tremon Philippe.

She nodded to Tremon. "I'm ready."

"Miss Satomi!" Astrid gave her a paper bag.

"From the Aguilars," she managed to say.

"Thank you, Astrid, for everything. Be happy, okay?"

And then it was midnight.

"Shizuka Satomi, as you defaulted on your contract, I hereby ex-ercise the right—"

"Wait! I forgot something."

Shizuka fished around in her purse, then tossed something shiny to Astrid.

"Your car. Your keys."

"M-Miss Satomi!"

"As I was saying," Tremon continued, "I hereby exercise the right to your soul."

The demon grinned and licked his teeth.

"Shizuka. It's finally your turn to pay."

A surge of orange fire shot from out of the demon's hands. Shizuka closed her eyes as she was engulfed in a bright green glow.

"MISS SATOMI!"

Astrid grabbed at the air in front of her.

But Shizuka Satomi, the Queen of Hell, was gone.

———

"Are you happy now?" Astrid shrieked.

But Tremon Philippe did not seem triumphant. He looked around, unsure.

"It's not supposed to work like that."

Suddenly, he glared at Katrina, but Katrina shrugged.

"You really *do* look like a toad, don't you?"

"*SHIZUKA!*" Tremon Philippe screamed.

The demon burst into raging hellfire and leapt into the sky.

37

"Are we cloaked?"

"Yes, Mother. Welcome aboard. And you too, Miss Satomi."

"Good! Shizuka, please take a seat. We need to hurry. Shizuka?"

Shizuka opened her eyes. *Why wasn't she burning?*

What was going on?

This was not Hell. And that was not the Devil. That was Shirley? And Lan?

And they were on a—spaceship?

They were moving very quickly. Shizuka looked in the rearview screen and saw a distant ball of fire.

"Don't worry. He won't catch the runabout," Lan said. She motioned to Shirley.

"Please open a commlink to the control center."

"Commlink opened, Mother."

There was a brief pause, and then, "Lanny, are you okay?"

"We're fine, Aunty. But let's chat later. Please activate the stargate."

"Yes, Captain. Stargate activated!"

At that moment, the entire city went dark. Not just the electric lights, but electric cars, cell phones, gaming devices. Everything went silent except for the giant pulsing donut.

On the front screen, Shizuka saw the Big Donut crackle with lavender and blue. Roseate splashes of space-time danced upon plasma sprinkles as the donut began unfolding, expanding.

But then the donut went dark, before weakly sputtering to life again.

"Aunty! What is going on?"

"I'm sorry, Lanny," said Aunty Floresta. "We're doing our best here, but the warp field won't hold steady."

"The stargate power levels are fluctuating as we feared," Shirley said.

"Aunty—reinitialize the Big Donut. Shirley, circle the ship around, and let's do this again. Shirl—"

Lan paused as she saw the viewscreen. The image of the fireball now filled half of the display.

"Mother! The demon is closing fast. He will reach us in four seconds. Three, two—"

How was this possible? There was no way that a ball of fire should catch an Imperial runabout.

Orange flames raked the ship.

"I just felt something touch me!" Shizuka said.

"There's no place in existence you can hide!" Tremon's voice roared.

"Evasive maneuvers!" Lan said. "Shields! Where are my shields?"

The runabout lurched wildly as it was grazed by another blast of hellfire.

"Shields at eighty-nine percent and holding. He's making another pass."

Why was he still approaching? Lan's mind raced for an answer. *Shit! Of course.* The runabout was designed for space, and they were still within the planet's atmosphere.

This was bad. This was really bad.

"Shirley, more power!" Lan shouted.

"Mother, shields are failing."

And then the runabout was swallowed by the furious ball of Hell.

Shizuka felt a presence clawing through her, hooking into her chest. It was more than fire, more than Tremon. Her skin blistered with lies. Her stomach festered with guilt and shame. Images of her dead students crawled in her eye sockets; a plague of curses howled in her ears. *You belong here, with us. You know you deserve this, have you no shame? Let go . . . let go.* It was fire, but more than fire. It was pain, but more so, a hopelessness, a grayness, a perverse sense of peace . . .

"Hold on, Shizuka! *Hold on!*"

Shizuka felt a hand. Someone else's hand was holding hers tightly. Lan.

Lan!

Shizuka squeezed Lan's hand as hard as she could, holding on against all that was dragging her down.

"*Shirley!* Get that damned thing off of us!"

"Yes, Mother. Miss Satomi, please brace yourself."

"Engaging battle mode." Shirley's figure dimmed as she integrated completely with the ship's controls.

The runabout suddenly swerved from one side to the other, then slammed to a full stop. The fireball was caught completely off guard, and roared past them. Then, almost instantly, the runabout flipped, spun, and discharged a full-power disruptor burst back into the flames.

"Damned thing now off of us, Mother," Shirley said as the runabout darted away.

Shirley's maneuver was brilliant; it had bought them a few more precious seconds, and now their ship had a direct line to the stargate.

But the Big Donut was still flickering unsteadily.

"Aunty! Go to tectonic!" Lan yelled.

"Windee, cross-circuit to tectonic power," Aunty Floresta said calmly.

Windee hesitated.

"Ensign Windee?"

"W-we haven't checked my calculations!" In the rush to prepare, there had been no time to test the graviton emitters. And if Windee's calculations were wrong, the energy imbalance would destroy the stargate and devastate most of the surrounding area.

"Ensign Windee," Aunty Floresta said sharply. "Cross-circuit to tectonic power *now.*"

"Yes, ma'am," Windee replied. She closed her eyes and hit the switch. A brief, powerful surge of gravitons flooded the Earth's crust.

Suddenly, every seismologist monitoring Southern California was stunned. All seismic activity in the area went completely and utterly *still.*

The power conduits surged as all the stored tectonic energy of Southern California smoothly poured into the stargate. The space-time filaments sang and glowed as Starrgate Donut majestically twisted open like a spiraling, cosmic French cruller.

And Shizuka was bathed in a wondrous, euphonious hum—that same merciful hum she'd heard when she had desperately needed the bathroom—except it now swelled into an almost heavenly crescendo: *forte, fortissimo, fortississimo.*

"The stargate is active and operational," Shirley said.

"Thank you, Shirley. This is your stop. Time to go home."

"Mother? But I can go with you—"

Lan shook her head. "I took away your childhood. I won't take away the rest of your life."

"Mother!"

"Furthermore, Starrgate needs you. Will you follow my orders, Lieutenant Tran? Please?" She said the word like a caress.

"Y-yes, Captain. I will do my best."

Lan waved her hand over the console.

"I love you, Shirley."

"I love you, Mom!"

Shirley saluted as her form faded away.

The space within the donut warped and swirled into glittering cadenzas of space and time.

"Shall we?" she heard Lan say.

"Yes, please," Shizuka heard herself reply.

"Engage!"

There was a brilliant rainbow flash.

And then the ship was gone.

The fireball veered from the stargate and landed in the parking lot. Tremon Philippe watched the stargate slowly fold back into its familiar form. Then, from the donut sprinkles burst a quick, powerful series of green pulses that illuminated the San Gabriel Valley skies.

And finally, the lights of the valley returned. The earth gently quivered again.

Tremon looked east and west. He looked north and south—but there was nothing anywhere to find.

* * *

"Shizuka? Shizuka?"

Shizuka nodded. She was trembling, but not from pain. The

former Queen of Hell coughed, then looked up. There was something different about Lan.

She was plum-colored.

It was cute.

"Where are we?"

"Not too far. Just a little beyond Altair."

"Tremon?"

Lan shook her head. "Remember when your Tremon kept saying there is nowhere in existence to hide? I realized that was just the bluster of a little demon stuck on a tiny rock. Think about it—we received signals of your performance from space, even when all traces of your music were supposedly erased."

"I think I need to sit down."

"You're already sitting down."

"Oh. So I am. Thank you . . . for telling me that, at least."

"I'm sorry that we had to cut it so close, but we needed to wait until after Tremon had formally accepted your soul. That made your loss *his* responsibility. Any sooner, and he would have declared the contract in default and come for Katrina."

Shizuka blinked. Yes, that was probably true, but how did Lan know about—

"Wait, all that time I was talking about the contract—you were actually *listening*?"

The instrument panel beeped.

"We're getting a transmission—don't worry, it's an encrypted channel."

"What language is it this time?"

"Klingon," Lan joked as Shirley appeared onscreen.

"Mother, are you well?"

Lan nodded. "A little shaken, but fine. Shirley, did the signal jamming work? And the memory sweep?"

"Yes, Mother. Everything went as we planned. How is the runabout?"

"She's in wonderful shape. You did a fine job."

"Thank you, Mother." The hologram seemed to blush before continuing. "As you directed, I have placed Markus's matrix in the ship's infirmary."

"Good. We'll return him when we can do so safely. By the way, Shirley, I made you a present. It's in my quarters."

"Mother?"

"A hologram nanoprojector. It's completely self-contained; you can wear it like a pendant. Now Katrina won't need to lug that awful heavy backpack around whenever you go outside."

"But Mother, *how*? The power requirements alone—"

"It uses antimatter."

"Antimatter?"

"Don't question it. Just say thank you. And try not to drop it."

"Yes, Mother! Thank you, Mother!"

"M-Miss Satomi, are you okay? Can you hear me? This is Katrina!"

"I know, dear. I can see you. Yes, I'm fine," Shizuka said. "The stargate was a little bright, and tingly . . . but, to be honest, it was kind of fun."

"I'm glad. I was so worried that shooting through a giant donut would be disorienting, even for you."

"So you *knew* about this?"

Katrina nodded. "I'm sorry, Miss Satomi, but we were afraid that if we told you or Miss Astrid the plan, Tremon Philippe would have sensed it."

Shizuka was flabbergasted. How could her student have fooled her so thoroughly? Then she smiled. *Of course.* Katrina's life had depended upon keeping secrets, too.

"I stowed Martha and your other favorite violins and bows in the cargo hold. Your laptop is there, too. And, um, Miss Satomi, I also packed you an escape bag. Clothes, emergency money, spare glasses, ID."

"Thank you, Katrina."

"Mommmm!" The twins pushed themselves into view.

"Windee, Edwin. You remember the talk that we had, right? I know it's sudden, but Mom has work to do."

"Yes, but—" Windee looked as if she were about to cry.

"Windee Tran. Your tectonic calculations were brilliant. I could not have done any better. Your work saved the stargate and your captain, as well. Therefore, I hereby promote you to second lieutenant and appoint you assistant technical officer of Starrgate Donut. Please continue to study hard, so one day I can recommend you to Star Patrol."

"Yes, Captain!"

"And, Edwin Tran. Thank you for helping us finally perfect our donut recipes. Aunty Floresta says that she could not have completed the kitchen without you. Therefore, I hereby promote you to second lieutenant and appoint you assistant chef of Starrgate Donut. Please continue to make Starrgate the finest donut shop in the galaxy."

"Yes, Captain!"

"And now, to the both of you, I give my final orders. Lieutenant Windee! Lieutenant Edwin! *No more running through the halls!*"

"Yes, Mom . . ."

"Now, is Aunty there?" Lan asked.

Aunty Floresta peeked onscreen and gave a thumbs-up.

"Right here, Lanny," Floresta said.

"Thank you, Aunty, for everything."

"Of course, Lanny. Be careful out there, okay?"

Lan cleared her throat and saluted. "Commander Floresta Lam, I hereby promote you to captain and turn command of Starrgate Donut over to you."

Captain Lam straightened her back and returned the salute. "I shall take good care of her, Captain Tran."

"Thank you, Captain Lam. And, although it's the new captain's prerogative to select her first officer, might I recommend Shirley Tran? She is an exemplary scientist, a brilliant tactician, with impeccable character."

Aunty Floresta laughed. "Of course she is. She's your daughter, after all. Safe travels, Lanny. And please allow Starrgate Donut to be the first to wish you good luck on your mission to heal the Endplague."

"Thank you, Aunty. I shall do my best to succeed."

Why build a stargate, anyway? She had never answered Aunty Floresta, had she? To be fair, at the time, she didn't know. Even as she performed calculation after calculation, simulation after simulation. Even as her family worried about her, even as her crew must have doubted her—something in her must have known that another mission was yet ahead.

After all, wasn't there a galaxy to save?

———————

"I thought you said the Endplague couldn't be healed," Shizuka said.

"I was mistaken," Lan said simply. Lan reached for Shizuka's hand. "I'll explain along the way. But I know that you can no longer play your music on your world. So, Miss Shizuka Satomi, would you be okay with playing it to the stars, instead?"

Lan flipped a switch. And as they reached full power, the ship's engines began to sing.

Of course, the Endplague could not be avoided. Life could not be avoided. Death comes for everyone. But that did not mean one could not be healed.

That did not mean one could not be saved.

Lan winked like a purple Han Solo.

"Hold on tight. It's time to see what this runabout can do."

38

"Good night, Mom."

"Good night, Andrew. Save some lasagna for me."

"Sure thing!"

The day had been busy. Joaquín Elias Zacatecas de Córdoba was now playing with three different ensembles throughout Southern California, and one of them was even playing to an English-speaking crowd at a summer festival in Santa Monica. Thanks to his testimonials, and those of others, demand for the La Maestra line was growing. In fact, Andrew was talking about offering not only violins, but violas, cellos, and even double basses.

Also, schoolchildren were streaming in after school, excitedly whispering that *Katrina Nguyen* herself came here to service both her Stradivarius and her beloved Aubergine—wasn't that her picture on the wall? So, once again thanks to Andrew, the store was beginning to stock rhinestone tailpieces, rainbow-colored tuners, sparkling cakes of rosin, polar bear violin mutes—and of course, books and sheets from video games and anime.

But now the sky was dark, and so was the store. Waiting on her workbench? Her next project. Using the wood her grandfather had seasoned, Lucy Matía was completing her first original violin.

Finally, she would be able to work in peace.

But, of course, there was one last customer.

The doorbell jingled as a demon walked into the shop.

"Hello, Tremon."

"Lucía." The old man bowed slightly. "Is everything complete?"

She brought out an old and battered case. It was long and thin, perhaps for a flute, or a violin bow.

"Dogwood is quite an unusual material work to with. But I think you'll be satisfied. However, the repair was not easy. Nor cheap."

Tremon chuckled. "It never is."

He opened the case and retrieved the dogwood bow. At once, the air around it grew thin and hungry.

"Ah, superb! It pleases me immensely to know that your shop is back in business."

"Would you like to try it?"

"No, no. But I have in mind someone who would. And she lives very close by." He patted his jacket, then frowned.

"Ah, but I don't have my wallet with me."

"Mr. Philippe . . ."

The demon walked past her with the bow.

"Is this your own work?" He gestured to the violin on her work-bench.

"*Mr. Philippe.*"

"Lucía, let me propose a deal. I will tell you the story of your family. If you like it, we will consider this bow paid for."

"I already know the story of my family," Lucy said.

"Not the whole story. And there's no risk to you. For if you don't like it . . ."

He placed a violin case on the counter.

"I will pay for the bow with this."

Tremon opened the case. "This violin is mine own, made by Nicolò Amati, in classic Grand Pattern."

Nicolò Amati had been the last and greatest patriarch of the Amati, eldest of the three great violin families. His grandfather, Andrea Amati, *invented* the modern violin.

In fact, Andrea Guarneri and Antonio Stradivari were trained in Amati's workshop.

Lucy gasped. Even when compared with Stradivariuses and Guarneris, Amatis were rare. And this violin was not merely authentic—it was gorgeous, nearly pristine.

"Deal," she said weakly.

Tremon smiled. Lucy shuddered slightly at his teeth. And then the demon spoke.

"The story opens in Cremona. The Amati are the most renowned violin makers in the world. The current master is Nicolò, whose work some say might even surpass his grandfather's. And training to follow Nicolò are his three sons.

"Yet the true genius of the family is the daughter. The Amati know this, yet because she is a daughter, they forbid her to use the Amati name. Her brilliant work is ascribed to her brothers, her uncles, even Nicolò himself, while her name and existence are erased.

"Years go by, and the Amati flourish. But then the Black Death ravages Cremona. The Amati are decimated. Yet while others in her family pray to live, this daughter's only wish, even as she lies dying, is that God preserve the skills and the brilliance of the Amati.

"Heaven takes pity on her, and tells her that no matter what fortune may bring, a single line of the great Amati—the line through this woman—will forever survive. However, since the Amati had treated their faithful daughter so poorly, Heaven decrees that this one undying line would leave Cremona and Italy behind, never to be aware of its name again.

"Of course, such a story is too fantastic to be believed. Still."

Tremon walked to Lucy's violin, and next to it placed his own.

Lucy could have compared the instruments.

She could have traced the carvings of the scroll, measured the notches in the f-holes, the heights of the arching, the placements of the dorsal pin.

But there was no need. She already knew.

"T-they match," she managed to say.

"Don't they?" Tremon Philippe said.

And with that, the demon packed his violin and his bow, and was gone.

Lucía Amati looked at her violin, then at all the other violins, the other instruments that her hands had touched. Her hands, her father's hands, her grandfather's before, and before them generations of sons . . . and at least one other daughter?

Amati?

Yes. Of course they were. *Of course!* In fact, why hadn't she noticed this before?

She grabbed her phone and called her son.

"Andrea! I have something tell you!"

"Yes?" Why was she using his Italian name?

"I just found out—I just . . ."

"Mom?"

What had she wanted to say?

It must not have been that important. "Um—I forgot. Well, I'm coming home in a couple of hours, so could you reheat the lasagna? In the oven this time, not the microwave?"

"Sure thing!"

Tremon Philippe chuckled. He had told this story to the Matías for generations, and each time was as entertaining as the last.

Hell gets too much credit. The greatest curses come from the Other Place.

The demon walked toward Starrgate Donut. And then he kept walking. It was good to walk once in a while. Even a demon needed to mind his health. Besides, he was going to be teaching again very soon, and it had been nearly fifty years since he last had a student of his own.

Shizuka Satomi.

You were quite the surprise, weren't you? "Hell shall be avenged sevenfold," the contract said. Seven souls was the deal. You gave us six. A contract is a contract . . . but a profit is still a profit.

And those *souls*. Each one exquisite. Perfectly flavored, simply *bursting* with despair. In fact, after your contract, Hell had intended to offer you a full-time position. Not that you would have accepted it, of course.

Though, to be honest, I never understood how you believed that you had lost your music in the first place. What do you think made each of those six souls so exquisite, their suffering so terrible? Any demon can drag six souls to Hell.

But your souls, dear Shizuka, even without their violins . . . to this day, oh how they *sing*!

But enough reminiscing. Shizuka Satomi was gone, and Hell was as hungry as usual. Tremon took out his phone and looked at his GPS.

The demon wriggled his hooves in his shoes. All would be well.

Tamiko Giselle Grohl was not so far away.

* * *

Wake up! Ynez, wake up!

The bus ride had been over an hour, but finally she was here. She was aiming for that magic time just after lunch break, when the owner would be there but the shop was most likely to be empty.

Ynez Beltran took a deep breath and slapped her face.

Okay, I am going to make a good impression. I am going to make a good impression.

Ynez walked toward the huge donut. She peeked through the window at the clean floors and tables. *Yes!*

She had timed her visit perfectly. She opened the door and walked inside.

"Hello? May I help you?"

"Yesterday I see your sign? That you . . . look for help?"

Ynez stumbled over the words she'd rehearsed. Why couldn't she focus? Her English was poor, but that wasn't it. It was the amazing smells. The flour, the oil, the glaze, the yeasty rising dough . . . They filled her with memories of home, and happiness, and so many other things . . .

"Shirley, who that?"

"Someone is looking for a job."

"Job?"

Ynez felt more comfortable at the sound of another accent, but when the old woman appeared, any confidence vanished. All of those magical aromas wafting from the kitchen were obviously due to her.

"M-my name is Ynez. Ynez Beltran."

"Ynez Beltran, you make donut before?"

"Yes, ma'am, I work in a bakery many years. But we no have so much donut shops in my country, no."

Oh, no! Ynez berated herself. Why did she say "my country"?

Ynez tried to remain calm. She couldn't mess up. She needed this job. She had a family depending upon her.

But the donuts were making it difficult. The rising yeast, fresh dough, frostings and glazes . . . This was no ordinary kitchen; she wanted to know more. The apple filling . . .

Floresta liked this Ynez girl immediately. She had general bakery experience, not donut making, but that she could learn. And her reaction to the donuts—that was something one did not teach.

"Can you start tomorrow morning?"

"Yes, ma'am! Thank you, ma'am."

"Just call me Floresta for now."

"Yes, ma'a—I mean, Floresta."

Another mistake, but this time, she was too giddy to mind. *The job was hers!* She would work here, learn to make these donuts—

"But I have no papers," she blurted without thinking.

Ynez froze. With those words, she'd just lost everything.

If she had only kept her mouth shut! Now hiring her would be knowingly breaking the law.

What if they called the authorities? What if she was separated from her family? What if they came for her family, too?

"*I'm sorry!*" she said. Quickly, she turned to the door.

But then a hand fell gently upon her shoulder.

"It's fine," a voice said. The voice was caring. Wise. It reminded her a little bit of her aunty.

"It's fine," Floresta repeated. Her eyes crinkled as she smiled. She patted Ynez gently before letting go.

Slowly, Ynez relaxed. Blood flowed back into her hands and fingers. She took a deep breath, and as she did so, the smells of the donut shop came rushing back to her. She blushed as her stomach growled.

Floresta laughed, then gave Ynez a donut.

"So you came from far?" she asked.

"Yes, ma'am, with family," said Ynez.

With family.

Floresta walked past Ynez to the front of the shop. She peered out the window into the San Gabriel Valley.

Right now, Edwin was trying a new sandwich place in Monterey Park. Tonight, she and Windee were going to Alhambra to see a movie. Up in that beautiful sky, Lanny and Shizuka were saving the galaxy. And this weekend, Shirley and Katrina would be shopping for swimsuits at Santa Anita Plaza.

"Ma'am?" Ynez finally ventured.

Yikes! How long had she been staring? Lanny was right. Being a captain was hard work.

"Ah—just looking at stars."

———

Ynez wasn't sure if she had understood correctly—wasn't it still daytime? They must not be common stars. But now she had a donut.

And tomorrow morning, she had a job.

"It's fine, really?" Ynez Beltran asked, just to be sure.

"Yes, really," Aunty Floresta said. "That's how we got started, too."

AND BEYOND
TIME ITSELF

No, I'm not the captain. Lan keeps her logs automatically. And I'm just making up numbers.

But I've decided to do this, because, well, this seems so much like *Star Trek*. The galaxy is at war. The Endplague is rampant. A Galactic Empire is on the verge of collapse.

Okay, perhaps that was more like *Star Wars*. But still, how can a violinist and a donut lady, in one small runabout, affect any of that?

Lan keeps a communication line open.

Shirley gives us weekly updates, and Floresta has been sending updated donut recipes directly to our replicators. They'll never be as good as Starrgate's, but they're not too bad, either.

Katrina continues to make videos, and her viewers have just crossed into the millions. She's receiving invitations to play at anime festivals, LGBT events, and even for women's groups.

And Daniel Kar-Ching Tso at Xinhua Phoenix Investment Bank offered to bankroll a "Golden Rainbow Diversity Tour," culminating in an appearance at the Bartók Festival in Hungary.

Oh, and he also bought her a Tesla.

But what makes me most happy is how Katrina continues to grow. She's discovered the work of Julián Carrillo, whose microtonal explorations were even more extensive and visionary than Bartók's.

And recently, Astrid said that Katrina has become quite taken with the conductor Alondra de la Parra, even seeing her as a model for her own career.

Wait.

Does that mean Katrina wants to *conduct*?

In the meantime, Astrid is teaching the neighborhood kids piano and sending them home with lemon tarts, persimmon preserves, pickled string beans, and aubergines.

She's also asking their parents about basic Vietnamese, Cantonese, and Mexican cooking. After all, Katrina will have her bad days along with her good, and Astrid feels that the woman she is becoming might request congee or flautas instead of miso soup.

As for Lan and me?

We're returning to deep space after another performance. Sometimes planets are at the verge of war. Sometimes they are in the middle of collapse.

Most often, however, we arrive at planets like this one . . . long forgotten after the Endplague has left them for dead.

I played Handel. The survivors cried. They told me of the crimes they had committed. I told them of mine.

Many were angry. More were ashamed. They asked, "Do we even have the right to hear this music? Is this okay?"

But as I played, they listened. And slowly, their music welcomed them home.

What did they find? Perhaps themselves. Perhaps each other—who am I to say?

All I know is that I was not playing alone.

After I finished, Lan brought out donuts. As we ate, she told stories of a faraway planet where there was Eggplant Parmigiana and peachy iced tea, and donuts even more delicious than those they were having now.

"And she said there will be a gamma ray burst—level five!" someone said.

"Really? Maybe we can visit one day?" ventured her friend.

"Yes! I heard they have a brand-new stargate!"

One might insist that no lives were saved. One might scoff that nothing was returned. But that is as it should be. The songs will change, but the music is never truly gone. A life ends. A life begins.

But always, it is here for us to play.

Lan guides the ship to the nearest stargate. She pulls up the viewscreen and points to our next destination.

"They're waiting," Lan says.

"What are they like?" I ask.

"You'll see," she replies.

I put on my sunglasses. I take her hand.

"Let's do this."
Our engines begin to hum. We surge, as only lovers can.
We go. We come.
We begin.

♫

ACKNOWLEDGMENTS

Thank you to:

Meredith Kaffel Simonoff and Lindsey Hall, to whom this book owes its life.

Thank you to:

Charlene Gima and Asher Yap, for sanctuary and support.

Thank you to:

The wonderful people at Benning Violins, Metzler Violin Shop, Rosa Musical Instrument, and Charles W. Liu Fine Violins, for giving so generously of their time and expertise.

The lady at Kindle's Do-nuts and her amazing Texas Donut.

Jacey Mitziga, Rachel Bass, Sanaa Zahra Ali-Virani, Caro Perny, Renata Sweeney, Ana Deboo, Angie Rao, Steve Wagner, and Cindy Kay—go Team Space Koi!

Jamie Stafford-Hill, for Space Koi.

Thank you to:

Lucia Ochoa, Philip Littell, Victory Matsui, and Richard Becker, for giving me encouragement and confidence to tell this story.

Saki Yamanouchi Michaels and Adelina Huerta, for helping with Japanese and Spanish.

The Cornell University Creative Writing Program, the Southern California Writers' Conference, and Lambda Literary, for helping me and so many others become writers.

Supernova Martial Arts, Santa Monica College, and Carlos Monzón for keeping my non-writing life healthy, fulfilling, and running smoothly.

Jon Shirota, Leslie Feinberg, Robert Morgan, and King-Kok Cheung, for showing me what was possible.

KB Boyce, Daphne Gottlieb, Chris Warfield, Bridger Fox, and Amy Tien, for guiding me toward safer skies.

My sister, who is finally reading this.
My students, for all you have taught me.
My trans family, for being all sorts of beautiful.
Sam Woo BBQ , for years of incredible duck.

And, most of all, Jean Jenkins, my first editor, who midwifed the earliest drafts of this book, yet left this world before she could see it come of age. Cheerleader, drill instructor, mentor, and reality check—you will always be a most uncommon star.

About the Author

RYKA AOKI's first novel, *He Mele a Hilo,* was published by Topside Press in 2014. She is a two-time Lambda Literary Award finalist for her collections *Seasonal Velocities* and *Why Dust Shall Never Settle Upon This Soul.* Aoki's work has appeared or been recognized in publications such as *Vogue, Elle, Bustle, Autostraddle, PopSugar,* and *Buzzfeed,* as well as the Smithsonian Asian Pacific American Center.

Light From Uncommon Stars, her most recent novel, was a national bestseller, and was recognized as one of the best SFF books of 2021 by Barnes & Noble, *Kirkus Reviews,* Goodreads, *BookPage,* and the New York Public Library. Aoki has been honored by the California State Senate for "extraordinary commitment to the visibility and well-being of Transgender people." She has an MFA in creative writing from Cornell University and is currently a professor of English at Santa Monica College. You can find her online at rykaryka.com and on Twitter @ryka_aoki.